Starburst

Tanya Dolan

RED HOT DIVA

by the same author:
High Art

First published 2003 by Red Hot Diva/Diva Books,
an imprint of Millivres Prowler Limited
Spectrum House, Unit M, 32–34 Gordon House Road, London NW5 1LP
www.divamag.co.uk

A catalogue record for this book is available from the British Library

ISBN 1-873741-90-1

Printed and bound in Finland by WS Bookwell

Distributed in the UK and Europe by Airlift Book Company,
8 The Arena, Mollison Avenue,
Enfield, Middlesex EN3 7NJ
Telephone: 020 8804 0400

Distributed in North America by Consortium,
1045 Westgate Drive, St Paul, MN 55114-1065
Telephone: 1 800 283 3572

Distributed in Australia by Bulldog Books,
PO Box 300, Beaconsfield, NSW 2014

One

The pretty girl was draped, exquisitely, by a red evening gown that came up from the floor and stopped just above the nipples of a pair of creamy, uptilted breasts. She walked from room to room like an advertisement for the greatest arse in the world. This was the first big showbiz party she had ever attended; no one had invited her. But it was late now and everyone had become so suddenly and stupidly drunk that she was unlikely to be asked for her credentials.

She was eighteen years old, virginal in a technical sense, and determined to be an actress. The incubation period she'd spent with a local drama group hadn't hatched her into stardom, but tonight she intended to peck her way out of her own shell. A month ago she had left Basingstoke as Pauline Manning and had arrived in London as Paula Monroe. The dark roots of her blonde hair said that the collar and cuffs didn't match. Still, with a glass of orange juice in her hand, she returned the smile of an ageing but still highly popular American singer. His shoulders were hunched as if he were at a microphone and he wore a permanent, engagingly boyish grin that was a contradiction on his tired old face. What if he should come over to speak to her? There had to be something she could talk about without bringing in the weather.

It was a beautiful house. The rooms were spacious and expensively decorated by an expensive interior designer. This main room had shiny black patent-leather walls. The general decor was an effective blend of gold, green and rose. The place was alive with music and wild with dancers. Those not dancing stood around in little groups that were as insular as secret societies. She looked around her and was certain that she was the only one among those here who hadn't been invited, and it was unnerving to be among people who all looked so wealthy, so confident, so celebrated. Yet, an hour ago, she had caught the eye of Matthew Wyndham. Paula wasn't kidding herself. It was either her boobs or her buttocks that had attracted the host. Men usually talked to her tits, ignoring her as if she were some kind of dull friend tagging along behind her own chest.

But the charming Matthew Wyndham had been different.

He had the looks of a 1940s matinée idol. His sprightly white hair was close-cut, his brown face was lean with a straight high-boned nose, a square jaw and a stubborn chin. What could have been an intimidating ruggedness was diffused by a pair of somehow sad, compassionate green eyes. Looking younger than his fifty-five years, he was a candidate for either a father or a lover. Paula instantly took the father option. And, though wanting to impress the wealthy boss of a gargantuan independent television company, she had been terrified that he would ask who had invited her, and there had been dry fear in her throat. Wyndham was a multimillionaire who took up slack time by organising celebrity charity events. Being in the company of ultra-sophisticated people such as Matthew Wyndham always had her acting like a schoolgirl on her first date, and she was neither quick nor confident enough to bluff her way through. When he had said nothing more than to enquire solicitously if she was enjoying the party, Paula had become so tongue-tied that she had missed her golden chance. He had smiled, his capped teeth gleaming, and then someone had called him away.

From time to time she had glimpsed Matthew Wyndham's

wife, the stunning star Karen Cayson, through the crowds of guests. The famous actress was everything that Paula had always wanted to be. Karen was exceptional in that she looked every bit as good in the flesh as she did on screen. Her hair was a natural red, her features perfect – small nose, big eyes, and good facial bones. But each time Paula saw her, the hostess was a little more loudly drunk on sherry mixed with champagne. As time passed, the opportunity to meet the hostess was irretrievably lost.

Now, the party had become crowded as more and more people – soap stars, singers, comedians, so many famous and a few remotely familiar faces – had flooded into the main room. Feeling increasingly out of place among the well-to-do and successful, Paula was relieved to be rescued from her isolation by a young guy who had a full glass of champagne in his left hand and had his right hand thrust out to her. Expecting him to introduce himself, she took the chubby hot hand that was tacky with sweat. The anticipated introduction didn't happen.

"Let's hit the bubbly, baby." He grinned at her.

He didn't have a known face. Hair slicked down, smartly dressed, he had the anonymity of the army of identical young men who sell computers and televisions in places like Curry's and Dixon's. But maybe he was someone who could further her cause. She decided to find out.

"Let's find ourselves a quiet place." He beamed at her. "I'll get you some champers to fix whatever's making you so sad."

"I'm not sad."

"Everybody's sad. This mob is too stupid to realise it. They never face the big questions in life: like can a mule have sex and why won't prostitutes let you kiss them on the mouth? Come on. Let us find an oasis of quiet in this desert of inanity. Then you can tell Uncle Jay your problems."

"I don't have any problems," Paula objected.

She followed him as he threaded a way through the milling,

heaving human mass. He was definitely mad, but he was funny and she could do with a laugh. Paula was prepared to spend a little time with him, be nice to him, find out if he could be useful to her. No doubt he had something else in mind, but she knew enough to fight him off without angering him. They went into a small room that was unoccupied.

The room was sparsely furnished. A little warm light from two wall lamps gave the atmosphere a cosiness. A large framed photograph of Clark Gable hung on one wall.

"Everybody has problems," he said, returning to their suspended conversation.

When he gestured her to a sofa, she obediently sat. She reminded herself that she had to control this performing-dog behaviour, jumping through hoops in response to any mildly authoritative command.

Walking back to the door, he said, "I won't be two shakes of a donkey's whatsit. And what's more, I'll return with a magnum of champagne."

"I don't want anything but orange juice," she told him, surprisingly firmly for her.

She managed to protest again when he returned with her drink and was closing the door. "Please leave it open."

Doing as she asked, he chuckled at her prudery as he sat beside her and they raised their glasses in a toast. He asked, "What shall we drink to?"

"I don't know."

"Let's drink to your not being found out."

"I don't know what you mean."

To cover her awkwardness, she lifted the drink, surreptitiously sniffing it. She was sure that he had doctored the juice – the lack of smell suggested vodka. She trusted neither the drink nor him, and disliked anything she mistrusted.

"You don't lie too good, baby, and I like that." Now he sounded like Austin Powers. "Whose guest are you, Matthew's or Karen's?"

"Both, really," Paula replied, speaking defensively round the rim of her glass. "We're old friends."

"Ah!" he nodded, apparently convinced. "Then you'll be one of the chosen few to have visited their houseboat on the Thames?"

"Of course," Paula replied with bogus confidence, adding authenticity with, "but just the one time."

He chuckled. "Matthew and Karen don't have a houseboat, baby. You gatecrashed this do! You've got straw in your hair, straight off the train at Waterloo, a country hick walking barefoot through stardust."

Lowering her head she dabbed with a finger at a real or imaginary tiny splash of drink on her dress. She had made a mistake, but didn't like being ridiculed. This guy was a threat to her daydream.

"Don't go all sulky on me," he complained. "I'm not going to shop you. If I wanted to, which I don't, they'd be too pissed to understand what I was saying."

Paula explained almost apologetically. "I didn't mean anyone any harm. I heard about this party and saw it as a chance to meet people in show business."

"It's too late for that this time, baby. But, *nil desperandum*, you've struck lucky. I haven't missed a Matthew bash in years. Stick with me and I'll make sure that you're my guest next time. I can introduce you to the top people. Look, I can't keep calling you baby. What's your name?"

"Paula Monroe."

He sounded good and she felt good. The night hadn't been a total waste after all. She may have gone unnoticed, but at least she had met someone with contacts.

Both his eyebrows had gone up sceptically. "Your real name."

"Pauline Manning."

"That's better. Where've you been, Pauline? The Monroe thing was done forty years ago. I bet you don't know what you were doing when Kennedy was assassinated. You'd have been a little speck with a tail swimming around with a billion other tailed specks in your old man's reproduction system."

The same would apply to him. She doubted that he had turned thirty yet. She staunchly defended her choice of name. "I thought enough time had gone by to make the revival interesting."

"You mean you think you look like Marilyn," he said, tapping her lightly on the tip of her nose with one finger. Paula blushed a deep scarlet. Then he covered one of her hands with his and added, "Don't let me embarrass you. You do resemble her, Pauline."

"Paula."

"Sorry, Paula. I'm Jay Clifford. How long have you been in London?

"Only a month."

"This is where either you lie and tell me you've struck lucky in a West End show, or admit you're on the dole."

"Neither." Paula felt smugly proud as she put him right. "I'm in a musical. Not in the West End, of course. It's only a small company, but Rick – that's the guy who runs it – says he's getting us a summer season at the seaside."

"And you're at this bash because you want to be Liz Hurley and Catherine Zeta Jones both," he smiled, "and you think coming here will make it happen."

Annoyed, she retorted, "I'm not that stupid." Then she toned it down a bit. "It's just that I heard this afternoon that Karen Cayson was giving this birthday party for her husband, and I thought if I kind of crept in it wouldn't hurt, and I might meet someone important in show business."

He sat close to her. It was a small sofa. His knees touched hers. Paula tried to put a distance between them but lack of space restricted her. There were traces of sweat on his fat upper lip.

"You've got ambition and you've shown initiative, Paula," he congratulated her. "Add your good looks to that, and I'd say you'll make it to the big time."

Was this flattery, part of a seduction plan, or could it be that he was in a position to know these things? As he had been boldly prying into her background, Paula felt justified in asking, "What do you do, Jay?"

She watched him reach to an inner pocket for a metallic business card. It reflected greenly in the artificial lighting. She had to tilt it slightly to read the silvered wording.

"You're a photographer," she acknowledged. "What, for magazines, newspapers, that sort of thing?"

"Nothing so common," he exclaimed, pretending that he was indignant. "I am an artist, Paula. My portfolios are a passport to fame."

"I couldn't afford you," she said with a shake of her blonde head.

"But you may need me, so keep that card somewhere safe," he said, slipping an arm round her shoulders. Then he said, mockingly, "Now, my little prude from the backwoods, I am going to kiss you. Keep your lips tight together so that I don't make you pregnant."

Starting to draw away, Paula looked at him. She searched his face. Uncertain about him and everything else. Feeling distaste, she struggled to hide it. She held herself stiffly but didn't resist as his mouth came against hers. An unwelcome kiss was better than missing out on an opportunity.

A woman giggled piercingly. It was the delighted kind of giggle that said she'd been touched up in the crowd. Though unable to see the woman, Cheryl Valenta detested her by proxy. She had to be the vain type who preferred being groped in public to being ignored. Aware that her cynicism set her apart from the mob, Cheryl didn't experience even a slight sense of loneliness. It gave her a strange feeling of superiority to be cold sober among stupidly drunken revellers. After spending hours trying to look seductive, the women with ambition were now getting in some soul snogging and lap sitting where the lights were low at the fringes of the room.

Feeling contempt for her fellow guests one moment, pity the next, Cheryl observed people she knew better than they knew themselves. They didn't realise any of this because they weren't really people. Cheryl knew that the whole lot of them were still acting off camera: there were the women and girls who had fornicated their way to pseudo-stardom. Then there were the big wheels, the male VIPs of show business who somehow retained an air of aloofness despite being as openly lecherous as they were drunk. To her left, speaking with the concentrated seriousness of the inebriated, Matthew Wyndham was addressing a bevy of would-be disciples. Standing close, looking up adoringly into his eyes, was Wendi Maylor, a lavishly beautiful young dancer, a singer, an actress and a rumoured call girl. Her blonde hair was lacquered; the midnight-blue dress she wore was cut so simply that it had to be costly.

One of Wendi's hands rested lightly on Wyndham's forearm. She blew a long column of smoke out between her red lips, her look cool and amused. Wyndham was holding a bottle by the neck with his left hand. He continually topped up his own glass and that of anyone around him requiring a refill.

Matthew Wyndham's wife mingled drunkenly with the guests. Laughing too often and too loudly, Karen Cayson was wearing a sleeveless, lacy, deep-cut, see-through dress that announced she wasn't wearing a bra. Cheryl was given an unnecessary reminder that Karen had no need of a brassiere's support. To Cheryl there was something unethical if not sacrilegious about a close-to-bare-breasted woman drinking vintage champagne in the company of men. Maybe that was sour grapes, as she'd never quite succeeded when trying to convince herself that she didn't fancy the gorgeous Karen. She had lost count of the number of naïve starlets Karen had sexually devoured. Cheryl had always regarded the top star's renowned jealousy of her producer husband to be an alibi. By what had to be a mini-miracle for someone always in the news, Karen had managed to keep her many lesbian liaisons secret.

The tabloid newspapers would pay a fortune for what Cheryl knew, but she wasn't about to tell. You sold more than a story to the gutter press: you sold your soul as well. Cheryl neither liked nor disliked Karen Cayson as a person. She *certainly* wasn't envious of the star.

Leaning over backwards to be modest, Cheryl was aware that she had a lot more going for her than Karen Cayson had. Both beauty *and* brains, together with a scintillating personality when she chose to switch it on. A diploma that labelled her a Master of Arts. While giving her a certain prestige and a superb self-confidence, the MA had not aided her career in any way. She was svelte, sleek, hard, burnished, an enamelled sophisticate able to hold her own in any company. A wiseacre with all the wise words, snappy with the quickies of repartee. In these circles she was an intellectual Amazon among mental pygmies.

Noticing her standing alone, the television producer Art Cooney made an overcasual approach. He was a short, stout, wet-lipped womaniser and his almost colourless eyes had a glisteny look. His tongue licked out toadlike, flicking at his lips. God's gift was how he saw himself. Cheryl had not met one woman who shared that view.

"It is the height of bad manners to leave a lady standing alone without a drink in her hand," he said. His tongue licked out at his moist red lips. "That's what my old daddy always told me."

"It surprises me that you know who he was," Cheryl said cuttingly, turning her back on him.

As she walked away she heard Cooney hiss angrily, "Lesbian bitch," and in her mind she said, Up yours, fuck-face! and kept going. There had been one man for her once, a very long time ago. Since they had split up, all the rest of the guys had the same kind of face, and she wasn't interested.

One of the catering staff hired for the evening held out a gleaming tray filled with drinks. Cheryl waved him away. She moved off in search of a much-needed spell of solitude before leaving. To go home without detaching herself from these people by means of a short indulgence in what could probably be described as meditation would mean that she would spend a sleepless night. She had long ago learned that mental contagion was as dangerous as the worst infectious disease.

There was a burst of childish cheering as a dropped glass shattered noisily. The music trailed away, and those on the floor released each other. They stood limply holding hands in the vague, stupid way people do when a dance ends.

Drifting from the herd that she held in contempt, Cheryl thought that she'd found a peaceful haven in a side room. But there was a scrambling sound as she went in through the doorway. A young woman, her bright blonde hair dishevelled, fear in her enormous blue eyes, stood up from a sofa. A bewildered Clark Gable looked down out of yesterday into a today that he couldn't understand. Cheryl didn't like photographs. They were reminders of passing time, of mortality.

Whatever was going on in the room was no business of Cheryl's. She was turning to leave when from the corner of her eye she saw a man surface from behind the sofa. Recognising him, she stepped back into the room. Cheryl looked at the girl, who smiled weakly. She had a passionate, full-lipped, sensuous mouth that didn't fit right with a slender but prominent nose. Strangely, the irregularity of features gave the girl a special kind of erotic attractiveness. Cheryl turned her gaze to the young man.

"The casting couch," Cheryl cynically remarked, indicating the sofa with a nod of her head. "Are you still pulling your stunts, Clifford. What have you been telling this kid, how Kate Winslet would never have made *Titanic* without your help?"

Jay Clifford had a tendency towards obesity that his skeleton hadn't been designed to support. Yes, in Cheryl's opinion he dressed well, but his suit appeared to be standing at attention while his body stood at ease. His eyes were feminine, dark-lashed and terribly innocent, but they were also terribly wise with a perverted wisdom that altered the innocence to mocking knowledge.

Clifford's much-boasted-about photography earned him a pittance on the periphery of show business. His main income came from pornography, and many a successful actress today would once have starved had she not performed in front of Jay Clifford's sleazy cameras. It was rumoured that he was gay. Cheryl didn't know if he was and she had never cared sufficiently to find out.

"At last, Ms Valenta, you've come to interview me." He grinned at Cheryl.

"You're a prick, Clifford," Cheryl said harshly, "and I don't do interviews in toilets."

She looked at the bewildered girl. A teenager! Good God, what an awful age! Had *she* been like that as a teenager? Had any other human being? That wasn't a fair question. The kid wasn't human yet. Her shapely body was as soft as her unformed brain. She was like those half-baked loaves you can buy. The kid should go back to where she had come from and finish getting cooked in the family microwave. If Cheryl didn't interfere, Clifford would tomorrow have given the girl her first role as an actress. Her leading man would be wearing nothing but shades, a moustache, socks, a wristwatch and an XL hard-on.

"This," an unabashed Clifford began, turning to the girl, "is the woman of my dreams. If I should die tonight and be reincarnated, she is the woman I'd want to spend the next nine months inside of."

An expression of disgust on her face, Cheryl said, "You can get lost, creep, or I'll have to tell Matthew Wyndham that you've crashed yet another of his parties."

Clifford hesitated. It seemed that he was going to refuse to go. He did some thinking, realised that Cheryl would humiliate him further in front of the blonde if he stayed. He went sulkily from the room.

Cheryl heard the girl's sharp inward sigh of shock. The kid owed her, though she didn't know it. Finding out early that Jay Clifford was a charlatan was a whole lot healthier than making the discovery too late.

Cheryl sat in a comfortable armchair and comfortably studied the girl. The blonde was a little agitated, looking as if she needed to escape. She sank into the sofa, her legs high. She crossed her knees, the hem of the red dress retreating to her thighs. That presented Cheryl with the minor problem of where to look. At the provocative legs or the semiexposed tits. The girl stood up.

"There's no need for you to leave," Cheryl said. The girl went back to the sofa. She tucked her feet under herself like a child, sitting in the lotus position. Cheryl thought it sweet, touching. But it revealed a vulnerability that was frightening to observe in a newcomer to London. The girl looked as if she was about to cry. Cheryl knew that she wouldn't be able to cope if the kid did crack up.

"I suppose that we should introduce ourselves. I'm Cheryl Valenta."

"Are you an actress?" the girl asked with such reverence that she caused herself to blush. The soft beams angled from the wall lights sharpened her colour and gave her a fragile transparency.

"No—" Cheryl began, pushing the shy girl into giving her name.

"Paula. Paula Monroe."

"Paula, that's nice." Cheryl smiled encouragingly. "No, I'm not an actress – I'm a journalist."

That was a fundamentally bare statement that didn't do Cheryl justice. She was a syndicated columnist with enough power to guarantee an invitation to every celebrity soirée such as this one.

But it would be pointless giving her full CV to someone like Paula Monroe. The kid probably didn't read anything that didn't have a computer-enhanced picture of Atomic Kitten on the cover.

"Ooh, you must be very clever."

"Actually, I'm very stupid," Cheryl said, putting herself down to make the girl comfortable. "I'd say that you haven't been in London for very long."

"That's right," the girl replied as if she were making a confession and being new were a shameful sin.

"And you're feeling homesick?"

"I am, yes." It was another confession, another sin.

"That sort of thing will pass when you're a bit older," Cheryl advised, her do-gooder side surfacing – a side that she detested but had no control over. "We may inhabit families, enjoy friendships, experience moments of love, but all of us live alone."

"You make it all sound very depressing," the girl remarked unhappily.

"On the contrary, acceptance of that fact is an antidote for depression. But you are too young to understand."

"I like to think that I'm fairly bright." Paula smiled at Cheryl. It was a nice smile. It was friendly, and her eyes were friendly.

Finishing her drink, Paula frowned at the empty glass. She looked around as if about to signal a waiter. But she and Cheryl were alone, somehow separated from the pulsing sounds of the crowded house.

"I'm sure that you are," Cheryl said consolingly. "But when we are young we tend to mistake arrogance for experience in life. The Big City can be a dangerous place for a young girl alone."

"I know, and I've been taking care of myself since I got here." Paula's pale-blue eyes studied Cheryl. "You talk different to anyone I've ever met. I know that I could learn a lot from you."

"I'm still wearing L-plates myself." Cheryl smiled, liking the refreshing simplicity of the girl. "I don't want to pry, Paula, but have you anywhere to stay tonight?"

"Oh, yes. I share a room with another girl, Nikki Graham. We're in a show together."

"That's nice," Cheryl said again, unable to stop herself. Her vocabulary had become as limited as that of most of the morons she had to interview to earn a crust. Scriptless, the majority had the communication skills of goldfish.

Tiredness caused Paula to close her eyes, her head giving a sharp little jerk as she fought sleep. She was very sweet and desirable. Cheryl wanted to help her, save her from the myriad perils in a big city. Did that mean that she wanted to save her for herself? If so, then was she being hypocritical? Not really, because Cheryl never went in for one-way relationships. If anything happened between them it would be with the girl's total agreement.

Cheryl found the contrived names these hopefuls chose for themselves to be pathetic. They began life as plain Jane Smith, or something like that, took on some exotic name for a brief period, then ended up collectively as hookers in Paddington. Changing their names was the first mistake that came before getting their time sense confused. Once they got their dreams and daydreams mixed with reality they became completely disoriented – real schizos.

This one was more immature than most, more innocent. No, that last bit wasn't true. You weren't born innocent. Innocence was something that had to be striven for and few ever achieved. It was an impossible target that Cheryl Valenta had years ago stopped aiming at. She had settled for neutrality, making sure that she harmed no one, while protecting herself against being hurt. In a little while from now some pimp wouldn't be able to believe his luck when this guileless child practically volunteered to be abused.

If she left the kid here, then someone would take cruel advantage of her. But Cheryl found herself questioning her own intentions. Her attention was focused on the girl's slack-lipped, made-for-kissing mouth. Paula came suddenly awake, and Cheryl changed desire for protectiveness. The uncertain smile on the girl's lips and the excessive brightness in her eyes were signs of fear – not the emotion to be sought in a potential lover.

Cheryl redeemed herself by saying, "You look as tired as I feel, Paula. I'll give you a lift home."

She saw that the suggestion didn't appeal. Paula Monroe, or whoever she was, had come here tonight for a purpose. It would be an anticlimax for her to leave without having been noticed.

"I was wondering..." Paula began hesitantly, looking longingly out through the open door.

The sound of music had become muted, the buzz of conversation had turned into a roar, and the laughter of women was now piercingly shrill.

"You go out there now, Paula," Cheryl warned, "and you won't find what you're looking for. What you will find is trouble."

A dubious expression on the girl's face looked ready to turn into disbelief. Cheryl waited for her to reach a decision. Cheryl's voluntary, or rather involuntary, social work stopped short of playing mother hen.

Standing, Paula looked at Cheryl with a temerity that she found embarrassing. The girl spoke hesitantly. "If I asked you for one bit of advice about getting ahead in showbiz, what would your answer be?"

"You mean generally?"

"Yes."

"Well..." Cheryl began, but stopped, shaking her head. "No, you're too young. I'd shock you."

"I'm grown up, and not easily shocked," Paula argued. "So please tell me."

With a resigned shrug, Cheryl advised, "Never fuck for free."

In the main private room away from the crush of guests, Karen Cayson tested herself. Selecting a straight black line in the pattern of the carpet, she walked it by placing one foot carefully in front of the other. Making the far end without even the hint of a sway, she congratulated herself. In a police station in the days before breath tests she would right now be shaking the hand of the duty sergeant before going back out to her car. But she wasn't at a police station. She was in her own home and the crowd was absolutely voluminous. Why were all these freeloading fuck-pigs here in her house? Where was Matthew? He should be at her side, feeding platitudes to the multitude. It would take more than a few loaves and fishes to satisfy this clamouring horde.

Minutes later, she recalled that today was Matthew's birthday and that she had arranged this bash for him. It had seemed the right thing to do at the time. But she had overlooked the fact that to be part of a drunken mob you needed to be as drunk as all the other party animals. Of late, alcohol had been letting her down. No matter how much she drank, she could get to only a certain stage of drunkenness and no further. It was like being in an alcoholic purgatory, a mental vacuum in which only vast despair and raging anger existed. She'd mentioned this state to Dr Alice Frayter, who hosted a televised health-advice programme.

"The problem is that your system has built up a defence against booze," Alice had explained.

Like all physicians, Dr Frayter was brilliant at telling you what was wrong, but not so good at fixing it. Fat Alice didn't even look how a doctor should look. She'd have been at home sitting at a supermarket checkout point, or squashed like a female Buddha in the pay box of a cinema.

In spite of her popular help programme, Alice Frayter was a flawed saviour. She had a cocaine addiction, and once during an examination she had woozily tried to kiss Karen's cunt. Though a devoted fan of cunnilingus, Karen had been revolted. Alice wasn't her type and she had – painfully, she felt sure – pulled the amorous doctor up by her ears.

Remembering that she was looking for Matthew, Karen continued her search. As she walked she disciplined herself. There must be no drama, no big scene. She mustn't make a four-star production out of it. Jealousy, a compulsion with her, was demeaning. Guests diplomatically looked the other way when their hosts had a blazing row, but they had a good old piss-taking gossip afterwards. This wasn't going to be yet another occasion on which her explosive temper would turn Matthew and herself into a laughing stock.

Maybe Matthew was in a dark corner with some half-arse wannabe, but Karen was determined to keep her cool. She saw their servants, Henry and Nellie Drury, filling glasses at a long table. They had been with Matthew's family for years. Both still spoke of his long-dead parents reverently, but both had to struggle to conceal the low regard in which they held Karen. Karen knew that to Henry and Nellie she was not the wife of their beloved master, but a whore who should have stayed for only one night.

Catching Henry's eye, she beckoned him over. Grey hair Brylcreemed and immaculately groomed, his short white coat as stiff as a straitjackets, he came to her in his foot-slapping walk. Henry's left ankle had been fixed with a pin after a motoring accident. With each step he lifted his left foot high and shook it as though he had stepped in something nasty. Even a short walk made him aggressive. It was as if he blamed everyone in the world for his lameness.

There was a mixture of anger and servility on his face as he came up to Karen.

"Do you know where Mr Wyndham is, Henry?"

"I haven't seen him for at least half an hour, madam." Servility had triumphed.

"Nellie?"

"She won't have seen him, madam," Henry said stiffly, miffed that his mistress believed his wife had time to stand and stare. He covertly censured Karen. "Nellie has been very busy."

"I know that," Karen said soothingly. To cause staff problems right now would be a bummer. "Where was my husband when you saw him last, Henry?"

"I do believe that he was going up the stairs, madam."

"Thank you, Henry."

That wasn't good news. Karen followed Henry as he returned to the table. She picked up a glass and drained it in a gulping series of swallows. Waiting, disappointed because the alcohol hadn't filmed her senses as constructively as she had hoped, she headed for the stairs.

Walking the landing, her anger rising as she progressed, Karen opened every door, looked into every room. She found Matthew finally, in the bedroom she used when she had to be early on set and hadn't wanted to wake him. That had been considerate of her, but right now he wasn't affording her any consideration.

Wendi Maylor, naked, not blonde but two-toned, lay sprawled on the bed on her back. Matthew was lying beside her, as naked as Wendi and with his slender penis at full attention. Oblivious to Karen's having opened the door, he was licking at Wendi's ear, and his right hand was passing down over a hillock of firm breast, along the plateau of flat belly, and down into the lush valley between her legs. Conversely for a cheated wife, a wide-eyed Karen felt excitement curling through her like a hot snake as she saw her husband's middle finger find the slot, slide in, slide up to the clit, and deftly massage it.

It was Wendi's soft moan that brought Karen out of her state of inertia. Realisation of what was happening drained her of her lust. The bottle from which Matthew had been pouring drinks for his guests downstairs was almost empty now. It stood on the dressing table. Leaping into action, Karen grabbed the bottle by the neck.

From then on she hardly knew what she was doing. The naked couple looked up at her, alarmed but not yet able to take in what was happening. Matthew had raised his head and shoulders up off the bed. Wendi was squirming around. Her eyes glistened and her breath was coming fast. She had caught the scent of violence and it had aroused her.

Karen swung the bottle like a club. There was a dull but hard cracking sound as the bottle connected with Matthew's head. Making a snorting, choking sound, he slumped back down, his body inert. Uttering a tiny scream, Wendi jumped off the bed. She staggered and her calves caught against the side of the bed. She toppled, but panic assisted her in righting herself. Having scooped her clothes up from the floor with the skill of a quick-change artist, she fled the room.

Karen, a fire blazing in her head, the redness of it blurring her vision, went out after her. The landing was deserted. Any pursuit of Wendi Maylor would be pointless.

A grey haze started to hem Karen in, stripping her of conscious thought. Then everything seemed to snap into place and her mind was crystal clear. Walking slowly along the landing, she reached where she could stand on the balcony with both her hands resting on the banister rail. The tinsel glare of the lighting made her squint as she looked down at the merrymaking mob.

The recent scene inside the bedroom lay on the fringes of her memory, to be recalled at will. A strange sense of power passed through her. She felt unique, even further separated from the rabble below who thought of themselves as her guests.

Karen shouted loudly. She intended to utter words, but hadn't decided what the words should be. It came out as a ridiculous sound, something like Tarzan's yell. The noise below lessened gradually, then faded swiftly to silence.

She saw a sea of faces looking up at her. Silly faces wearing the stupid smiles of people who don't know what to expect but are ready to join in happily once enlightened. Mass adoration was there, too. Karen could have been Queen Elizabeth II on the balcony of Buckingham Palace, about to give little circular waves with a hand held upright. Her loyal subjects waited and they wondered, but not one could have guessed what Karen Cayson's announcement would be.

In a clear, shrill voice, she cried down at them, "You can all fuck off."

Below her there was a moment of utter numbness. Here and there an expression of mild disbelief showed through.

"I want each and every one of you bums out of my house," Karen continued. "You've drunk my booze, eaten my grub, and dropped ash all over my carpets. I didn't want one of you freeloading bastards here in the first place. Get out of my house, the fucking lot of you. Right now."

Her message instantly got through. Everyone grasped at once that she wasn't kidding. Within minutes, every one of the guests had left.

Karen looked down on a view that was desolately empty of friends.

Two

Paula sat in the front passenger seat, huddled within herself, gazing blankly out through the windscreen. Shattered by Karen Wyndham's abrupt, foul-mouthed dismissal of her guests, the girl had been silent since they had left the pretentious Wyndham home in New Malden. Cheryl Valenta left the kid to adjust to the neurotic reality of celebrity life. Fame and riches made it unnecessary to keep within the boundaries of convention.

The party had dragged on interminably. Cheryl could never understand why the days and the nights were so long, yet the years went by so quickly. As she drove her Mercedes SL towards London, she was in a reflective mood. A nonsensical mood, more like. She looked along the beams of her car's headlights, which probed far ahead into the night. They were a lesson in physics. No matter how fast you drove you would never catch up with your own lights. Maybe you could if you travelled at more than the speed of light. Where would your headlights be then? Trailing out behind you like an illuminated smoke trail? Or would they go faster in ratio to your speed? In that case they would stay up ahead, big blobs of solid light hanging in the darkness.

"What on earth was all that about?"

Paula's voice startled Cheryl out of her ludicrous reverie. She was aware that she would have to compose her answer carefully. Finding out how the other half lived was always traumatic, regardless of your social standpoint. Seeing another side of Karen

Wyndham/Cayson had pierced Paula's emotional armour. She could be so easily wounded now. That was something that Cheryl wanted to avoid. Fan worship was psychopathic, and it was a mistake not to treat it seriously.

"I've never known a Wyndham bash end without either Matthew or Karen throwing a wobbly," Cheryl smiled. "I remember one time when they turned on each other first, then rounded on their guests together."

"But that was very rude tonight, Cheryl, ordering everybody out after they'd been invited."

"Who was invited?" Cheryl teased. "I must see my shrink in the morning, get my memory checked over."

"That's not the point." Paula's voice was quiet, colourless. "She's always been my idol, and to see her raving like that really shook me up. As for the language – well! Who would believe it?"

Who indeed? Anyone who knew Karen Cayson, the hottest actress in Britain today. Unbalanced, explosive Karen Cayson, flawless body, perfect face, full of charm and original wit. Mrs Matthew Wyndham wrongly suspected to be a whore, totally unsuspected of being a lesbian.

"She's so beautiful," Paula was enthusing at Cheryl's side. "I've got a big colour still of her from that comedy, that American movie – what was it called?"

"*Living Forever but Dying Young.*"

"That's it." Paula turned her face to Cheryl, impressed by her knowledge. "Cost me twelve pounds, the photograph did, but it was worth it. I even brought it to London with me. I've got my scrapbook here, too."

It was like hearing a child relate what she'd had for Christmas. Paula would have studied the photograph of Karen Wyndham until it had become imprisoned in her mind like a convict in solitary confinement. Cheryl's rising carnal interest stopped rising, began to steadily fall back. Though she hadn't had sex in mind when she'd offered to run Paula home, she had since considered it. Cheryl had the kind of sexual fuse that couldn't be put out once it had been lit, and her arousal had been on the increase since they had left the aborted Wyndham bash.

More out of courtesy than anything, Cheryl had snogged Julie Stanmoor on the Wyndham terrace while waiting for Paula. Julie, an ageing hostess from a long-gone television quiz show, had turned a few snatched minutes in the exotic shadows of a Japanese garden into a torrid encounter. Serenaded by the somehow delightfully tuneful splashing of a miniature stream tumbling into a pool encased in bamboo and stone, using an older woman's experience and expertise, Julie had roused Cheryl into a trembling state of desire. Paula, on the other hand, was unknown sexual territory, but she was the reason why Cheryl had turned down an invitation to go home with Julie. Cheryl had forsaken the certainty of what was arguably the tastiest and liveliest 69 in London, for the possible seduction of a young country girl.

Now, going over Kingston Hill, she saw the centre of London and felt it, a surf of neon lights breaking against a neutral sky. The tourist traps, a pulsing sheet of stained lights stretching from Hammersmith to the City. Traps of stainless steel and polished glass where foolish people from out of town paid high prices for food they wouldn't touch with a bargepole back home. There were a few good places, but the throbbing, bragging, beckoning neon made everything look alike.

Cheryl drove into Battersea, where she had lived on leaving college. She had shared a bedsit with Sheena, a West Indian girl who was in public relations. That had been fifteen years ago. Though she had difficulty recalling her face, the memory of Sheena's kisses hadn't yet gone cold on Cheryl's lips, and she could still feel Sheena's long finger sliding into her to unerringly and arousingly locate her G-spot. She'd had many lovers since, but none of them came anywhere close to equalling Sheena. After exchanging cards for the first four Christmases, they had lost touch.

In those days, Cheryl had freelanced, profiting little, but securing valuable contacts. She had earned money for her keep by writing pornography for French and Swedish magazines. That was how she had developed the style that brought success. She'd even held aspirations of becoming a novelist.

In her Kensington apartment now were two typescripts for novels she had written in those tough days. One was a tour de force entitled *Nights with the Knights*, about an oversexed maiden who, disguised as a man, joined the Crusades. The other novel, entitled *Long Grass – Short Memories*, was a contemporary lesbian romp that revolved around Battersea Park. At the time, Cheryl had considered the first to be too boring, and the second too embarrassingly autobiographical to submit to publishers. The time was probably right now, but she had learned a lot since, which meant that both manuscripts would need rewriting. That was a prospect that she couldn't face.

These days, although coaxingly solicited by agents and publishers, she wasn't given to literary thinking. The writers she met were either excruciatingly boring or downright embarrassing.

"There it is, over there on the right," Paula said suddenly, temporarily blocking Cheryl's view through the windscreen by pointing.

In Streatham there were some nice houses and then some worse ones and then some truly horrible ones. The place Paula was pointing at most definitely belonged in the last category. The "Hotel" on the half-illuminated sign outside was a misnomer. Inside, sheets of hardboard would have been used to divide the original rooms into three or four cramped compartments. These were let at a high rent to no-hopers who carried all their worldly belongings in Tesco plastic carrier bags. A cardboard box under Waterloo Bridge would be preferable.

Cheryl felt a vast despair for Paula. The kid would get nowhere living in a place like this. You had to have some space around you.

Otherwise you felt oppressed, defeated, and spent your life bogged down worrying over trivial things. It didn't have to be a tent in the middle of the Sahara desert, but everyone needed room to breathe, to expand.

Having switched off the car's ignition, Cheryl sat in the new silence, waiting. The tall houses on each side of her were slightly claustrophobic. The road in front of them narrowed and curved into more depressive greyness. Cheryl looked at an unmoving Paula. The girl spoke.

"Thank you for the lift. I'd better go in."

"Take care now," Cheryl said as she leaned across in front of Paula to grasp the handle of the door, ready to let her out.

The girl gave a little laugh. Her breath lightly kissed Cheryl's cheek. There was just enough illumination from the street lamps to provide an intimate orange glow inside the car. Still holding the door handle, Cheryl turned her head to look at Paula. The girl looked into Cheryl's eyes. Their faces were close, almost touching. Catching the scent of the girl, Cheryl inhaled, liking it. For all her youth and girlish manner, Paula Monroe had a knowing look, and Cheryl was drawn to her by a hypnotic charm.

"When you leaned across," Paula said with a self-conscious little laugh, "I thought for a moment that you were going to kiss me."

"So, I almost got my face slapped?" Cheryl questioned softly, her mouth very near to the full, sensual lips of Paula."

"No," Paula protested quickly. But it wasn't a protest. It was an invitation.

Cheryl kissed her. Lightly on the cheek at first and then on the lips. She felt Paula pull away slightly, then the girl was returning the kiss passionately. The kiss lasted a long time before their lips parted. They were both breathing heavily, and Paula gave what sounded like a sigh of appreciation. Cheryl kissed her again, her tongue in the girl's mouth this time.

The dress barely needed the touch of Cheryl's hands to fall away from Paula's breasts. They thrust out proudly, the left one firm and responsive to Cheryl's gently exploring hand, the nipple pressing hard into the centre of her palm. Lowering her head, Cheryl found that the breasts were powdered. She kissed them, enjoying the perfume that was radiated by the warm, soft skin. She circled the poking-out nipple with her tongue, teased it with her lips, took it into her mouth and sucked it.

But this wasn't right. The dashboard of her car was boring painfully into Cheryl's back; the position of her legs was giving her pain. She sat back up in her seat. She stroked Paula's hair, and there was a sultry, parted-lips look on the girl's face. Cheryl wanted her, lusted madly for her.

Glancing over at the tall house, Cheryl said, "Don't tell me that you have a dragon of a landlady who won't allow visitors."

"I haven't, but I do have a roommate." Paula held up her arm to the car window, checking the time on her wristwatch. "It's gone half past three. It wouldn't be right to disturb Nikki at this time."

It wouldn't, Cheryl silently and disappointedly agreed. Opening the glove compartment, the little light inside coming on to light Paula's face dramatically, Cheryl took out a ballpoint pen. Clasping Paula's hand, she wrote her telephone number on her wrist.

"You be sure to call me, Paula."

"I will."

They kissed again, feverishly devouring, tongues exploring each other's mouth. They drank of each other hotly, and Cheryl knew that she was being carried away by the kiss. She needed more of Paula, wanted everything of Paula. It would be uncomfortable and risky in the car out here, even though the street was deserted.

Cheryl was reaching for the lever to tilt the passenger seat back, when Paula pulled away. The girl's breaths were coming in mighty sobs, her naked breasts rising and falling as she pulled her dress up over them. Finding the handle herself, she opened the door and clambered out into the night. Turning, she looked in at Cheryl, desire contorting her face, her voice husky when she spoke.

"I'll call you, Cheryl."

"Don't leave it too long," Cheryl half ordered, half pleaded. As the girl was about to shut the car door, she called her name sharply: "Paula."

"Yes?"

"You're not new to this, are you?"

"I am, honestly," Paula replied. "I couldn't help myself. I don't know why, but it just seemed so natural."

"Good." Cheryl smiled. "Like I said, ring me soon. Goodnight."

"Goodnight, Cheryl."

Watching the girl go up the broken steps and in through the door without turning, Cheryl didn't start the car's engine. Though it was Saturday and she could enjoy a lie-in, there was no point in her going home. In her aroused state she wouldn't be able to sleep.

Opening the glove box again, she took out her mobile. She ran her tongue over her lips to moisten them and fingered Julie Stanmoor's number.

Turning from the balcony, Karen started along the landing towards the bedroom. A wave of giddiness came over her. She staggered, slamming against the wall with a force that painfully jarred her whole body. Expecting to fall, she clung against the wall with both hands to stay upright. In that position she became suddenly and unexpectedly stone-cold sober. It must have been the impact with the wall, she told herself as she hurried along to the bedroom where she had left her husband.

She remembered the awesome sound of the bottle cracking against his head. Clenching her fists as she hurried along, she thought of him dead. At the bedroom door her heart squeezed tight, and her breath caught in her throat. She took three little running steps into a room that smelled of drink and sex, and a third smell that she couldn't identify. Matthew still lay on the bed in the same position as before. His face was grey-white and his head hung a little over the side. She went to lift it gently, to settle him more comfortably, but she shrank back as she saw the trickle of blood leaking from Matthew's ear. This was bad. Either she'd read it somewhere, or seen it on a television programme, that blood from an ear denoted a fractured skull.

Matthew wouldn't move. It wasn't right. The man was a powerhouse, not only in show business, but also in politics and the media. Dynamic people such as Matthew Wyndham were always on the move, never still. Clutching at him, her fingers going strangely weak, Karen raised him a little from the bed, calling his name. She shook him, but he was appallingly still.

"Wake up!" she said. It was a funny, small, scared voice. Then it cried out from deep inside of her. "Matthew, wake up! I didn't mean to hurt you. You know I'd never do anything to hurt you!"

What had she done? Anger rubbing against libido produces nasty sparks. The sparks couldn't get nastier than they had this night. This would make giant-sized headlines. Like kings, queens, presidents, heads of state, people like Karen Cayson and Matthew Wyndham were allowed no privacy – they were everybody's business.

Holding her husband in her arms, Karen rocked him back and forth. He would come round in a little while and they would laugh at this as they had laughed at all their little fall-outs. Dawn wasn't far away. When the sun comes up in the movies, everything comes up right with it. They would both take a rest, and then drive up West for lunch. "Come on, darling, we're a team. When Karen Cayson and Matthew Wyndham walk into that restaurant all heads will turn, just as always. Come on, darling."

Karen hadn't prayed since attending Father O'Malley's catechism classes as a child. There was a rosary in one of the drawers in her room. There was no time to search for it. She remembered a prayer: "Hail Mary".

She said it aloud in the velvety voice that she reserved for emotional scenes in front of the cameras. She regarded her image in a wall mirror. "Hail, Mary, full of grace, the Lord is with thee; blessed art thou among women, and blessed is the fruit of thy womb..."

Jesus!

Karen gave up. It was pointless. A God checking on fallen sparrows and counting hairs wouldn't put himself out to help a television tycoon and a top actress. Anyway, she liked instant, positive results, like when you called a servant, or ordered something over the telephone.

Time passed and he still wouldn't move. Holding him was a strain. Her thigh muscles ached and screamed for relief. Her face felt old and worn out from the hours of false smiling for their guests. She shut her eyes tight, trying to pretend that she didn't feel the dread that had started throbbing and was spreading, reaching out all through her. There was a distant clatter from somewhere in the house. A cold chill ran along her spine and she twisted round, not knowing what she expected to see. There was nothing for her to see.

Lowering Matthew back down onto the bed, Karen rose dazedly to her feet. Her legs felt numb, her knees stiff so that she walked zombie-like along the landing to the balcony. She leaned on the rails for support, breathing hard, her heart lurching wildly. The party had left a smell behind. It was the sickening smell of a pub in the morning. The reek of stale alcohol, the stench of stale people.

There were no guests now, just a ghostly emptiness. It was as if nobody had lived down there for a long time, and the place had died while she'd been gone. The house had got bigger. Houses swell up at night like those inflatable buildings. They swell up so that when you creep around you can't find anywhere to hide. She intended to call down the name of the servant, but it came out as a frantic scream: *"Henry!"*

*

The voice sounded mechanical. It had the usual stiffness and self-consciousness of a telephone-answering machine: "Hello. Thank you for calling Julie Stanmoor. I am sorry that I am not at home right now – unless you happen to be a randy bitch by the name of Cheryl Valenta."

Though a has-been, a victim of the fickle nature of show business, Julie still had a terrific sense of humour. Taken over by a giggling fit, Cheryl couldn't speak for a moment. When she recovered, she said, "Julie, you cow! You had me going for a moment. How did you know it was me?"

Waiting for an answer, she looked out through the car windows nervously. Cheryl was still outside of Paula's "hotel", in the kind of street where you would expect to be mugged. Even the most loyal guardian angel wouldn't venture into a road like this. She was on her own, and hoped that it would stay that way.

"It doesn't take a Sherlock fucking Holmes to work it out," Julie's telephone voice said with a tinkling little laugh. "Who else would be ringing me at four o'clock on a Saturday morning? Anyway, when I French-kiss 'em they always come back for more. I take it that's what you're after, you exquisite piece of arse."

"Not really. I'm not sleepy and I thought we might share one of those bottles of Haig whisky that you hoard."

"Oh, I see. You just want to talk?"

"That's all."

"Liar!" Julie sounded angry, but Cheryl knew that she wasn't. "I was just about to take a shower."

It was an impossibility, but Cheryl felt certain that she was breathing in the sweet scent of Julie's flesh. "Wait for me and I'll join you."

"I say, Cheryl, that's rather suggestive." Julie now sounded shocked. "How long will it take you to get here?"

"Half an hour, tops."

"Fine, I'll be waiting," Julie promised, then she called Cheryl's name swiftly before she could ring off.

"What is it, Julie?"

"Give me the catchphrase of the show I was on."

Doing a rapid surf through her memory, Cheryl came up with a blank. Reluctant to admit it, she said, "I'm sorry, Julie, I just can't remember."

"Neither can any other fucker," Julie morosely complained, and hung up.

One side of Karen Cayson knew that she was in deep trouble, and another side denied this. Who could point an accusing finger at her? Only Matthew. The paramedics had done what they could for him in the house, and had then rushed him to hospital. They had put something round his head and a supporting collar round his neck. Why were ambulance crews obsessed with collars? Break your fucking leg and you ended up in a collar. If Matthew died, then that was an end to it. Should he survive, then he would keep schtum rather than stir up a scandal involving Wendi Maylor. The two young constables, male and female, who had arrived with the ambulance, had accepted Karen's story. They'd had to walk through the debris of a drunken bash to reach the bedroom, and had no reason to doubt that an inebriated Matthew had fallen and hit his head. There had only been Matthew and herself in the bedroom at the time. She had called Henry Drury upstairs afterwards.

Karen had not been caught in the act, but the arrival of Detective Inspector Collings made her uneasy. The detective put his identification away. It jammed against something in his pocket and he kept his hand in there. Without being invited, he settled into Matthew's high-backed swivel chair. For some odd reason, Karen regarded this as an affront. His face was brown, strong-boned and tight-skinned with heavy black eyebrows, black eyes, and a hawklike nose. He didn't act as if he planned on missing anything, for all his look of weariness.

Henry poured a drink and passed it to the policeman. Collings took the glass eagerly. It had to be only television cops who never drink on duty. The detective drank Scotch and over the rim of the glass observed Karen while speaking to Henry. His voice was not only harsh, it was totally unmusical. He managed to sound very bored in spite of the monotone.

"Constable Houston tells me that you don't think this was an accident, Mr er..."

"Drury," Nellie filled in for her husband. She stood there like something out of a horror film. She was a raw-boned, grim-visaged woman whose excessive use of powder made her face as white as a clown's.

"Drury," Collings acknowledged aloud.

Bastard, Karen said in her mind. She experienced a touch of the occult, a shimmer of intuition, a metaphysical portent of what was to come. The prognosis wasn't good. Henry Drury was about to point the finger. Had it been the other way around, and she was in hospital, this pair of treacherous bastards would be perjuring themselves right, left and fucking centre to help Matthew. Henry was in a nervous state, his body jerked and he had difficulty getting his words out. Without asking Karen's permission, Nellie poured her husband a stiff drink.

How swiftly the cure worked! Henry Drury was revived. The twitches were gone, the eyes were clear, the expression on his peasant's face as lively as a gypsy dance. Henry's words flowed to condemn Karen. Matthew Wyndham hadn't fallen, but was lying on the bed, his head bleeding.

A frown laddered Collings's forehead and the knuckles of a fist rubbed at his strong chin. He shrugged, and the hands came out to move as if coaxing words out of Henry.

"Isn't it possible, Mr Drury, that Mrs Wyn— that Ms Cayson, picked Mr Wyndham up from the floor and placed him on the bed?"

Good point, Inspector. Collings had big feet, but that wasn't his fault. Henry swung the finger of suspicion back towards Karen by saying that his master had definitely not been moved. There was blood on the pillow from the head wound, but not a speck of blood elsewhere. Waiting her turn, Karen decided to rely on her mystique, part of which was an aura of obscurity. An actress earns her living in that aura of obscurity.

It didn't work. Between them the Drurys had damned her without even the courtesy of faint praise. Where did that come from? Ah, yes, Erica Jong: "Tell the truth and you are likely to be a pariah within your family, a semi-criminal to authorities and damned with faint praise by your peers."

Detective Inspector Collings was saying something about her being able to call a solicitor. Ha-bloody-ha! There was no need to ask whose side Richard Neehan would be on. The solicitor was a thousand times more partisan than the Drurys. He was fawned upon, licked, lapped, and treated with trembling obeisance by the Wyndhams, because Neehan knew where all the family's important dead horses were buried. Karen heard the detective's final sentence.

"I'm afraid that I'll have to ask you to come down to the station with me, Ms Wyndham."

Julie's home was a three-room penthouse in St John's Wood. It was at the top of a tall, narrow, expensive house, in which her apartment was the most expensive. Though the public no longer remembered her, Julie was the head of a thriving model agency. She now had an affluence that appearing on television could never have brought her. Even so, she would willingly trade half of her wealth, perhaps all of it, for a return of the fame she had once enjoyed so much.

They were in the shower together. They had entered like a couple of innocent water sprites. Now Cheryl soaped Julie and Julie soaped Cheryl and hissing water washed them clean. They kissed as water rained on them warmly.

She had been waiting for Cheryl with the lights down. Only a single table lamp had been burning, and Julie had been standing barefoot in bra and briefs. She was beautiful, exquisite, gorgeous, divine, the whole bit. A white-skinned figure that was big, but nowhere was an ounce of fat overhanging. Julie was tall, taut and wonderfully proportioned.

Now Cheryl saw Julie's eyes darkening as she reached for her. The fooling, the laughing, the preliminaries were over. Cheryl drank in tiny breaths of steamy air. Her hands did a sensuous sliding over the wet skin of Julie's back. Julie's hands fastened upon her buttocks, pulling Cheryl to her. Their breasts, soft but firm, came together in the sweltering mists, tingling nipple against tingling nipple. A thrilled moan escaped from Cheryl as Julie's sweet tongue insinuated itself between her greedy lips.

Suddenly, Julie moved down, her hands coming up to squeeze Cheryl's breasts together as her mouth suckled at the nipples, going from one to the other in rapid succession. Hands going up to clench Julie's damp hair, the liquid heat between her legs threatening to reach boiling point, Cheryl dropped one hand to Julie's flat stomach. Her fingers traced down through the fine-haired inverted V, then moved into the forest of thick pubic hair. Finding the swollen, drooping lips, Cheryl held and gently fondled them. Then a sharp intake of breath came from Julie as Cheryl's fingers ventured into the hot slit, sliding up and down the full length, from the anus end to the clit.

Bending her thumb, Cheryl found Julie's clitoris with the knuckle and set up an on/off pressure at a slow rhythm. She opened her legs, pressing her own wet cunt against one of Julie's thighs, working her pelvis against Julie in time with the manipulation of Julie's clitoris. It was sexually exhilarating. Julie, her head tilted back, was biting her lip. She liked to bring arousal to the edge of the precipice, but Cheryl was thinking that if they didn't fuck soon they would be too exhausted to do anything.

Then Julie had her by the hand, pulling her out of the shower. With huge bath towels they dried themselves, they dried each other. They swigged martini from a bottle as though it were Pepsi Cola. Dropping to her knees in front of Cheryl, Julie held her by the buttocks and buried her face against Cheryl's stomach. With her lips gently sucking and savouring Cheryl's skin, Julie's voice was muffled. Cheryl could just understand what she was saying.

"I'm orally orientated. Do I know how to suck a cunt, Cheryl?"

"No one can do it like you," an appreciative Cheryl replied, opening her legs, thrusting her pelvis forward, holding Julie's tousle-haired head as it went down further.

Then Cheryl threw her head back, groaning in pleasure as Julie sucked and lapped at her cunt. She felt her labia sucked into Julie's mouth, and kept there hotly. Then her lips were released and Julie's tongue entered her slit, stiffening as it invaded her vagina, while Julie's top teeth lightly worked against her clitoris. Hotly throbbing down there, Cheryl was sure that she was pumping out love juice faster than Julie could gulp it down.

Julie released Cheryl's bum and stood upright. Face close to Cheryl's wetly glistening all round the mouth, she let Cheryl lick and kiss her own juice before passionately kissing Julie. They were breast against breast once again. Their skin was dry this time, as they exchanged tongues, lapping greedily at each other's saliva.

That deep kissing went on and on until neither could stand it any longer. Julie was so worked up that her voice let her down. Several times she tried to speak, and when she eventually managed it her voice was slurred as if she were drunk.

"Are you ready to do it?"

Not expecting her own vocal cords to obey her, Cheryl merely nodded. They rushed to the bed, moving themselves and each other into position. They curled their heads between each other's thigh. Their bodies formed a sexual yin-and-yang symbol. It was a "69", Julie's speciality.

Nose against Julie's anus, Cheryl kissed the hot, hairy cunt that was presented to her open. Thrilling as she felt Cheryl's tongue find her back hole, she reciprocated by using her hands to part the firm cheeks of Julie's bum. Her tongue flicked and darted, darted and flicked, rimming and reaming as Julie did the same to her. A mighty shiver of excruciating pleasure went through both of them.

They moved hungry mouths rhythmically against thrusting cunts. As her excitement threatened to explode off the human scale, alternating colours filled Cheryl's head. There was a green, then a blue, then finally a brilliant orange that flashed like lightning as she reached orgasm. An extra discharge, a slight change of taste, told her that Julie had also come.

For a while they lay as they were, breathing in the fundamental body perfumes of each other. Then they parted temporarily to move up and round and lie properly on the bed, arms around each other, mouths resting lightly together, sharing their breath.

"It's Saturday," Julie murmured contentedly. "We can stay like this, go to sleep while holding each other, all day if we wish."

Mention of it being Saturday had Cheryl struggle to free herself from Julie's embrace. She didn't want to break away from her lover, but duty might be calling. Sometimes the editor of a Sunday newspaper needed something from her. At this stage they were usually desperate enough to pay well.

"Where are you going?" an annoyed Julie mumbled sleepily.

"I won't be a couple of minutes," Cheryl assured her. "I just want to ring my answering machine to see if I have any messages."

Naked, aware of Julie's hot eyes on her, she found her mobile, did the necessary, and waited. There was just one message, a startling one.

"Hello," said the female voice. "I'm sorry to disturb your weekend, Cheryl. This is Karen Cayson. I realise that we don't know each other well enough for me to ask a favour, but I really need help. Matthew is in hospital, and I've been charged with causing grievous bodily harm. The detective inspector says there's a possibility of it being reduced to 'actual' bodily harm, but that's as much as I can hope for. Maybe when Matthew comes round..."

Karen made a choking sound here and a few seconds passed before she continued speaking. "Maybe when Matthew comes round he'll see that the charges against me are dropped. But right now the tabloids are going to tear both Matthew and myself apart. This could well be the kind of bad publicity that neither of us will ever recover from. What I'm asking, Cheryl, is for you to handle my public relations, as it were. You could put the story across in a way that would counter a lot of the damage the newspapers will do. As I said, I realise I have no right to ask this of you. But could you give me a ring as soon as possible? They've allowed me bail so I will be at home all over the weekend."

Three

When Paula Monroe awoke, the room was warm and sunshine glowed on the drawn blinds. She looked at her travel clock on the dresser. It was nine thirty, although that wasn't important on a Saturday. As long as they got to the theatre by five, the day was theirs. Then another night of humiliation would commence. Paula was forced to admit to herself that the show stank. It was a brash, noisy revue, but the audience was more noisy than the people on the stage.

She stretched, catlike, releasing something into her system that made her feel good. Saturday morning in London wasn't cool and inviting and purposeful like Saturday morning in Basingstoke. Having left home a month ago, Paula was still insecure. She suffered an absurd loneliness in overcrowded London. Often fear closed round her like a sodden blanket. A sick-scared feeling would come over her. It was hot when she woke up in the pitch black of night. Ice cold in the day, as if the sun had been switched off. You had to wait for it to pass. It was useless to try to fight it.

Cheryl Valenta came stirringly into her mind. She could taste the woman's kiss. She could find Cheryl's perfume about her now, hours after they had separated. Meeting the journalist had been a strange experience. Strange but exciting. On arriving home, more aroused than she cared to admit to herself, Paula had expected to feel regret in the morning. Possibly more than regret – guilt, shame, maybe even repugnance. But none of those things afflicted her.

Rather than upsetting, her memory of Cheryl was warmly pleasant.

Lifting her arm, she gazed through half-open eyes at the telephone number that Cheryl had temporarily tattooed on her wrist. Did this make her a captive, a prisoner of love? This was a touch of childish drama, but it made Paula feel good. After making a note of the number she would wash it off. She had nothing to be ashamed of, but didn't want to be questioned by Nikki. Not that she had to explain herself. But when two of you lived together and worked together, a certain amount of possessiveness crept in unnoticed.

There was a knock on the door. Let Nikki answer it. Paula was still relaxed by a residue of sleep. She rolled onto her side as the knock came again. Paula blinkingly looked about. The room was unoccupied. She looked towards Nikki's bed. It was unoccupied. Puzzled, Paula sat up. Swinging her legs out onto the floor, she stayed sitting on the edge of the bed. Though not such a sleepyhead as Paula, Nikki was not usually up at this time on a Saturday morning. For her to be up and out was remarkable.

The knock came again. It had an insistence now. There was more than a hint of annoyance at being kept waiting. Paula put a full-length coat on over her nightdress. She could hear distance-muffled sounds coming up from the hall.

Paula braced herself as she opened the door. The noises far down below changed into indistinct voices. A door a long way off squealed as someone pushed it open. The smells rose up three floors to sicken Paula. You could never get used to the stench. The odours of decay and cooking and poverty. The walls were wood-panelled, the floor of the landing and stairs covered with worn and cracked linoleum. Paula didn't really see her surroundings. She didn't have to. These places were all the same. As with rows of houses on an estate, you know what they look like without looking at them.

Nikki stood there, staring unblinkingly. "I forgot my key."

She made that a statement of fact and not an apology as she

walked past Paula into the room. She had long, straight, golden hair that framed a schoolgirl's face. Her slender build added to the youthful illusion, and her long-lashed eyes were filled with pseudo-innocence. From a small distance she had the slim, honey-haired look. In closer, the girl-child looked older and more tired. Her mouth wasn't young. She always held herself tight, stiff. Even though a strong friendship had evolved between Paula and herself, Nikki's eyes never lost a wary unfriendliness.

Unzipping her fleece, Nikki sat on her own bed. She looked up miserably at Paula, who stood waiting, mystified.

"No need to get yourself washed and polished today, Paula." Nikki's voice was flat, dispirited. "You and me and the others in the line aren't going back on tonight."

Knees giving way, Paula plopped down to sit on her own bed. She could hear the clock ticking, and it sounded too loud. The stained mirror affixed to the wall looked back at her, imprisoning her in hopelessness, mocking the way she looked, hair dishevelled and face white and twisted by disappointment.

"You mean the show's folded?" Paula at last managed to ask. "I know that the audiences have been rowdy, but the place was always crowded. We were taking money. Rick said that—"

"*Rick* has run off with the proceeds."

"No!" Paula felt about a thousand years old. "But Rick said—"

"Rick said a lot of things, but he forgot to say goodbye, Paula."

"But what about our money?"

"Forget it," Nikki advised. "Rick took everybody's earnings with him. I've been through this sort of thing before. There's a bastard like Rick round every corner in this business."

Paula felt desolate. The money she had would last until about the middle of next week. And that didn't include paying the rent. The prospect of going on the dole loomed. That was what most of the people back home had predicted for her when she had left.

The fear had returned. Its icy fingers gripped Paula's brain, numbing it. She asked, "What are we going to do, Nikki?"

"You've got a home you can go back to," Nikki pointed out.

That wasn't an option. Paula clasped her hands and squeezed them together. She had left Basingstoke just four weeks ago after boasting, "I'm going to make it as an actress, a rich actress." Her parents would be sympathetic. It would probably be a relief for them to have her back home. But the neighbours would be gloating, and her former workmates at Sainsbury's would ridicule her mercilessly.

"I won't be going back home. What about you, Nikki?"

Shrugging narrow shoulders, Nikki replied, "I've no home to go back to. I'll give it a few days, then if nothing turns up I suppose I'll go to see Jay Clifford. He's a photographer, a sleazy kind of guy, but he helped me out before when times were hard. You might as well come along if you're staying in London."

Coincidence. Paula remembered the name, remembered the man. She couldn't see how having photographs they couldn't afford taken would be a cure for their unemployment. She was about to enlarge on this to Nikki, but something stopped her, warning that if she did so she would make a fool of herself. Paula stayed silent.

They met in an amber-lit club in Soho. It was a subtly attractive place with oak-lined walls, blue carpeting and blue velvet draperies. The lighting was pleasantly discreet, and the piped-in music was not the harsh stuff of discotheques, but soft, sweet, romantic ballads and instrumentals. It was late when Cheryl came in through plate-glass doors that were like polished air. The place was only about a third full. Most of the pairing up and departing had been done. There was still a lot of leftover smoke, but she spotted Karen Cayson sitting alone at a small oak-wood table close to a long oak-wood bar. She looked cool but Cheryl knew that Karen had to be on red alert.

The newspapers had swiftly got hold of the story. There were sensational headlines such as DID HE FALL OR WAS HE PUSHED? and

MATT WYNDHAM BASHED AT HIS BIRTHDAY BASH. On one front page, over a photograph of Matthew Wyndham being stretchered into an ambulance, was the heading BOTTLED OUT!. What puzzled Cheryl was the photograph of a well-known dancer inserted in the text of one story, and was captioned, "Wendi Maylor – bottle blonde?" All this was in the Saturday dailies! What would the Sunday papers do to the story in the morning?

Sitting at small oak-wood tables along the far wall were unaccompanied young women, some of them not so young. They were the house whores, which strictly speaking was not quite true. The club owner neither pimped for them nor had any personal connection with them. The girls all paid Ralph Remington a nightly fee in advance for permission to work out of his club.

Resplendent in a velvet tuxedo, a lace shirt and a drooping bow tie, the club owner was suspicious now of Karen, who was sitting alone, and of Cheryl as she walked across the big, softly carpeted, softly lit room. To set his mind at rest, Karen ordered a martini for herself and raised her eyebrows questioningly at Cheryl, who nodded to say that she'd have the same. Ralph Remington was satisfied. Square, yellowish teeth showed in a smile. They were customers, not toms trying to muscle in.

"Sit down, please. It was good of you to come, Cheryl."

Though she was casually dressed in a red three-quarter-sleeved cashmere jumper with a slash neckline, and a tight black skirt, Karen looked absolutely stunning. She had a gorgeous face, gorgeous breasts and gorgeous legs. There was a depth to her soft brown eyes that held Cheryl rooted, and she could even flash a dazzling smile through her troubles. Karen's teeth were big, big and white. They gave her full-lipped mouth an additional prominence. Cheryl liked that.

"The house is under a media siege," Karen explained, less calm now. Worry was melting the steel that had hardened inside her over the years. "I didn't want us to meet there, so I escaped."

"This is fine by me," Cheryl said genially.

"I feel pretty bad about begging favours from a friend." Karen looked at her, then stopped for a moment. Cheryl waited, anxious to learn how Karen defined "favours". Usually they were requests for journalists to write lies, which was something Cheryl wouldn't do. Then she heard Karen say in a tone of contrition, "If I may refer to you as a friend."

Cheryl's unease made it her turn to pause. How could she answer that? Professional respect and friendship are not necessarily joined to the same body. The minutes dragged by as the air-cooled air and the low music soothed Cheryl.

Remington brought drinks that he had donned rimless spectacles – like a preacher's – to mix. He had made a good job of the martinis, but the glasses spoiled his image. Cheryl was still wondering how to reply when Karen took the onus from her by continuing.

"I have regretted not thanking you for that piece you wrote about me last month. I've always admired the way you are objective but not cruel, justifiably critical without depriving your subject of either their self-respect or dignity. What you said about me encouraged me to regard you as a friend, or at least a potential friend. Am I mistaken?"

"No. I suppose that's a logical conclusion."

Though she had agreed, Cheryl was on guard. Talk, phraseology, appearances – they didn't mean a thing. Often people who used the nicest-sounding language had the meanest hearts. In modern times nice talk had somehow become a status symbol.

On a slack day a month or so ago, the news that Karen Cayson was signing up to star in a Hollywood blockbuster had prompted Cheryl to devote a full column to Karen's career and the considerable contribution she had made to films and television. In retrospect, she realised that she may have gone over the top of Sugar Hill, but that was how Cheryl had felt. To use your pen to knock genuine talent is to reveal your own inadequacies and jealousies.

"I learned ages ago to stay clear of all writers." Karen made a little face of recorded bad memories of the press. "But I regard you as the only exception, Cheryl."

"We'll exchange autographs in a minute or two," Cheryl laughed, "but, before we form this mutual-admiration society, I gather there's something I can do for you."

With a small, self-conscious smile, Karen moved her elbows further in on the table, bringing her face closer to Cheryl's. She lowered her voice to what was almost a confidential whisper. "I take it that you've read all about what happened last night?"

Useless tears brimmed her eyes. New sensational headlines would be on her mind. Karen would be dreading the newspaper delivery tomorrow. But tomorrow would come and she would get through it. Everyone gets through all their tomorrows in some way.

"Yes," Cheryl replied guardedly.

"Most of what they've printed is utter balls, Cheryl. I want you to put the right story over."

"What is the right story?"

"Matthew regained consciousness earlier today," Karen said, her relief evident.

"I heard that on the radio."

"I'm thankful for that, of course," Karen nodded. "But, although Matthew wants to tell the police that he had fallen last night, Henry and Nellie Drury, our blasted servants, are eager to have me hung, drawn and quartered. How can a toadying butler and his wife be snobs, Cheryl? I've never fitted into that house, solely because of them. They have never considered me good enough for Matthew. Henry in particular looks down his nose at me."

"Surely Henry could persuade them to change their story, Karen."

Karen shook an unhappy head. "Matthew comes from a very old-fashioned family, Karen, in which the butler rules. But that's not the worst of it, really. Some of the tabloids have picked up on Wendi Maylor."

"I saw her picture in one of the papers." Cheryl was intrigued. "Where does she fit into this?"

"She was on the bed with Matthew."

"When you hit him," Cheryl guessed with a wry smile.

"Yes, with a bottle," Karen confessed.

"Oh, fuck!" Cheryl sighed. She took a sip of her drink and did some rapid thinking. A group of men had come into the club and there was some animated conversation going on between them and the lively ladies with bodies for hire. "You're scared that Wendi will get an offer she can't refuse to tell the full story?"

"Something like that." Karen was looking shaky. She fumblingly lit a cigarette with a tiny gold lighter. She sipped her drink. Her fingers were trembling but her eyes improved.

"Then there's no problem, Karen. You and Matthew aren't exactly on the breadline. Find out how much she's offered to tell, and pay her more to keep her mouth shut."

Before answering, Karen bit her heavy bottom lip enough to leave teeth marks. "This is going to sound like a line from a corny script, Cheryl, but it isn't that simple."

Cheryl sighed inwardly. There were complications, and complications don't come anywhere as complicated as they do in celebrity life. Richard Neehan, the Wyndhams' solicitor, could fix just about everything, and Matthew had pull with members of Parliament from both sides of the House. Although, of late, MPs seemed incapable of keeping the lids on their own scandals.

"Tell me the worst, Karen."

"Wendi Maylor."

"What about her?"

"She and I have been lovers for the past two years or so."

That figured. Cheryl had herself long been an admirer of Wendi's high hips, the big round firm dancer's arse, the buttocks enticingly undulant. Aware of Cheryl's interest, Wendi had given out the right vibes in return. The opportunity for them to get together had not occurred – yet. Releasing a long, low whistle between her teeth, Cheryl said, "Fuck a priest! You need a magician, not a journalist, Karen. I thought you caught her on the bed with Matthew."

"I did." Karen gave a confirming nod. "Wendi goes both ways – one for gain, the other for pleasure. She's looking to star in a musical Matthew is planning to stage in the West End."

Frowning, Cheryl said, "I see your problem. Some reporter is going to follow up the Wendi Maylor thing and—"

"Expose me as a lesbian." Karen finished Cheryl's observation for her.

"But surely in these liberal times that's not going to do you any harm."

"That's not the point, Cheryl," Karen said hollowly. "Second to Princess Anne, or whoever, I'm the most wanked-over woman in the western hemisphere. I'll end up without a single fan."

"Not necessarily. All it will mean is that you'll have female instead of male followers," Cheryl argued.

"Look at me, Cheryl." Karen patted herself under the jawline with the back of one hand to give emphasis to what she was about to say. "I looked in the mirror this morning and I'm sure I detected the start of a double chin. I don't have the time left to change sex horses in midstream. Apart from that, it will be Matthew who suffers the most. He'll be subjected to all kinds of ridicule. Some people already refer to him as 'Mr Cayson' behind his back. They'll be openly calling him 'Mrs Cayson' if I'm outed as a lez. It would finish him, Cheryl."

"The implications would be grave for you both," a serious Cheryl acknowledged.

Cheryl took time out for consideration. She was made hesitant by a premonition that she couldn't discourage, a certainty that Karen was heading for disaster. But she knew that she mustn't tell her. Intuitions and hunches are either misunderstood or unappreciated. Guess wrong and it will be forgotten. Get it right and you're under suspicion.

Karen was showing ill-concealed fright at her patent indecision. There was nothing she could write that would successfully refute an allegation that Karen was a lesbian. But she had never yet met a problem that she couldn't get the better of. There was no reason why this one should be any different. She genuinely wanted to help. A bonus came with the realisation that she wouldn't kick an extremely grateful Karen Cayson out of her bed.

"Any help I could give through my column would be minimal," she warned Karen, going on dubiously. "But there might be something that I can do. No promises, Karen, but I'll do my best."

"I'll rely on you, Cheryl. You are my only hope."

She didn't fly well. Seated midway in the plane, next to a window, Wendi Maylor forced herself to watch the ground go speedily past as they took off. In an unsuccessful attempt at curing a sudden dizziness, she closed her eyes. Then within minutes the plane was airborne. Opening her eyes, she saw the airport far below. The plane turned a three-quarter circle and headed north. Wendi's sigh of relief was audible enough to embarrass her. That was the worst over until the landing. As someone living perpetually in a state of expectation, she had accepted an invitation to guest on a live television chat show that Sunday evening. Having weighed the strain of driving to Manchester against the fear of the flight there, she had opted for the flight. Nevertheless, she had, as she had known she would, rued the decision when the plane had been taxiing for take-off.

"Good morning, Miss Maylor," a resonant male voice said into her ear.

Startled, Wendi swung her head round. A little lightweight jockey of a man was leaning over the empty seat beside her. He had grey hair, grey eyes, a grey face, and was dressed in a grey suit. Wendi idly wondered if he wore grey underwear. He was the first visible invisible man she had seen, able to blend with any background. A human chameleon, he would be lost to a firing squad from the moment they put him up against a wall for execution.

It wasn't an attempted pick-up, as he had used her name. That was a relief. Having to put up with the advances of men for the sake of her career had always made her skin crawl. It wrapped her in a second-hand feeling, making her wish that things could be different. Whoever the men were, it was invariably cheap and degrading. "Permit me to introduce myself. I am Richard Neehan, Mr Matthew Wyndham's solicitor. May I?"

Having gestured at the empty seat, he slid into it on Wendi's consenting nod. She knew this wasn't a chance meeting. Neehan was here for a purpose. The fact that he was taking a probably unnecessary flight to Manchester evinced how serious that purpose was.

A brightly smiling stewardess was passing down the aisle. Wendi always watched the faces of aircrew. They were trained not to show any alarm, but she was confident that if anything was going wrong she would be forewarned by their manner. This one turned a pretty face to them as she passed.

"You may smoke now, if you like," she said.

Making a determined effort to cut down on cigarettes, Wendi hoped that Neehan wouldn't light up. He didn't. Instead, he rose up in his seat to look past her out of the window, saying, "A most unfortunate business."

Turning her head, Wendi followed his gaze out through the glass. She could see nothing but cloud, a grey widespread mist. If there was some kind of business out there, unfortunate or otherwise, she couldn't see it. She turned questioningly back to him. The lines in his skin broke his face up into sections of different shapes and sizes. It put Wendi in mind of a child's paint-by-numbers picture. She was mentally filling in various colours when he screwed up the pattern with a smile.

"Forgive me, Miss Maylor." He shook a self-deprecating head as he spoke. "I have this silly habit of speaking partway through my thoughts. I was, of course, referring to the fracas at Mr Wyndham's house on Friday night."

Fracas! That was a mild way of putting it. If Wendi had caught the clout from the bottle that had felled Matthew, she would be dead now. Karen drunk was frighteningly different from Karen sober. Wendi knew that she was the only witness and this guy was here to prevent a scandal. Did they want her to keep quiet about being bollock naked with Matthew, or had they learned about Karen and herself? Perhaps the invisible man was Godfather of the lesbian Mafia. Was she about to be tossed in the river, weighted down by dildoes?

She was feeling better about the flight now. The steady hum of the plane was calming to the point of inducing drowsiness. Across the aisle a man was groping his companion's breast, and she was giggling hysterically. Neehan didn't notice. His piercing grey eyes were looking into Wendi's.

"As I said, Miss Maylor, an unfortunate business indeed. Best forgotten, don't you think?"

"I've already forgotten it," Wendi convincingly lied. She saw that night's incident at the Wyndham home as a turning point for Karen and herself. It would also allow her to make a huge donation to the children's charity that she wholeheartedly supported. The deal she was about to enter into with a Sunday newspaper would benefit a lot of needy kids.

"We don't doubt your integrity, Miss Maylor." Richard Neehan gave her a smile that died just as it reached his lips. "But you can understand that Mr Wyndham, with the media taking such a huge interest in this, is concerned that you may be tempted by the, er, thirty pieces of silver, as it were."

It was going to be a whole lot more than thirty pieces of silver.

There would be thousands of lovely folding notes, all put to a mighty good cause. She said, truthfully, "I give you my word that I won't say one word about Matthew."

"Thank you, my dear girl."

Your thanks are premature, my dear Richard. Matthew won't be mentioned, but Karen will. Wendi saw it that she was about to do the star a big favour. The beautiful Karen Cayson – superb actress, skilled self-promoter, with the courage to face any audience or camera in any challenging situation – needed Wendi's help. A committed lesbian, an unbelievably passionate lover, Karen lacked the nerve to come out. Many times she had told Wendi that she despised herself as a hypocrite, but still couldn't face the prospect of publicly declaring her sexuality.

Now, because she was very fond of Karen, Wendi was about to make everything right for her. It was a ludicrous situation, really, with Wendi, the new recruit to lesbianism, so to speak, forcing the veteran Karen to stand up and be counted. They had first met a couple of years ago at the television studio where they were appearing in the same programme. Wendi's involvement was strictly as a dancer. Fascinated by Karen's talent, she had watched her brilliance in every scene, catching all the cogent details. The two of them had become close. At Karen's suggestion they had gone shopping during a daytime break in rehearsals.

As they had chosen cosmetics and the like, Karen had invited her to go with her to her favourite club that night. Thrilled at the thought of being seen on the town with the adored Karen Cayson, Wendi had readily agreed.

Perhaps not so worldly-wise as she had pretended to be, Wendi hadn't noticed how, after she had accepted the invitation, the direction of their shopping had changed. Neither had she been aware that Karen had surreptitiously steered them into purchasing exotic underwear. Looking back, she realised that Karen had been a veritable Svengali and she a gullible Trilby. When they reached the club that evening, Wendi had on a new soft lacy bra, which showed no seams through the elegant, clinging, yellow dress that, so Karen had remarked, bisected and showed off an admirable arse. For the first time ever Wendi had been wearing sheer stockings and suspenders. Under Karen's aubergine velvet cowl-neck dress, she had worn no underclothes except for the wispiest pair of silk French knickers.

All unsuspecting, Wendi had glanced up briefly at the green canopy above the shabby entrance to the Starland Club. From behind a desk in reception a pretty Asian girl with dimples had smiled at them. They had gone up a wide stairway to the second floor. As they entered a spacious room they had to gingerly step over a brunette who lay peacefully asleep curled on the floor. This had been something Wendi hadn't expected.

The lighting had been so dim that at first the room seemed to be in darkness. This was her second discovery, her second shock. She wasn't going to be seen on the town with Karen Cayson, because Karen Cayson had deliberately chosen a place where Karen Cayson would be neither seen nor recognised. There had been something different about the couples gyrating in time with tinny music that grated on Wendi's ear. Wendi fathomed what it was. This had been her third and most shocking revelation of that evening. Karen had brought her to a gay club.

They got themselves drinks from a surprisingly well-stocked bar. The assembly was happily homogenised in the close-give-and-take of clubland. When they were sitting at a table, Wendi had found herself relaxing. The atmosphere was pleasant, with the women much more friendly towards them than the men. Karen's gaze continually strayed to a tall black girl seated on a bar stool not far from them. She had short-cut black hair, slender shoulders, slender arms and long slender legs. When Karen caught her eye, the girl stared back, smiled and placed her glass on the bar. Then she came over to their table. Her swaying walk was an elegant dance, even though no music was playing at that time.

As she reached them the band had recommenced playing. Leaning over, she had slipped a long-fingered hand down inside the front of Karen's dress. "Our dance, I believe," she murmured, brushing Karen's cheek with her slightly parted lips.

Leaving a bewildered, disbelieving Wendi at the table, Karen and the girl moved onto the dance floor. They held each other close, moving body pressed against moving body for the whole of a long, slow dance. A trio of young men sitting with arms round each other at a table to Wendi's right had disgusted expressions on their faces at the sight of the two women dancing sensually together. Two girls had watched the dancers in a way that left Wendi in no doubt that they lusted after both Karen and her dance partner. This was an alien world to Wendi, and she felt out of place, possibly even disoriented, in it.

They both appeared slightly hot and flustered when they came back to the table. "This is Frankie, Wendi," Karen said, introducing her dance partner, who looked at Wendi as no woman had ever done before. Karen continued, "Frankie, this is my best friend, Wendi."

Slipping her left hand round Karen's waist, Frankie took Wendi's hand in her right one. The hand was warm, strong, the long fingers wrapping themselves possessively and excitingly around Wendi's hand. Frankie's and Karen's bodies were still in contact. Terribly ashamed of her thoughts, Wendi found herself wanting to see them doing much more than just dancing.

Covering her discomfort, Wendi lit a cigarette. Karen didn't smoke, but, smiling her thanks, the other girl put a cigarette between her lips. Wendi's gaze was held by the white knuckles of a hand that otherwise might have been carved from beautifully polished mahogany. Frankie leaned forwards to light her cigarette from Wendi's. The two ends touched, the little glow that united them revealed and accentuated her features in close-up. Wendi was forced to notice the fullness of Frankie's lips, her small nose and the brown watchful eyes.

"I always call that a smoker's kiss," Frankie then said huskily and suggestively.

Standing upright, Frankie moved naturally into a provocative pose. The tight white sheath she wore showed off her ripe curves to breathtaking advantage. Though earlier that day she would never had believed it of herself, Wendi had been excited by Frankie. She heard Karen speak to leave no doubt that she, too, was aroused.

"You really are lovely, Frankie," Karen commented, her assessment sounding the awed discovery that it was. "I'll bet nobody else in of London, no, the whole United Kingdom, could do what you do for that dress."

Giving Wendi a sharp look carefully softened by an intentionally flattened smile, Frankie said, "It doesn't come on too strong for the uninitiated, I hope."

How could Frankie know that she was an outsider? Wendi marvelled at this and the easy way in which Frankie, a total stranger, had moved in on Karen and herself. It was all very bewildering. Until that moment Wendi hadn't realised that for some days she had been careful not to let Karen know what effect she had on her. In fact, until that moment Wendi hadn't realised that Karen *had* an effect on her.

"Do you two want to stay here or shall we go back to my place?" Karen asked casually, her eyes sparkling.

"I don't mind," Wendi replied.

Karen had a flat close to the studio for use when her work kept her in town. Wendi hoped that Frankie would opt to stay at the club. Both she and Karen seemed so sophisticated, so worldly-wise, compared with her, that the thought of being alone with them brought a strain of edginess to Wendi. Her heart sank as she heard Frankie speak.

"Let's hit the road, Karen. You want me to get a bottle to bring along?"

"Just bring your luscious self, Frankie," Karen had replied, causing Wendi to feel the rise of libido in her loins. She tried to quash the feeling, and failed.

They had left the club hurriedly. To Wendi there was something shameful, indecent, perhaps even obscene about their hasty exit. The music volume had been up as they left, blasting rocks out of the quarry.

At the corner outside her tall apartment building in Holborn, Karen overtipped the taxi driver. The ride up to the fifth floor was made restless by what a worried Wendi suspected was sexual tension. Sharing the lift with a middle-aged man and woman, the three of them stayed a little apart, unspeaking.

Karen's was a corner four-room apartment. Though she was Matthew Wyndham's wife, her town home was a bachelor-girl pad with all the snazzy furnishings. Going straight to a drinks cabinet, Karen poured brandy for each of them. The bouquet filled the centrally heated air for a second.

Wendi looked out through a window at the London skyline. The sun was out of sight now, but it had left a memory of gold where it had set. The molten shadow that was night blended through the spectrum to the black silhouettes that were then the distant buildings. She heard Frankie's excited, appreciative squeal.

"Wow! What a place! Is it my birthday or Christmas?" Frankie laughingly enquired. Her head swivelled to take everything in.

"Probably the fourth of July," Karen vaguely suggested.

"It ain't even that." Frankie shook her head, revealing an attractive smile.

"Who gives a flying fuck!" Karen remarked.

Frankie stood with her back against a wall, and Wendi watched Karen move to Frankie, put her arms round her and kiss her tenderly. Next she kissed Frankie's fingers, palms, bare arms and shoulders. Then, murmuring soft words of endearment, Karen drew the other woman close. And then she sought Frankie's mouth once more, this time passionately. Within a few minutes the two women were urgently pressing soft body against soft body.

Frankie's open-mouth kissing affected Karen strongly. Her hand caressed the two magnificent mounds that strained so enticingly against the bodice of the other woman's tight white sheath. Then Karen's hand strayed down to Frankie's knee, moved stealthily in under her dress and slowly up her thigh. Beginning to squirm violently beneath the caresses, Frankie thrust herself towards Karen. Her dress worked up around her waist like a thick white rope.

"Love me!" Frankie called out wildly.

Moving hesitantly towards the couple, Wendi was beside them when Frankie turned a sultry face to her. Karen was kissing and sucking at the skin of Frankie's neck and, tentatively, Wendi had kissed Frankie's scented hair, and the way she moved her head tickled Wendi's lips.

Putting her hands on Frankie's soft cheeks, Wendi brushed her eyes spasmodically with her fingertips. Wendi's mouth softened and she opened it a little to meet Frankie's. With the aroma of Frankie's sex rising as Karen continued to finger the other girl, a shuddering thrill went through Wendi as she kept hold of Frankie's cheeks and drew her lips back and forth across hers.

Frankie's cheekbones became accentuated as she shaped her mouth for a long, tongue-exploring kiss that left Wendi's legs trembling so much that she was in danger of collapsing.

Having watched the deep kissing between Frankie and Wendi from the corner of her eye, Karen took her mouth from Frankie's neck. Lips travelling slowly and lightly over Wendi's face, Karen's mouth grew moist and warm as it sought Wendi's. Then they were kissing, hotly, demandingly, passionately. Karen's moans of ecstasy affected Wendi like a powerful drug. She felt her whole body trembling with desire.

How the three of them moved from there into bed was to remain a blur in Wendi's memory. She did remember that all three of them had been naked. Lying on her back under a silky black sheet with Frankie on one side of her and Karen on the other, Wendi had looked up at an ornate ceiling as the two experienced women had introduced her to the magic of lesbian sex. They had both caressed her gently, taking a long time to trace the curves of her nude body with the tips of their fingers. As Wendi's breathing had first quickened and then become a panting, they had begun to trace her curves again, this time with the tips of their tongues. From that moment...

"Mr Wyndham, Matthew," Richard Neehan's voice echoed in Wendi's head, pulling her out of her reverie, "instructed me to tell you that you will have star billing in the West End show."

"But..." Wendi struggled to get her talking equipment into gear. The thought of that night with Karen and Frankie, the distraction of that night, made her shake. Her voice was squeaky. "But what about Della Hurst?"

Della had a fine singing voice and could dance. Wendi was a superb dancer, but came a poor second to Della as a singer. Della just had to be the star, and deservedly so.

"Matthew is the boss," Neehan replied with a smile and a shrug of his jockey's sloping shoulders.

Wendi's interest in the conversation fled then. It was chased out by the return of old fear as the signal to fasten seat belts was given. Manchester was down below them. They would soon be landing. Trembling with fright once again, Wendi closed her eyes tightly.

Four

The weather forecasters had got it wrong again. The Sunday night air was unannouncedly chilly and London's pedestrians to the left and right of Cheryl Valenta's passing car were walking briskly. As expected, the newspapers that morning had hung out all the Karen Cayson–Matthew Wyndham dirty washing they could find in a short time. The reporters had dug and they had learned. They would go on digging and learning, and telling the world what they found. Most of the papers had a fuzzy photograph of what could have been Matthew Wyndham, half sitting, half lying in a hospital bed. Not out of sympathy, liking for Matthew, or even plain old curiosity, Cheryl had felt compelled to visit him in hospital. That had been a depressing mistake. The suave, sophisticated tycoon had looked as ghastly as something that the police might have pulled out of the Thames after three days.

Nobody had brought the Wyndham servants up to speed. In a flash photograph that made the front page of a couple of tabloids, Henry and Nellie Drury had the one-dimensional appearance of a married couple who no longer engaged in the sensational act of copulation. Probably motivated by a bitter sense of inferiority that came chiefly from his dragging foot, Henry had told the papers, "I found Mr Wyndham lying on the bed, unconscious from a blow to the head." Nellie had supported her husband with, "If Mr Wyndham had taken a fall, we would have known. He most definitely hadn't fallen."

Through Richard Neehan, Matthew had countered this with a statement to the press: "I want to make it clear," he was quoted as saying, "that I am in hospital because of my own foolishness. I learned a lesson last night, that an old man can't celebrate his birthday the way he did when young. I fell because I had too much to drink. Fortunately, my wife was there to assist me and call medical help. It is my servants' loyalty, their well-meant efforts to protect my reputation, that prompted their false allegations against Karen Cayson. She is the finest wife a man could ever have, and when I leave this hospital we will be continuing our most happy married life."

There were some glamour shots of Karen in the main text, while she had a separate story of her own under the heading KAREN CAYSON: HER LIFE, HER LOVES, HER TRAGEDIES. This was just a brief, well-known biography with an attempt made at disguising its familiarity in a wrapping of journalese. In her teens she had metamorphosed from East End urchin to superstar. Much was made of her first stormy marriage to a young actor and the trauma of a bitter divorce. There was her friendship with top people, including royalty, and the late-night mini-Chappaquiddick-type car crash in which Karen had been badly injured. Before daylight the wrecked car had been taken away, and the truth of the accident had gone with it. The 28-year-old star's marriage to the 55-year-old television tycoon came last, under the cynical cross-heading of MATT WYNDHAM'S GENERATION GAME.

It seemed that neither of the Drurys had mentioned Wendi Maylor by name, but at least two of the more daring tabloids reported that it was alleged that a mystery blonde had been seen running naked from the bedroom shortly before Matthew Wyndham had been found injured. Mixing rumour and innuendo, these newspapers printed photographs of Wendi Maylor, merely stating that she had attended the Wyndham party. Wendi's face was delicately lovely. It was the kind of face that went with small breasts. Girls with big tits often have coarse faces, Cheryl had discovered. Nature loves to play games.

Media experience convinced Cheryl that Wendi would soon be hitting the headlines. From what Cheryl knew of her, the dancer had no sweeping interest in anyone or anything except getting ahead. Determined not to go back to being poor, Wendi was careful never to make a move that didn't pay off. She had ripened in several short-lived musicals that had meant disaster for all those around her. Wendi was an opportunist with style, and she had the brains to prosper from the possible downfall of the Wyndhams.

Matthew Wyndham was a man with political connections so powerful that they inspired fear. Wendi Maylor was the major protagonist in this affair, but he couldn't put muscle on her, because Matthew would be aware that Wendi held all the trump cards. What Cheryl knew, and Matthew didn't know, was that there were a lot more trump cards that could fall into Wendi's hand.

Cheryl was heading for Barnes now and the home of Deborah Hurley, her researcher. She had telephoned Deborah that morning with the instructions, "Get me everything you can on Wendi Maylor. Not the professional items, the reviews and the bullshit, but everything that has ever been printed about her."

"Everything?" Deborah had complained, Sunday morningish.

"Everything, and by tonight."

Deborah was a weird, complex character. She was not a lesbian, as most of Cheryl's friends were. Until meeting Roland Reader, her boyfriend, a year ago, Deborah had been disappointed with life, hating it all – herself, her colleagues, her work, her aimless existence. All that had changed since she had become intimately acquainted with Roland. Now she just hated him.

Though she hardly knew Reader, who worked as an engineer for Richmond Council, Cheryl disliked him intensely. She was jealous that he was sampling what she had always wanted to make her personal property. She just couldn't stand the thought of his pawing Deborah's exquisite breasts, or running his ugly hand up between her breathtaking legs.

Deborah's house was an old-timer, one of a terrace of tiny houses in a narrow street. There was a small gate and a walk-up, and the type of doorbell that rings somewhere so deep inside the house that after waiting a couple of minutes you are convinced it isn't working.

It was. The door was opened by Deborah, wearing just a pair of red shorts and a white bra. "I've been doing callisthenics," she explained as she let Cheryl into a small hall and preceded her into a room of reasonable size. "I reckon my figure's just the same as when I was a girl, apart from my backside. There's not much you can do about your bum when it starts bulging up on you. You take a look at those freaks who work out regularly in a gym. They've got arses like fucking baboons."

Agreeing with an uninterested nod, Cheryl sat in a chair Deborah had pulled out for her. "I'll just boot up," Deborah announced, switching on her computer. This was more of a workplace than a living room, and scattered cardboard files made odd splotches of colour around the place. They untidily decorated every piece of furniture.

Cheryl studied Deborah as she intently watched a regiment of icons dutifully line up on parade on the blue screen of her computer. Deborah was not pretty. Her nose was long, her wide mouth thin-lipped, and her complexion sallow. But she had good teeth, and her smile brought out dimples that stayed buried most of the time. There are things that happen inside, under the skin, and are reflected in the eyes and the set of the mouth that rob a woman's face of beauty. Deborah must have been beautiful once and she could be lovely again. Her bare arms were smooth and firm. Held in check by the white bra was a crazy, wonderful pair of tits. Deborah had nice white flesh that was firm and young, but her face was old with knowledge she hadn't got from books.

"You're a very attractive woman, Debs," Cheryl complimented her.

"Never try to kid a kidder, Valenta."

"You are truly lovely."

"In the eyes of the beholder," she reminded Cheryl, moving the mouse and clicking it. She had elegant hands, long fingers tipped with deep-coloured nails perfectly kept.

"You have a great figure."

"What's with this crap?" Deborah asked. "I've spent all day on this project, so you're out of luck if a discount's what you're after."

"I'm not sure what I'm after," Cheryl said suggestively, wishing that Deborah had been wearing one of her usual shapeless dresses when she'd arrived. The researcher's seminudity was distracting. Deborah's clothes were always last year's fashion, old-looking and ill-fitting. "What have you got for me, Debs?"

Deborah's laugh was a tinkle of sound. "I take it we're talking information?"

Was she mocking Cheryl's lesbianism or opening up a channel for Cheryl to pursue? With Deborah it would take an expert psychologist weeks to find out. The Karen Cayson thing was too pressing for Cheryl to allow herself to be sidetracked.

"We're talking Wendi Maylor."

"Let's see." Deborah slid into an office chair and studied a line-filled computer screen. "Wendi's a girl in a hurry." She read off some facts. "Born in Bristol, bus-driver father, housewife mother. Attended Manchester University, where she read history and philosophy. Left before graduating."

"Why?"

With a shrug, Deborah replied. "I can't be sure. It seems she was something of a rebel at the time, spending a season with a travelling funfair show. What I can make of it she danced on the platform outside to pull the punters in, and stripped inside to please them."

"Quite a girl," Cheryl remarked admiringly. "But by all accounts the waste of a brilliant mind."

Turning her face to Cheryl, Deborah said, "I've never met Wendi, Cheryl, but I've got to like her from all this. There are times when I think I've lost the power to like anyone, but I like her."

"Where did she go from there, Debs?"

"There's a couple of blank years." Deborah made her reply sound like an apology. "There's the implication, but no proof, that she may have worked the big London hotels."

"As a call girl?"

Deborah nodded, but Cheryl shook her head. That didn't fit in with the Wendi Maylor that she knew. "I don't think that's very likely."

"Probably not. But she did work as an accountant and left under a cloud."

"Embezzlement?" Cheryl asked in surprise.

"Nothing proven. She could well have been a scapegoat."

It was of no consequence. There was nothing here that a disappointed Cheryl could use to dissuade Wendi Maylor from destroying Karen and Matthew. Parliament had condoned its members' misconduct so many times that financial irregularities and sexual indiscretions were no longer scandalous.

"Don't give up, Cheryl," Deborah cheerily advised. "I saved the good bits until last."

"You really don't know, do you?"

Nikki's amazement made Paula cringe with embarrassment. Ever since that morning when Nikki had made an appointment for them for noon the next day with Jay Clifford, Paula had wanted to enquire what it was all about. Now, as they were preparing for bed, she had plucked up the courage to do so. Nikki's reaction had been one of total incredulity.

"It may sound like I'm prying, Paula," an apologetic Nikki said, "but I don't want to involve you in something you may not want. I have to ask. How sexually experienced are you?"

Paula could not help flushing. "Not at all, really."

"What, were you living in a convent down in Basingstoke?" Nikki's tone expressed her disbelief. "You're not saying that you've never been with a man."

"I have, but only once. Then it wasn't my idea."

"I don't get it."

"I don't like talking about it, really," Paula began, aware of the familiar pain and the disgust that recall always brought her. There was self-loathing, too. This was totally unjustified, but she had never been able to convince herself of that. "It was on Saturday afternoon when I was working in a supermarket. We had a relief manager. All the girls were crazy about him. He looked something like Hugh Grant."

"There's no accounting for taste," Nikki said, an expression of revulsion on her face. "And he tried it on with you?"

Nodding unhappily, Paula said, "Yes. I was on my own in the storeroom and he came in and, well, he first started feeling my – my breasts. But I was able to push his hand away."

"But he didn't stop there," Nikki prompted.

"No. Then he put his hand under my skirt. It was between my legs," a horrified Paula said, her voice creaking from the stress that remembering was causing her. "It was really awful, Nikki, it was dreadful. I couldn't fight him off. I couldn't get away from him. It was when he was trying to pull my panties down that I screamed. I don't think that I meant to scream, but I knew that he was going to do something horrible to me."

"What happened then?"

"Mrs Forster, one of the supervisors, came running in. She telephoned head office and he was instantly dismissed."

"Is that it?"

"Is that what?"

"I'd hardly call that sex. In fact, scratch that – that *definitely* wasn't sex. Is that the total of your experience?"

"Not really," Paula defensively replied. "I haven't liked men since that time. I'm not sure that I liked them even before then. But me and Erica, my best friend, we... did things to each other."

"The two of you had sex?"

Paula nodded. "Yes. We kissed a lot and sort of examined each other – you know."

"Oh, bloody hell!" Nikki gasped out her astonishment with a mirthless little laugh. "Is that it?"

Either due to her reminiscences or Nikki's attitude, possibly both, Paula felt tears stinging her eyes. Since coming to London she had been striving to appear sophisticated, but she hadn't even fooled the girl with whom she shared a bedsitter. Turning away so that Nikki wouldn't see how close she was to weeping, she heard a contrite Nikki speaking kindly to her.

"Don't upset yourself, Paula. We'll talk about this in the morning. Get undressed and into your bed."

Hesitating, though never having before been bothered about undressing in front of Nikki, Paula felt foolish about her hesitation. She slowly took off her clothes, sensing that Nikki was avidly watching every movement. A perplexed Paula felt sure she heard her friend's sharp intake of breath as she released her large, silky-skinned breasts from the unclipped brassiere. Dropping her panties, Paula stepped out of them, glowing and heady in her nudity. Then, blushing and too self-conscious in her nakedness to prolong her discomfort by putting on her pyjamas, she quickly slid into the bed and pulled the covers over her.

Lying with her eyes closed, Paula tensed as Nikki eased herself under the covers and got into her bed with her. Feeling Nikki's soft-skinned limbs against her, aware of the warmth of her body, a startled Paula realised that her friend was as naked as she was.

Nikki comfortingly patted her on the shoulder, at the same time managing to touch the rise of her breast, apparently by accident. "Go to sleep, Paula. Like I said, we'll sort it all out in the morning."

Murmuring something in return, Paula must have nodded off to sleep. When she woke, Nikki was lying on her side, cuddled against her. One arm was lying across Paula's bare breasts. With her eyes closed, Nikki's face nestled against Paula's shoulder.

Suspecting that Nikki was awake, Paula pretended to be still asleep. This dual charade went on for a dragging fifteen minutes. Then Nikki, acting as if she were stirring in her sleep, moved her arm so that her hand rested on Paula's breasts. It shocked Paula to feel her nipples respond. They became tight buds thrusting up from the tips of her swelling breasts. Cuddling tighter against her, Nikki murmured in imitation drowsiness: "Oh, this is nice. Are you awake, Paula?"

"Yes."

"Do you mind if I stay here awhile?"

"I'd like you to."

Raising herself slightly, Nikki kissed Paula lightly on the cheek. "Thank you. You're a very sweet girl."

"I don't know why you think that."

"Because you are." Nikki kissed her again, lightly cupping Paula's left breast this time.

Involuntarily, as Paula liked to think at the time and since, she moved so that Nikki's and her bodies were together at full length. Nikki's hand moved to caress the breast it was holding, and she kissed Paula's cheek a few more times. Paula felt the body against hers give a little shiver. Then Nikki was up over her, looking intently at her before brushing a kiss across her lips. Nikki's mouth touched hers as lightly as a feather. It was a probing kiss, testing for Paula's reaction. Uncertain of how to respond, of how she wanted to respond, Paula lay passively in Nikki's arms. Nikki kissed her again, longer and more deeply, now with Paula's hard nipple between her manipulative fingers. Her third kiss was raunchily demanding, a kiss that was a totally new and arousing experience for Paula.

"Did you like that, my darling?" Nikki asked in husky tones.

Pressing her face against Nikki, her voice barely audible, Paula confessed, "Yes, I – I loved it."

This was the only incentive Nikki needed to kiss her again. Now she did not hold back. Mouth hotly against Paula's, Nikki's tongue came out to try to gain entry, but Paula kept her mouth closed. Then, needing more of Nikki, wanting to savour more of the delicious taste of her, Paula did part her lips. When Nikki's eager tongue entered, Paula's tongue met it. But it was a timid meeting. Soft and wet, all Paula's tongue did was accept the darting probes made by Nikki.

Fearing that the pleasure was about to end when Nikki took her mouth from hers, Paula grabbed and held the honey-blonde. But Nikki only wanted to whisper instructions. "Move your tongue against mine, Paula. Let me show you how."

Capturing Paula's mouth with hers once more, Nikki showed her how to use her tongue erotically. Paula tried but was hampered by her inexperience and timidity. Even so, tremors of delight ran through her as she felt the warm wet texture of Nikki's tongue. Instinctively, she opened her mouth wider and Nikki's lapping tongue explored the insides of her lips and cheeks.

As Nikki's hands squeezed and teased from one of Paula's breasts to the other, Paula's nipples hardened until they pleasurably ached from the momentous thrill of it.

Suddenly pulling back from the kiss, Nikki crouched above Paula and lowered her head to take one of the Paula's thrusting nipples in her mouth, gently pressuring it with her teeth. Next, moving to the other breast, she slid a hand down over the smooth skin of Paula's stomach. Paula felt the tips of Nikki's fingers playing in the fringe of her pubic hair at the top of the triangle. The fingers played and delayed, delighting her, making her groan with pleasure when at last Nikki's middle finger partly entered her slit.

Then came a coldness and a terrible disappointment as Nikki took her hand away. She moved up over Paula, her breasts a fraction of an inch away from Paula's mouth. She whispered, "Now you do it for me, Paula. Suck mine the way I sucked yours."

Trembling, Paula got the wonderful scent of Nikki's breasts, then she took the long, taut nipple in her mouth. Ripples of sensual delight ran through her again and she sucked hard as if trying to get the whole breast into her mouth. Nikki's hands came against Paula's face, gently pushing her a little away.

"Not so hard, darling," she cautioned softly. "That was hurting. Suck on the other one, and put your hand down there and feel me. I'm dying to feel your hand on me."

Clumsily aware that she was a novice at this, Paula put her hand between Nikki's legs. She moved it up over the soft silkiness of the inner thighs. Hair, long and wet, brushed against the back of her hand. Turning the hand, Paula found that Nikki's pubic hair was so thick that it obscured the entrance to her. Paula's fingers went inexpertly on safari through the jungle of it. Nikki's kneeling position caused her heavy, hot, juice-oozing lips to hang down. Paula's hand captured them, first taking the weight and then her fingers parted them. Running two fingers up and down the greasy slit, Paula felt them come up against an obstacle. Maybe she was inexperienced, but she wasn't ignorant of the facts of life. This had to be Nikki's clitoris – the man in the boat, as she had heard the boys at school refer to it. Taking it tenderly between a thumb and forefinger, Paula gave herself pleasure and brought a groaning ecstasy to Nikki by caressing the clit. Then Nikki squealed in delight as Paula continued to play about with her hole.

Suddenly, Nikki took her breast from Paula's mouth, and moved her body away from Paula's pleasurably torturing hand. Nikki cried, "Enough. I want more fun before I come. I've wanted to kiss you down there since the first moment I saw you, Paula, and I'm going to do it now."

Moving down under the bedcovers, she used both hands to spread Paula's legs wide. She kissed her way from the knees right up the inside of Paula's thighs. Then Paula was aware that Nikki was kissing her stomach, mouth open, sucking in the skin. Nikki's mouth slid slowly down, and a wonderful sensation had Paula in its grip as Nikki's mouth opened her up, tongue sliding in, probing, licking. Paula's clit responded to Nikki's tongue. It was being licked, sucked, titillated so that Paula experienced an ecstasy that was in contradiction almost unbearable. She felt Nikki sucking her swollen cunt lips into her mouth. Then, releasing the lips, Nikki slid both hands under Paula. Paula was aware of her buttocks being held as she was lifted a little and her cunt pulled tightly against Nikki's mouth.

Paula was held as Nikki built up a rhythmic on-off-on-off pressure against her open cunt. Guided by Nikki, Paula began to move her lower body in time, thrusting and jerking in the exhilarating rhythms of love. Hearing a scream of pleasure, Paula realised it was hers as her body arched violently, writhing from side to side. Then she let out another wild shriek as she reached orgasm.

Absolutely spent, Paula fell back on the bed, quivering from head to toe. Nikki moved up on her. Lying in between Paula's legs, Nikki reached down between their stomachs. First she opened the lips of Paula's juice-dripping cunt, then she opened herself up before lowering her hips so that their gaping quims were joined wetly and tightly.

They lay together with Nikki on top, panting into each other's mouth, tongues mingling. The warmth of each of them flowed into the other. They fucked, pelvis upon pelvis, clitoris on clitoris. Paula thrust herself upwards to meet Nikki's downward thrusts. Paula was a fast learner. Aroused again now, she was determined to come when Nikki did.

Nikki cried out. She howled, "Now! Oh Paula, darling, Now!"

Her tongue thrashed crazily inside Paula's mouth and Paula's tongue met it lash for lash as they came together in an earth-shaking shared orgasm.

Sliding off on to her side, Nikki held Paula lovingly in her arms. Paula felt more relaxed, more at one with the world than she had ever been in her life. Nikki was good for her, really good. Always more than a little afraid of sex, Paula now knew that it could be enjoyed to the full without any risk whatsoever.

Then her body tensed and she was dragged back into reality by what Nikki must have regarded as reassurance. Close to Paula's ear, she whispered, "You've no need to worry now, Paula. You'll be fine at Clifford's place tomorrow."

"What do you mean, Nikki?"

"He'll be ready to pay to film us doing what we just did," Nikki explained.

"I couldn't possibly do that," Paula protested.

"We don't have much choice, Paula. We are both desperately in need of money."

Nothing more was said, and a few minutes later Paula gently freed herself from Nikki's arms. Then, sliding from the bed, scarcely disturbing the covers, she reached for her pyjamas. She got into them and took her coat down from the rack inside the door. She was putting it on when Nikki called sleepily to her.

"What are you up to?"

"I'm just going down to the hall to ring Mum and Dad."

Alarm brought Nikki instantly awake. "You're not thinking of going home, Paula?"

"No, I just owe them a call," Paula replied as she sought and found the slip of paper she had written Cheryl Valenta's telephone number on.

"It's her, there's no doubt about that," a relieved Cheryl said as she looked over Deborah's shoulder at the computer screen.

On display was a newspaper page with a photograph of policemen making arrests at a dingy-looking terraced house. Held between two uniformed officers, a girl glared angrily at the camera. It was Wendi Maylor. Her picture appeared below the banner headline POLICE ARREST STUDENTS IN DRUGS SWOOP.

"How will that do you, Cheryl?" Deborah asked, raising one eyebrow high.

Shaking her head doubtfully, Cheryl said, "Not enough in this day and age, Debs. Celebrities in show business who've been busted for drugs have received knighthoods."

"Don't let that worry you," Deborah chuckled, moving the mouse about, clicking it repeatedly. Copies of newspaper pages flicked past too speedily for Cheryl to read, but Deborah gave a running commentary. "Celebrities can afford drugs, but few students can. This is how Wendi tried to fund her habit. Look – theft of a fellow student's credit card and credit-card fraud, three months' imprisonment."

Unable to believe her good fortune, Cheryl sat down, letting the full impact of what she had just learned find its rightful place in her mind. Pleased that she could use Wendi Maylor's criminal past to save the Wyndhams from scandal, she felt sad for Wendi. It was easy to go wrong when you were young, and it was to Wendi Maylor's credit that she had put it all behind her to become an acclaimed entertainer.

Yet business was business, and Cheryl asked, "Can you print me off copies of those reports, Debs?"

"I'll run them off now," Deborah said obligingly, coming across to where Cheryl sat, leaning over her as she reached for a part-ream of paper on a dresser behind Cheryl.

With Deborah's bare shoulder close, and breathing in the womanly scent of her, Cheryl felt a need stirring deep within her. It was the very familiar, yet ever-new birth of desire. At that moment it was no more than a faint tendril of sensation but she was aware that soon it would come in a hot gush.

Unable to help herself, Cheryl reached up with her right hand.

Hooking a finger into the top of the left cup of Deborah's brassiere, she gently pulled it down. The flesh of the white breast swelled up, proud to be free and on show. The erect pink nipple was caught at first, but then it sprang out, stiff and inviting. There was a faint smile on Deborah's face and a knowing look in her eyes. Cheryl flicked a tongue over her lips to moisten them. She let her lips part, hungry for the rigid nipple.

Deborah bent obligingly and the tip of her nipple touched Cheryl's bottom lip just as the buzzing of Cheryl's mobile telephone instantly dispelled the sensual magic of the moment.

Cheryl reached for the handset as Deborah stood upright and pulled her bra out. When the boob popped automatically back into hiding, Deborah released the cup. It returned to normal with an elasticated little snapping sound.

"Hello? Cheryl Valenta."

"I'm sorry to bother you on a Sunday evening," a far from confident female voice crackled into the earpiece. "It's me, Paula Monroe."

With Deborah's breast still present in her mind as an erotic image, Cheryl couldn't initially place the name. Then she remembered. It was the pretty but incredibly naïve country girl at the Wyndham bash.

"What can I do for you, Paula?"

The girl's words came out in a rush. Deciphering rapidly, Cheryl understood that the show, whatever it had been, had folded. The girl was all but destitute, and her friend was taking her to Jay Clifford's place in the morning.

"I do need the money, Cheryl, but what do you think?"

"You do understand what Clifford will be paying you for, don't you?"

Cheryl asked. Deborah had the computer's printer in action not far off, but the rumbling little sound it made didn't interfere with the telephone conversation.

"I didn't until just a little while ago," Paula admitted, "but I do now."

"And you're still going to do it?"

"I don't know. I wanted your advice."

"My advice is to stay well away from a creep like Jay Clifford," Cheryl said emphatically.

"But I do desperately need money," Paula protested. "The alternative would be to swallow my pride and to go back home as a failure."

That was the only real option the kid had. Cheryl, annoyed with herself for always getting involved with the problems of others, found that she wasn't hard enough to give the girl the bum's rush. Instead she got herself in deeper by saying, "Look, if I remember rightly, Clifford's place is at the rear of Olympia. When are you supposed to be going there?"

"At noon."

"Do you know where Olympia is?"

"I'll have to find it," Paula answered, "because Nikki – that's my friend – has to go somewhere first, and I'm meeting her outside Olympia."

"What time are you meeting her?"

"Half past eleven."

"Right, now listen, Paula," Cheryl said firmly. "I'll meet you there at eleven o'clock, and we'll find a way for you to get by without getting mixed up with scum like Clifford."

"Oh," Paula sighed. "You don't know how pleased I am that you're going to help me. Are you sure that you don't mind?"

"I don't mind. Be there at eleven tomorrow."

Ringing off, Cheryl turned to see that Deborah had put on one of her baggy old dresses. She wasn't going to take any further risks by being seminude. There was an awkwardness between them now that hadn't existed before. Cheryl took the hard copy and thanked Deborah. They spoke the way strangers do until growing familiarity rubs off the rough edges between them.

Strange though it was, Cheryl, who was still aroused by the earlier incident, felt certain that Deborah was also still affected by it. They both desired each other, but neither of them wanted to risk taking the other by the hand to walk into the sexual wonderland from which there was no return.

They said stilted goodbyes as Deborah held the front door open for Cheryl. She went down the path to the car. Deborah was still there when Cheryl pulled away and waved. In the rear-view mirror, Cheryl saw Deborah wave back.

Replacing the telephone receiver, Matthew Wyndham looked anxiously at his wife. He had been discharged from the hospital that morning, but had stayed in his pyjamas and dressing gown all day. It was as if he was expecting a relapse and wanted to take the difficulty out of going back to bed. Karen noticed how pale he was, but the only indication that he was wounded was the small patch of skin where his head had been shaved, a long red snake of a wound that had been stitched together, and the rusty stain of iodine that contrasted with his grey hair.

"That was Richard," he told her bleakly as he poured them both a drink. "The rumours are thickening."

"But that's exactly what they are, rumours," Karen argued. "The public has a very short memory, Matt."

"Maybe so, Karen, and your fans will soon forget, but it's business that worries me," he said, reaching for her hand as he sat. She gave it to him.

"What does Richard say?"

Shaking a glum head, Matthew said, "He thinks the best way may be for us to make an admission."

"What does he want us to admit?" Karen feared the answer. If she was going to be forced to come out, then no matter how short the memory of the general public was, she didn't have the time to wait for her fans to forget.

"A simple admission that you struck me." Matthew Wyndham tried to make this sound like a wise idea. "Richard has someone ready to swear that he spiked your drinks at the party. That way it will be seen that you were not responsible for what you did."

More lies. What a profession! One of Karen's major regrets was that she had learned to lie with the ease that decent folk told the truth. Though he made this sound like a simple solution, she doubted that Matthew believed that it was.

"What about Wendi Maylor?" she enquired. "She can get million-dollar publicity by saying that I whacked you because you were about to slip her a length."

"Richard has taken care of Wendi. He assures me that she won't say a word about me," Matthew said consolingly.

Maybe Wendi might be prepared to say nothing about Matthew, but Karen doubted that Wendi's promise extended to her. The dancer was one of those deluded people who confuse sex and love. For a long time Karen had more than suspected that Wendi had fallen in love with her. That created a dangerous situation, an extremely dangerous situation. Jealousy was probably the motive for most murders. Not that Karen thought for a moment that she was likely to be a victim of homicide. It was her career that was most likely to be slaughtered.

"So, what do we do?" she asked.

"Richard wants us to meet in his office in the morning. For some reason he's asked Cheryl Valenta to be there."

That made Karen feel better. She silently congratulated Richard Neehan. Great minds did think alike, but she was glad that she had thought of Cheryl before the solicitor had.

Five

Richard Neehan's offices occupied the entire sixth floor of a lofty building just off, and overlooking, Kingsway. It was a private world high above the asphalted, pedestrian-thronged, traffic-jammed, fume-spewing madhouse that was London. Cheryl Valenta hated the city, but wouldn't want to live anywhere else. How was that for a split personality? Deborah reckoned that too much looking into a full-length mirror led to schizophrenia. Cheryl stepped out of the lift into an oppressive library-like hush. The whisper of her feet on the thick-pile carpets was a mini-riot. Girls wearing headphones timidly tapped at computers, wincing at the sound of every tiny click. There was a churchlike smell of old leather and old people. The scent of furniture polish had the acrid quality of incense. An ageing secretary rose up from behind an ageing desk. An ageing secretary, because she didn't look like anything else. Women working in these places never did. You don't see them climbing little steel stepladders in shoe shops, or dragging bar codes over a bleeping checkout in Sainsbury's.

"Do you have an appointment?" She peered over silver-rimmed glasses, imprisoning Cheryl with an invisible peripheral glance.

Cheryl had less than an hour to spare before meeting Paula at Olympia. She stood there, very conscious of the sour smell of the secretary's virginity, able to feel the force of the woman's hostility.

"Mr Neehan is expecting me."

That was true. Richard Neehan had telephoned her last night.

Only fools believe what lawyers and politicians tell them, but Cheryl knew that what Neehan had told her – about the hospital's diagnosis that Matthew was suffering from what was probably a terminal illness – was true.

The secretary shook her head, her hennaed hair flapping. Her smile was very condescending. "I don't think so, madam. Mr Neehan will be unavailable throughout most of the morning. He has someone with him."

"I assume that would be Matthew and Karen Wyndham," Cheryl said.

Taking off her glasses with a dramatic gesture, the secretary managed an indulgent little smile. The plebs had to be kept in their place. "You really don't expect me to divulge that kind of information. Mr Richard Neehan—"

"Is expecting me," Cheryl repeated, raising her voice. "Matthew Wyndham is expecting me, Karen Cayson is expecting me."

The lines of discontent and bitterness on the secretary's face became deeper and more distorting. They made her face look shallow, as though it were just a little way under water and the ripples on the surface were putting it out of focus. Anticipating more obstinacy, Cheryl was relieved to see a door open ajar and a frowning Richard Neehan peer out. He spotted Cheryl. His face lightened into an easy smile and the trouble lines were gone.

"Miss Valenta. Do please come in."

Cheryl exchanged a parting hostile glance with the secretary. Neehan noticed, and, when Cheryl got to him he said, "Pay no mind to Elspeth, she's very protective of me. She's been with the firm since—"

"Before she was a virgin," Cheryl filled in for him.

He laughed, a genuine explosion of laughter. "Something like that."

They entered a room where Matthew Wyndham was sitting facing the door. The T-shirt he wore was eggshell-white, with yellow stitching, tailor-made, with his initials embroidered over his heart. His trousers were moulded to his figure like a scuba diver's wet suit. He was an anachronism carrying the 1950s through to the twenty-first century. It struck Cheryl that this was how James Dean would have looked had he lived.

Matthew was his old self once more, bland, composed and damned handsome in a mature way. He didn't have the appearance of a man who had just learned that he was seriously ill. But his fingers betrayed him. With elbows resting on the arms of his chair and his hands together as a steeple pointing at the ceiling, his fingers were tapping against one another.

As Cheryl soundlessly crossed the thick carpet to take a seat, she smiled at Karen. The actress was submerged in an overstuffed easy chair, legs crossed, lots of thigh on display. Her eyes asked Cheryl to say nothing of their meeting at the club. Cheryl tried to send Karen a silently reassuring message back. By just using your eyes it was difficult to convey that you would keep schtum. Cheryl hoped that she'd made it.

Inflated by self-regard, Richard Neehan took centre floor as if he were Albert Einstein and the three of them were new physics students. Cheryl sat, waiting. The undersized lawyer was far more evasive now than when he had telephoned Cheryl. People found it easier to lie on the telephone when their body language couldn't be observed. It warned Cheryl that Neehan was about to lie now, which wasn't remarkable for a solicitor. Neehan had told her that he knew about Karen and Wendi Maylor. The big question was whether or not to tell Matthew Wyndham, whose newly discovered illness complicated things.

The virginal viper of a secretary entered carrying a tray with four cups of coffee. There was a plate of slender biscuits, too. Cheryl sipped coffee but left the biscuits. She'd learned, or had most probably read, that eating in some company could be psychically dangerous. There was a lot of tension here. Really bad vibes. These three were big wheels, hard workers and hard relaxers. They were people who lived on the verge. They slept on perches and had to stay partly awake so as not to fall off.

"We have a problem," Neehan announced from around the rim of a raised cup. He was a talker. He was a sophisticated man, a garrulous man, an awful bore. "We have you at home again, Matthew, and we pray that your problem will respond to treatment. But you are still on the media's critical list. Mainly due to the testimony of your servants, which, incidentally, they refuse to retract, the press won't accept that you fell."

"Well, then." Matthew's finger-steeple parted. His hands lay twitching slightly in his lap. "We must go ahead with what you proposed last night. Somebody spiked Karen's drinks and she struck me without knowing what she was doing. Karen is happy to go along with that. I've a lot of money invested in a heap of projects, Richard, and a whiff of a real scandal could finish me. That's no exaggeration."

Neehan accepted this with a nod. He looked weary. A lawyer to the rich could never take a holiday, not even have a day off, because his clients never did. Pushing fifty, he was a Cambridge graduate, once married, once divorced, never remarried. His and Cheryl's paths had crossed many times in the past. He had some time ago grabbed Cheryl and kissed her, his vicar squirming against her pulpit. She had ensured that it was a nonevent. "Of course. But after I telephoned you I realised that something had slipped my mind. We overlooked the fact that Karen was charged and convicted of actual bodily harm against Ralph Redfern, her first husband."

This was news to Cheryl. Wanting to know more, she heard Matthew Wyndham objecting.

"That was a long time ago, Richard," Wyndham protested. "Also, it was self-defence. Redfern was a brutal bastard who used Karen as a punchbag when in his cups."

"Maybe so, Matthew, maybe so." Neehan shook a wise head.

"But, with all due respect, it's verdicts that matter, not personal opinions. The tabloid hacks will enter the newspaper tomb and drag out the rotting corpse of that story. It'll be back on its feet quicker than Lazarus was. Karen's good name is at risk here. She'll be branded as a violent person, and it will be suggested that she's unstable. They'll portray you, Matthew, as a silly, weak old man ready to tolerate anything to keep the beautiful young wife who has – forgive me for quoting an oft-repeated observation – castrated you."

"So we stick to the original story," Wyndham sighed. He was clever worldly, and blessed with a whole lot of native intelligence. The ambitious kids eager to get into show business scrambled for the unlikely chance to touch Matthew Wyndham's cloak. But right then he wasn't so powerful, wasn't so "lord of the mountain" as he usually was. Turning his head to Cheryl, he said. "You've been in the newspaper business a long time, Cheryl. Your work is admired, you command respect. You can counter much of what will be said about us, and you'll be believed."

"I'll do my best, Matthew," Cheryl promised, but added a warning. "You must remember that I'm syndicated in the quality papers. Though I have no wish to offend anyone, Karen in particular, I have to say that the fans of television and pop stars often don't read serious newspapers."

"That is a generalisation, of course, but I would be foolish not to agree with you." Wyndham gave a self-pitying sigh. "It is to our great advantage that you cater for the people who count, Cheryl. They will read and take notice of what you write."

Cheryl found it difficult to even feel sorry for him, even where his illness was concerned. Whenever she was in Matthew Wyndham's presence for more than ten minutes she found dislike of him beginning under her skin. It had to be something either intuitive or instinctive, as it defied analysis.

Neehan looked uncomfortable. "We can rest assured that Cheryl will ably take care of that side of things. However, I am afraid that's not all, Matthew."

"Break it to me gently, Richard. These past few days I've had enough shocks to last me a lifetime," Wyndham said gloomily. "What's the problem?"

"Wendi Maylor."

"She's nothing, Richard. For a whore to be a whore she has to be a whore, and that girl is a born whore, greedy for fame. Forget her," Wyndham advised dismissively. "She can't prove she was with me. Anyway, an adulterer is always admired, never condemned. It will enhance my reputation." Wyndham paused a moment in thought, then remarked testily, "Don't I remember you telling me last night that Wendi had agreed to stay quiet?"

"It's not you that she's threatening to blow the whistle on, but Karen," Neehan said in a low voice.

"But..." Karen began, but didn't know how to continue. She uncrossed her legs and crossed them again and her skirt hiked higher. Cheryl's mind went up between Karen's thighs, imagination excitedly toying with a hairy cunt that she had never had sight of but was yearning to see and to touch, to grope. A sudden paralysis seemed to strike Karen. She was the type of woman who needed to have a legal, permanent hold on a man so that she could smother him with possessiveness knowing that he couldn't escape. There was every sign that she was about to lose that security. When the rigidity released her body she was trembling. Cheryl knew what was troubling her. Betraying fans was a threat to her income, but it was an impersonal thing, while disloyalty to a husband was close to home, emotional dynamite.

Karen lit a cigarette and blew a column of smoke up towards the ceiling, watching it rise as though it were something of importance.

With a little shake of his head, Matthew said, "You smoke too much, Karen."

This was an incongruous remark in the circumstances, but it

did nothing to ease the tension that was gripping everyone in the room. They waited, poised like predators, painfully aware that Karen was the prey.

Matthew Wyndham wrapped his fists into hard knots and pressed them against the arms of his chair. When he did speak it was to shock them. He cautioned, "To make denials will be both futile and unnecessary, Karen. I've known about Wendi, and all your other women, right from the start. When we married I was aware that I would never hold you to myself alone. Maybe my logic is odd, but I've never considered a wife having sex with a woman to be anything like as serious as her being unfaithful with a man. I was immensely relieved when, if I may put it crudely, you chose cunts rather than pricks."

"But she'll finish me," Karen gasped. She brushed aside the soft curtain of red hair that had fallen over her cheek. The actress had two enormous jewels, one an emerald and one a diamond, on her fingers.

"I'm pretty sure that she won't," Cheryl said brightly. Karen had miraculously escaped a serious confrontation with her husband, and Cheryl wouldn't permit her to be demolished by merciless media. "I'll be seeing Wendi later today, and I'm sure that I can persuade her not to cause you any distress, Karen."

Glancing at her watch, Cheryl was horrified to see that it was twenty-five minutes to twelve. She had missed Paula Monroe. The kid was in real need of protection and she had let her down. Cheryl stood, ready to leave.

"We'll be eternally grateful. Just name your fee, Cheryl," Wyndham said. "I want that Wendi bastard off my back, and you're the girl to do it."

"A whore is a whore," said Neehan, wagging a sad head, currying favour with Wyndham.

"No fee. It's on the house." Cheryl smiled at the television tycoon.

She flashed Karen a telepathic message. Receiving the silent communication, the lovely Karen confirmed that she understood with a look that said she would show her gratitude when the time came.

This pleased and excited Cheryl, but she felt terrible about having failed Paula. She said, "I have to go."

"The interminable battle for the mighty buck," Neehan said with a sympathetic laugh.

"That's a cynical way of looking at it, Richard," Cheryl remarked.

"Forgive me," he said with a smiling little bow. "Cynicism increases with age, and in my business you age fast. You will keep us informed on this Wendi Maylor business."

"I'll be in touch."

"Thank you, Cheryl," Karen called. Her voice sounded different. Deep. Throaty.

By the door, Cheryl turned to look back at her. They exchanged warm smiles.

Jay Clifford occupied the basement flat in a four-storey building. With the caution of someone expecting a hit man, he opened a door fitted with a chain lock. Shutting the door again, he released the chain and let them enter. Inside it could have been really classy, but it was a real mess. The main room was cluttered and he had to push a television set to one side and use a sideways sweep of a foot to shove video cassettes under a settee. Apart from a pair of jeans he was naked and barefoot. Paula noticed that Clifford's excess flesh showed more than when she'd met him suited. He had a pair of ludicrously floppy man-tits. Nikki, who seemed to know him well, pulled a disgusted face.

"This place is a tip," Nikki said.

"What are you, the fucking home help? I was a good friend to you when you were in need," Clifford retorted. Slipping an arm round Paula's waist, he brought a hand up to cup a breast and squeeze it. He reported to Nikki. "She'll do."

Pulling herself from his embrace, Paula felt really low. Slowly but disturbingly, she'd been getting feedback from making love with Nikki. Though thrilling, both at the time and retrospectively, the present situation increased her uneasiness about it. The dragging waiting time outside Olympia had ended in disappointment. Even now she still hoped to be rescued. One of those last-minute miracles like in the movies. She didn't need the Seventh US Cavalry. The sensible, self-contained Cheryl Valenta dashing up with an apology for being late would do.

Nikki spoke impatiently. "We're here, Jay, so what's the deal?"

"I don't do deals," Clifford replied with an emphatic shake of his head. "You should be asking what's on offer. Both of you need my money a whole lot more than I need your bodies. When I see what the pair of you can do, then I'll decide what you're worth."

"You'll have your film then, and it'll be too late for us to argue," Nikki objected angrily.

"With this 'money first, love', you sound just like a prostitute. If that's what you want, then I suggest you go on the game. Otherwise" – Clifford shrugged his fat shoulders and his male boobs jiggled – "you do as I say, and on my terms."

Not knowing what it was all about alarmed Paula more than the argument between her friend and Clifford. The place made her uneasy. It smelled of the photographer's sweat and something else that was less unpleasant. The second aroma had an appeal to it, but Paula resisted breathing deeply in an attempt at identifying it. She feared that the discovery would prove to be distressing.

Having been quiet and thoughtful for a minute or two, Nikki gave a nod. "OK, but don't you try to short-change us, Jay."

"What do we have to do?" Paula asked tremulously. She could actually feel the tiny hairs rise on her forearms, and an icy-cold prickle ran down her spine. There was dread in her veins, toxic and deadening. Coming here had been a mistake.

She noticed that Nikki seemed to have suddenly hardened, as if she were withdrawing something of herself. Paula fought for composure. She felt hesitant, frightened. Strangely enough, she was not even sure why she was so scared. Maybe Nikki was to blame. Had the situation they were in actually changed her from a friend into something else, albeit temporarily?

Clifford answered her question: "Nothing that will frighten the horses." He pulled aside a threadbare curtain covering a doorway. "Watch and learn, dear, watch and learn."

A shocked Paula found herself looking into an untidy room from which issued the smell she had earlier noticed. A girl lay on her back on an unmade bed, with the top of her dark, curly-haired head facing Paula, Nikki and Clifford. With both hands the girl was holding the white buttocks of another girl who was straddling her head, sitting on her face. The buttocks were being held apart, with every detail of the hairy crack on view.

At the sound of the curtain being pulled aside, the girl on top turned her head to speak over her shoulder to Clifford. "If you're not ready to start filming, at least turn the heating up, you tight cunt."

"Tight cunt is something you'll never be called, dear," Clifford said with a haughty sniff and a toss of his head. Turning to Paula, he pointed to where the dark-haired girl was making gasping, sucking noises as she fed off her partner. "See that, Paula? It's more fun than work. I haven't even thought about switching on a camera yet, but Suzie is really enjoying herself. Take Paula into the kitchen and make some coffee, Nikki. When I've finished with Suzie and Noreen, then you two can have the bed."

Clifford picked up an expensive camcorder, holding it against one eye. "Thank fuck," said the girl on top, rising up a little so that her cunt and arsehole came fully on show.

"Wow! That is one awesome cunt!" Clifford sighed in admiration. "I wouldn't be able to resist it myself if that was my scene. Which it isn't." Distaste showed on his face and he made a sound of disgust. "Ugh!"

It suddenly hit Paula that he was gay. His hitting on her at the

Wyndham bash had been an act. That made her feel a little better. Just a tiny bit better.

"Let's go have a coffee," Nikki said to Paula, giving her a reassuring smile.

"I'm – I'm not sure that I'm going to be able to go through with this," Paula stammered, watching the girl who was underneath tongue her partner's anus, keeping her head to one side so that Clifford could record the action.

Mouth twisted by his squinting through the viewfinder, Clifford almost overbalanced as he went down on one knee. He uttered a curse. "The punters will complain if the angle of a suck or a fuck isn't right," a petulant Clifford explained, as if terrified that one of his porno films might be criticised on the BBC's *Points of View*."

Trying to move Paula away into the kitchen, Nikki was aware that her friend was sickened by what was going on. She whispered a reminder. "We really need the money, Paula."

"This isn't for me," Paula said quietly, speaking more to herself than to Nikki. This wasn't what she had spent hours at home in Basingstoke for, practising possible and impossible facial expressions in front of a mirror. "I came to London to get into television."

Overhearing, an annoyed Clifford used his free hand to scratch at his bare left breast, leaving bright red tramlines. "That's great! You're in the wrong place if you're looking to be Julie Andrews. This is all about shagging, I'm not shooting *Okla*-fucking-*homa*."

This cruel remark made Paula starkly aware of how degrading this all was. Her mouth was tight, her lips dry. Turning, she ran from the room and out of the front door. After stumbling up the steps, half blinded by tears, she had reached the pavement when Nikki caught up with her.

"I'm sorry that I brought you here, Paula," Nikki said as she gave her a one-armed hug.

Still shaking a little, Paula said, "You've been here before, haven't you?"

"Only once."

"Who with?" Paula asked, puzzled as to whether she was just curious or perhaps jealous.

"I was on my own," Nikki answered. "Clifford filmed me while I was wanking myself."

"Weren't you terribly embarrassed?"

"At the start. But I forget everything, even where I am, when I get worked up."

They linked arms and walked down the side street until they came out at Olympia. Paula looked around, hoping to glimpse the striking Cheryl Valenta standing waiting for her. There was no sign of her. They turned left and went over the railway bridge into Kensington High Street.

"What will we do for money now, Nikki?" Paula worriedly enquired.

"We'll get ourselves work somewhere," Nikki replied with fragile optimism.

They were passing the Hilton Hotel, two destitute girls trespassing on the territory of the rich and famous, when Nikki giggled.

"What's so funny?" Paula enquired, mystified by the sudden mirth.

"I was just thinking," Nikki chuckled, "that I wouldn't have said no to a taste of what that girl on the bed was licking."

An admonishing Paula gave her friend a playful shove. "Nikki, you are absolutely awful."

Then both of them were laughing. Each slipped an arm round the waist of the other as they went on their way.

She had even failed at that. It was all too much. Wendi Maylor took her hand from between her legs. Her fingers had stroked and explored every intimate part of herself, all to no avail. She curled up in the foetal position, miserably. Any kind of problem, the slightest of worries, stunted her sex drive. The Karen Cayson thing had got to her so badly that now she couldn't even masturbate. She felt hot down there, but it was the wrong kind of heat. An uncomfortable heat. Her lower belly felt stretched tight and heavy, as if she were about to give birth to a cannonball, and her cunt felt tender and twitchy. She wanted either to scream or to weep, but even making a choice between the two was too much for her. Her life seemed to be as empty as her yearning quim, and her hand and wrist ached.

Even when the guy from the *Sun* had called to fix an appointment with her for Wednesday, Wendi had been certain she was doing the right thing. Now she was plagued by doubt. What Cheryl Valenta had written in her newspaper column had caused Wendi to do a major rethink. She held the evidence to out Karen Cayson, but had she the right to do so? What she had considered to be best for the lovely star might well be exactly what Karen didn't want. By selling the story to the press she would possibly be ending Karen's marriage, killing off her career. Cheryl's account of Matthew's illness had made her realise the terrific power that she held. It was no exaggeration to say that it was the power of life and death. Wendi knew that the revelation she had to make could even push the often neurotic Karen over the edge into suicide. All of it was daunting. It would be easier if she could talk it over with Karen, but there was no chance of that, the way things were right now. Being apart from Karen was why Wendi was frustrated. Being unable to bring herself off must surely mean that she was at the end of her sexual tether.

Pushing her skirt down from around her waist, not bothering to recover her panties from where they lay on the floor, Wendi reached out for the newspaper. It was folded so that Cheryl Valenta's "Stage Door Whispers" page was uppermost. Wendi had read it before, but she read the passage that interested her again.

> ... but when the rumourists have fallen silent and the ink of the last lie has faded, the worry won't end for Karen Cayson and Matthew Wyndham. Trial by tabloid is no threat to their long and happy marriage, but, sadly, illness is. When Matthew Wyndham had confessed that he had become drunk and had fallen at his birthday party, he believed that he was being honest. But hospital tests show that he is suffering from an incurable disease of the blood. It was weakness, not alcohol, that caused Matthew Wyndham's fall. This couple deserves our sympathy and our prayers, not our malicious scandal-mongering.

Wendi was confused by the article. Cheryl Valenta's reputation as a journalist was unassailable, but she couldn't know how Matthew had sustained his injuries that night. Only Matthew, Karen and she knew the truth. There was no reason why Cheryl shouldn't accept the version given her by the Wyndhams, but the worrying bit about the blood illness had to be true. Cheryl would have insisted on seeing proof before she would put the story in print.

At least Wendi wouldn't have long to wait to find out what it was all about. Cheryl was coming to see her that afternoon. The reason for the journalist's visit was a mystery, but, when telephoning Wendi, Cheryl had given the impression that it was of the utmost importance.

Leaning over, Wendi recovered her panties and stood up from the bed. Frustration was a big hole in her head. It was a huge hole that could grow until there was nothing left of her, only that huge hole. She picked up her mobile phone and crossed the room to place it on an occasional table. Once a prize possession, it was now something from which she wanted to distance herself. The intrusive, invasive mobile phone was the most ghastly of modern inventions. She'd had everything in that Manchester hotel room. They had kissed and found their place in time and in distance, two naked people lost in a sexual Paradise, enjoying the whispering sensual pleasure of skin against skin. Both with raging appetites, they had been savouring the appetising food of flesh when the telephone had buzzed demandingly. And now the hole was all Wendi had left.

Manchester had been generally disastrous. The television discussion had been about the council-enforced closure of a home for disturbed children of which Wendi had been co-founder. Expecting a Michael Parkinson-style one-to-one interview, Wendi had been ushered into a tatty studio that amounted to nothing more than a small, semi-derelict warehouse. In one corner a large oblong table had stood on an irregularly cut carpet. The illusion that was television.

Already at the table was the programme host, who smiled meaninglessly, a practised, yet unconscious gesture for anyone watching. There was no warmth in his eyes. He seemed only half human, an example of what self-regard can do to a man. He had beckoned a makeup assistant to have her pat extra powder on his nose and check that his wig was securely anchored.

Also at the table had been Father O'Leary, a priest whom Wendi knew, and two strangers. One was a pudgy man in his forties, with eyes like glass marbles and a head of hair that looked painted on. There was something vaguely familiar about him. He had a furtiveness about him and a neutral; face. He was one of those third-rate politicians to whom you can put a face but not a name – the same as it was with actors doomed for ever to playing supporting roles to the fortunate famous.

Giving up the game of identification, Wendi had switched her gaze to the woman sitting at her left, a smartly dressed American woman who was a professor of psychiatry.

With a dramatic gesture, a fussing floor manager had indicated that the broadcast had begun. An audience of freeloaders applauded listlessly, and the host smiled insincerely into a camera, and the show was on the road. Opposing emotions turned the televised debate into a shambles. Within minutes the presenter had taken the side of the politician against Wendi and the professor, with an uncomfortable O'Leary trying to find some neutral ground. It ended with the *hoi polloi* in the free seats having totally lost interest, and the host embarking on an ego trip.

Probably due to the acrimonious discussion, Wendi's gaydar system had failed her. Professor Nancy Lake was a beautiful woman. Frowning thoughtfully and teasing at her lower lip with her teeth, she had been staring off into nowhere. The professionally severe blue costume that she wore couldn't completely conceal a more than passable figure. She had tousled hair, full lips, a lascivious smile, and a dynamic sex appeal that Wendi felt had made even the priest a trifle off balance.

It was in the bar later that Wendi had learned the truth. She had come out of the ladies' and had been about to join the professor and the obnoxious politician at the bar, when she had overheard two male technicians commenting on Nancy Lake.

"I'm interested in that Yank," one of them said, eyeing the long-legged professor hungrily.

"Forget it," the other man advised.

"Why?"

"She's a dyke, mate."

An astonished Wendi, motivated by what she had overheard, returned to the bar, where she secretly signalled an eye message, the lesbian equivalent of a Masonic handshake. The American woman's eyes first narrowed in thought then widened in delight. She gazed directly into Wendi's eyes, and an unspoken agreement had been made between them.

Amused by something the politician had said, Nancy had laughed a low and throaty laugh. She had thrown back her head a little and Wendi had wanted to grab her and kiss the beauty of her throat. Now all that remained for her to think of was Nancy's face and her lovely body. The way she had kissed and the intensity in her eyes. These memories made Wendi's frustration painful.

Escaping from the politician, too hastily to be polite, they had booked into the Mon Ami hotel. Sandwiched between a public house and a taxi office, it was a place for showbiz second-rates and retreads. It survived solely because it was convenient to the television studio and the rooms were relatively cheap. The lobby was lengthy and dim, with potted cacti sticking up dangerously along the route. There had been a stale, cloying smell of cigars, expensive women and cheap alcohol. The desk clerk had looked like an ex-actor. He had probably worn a muffler and said, "Leave it awf, guv" in *Dixon of Dock Green* or something similar way back in the 1950s. Now he and his clothes had a seedy look. The bald spot at the top of his head was spreading, and wrinkles of defeat framed his eyes. He must have known the situation between them when he had booked them into a room, but he had probably seen it all in his time.

Once they were alone, there had suddenly been no space for small talk between the two of them. No neutral topic for conversation. The awkward silence had been broken by Nancy's self-conscious little laugh about the room. It had been small, with just one window – an old-fashioned room, the only other furniture being a worm-holed chest of drawers. But it was clean, and that was all that mattered to Wendi. She had been alone with the luscious Nancy Lake. The American had wet her lips in a deliberate gesture and her smile had been purposely inviting. All Wendi had wanted to do was satisfy the aching torment between her legs by drawing Nancy down on the bed.

They stood facing each other for a long moment, bodies only inches away from one another, and then she was in Nancy's arms. Their lips met for the first time. It was a long, slow, deep kiss. Then Nancy released her and stepped back a little. Holding both of

Wendi's hands, the American narrowed her eyes so that they became smoky slits. Her lips were shining wet, slackly apart, beckoning to Wendi, begging Wendi. Wendi studied her hungrily. Nancy stood smiling, her breasts rising and falling rapidly.

Once more Wendi was in her arms. Nancy's arms went behind Wendi to clasp her buttocks and caress them. She teased Wendi by brushing her mouth with lips that were gently damp and sweetly warm, the tip of her tongue a swift dart of flame. Then they kissed again, holding each other tightly, body against body. Breaking the kiss, Nancy's lips made light contact Wendi's face, breathing hotly on her cheek. Wendi kissed her neck, biting her once, sinking her teeth in. She held Nancy tighter and had heard her breath turn into a gasp. The professor was squirming against Wendi, trying to release the passion that was storming inside her.

What had followed was now a misty but ever-arousing memory for Wendi. Her body still reacted throbbingly to that session of abandoned sex, tantalising her, but she couldn't tune her mind in for a detailed action replay. Professor Lake, a naked psychiatrist, had paraded before her. The professor was a superbly beautiful woman. She had big beautiful tits that had made Wendi envious. Now Wendi could recall an outline of that wonderful experience. Nancy had been patient, so very patient and delicate, kissing Wendi so delicately, her lips, her ears, her neck, her breasts, her belly – oh, fucking hell, her cunt! Nancy Lake had been something. Bloody hell, what a lover; what an expert, loving lover!

It was coming back to Wendi now. Raunchy pictures were sharpening as they came out of a fog in her mind. Having intended to put her panties back on, she tossed them onto the bed and slid a warm hand up between her own thighs. It was great having somebody else do it for you, but they could never know exactly what you liked – what to do, where to do it, and when. She parted the drooping lips of her cunt to slide a finger in, slipping and sliding up herself, creating suction and causing an arousing sucking, slopping sound.

She had been a little frightened at the time. Not of the lovely Nancy, but of her own passion, which was strong to the point of being overpowering. Daft though it was in retrospect, she had been scared at the time that she might be driven insane by arousal.

That was what had made her try a joke. She had been lying on the bed with the professor's head moving up between her legs. Wendi had asked, "What would Freud say about this?"

As she had opened her thighs she'd heard Professor Lake's muffled "Fuck Freud" before she closed her legs and Nancy's head had disappeared from view in the scissored clasp of Wendi's hot thighs. Held against the steaming recesses of Wendi's fuming genitals, the professor had demonstrated her expertise. She had been a one-woman band, with her tongue a moving, thrusting, jerking baton, and her mouth, nose, lips, chin, the instruments playing a wonderful tune that had the whole of Wendi's body singing to the tune that Nancy had been playing. The music went on, the baton that was Nancy's tongue going deeply in Wendi's vagina, occasionally hitting the high notes by moving to enter her anus. Then Nancy's mouth alone took over for the grand finale. She sucked on the juice-oozing lips, her hotly wet tongue strumming on Wendi's erect and receptive seat of passion, her clit.

A swooning, moaning Wendi had started to build to orgasm, shivers of sensation running through her, when Nancy's mobile telephone lying on the chest of drawers began to buzz urgently. Pausing, her head still held between Wendi's sweating thighs, Nancy had been torn between business and pleasure – total enjoyment and the call of duty. Her professionalism ensured that duty won. There was an emergency at the hospital and she was needed at once.

Left alone and unsatisfied, Wendi had stayed lying on the bed.

Strangely, she had found the anticlimax more debilitating than probably the crescendo of the abandoned orgasm would have been.

But it was about to happen for her now. The movement of Wendi's finger quickened as a clear image of Nancy Lake appeared in her head. It was when the professor had stood up to answer the phone. Her thick black pubic hair had been dank and long. The memory of seeing it got to Wendi. Head back, eyes closed, top teeth bared, breath sobbing, she furiously masturbated. Crouching a little, legs spread wide, knees bent, she was applying the fast, demanding vinegar strokes – when the doorbell rang.

Sliding rapidly down from the dizzying heights of sexual arousal, Wendi sighed. Wiping her spunk-soaked hand on the bedcovers. Telephones and frigging doorbells! She pulled on her panties and went to answer the door. Her hand was shaking as she reached for the door handle. Meeting an intellectual like Cheryl Valenta was a daunting prospect. Taking a deep breath to steady her nerves, Wendi opened the door.

A smiling girl in a green kind of uniform asked, "Miss Wendi Maylor?"

"Yes," Wendi replied, and a huge bouquet of flowers was passed to her.

Calling "Thank you" to the girl, who was returning to a florist's van that was parked by the kerb, Wendi read the card attached to the flowers: "I have been unavoidably delayed. Please accept the flowers as an apology. Cheryl Valenta."

Six

It was night once again, with London coming into its nether with the hint of menace darkness always brought to the city. Gone was the daylight that had stripped away the facade of illusion and revealed the grime and the ugliness of the streets. Sitting in the front passenger seat of the car, Paula Monroe looked out wide-eyed at dirt that had been magically changed by artificial light into a pleasant blending of colours. Cheryl drove, saying nothing. She knew that for the girl the unreal had become real, just as it did for tourists and all newcomers to London. In Cheryl's opinion the vast collection of asphalt, concrete, stone and glass that was London should be nocturnal like Dracula. The city had been designed to live only at night. It would be better for everyone if the monstrous metropolis clambered back into a vast coffin before the first streaks of dawn were painted across the sky.

Having parked the car at the kerbside of the semilit road in Shepherd's Bush, she switched off the engine. The new silence was somehow painful. Cheryl could sense arrival draining the elation of the journey out of Paula. Cheryl questioned what she was letting herself in for. If she had to be so bloody charitable she'd be safer abroad somewhere rescuing people from earthquake-shattered buildings, or feeding a starving child with spoonfuls of sloppy rice. This had to be a guilt trip over having let this girl down. It had been a shock to discover how close Paula had come to falling into the clutches of the vile Jay Clifford. It was a familiar pattern. If not helped, Paula would be forced to give up trying to peddle her talent and settle for selling her body. With both hands resting on the steering wheel, top teeth digging marks into her lower lip, Cheryl sat thinking of all the things she should have thought of earlier.

"Are you sure about this?" she eventually asked Paula.

Looking pensively out the car window at the strange street, Paula replied weakly in a small voice, "I think so. I'll miss Nikki, being here all on my own, but I want to make something of myself. This will work, won't it, Cheryl?"

"I do hope so," Cheryl replied, wondering if she was doing the right thing. The final solution, so to speak, the ideal, would be to persuade the girl to go home. She decided to add a warning. "I can't guarantee anything, Paula. You'll have a comfortable room at Gina's, and I'll pay the rent for you until you find your feet."

"Why will you do that for me?" Paula frowned.

Shrugging, Cheryl replied, "I'm not sure. I suppose that I've always had a soft spot for the underdog. Anyway, you're a nice girl who deserves a break."

"Once I'm fixed up with Alan Marriott I'll be able to pay my own rent and repay you. That'll be soon, Cheryl."

Jeez! The kid was so credulous! If she didn't toughen up she'd be spending more time in Heartbreak Hotel than Elvis ever did. To paraphrase Oscar Wilde, Paula Monroe was so busy looking up at the stars that she'd forgotten that she was lying in the gutter. The fact that Alan was a top theatrical agent was probably a minus rather than a plus for the kid. An ambitious man, a big wheel in the business, although way behind Matthew Wyndham, Alan was ruthless.

"Look, Paula," Cheryl cautioned. "I haven't worked any miracles for you. Gina's a friend, so I know that she'll take care of you. Marriott's grateful for past favours, so he's agreed to see you. That's all it is with Alan, an introduction. Knowing someone is helpful, but it's not an open-sesame to stardom. If Alan Marriott doesn't think that you have the necessary talent, then he'll tell you bluntly."

"Don't worry." Paula smiled confidently. "I know that I have what it takes."

With her attempts at giving a warning thwarted, Cheryl got them out of the car. It was raining. Cheryl couldn't understand why people complained about the rain, especially in a city. Rain was good to walk in, easier to think in. Rain gave you a strange anonymity in the city. You felt alone even though you weren't alone. In the dry hot days of summer she was nostalgic for rain. It obscured visibility and put a soothing quiet on everything. You couldn't hear the sound of your own feet, and passing traffic became a muted swish instead of a roar.

They walked slowly together. Though she was already half an hour late for her appointment with Wendi Maylor, Cheryl didn't hurry. Paula had fallen nervously quiet, and Cheryl guessed that the kid's recent bad experiences had caught up with her. She seemed more reluctant than ever to reach their destination. It was as if the night were the only thing she had left, and even that wasn't doing much for her.

She didn't brighten up until they were in the hall of Gina Bey El Araby's house. Either a widow or a divorcee – Cheryl had never discovered which – Gina had auburn hair that didn't come from a hairdresser, high cheekbones, a Slavic cast to her dark-brown eyes, and a wide, expressive mouth. Once a highly regarded playwright, Gina in recent years had lowered her standards and swelled her bank balance by penning infantile scripts for television.

She was not a close friend of Cheryl's, more of a cross between a friend and an acquaintance. Every woman was a different woman when she woke up each morning. Saturday's whore might be Sunday's churchgoer; and Monday's blockhead Tuesday's mastermind. It was impossible to really know Gina because she changed more often than most people.

When Cheryl had made the introductions, Gina took two stiff-kneed steps towards a startled Paula. Grabbing both the girl's wrists in turn, Gina pushed each sleeve up to the elbow. Cheryl saw the fingers biting into the forearms and noticed the quiet pain in Paula's eyes. Satisfied that there were no track marks, Gina released the girl, sucking air deep into her lungs in a reverse sigh as she apologised. "Sorry. I don't have many rules here, but 'no drugs' is one of them." Rubbing her arms, Paula looked blankly at the woman.

Gina gave them coffee in her lounge. Cheryl let three sugar lumps drop into her coffee with soft plops. The sound was somehow far away in distance and time, reminding Cheryl of something that she couldn't recall. Whatever it was it brought on a feeling of depression.

"So, Paula" – Gina raised her eyes to study the girl – "you're a protégée of Alan Marriott, are you?"

Cheryl answered quickly for Paula. "Not exactly. He's agreed to see her tomorrow, so there's nothing definite right now."

As she nodded sagely, Gina's eyes danced a little solo as she looked at Cheryl. "I see, so that makes her your protégée, Cheryl."

"Not at all," Cheryl protested, slightly irritated by Gina's innuendo. "She's new in London and I'm just helping her out."

Finishing her coffee, Gina placed the cup in the saucer and began gyrating it in slow circles with a forefinger. "'Children in Need'. Even with a patch over one eye you wouldn't look much like Pudsey Bear, Cheryl."

"You would seem to be implying something, Gina."

Gina made a move and gave what could have been an apologetic shrug. "Please don't be offended, Cheryl." Her eyes went inward as she thought for a few seconds. "You've always been kind when you write of my work, and I don't want that to change because I've upset you."

"I'm not one for revenge, especially in my column." Cheryl watched Gina lower her head. "If there's something on your mind, spell it out and we can deal with it."

The cup turned under Gina's finger for over a minute before she looked up again and nodded. "All right, Cheryl. No disrespect, but as you well know, I'm straight. In my line of work I am beset by gays. I judge them not, neither do I discriminate against them, but when I come home from the theatre or television studio I leave them behind, switch off from them completely. I've always made a distinction between work and home, and that's the way I intend it to stay."

"I'm not going to change that for you," Cheryl assured her, guessing that Gina, with her customary cynicism, feared that her house was to be turned into a love nest for dykes. "All we're looking for is a place for Paula to stay."

"Then that's fine," Gina said, turning to Paula. "I'm sure that you'll like your room."

That was an understatement. Paula was so delighted when she saw the room that was to be hers that she hugged Cheryl in gratitude. Minutes later, when Cheryl was ready to leave, Paula's arms reached out to encircle her. Her hands held Cheryl's head, fingers tight in her hair. Cheryl could feel every inch of Paula's body pressing against hers. Paula's eyes grew soft and her tongue wet her lips. Slowly, with an insistent hunger, her mouth turned up to Cheryl's, she asked huskily, "Do you want to kiss me?"

Cheryl wanted to, desperately. She wanted to taste Paula again, to know her, to feel surging desire go through the girl and through herself, too. Though the door of the room was closed, the thought of Gina downstairs had a cutting edge that sliced away Cheryl's passion. Her insides felt hollow all of a sudden.

Raising her right hand, fore and middle fingers together, Cheryl kissed them lightly then touched the fingers against Paula's lips. At the door she looked back over her shoulder. The dull disappointment in Paula's eyes was easy to see even in the dim light on the landing.

Matthew Wyndham had to squint sideways at his wristwatch when he entered his study. It was either half past ten or ten minutes to six. He applied a fuzzy-headed logic to come up with the answer. It wasn't yet dark outside, so it had to be ten minutes to six. That was good enough. Time wasn't important when you had money and power. Richard Neehan was talking to Archie Peters, Wyndham's accountant, and this evening would be coming to him to report. Finding Wyndham slightly drunk wouldn't please the solicitor. That was too bad. Neehan hadn't been coshed by a neurotic wife, he hadn't been told that he had started to die on the inside, and his business was not under tremendous pressure.

Wyndham had spent the last hour on the telephone probing what was happening on the stock market. It had to have been more than an hour, because, while he was listening to the bad news and the not-quite-so-bad news, he had emptied a bottle of Barcardi, and even *he* couldn't do that in one hour or less.

It hadn't made him drunk. He was teetering a little from tiredness and disorientation from all that had happened to him recently. He realised that both Neehan and Karen thought that he was overreacting. It wasn't as if he were under any kind of financial threat. In fact, his success was the cause of his problem. In this modern world of business there was no place for an individual entrepreneur. The greedy big syndicates had become jealous and wanted to take him over. If he agreed he would overnight become fabulously wealthy. But in doing so he would surrender all control over his self-created empire, and being in charge meant everything to Matthew Wyndham.

These Johnny-come-latelys who were moving in on him had no idea what he had once been. As a film producer he had been a legend in the cinema-oriented world of the 1950s and early 1960s. Even today in his inspired moments he could humble the young men of television. They had overdosed on education, ruining their minds, whereas his imagination and naturalness had been untouched by the system.

Yet he strongly suspected that he was now regarded as a silly old cunt with a desirable young wife. They couldn't know that it was his dynamism that had drawn Karen to him, and held her there.

They had first met at the pretentiously named Tivoli Gardens on the southern perimeter of Birmingham. Wyndham had been a regular customer there when on business in the area. On that occasion a whingeing Richard Neehan had accompanied him. That evening, Neehan had been moaning about his ex-wife, who looked ready to clean him out. Only half listening, Wyndham had looked around a bar that had only one other customer, some kind of manic depressive who was sitting hunched over the far end of the bar with his back to them. Peter, the landlord, had been polishing glasses behind the bar in anticipation of a rush of business that never came. His wife, Rita, had been concentrating on the numbers on the jukebox as if she were about to press the button that would commence World War Three.

Neehan was saying, "I was just getting things straight, but..." when he had stopped talking to stare past Wyndham to the entrance of the bar. Turning round to see what had caught his attention, Wyndham had promptly forgotten Neehan and his marital difficulties. Coming in through the doorway was the luscious Karen Cayson. Wyndham had instinctively placed her as an actress before recognising her. She was physically big in all the places Wyndham liked his women to be big. Her most striking feature then as now was her hair. It was a brilliant red and cascaded to her shoulders like a waterfall at sunset.

After walking direct to a corner table, she had sat down and ordered a Pernod and black. Wyndham had asked Rita to bring him and Neehan more drinks, and to put what the redhead had ordered on his account.

Karen had turned towards him. "I don't normally accept drinks from strangers."

"If I'm a stranger to you, then you haven't been in the business long. I'm Matthew Wyndham," he had told her as he moved to join her at the table. He had then called to Neehan, telling him to put something romantic on the jukebox.

She had stared at him for a full minute, coolly making an inventory. Seemingly satisfied, she had spoken and he had noticed her voice for the first time. Low and sexy. Really sexy. It had sent a tingling from the nape of his neck down his spine to set up a vibration in his balls. She had smiled. "You don't waste much time, do you?"

"I don't have a lot of time to waste."

Neehan, tuned into Wyndham's understanding of women and romance, had chosen Al Martino singing "Spanish Eyes".

"How about it?" Wyndham had asked.

"How about what?"

"You and me. Nothing heavy."

She had changed the subject by saying, "I like your friend's choice in music."

"He's my solicitor, not my friend, and he has a problem. So have I," Wyndham had told her.

"I thought rich men didn't have any problems," she had said with a frown. "What's yours?"

"It's probably biological, perhaps my hormones. I want to take you somewhere and fuck you."

Karen had neither winced nor flinched. "Do you normally behave like this, Mr Wyndham?"

"It's the new direct approach," he had informed her, "designed to help men who haven't a lot of time *not* to waste the time that they do have."

"Perhaps I'd better leave."

"Not without me. I was going to suggest that..."

He could have killed Neehan right then, when the gloomy solicitor had come over to say, "We'd better be going, Matthew."

"Don't let me keep you," Karen had offered laconically.

Doing some quick thinking, Wyndham had come up with an answer. "Tell you what, Richard. We'll sort everything out in the morning. You take the rest of the night off. Enjoy yourself."

Enjoyment had probably been out of the question, but Neehan had looked a little happier when leaving for the hotel and what Wyndham knew would be a night made sleepless by worry. Peter had still been polishing glasses behind the bar. For a guy who wasn't doing much business he certainly had a lot of dirty glasses. Al Martino having ended his song, a glum-faced Rita had gone back to studying the music menu once more. Karen was still sitting beside him, but so detached that he might as well not have been there.

"Now, where were we?" he had asked her.

"You were just getting ready to proposition me."

"Oh, was I? I thought that I was about to suggest that we go to my hotel room and partake of some vintage champagne I happen to have."

"I'm not sure." A dubious Karen had pursed her kissable lips.

"I promise to be a perfect gentleman."

Smiling archly at him she had asked, "What fun would that be?"

"I'm renowned as a man who can't keep promises." He had grinned, standing up from the table.

Karen had got to her feet, too, ready to leave. "I'm known as an actress determined to get to the top," she countered.

"Then we both have a vested interest in the next few hours," Wyndham had smiled.

That had been the easy way it had begun. It had continued in the same way ever since. But Doc Williams had strongly advised him against marrying her. "Your age is against you, Matthew."

"That's balls, Doc," he had rejoined. "I've been shagging nonstop since before Christopher Robin went down on Alice, and I'm still as fit as the proverbial fucking jackrabbit. Putting a ring on the girl's finger won't make ha'p'orth of difference."

"I wasn't thinking of the physical but the psychological consequences," Williams pointed out in the superior way of physicians, solicitors, politicians and the like. "There'll always be young men sniffing round her, Matthew, and jealousy can become debilitating. You'd serve yourself better by offloading her and staying off the drink. You are an alcoholic, Matthew."

"Well, you're the doctor, Doc. Cure me."

"I can't do that. You must want to stop drinking."

"I don't want to, I like it."

With a shake of his head, Williams had said, "In that case, you've got to eat, like I told you. Hard-boiled eggs, pasta, creamed spinach."

"I'll give it a try." He had given a false promise as he walked to the surgery door.

"Matthew."

He stopped and turned only his head to the doctor. "Yes, Doc?"

"You either follow the diet I gave you, or you stop drinking. If not, the next thing requiring my signature will be your death certificate."

"That bad?"

"Worse."

That had now proved to be true. Doc Williams was either a gifted physician, a clairvoyant, or a lucky guesser. The first was probably the same as the last, for the medical profession worked on one per cent science and ninety-nine per cent guesswork. You never heard a doctor say he didn't know what was wrong with you. The egotistical bastards probably had it wrong about him now, and he would live to be one hundred and ten.

He was snapped back to the present by the appearance of an ultra-respectful Henry announcing that "Mr Neehan" had arrived.

"Well, Richard," Wyndham said, greeting his solicitor, "what am I up against?"

"I couldn't say, to be precise."

"I pay you to be fucking precise," Wyndham said angrily. "What am I facing, and who's the main man?"

"There's big money involved. You're not going to like this, Matthew," Neehan said, placing a comforting hand on Wyndham's shoulder.

The hand fell away at Wyndham's cold glance. He had to make an effort not to examine the shoulder that had been touched. He shrugged off the nasty notion that something horrible had permeated the material of his jacket to stain and infect the skin of his shoulder. Wyndham hated, but forced himself to tolerate, parasites like lawyers, accountants, and financial advisers

"You can advise me on the law, Richard, but I'll make up my own mind what I like and don't like."

"At the head of it all is Alan Marriott," Neehan announced sombrely.

His voice was a thin sound that touched Wyndham's spine with a cold finger. As the comforting effect of alcohol began to ebb, so did the kind of uneasy truce between himself and his worst fears end.

"That cross between a jackal and fuck all," Wyndham snarled.

Wendi greeted Cheryl in the entrance hall of her tenth-storey flat. She was the picture of lithe, sinuous beauty. Her blonde hair was shiningly drawn back in a bustle of baby-fine curls; her perfectly clear skin glowed and her greenish eyes were full of the sparkling love of life. Casually dressed in a short, blue-denim skirt and a white blouse tied round her waist, just under the moderate curve of her breasts, she betrayed an attitude that was slightly nervous.

"Good evening, Miss Valenta," she said respectfully.

"Good evening," Cheryl answered formally, adding, "Call me Cheryl, and please accept my apologies for being late. It was unavoidable, I assure you."

"Of course. Thank you for the lovely flowers." She turned to look at the flowers she had arranged in a tall vase. The arrangement was a fabulous explosion of brilliant colours. "Won't you come in?"

They moved into a lounge that was small enough to be cosy in spite of the blandness of modern furniture. Gesturing for Cheryl to be seated on a settee, Wendi asked, "White wine?"

"Thank you."

"I can get you something else if you wish."

"No, white wine will be lovely," Cheryl assured her ill-at-ease hostess. "I feel that I am intruding."

"On the contrary, it's lovely to meet you," Wendi said, then with a touch of heroine worship she added, "I read every word that you write, but I would never have believed for one moment that I'd ever be talking to you in my own apartment."

She laughed at herself, and Cheryl noticed how pretty she was. She had a delicate kind of loveliness that was serious in repose, registering intelligence. Between the attractive smile and the thoughtful expression was a great deal of character. Cheryl took an instant liking to her.

Modesty made Cheryl scoff. "Nonsense. The fact that I have for some time been intending to interview you is proof that you are much more of a celebrity than I'll ever be. But I'm not wearing my journalist hat tonight. You've probably guessed why I'm here, Wendi."

Enjoying the blonde's company, she dreaded the moment when she would have to shatter their relationship by threatening Wendi with her past. The old adage claimed that you had to be cruel to be kind. Cheryl was sure that bringing up the sordid period of Wendi's past would be kind to no one, not even Karen Cayson. She prayed that blackmail, for that was what it was, would not be needed.

"I guess that it's about the Karen-and-Matthew thing, but I'm uncertain where you fit into this, Cheryl."

"As a friend of the Wyndhams, I suppose." Cheryl gave a little shrug. "Plus the fact that I advise them on public relations from time to time. I think it best if I cut to the chase, Wendi. Matthew and Karen, particularly Karen, are afraid that you will—"

"Tell the world that she's gay," Wendi sighed. "That wouldn't be sensational in these enlightened times, especially in our business."

"It could well have dire results for Karen."

"I fully realise that, Cheryl."

"Of course you do," Cheryl accepted, "but I also know the sort of figures the tabloids offer for the kind of story you have. I take it that you have been approached?"

Wendi gave an ashamed nod. "In a silly moment I agreed to cooperate with one guy from a daily. I didn't do so for personal gain, but I'm involved with a children's home in Manchester that is desperately in need of money."

"I can understand your dilemma," Cheryl acknowledged.

"That would easier to solve if a true set of values existed," Wendi concurred.

Cheryl was very aware that she was likely to have to let Karen and Matthew down within the next few minutes. There was no way that she would be able to bring herself to threaten the good-hearted Wendi Maylor.

"But loyalty comes into it, too, and I can't bring myself to betray Karen. So, I've decided to cancel my interview with the newspaperman."

Wincing from a stab of guilt, Cheryl said, "I hope that my calling on you hasn't influenced your decision in any way."

"Not at all, Cheryl. I reached my decision before you got here."

"That's definite?" Cheryl had to be sure before reporting back to Karen.

"Absolutely," Wendi confirmed. "I telephoned the newspaper office about twenty minutes ago. You can tell Karen that she has nothing to fear from me."

"That's most kind of you, particularly in view of the good cause for which you need money," Cheryl said. "I'll leave you in peace now. I'm sorry for taking up your time."

"I've enjoyed having you here, Cheryl."

Cheryl glanced at Wendi and saw that her expression had far more meaning than her voice or her words. Encouraged by this, she laid plans for a future meeting between them.

"I didn't know about this charitable venture of yours," she mused, then adjusted the recent events linking Karen and Wendi in her head, then went on. "I wonder if..."

"Yes?" Wendi asked eagerly.

"Well, Wendi, I think it would make an excellent angle for a story on you. I have several projects that need finishing at the moment, but can we get together to discuss it some time soon? Perhaps I could treat you to dinner."

"You needn't go to that trouble," Wendi said, blushing a little.

"I can claim it on expenses, Wendi."

"You could come here." An embarrassed Wendi almost blurted out her words. "Cooking is one of my hobbies." She gave a smile that had an unexpected mischief. "I'll either kill you or impress you. I can't promise which."

Wendi's shyness, so unexpected in an entertainer, had an erotic effect on Cheryl. In her mind she said, Why don't you just fuck me and make us both happy? – but aloud she said, "I'm willing to take a chance."

"I'll be away for the next few days," Wendi said solemnly. "My mother's ill so I have to go home to Bristol."

"I'm sorry to hear that, Wendi. I hope that it's nothing serious."

"I don't think so. I should be back by the beginning of next week. Will you call me then?" Wendi asked almost pleadingly.

"You can rely on it," Cheryl promised.

"Miss Monroe?"

"Yes."

Paula put down the film magazine she had been leafing through, stood and walked over to the receptionist. An obese woman in her fifties, she wore a size of dress that matched her age but it was still under strain in places.

"Mr Marriott will see you now," the woman said, flashing her a plump-faced smile. "His office is on the left at the end of the corridor.

Thanking her, Paula pushed open the chromium-framed opaque-glass door that led away from the sleekly modern reception area. She had been a little overpowered by her surroundings since first arriving. Now her legs felt shaky as she walked along the carpeted corridor and knocked lightly on a stained wooden door.

She hesitated for a moment when a male voice brusquely commanded her to enter.

The office combined the modern look of the reception with a more refined appearance of opulence. The walls were a clean pale blue and decorated with narrow-framed photographs of the stars of today and yesteryear. Paula would love to have studied them, but she was so nervous that she barely recognised anyone in the photographs. The desk was huge and uncluttered, on display rather than in use. In front of the desk, with his hands, behind grasping it to support himself in a half-sitting position, was Alan Marriott.

In spite of all the frightening stories she had heard about him, Marriott was not plug ugly. He was palpably attractive, beautifully attired in a suit of dark material, and though his welcoming smile was restrained it was far from daunting. He had a presence that Paula found to be unsettling. She was aware of a high-voltage personality, a macho male charm that exuded from him like sweat from a heavyweight boxer in training. Dark-skinned, he had a heavy-set body. From the photographs she had seen of mobsters in America's prohibition days, Marriott could be a reincarnation of Al Capone. Paula felt intimidated.

She chided herself for being silly. The fact that a respected, influential impresario looked like a gangster didn't mean that he wasn't a respected and influential impresario. Paula reminded herself why she was there, and how lucky she was to be there. A chance meeting with Cheryl Valenta had been the turning point for her. If everything went right here, then she could well be on the first step of the stairway to stardom.

"You like the place?" Marriott's voice had a whispering hoarseness that suggested his throat had been injured at some time.

It was as if he were an estate agent and she a prospective buyer. The unexpected question puzzled her, throwing her carefully rehearsed interviewee plans into turmoil. It was a mistake to spend all night rehearsing what you were going to say. You were left floundering around when nothing went according to your invisible script. All she could do was nod energetically and say, "It's very nice."

Maintaining his tight smile, Marriott looked her up and down. She straightened herself, unconsciously, under his scrutiny, blushing as the movement caused her breasts to thrust themselves against the confining cloth of her white dress.

"I'm not sure myself." He shook his head in doubt. "Had the whole place decorated a couple of months back, from the front door to the back gate, so to speak. It cost me a fortune, yet I'm still not sure."

Paula knew that he was waiting for her to comment. Though she enjoyed his friendly approach, she wasn't going to toady. Holding his gaze, she said, "I don't know enough about interior decor to make an observation. To say I don't like it would offend you; to praise the place would have me appear a sycophant. So I'll stay neutral, Mr Marriott."

The stocky agent laughed, suddenly. "I like it! I like it! I've a gut feeling that you're going to suit just fine," he chuckled. "I have arse kissers coming in here all the time, and you sure are a refreshing change, Miss Monroe."

Paula felt her face flush as Marriott pushed himself up from the desk and went behind it to lower himself into a swivel chair. Swinging the chair a little from side to side, he motioned for her to take a seat. Conscious of his downward glance, she smoothed the hem of her dress over her slim legs.

Abruptly breaking off his gaze, he picked up the application form that Paula had earlier completed. He studied it for a few moments. "You can dance and sing – that reminds me of the Fred Astaire story – but your principal interest is in acting."

"That's right," Paula heard a voice say and recognised it as her own. She was pleased by the confident ring it had.

"You've got the looks, and I don't doubt that you have talent, Miss Monroe," Marriott complimented her, "but you'd have to admit that you lack experience."

"I agree, Mr Marriott. But there is only one way of gaining experience. Even Sarah Bernhardt had to start at the beginning."

This was going easier than Paula had imagined. Having expected to stutter and stammer and make a fool of herself, she was handling things well. She was being rapidly filled with a self-confidence she had never before known. A lot of that was down to Alan Marriott. He may have the looks of a sophisticated thug, but he was surprisingly easy to get along with.

"Meaning that someone such as me should take a chance by giving you a break." Marriott nodded, as if answering a question he had silently asked himself. "That makes sense. Should I make an investment in you?"

Paula blinked, caught off her guard by the question. "Only you can decide that, Mr Marriott."

He reread her application form for a few minutes, then looked at her. "It is my decision, that's correct, but I need your input, Miss Monroe. Unfortunately for me, and possibly fortunately for you, I made the mistake of placing a young actress solely on the recommendation of a friend. That was one foolish lapse in a lifetime of professionalism, Miss Monroe. Now I'm stuck with her – unless... Let's say for the sake of discussion, and I stress that this is hypothetical, that I was to cast you in a television series that work begins on in two days' time."

"A speaking part?" Paula held her breath, not daring to hope that she would have a line or two to say.

Closing her eyes for a moment she ecstatically imagined her family and friends in Basingstoke watching her on television. Not at any time in the daydreams would she have risked going to such an extreme. She couldn't believe that the magic was still working as Marriott continued to speak.

"A little more than that, Miss Monroe. You would be second only to the principal actress, Karen Cayson."

Hearing the name of her heroine, her role model, her goddess, rendered Paula both speechless and breathless. She was aware that Marriott was studying her, shrewdly and keenly, but she could only do a goldfish impersonation with her mouth. No sound came out.

"I seem to have caused you some difficulty," Marriott said after allowing her time to reply. "Would you prefer a less demanding part at this stage?"

"No, no." Paula found her voice. "It's just that I never for one moment expected to work with Karen Cayson."

"You have no need to be overawed by Miss Cayson. I'm told that she is by no means a temperamental artiste, a prima donna. By all accounts she is extremely easy to work with."

"It's not that," Paula swiftly explained, wondering why he was watching her so intently. "I suppose it's just that I've always been a huge fan of Karen Cayson."

"Then this will mean a great deal to you." Alan Marriott smiled encouragingly. "Now, I will put you in that show if you're confident that you can handle it. It will mean that I let go the girl who has already been prepared for the part, so if you let me down I'll personally see to it that you won't ever work again in the business, not even as the asshole-end of a pantomime horse."

"I can do it, Mr Marriott."

"Fine. Now, you will want to discuss terms. I should caution at this stage that very little is open to negotiation. However, you will appreciate that most newcomers fall by the wayside, as it were, and the few who don't rarely get the opportunity that I am giving you today."

"I'm well aware of that, Mr Marriott, and I can't tell you how much I appreciate what you are doing for me."

"For you and me both, Miss Monroe: you will be earning money for me as well as you, " he corrected her. "Now, you will want to hear what kind of money we are talking about."

With a swinging shake of her head, Paula told him, "Whatever it is I'll be content, Mr Marriott."

"I wish everyone who comes into my office was as easy to deal with as you are." Alan Marriott smiled. "If that's how you want it, then if you'd like to go back to reception, Miss Monroe, I'll have contract drawn up. I won't keep you waiting for long, I promise."

"Thank you, Mr Marriott." Paula started to leave.

"My pleasure. Good luck. I'm sure that you will make it."

Seven

The television studio was in Holborn, a modern slab of polished concrete and blue-toned glass. It was presided over by a uniformed doorman with a pugilist's face and calculating eyes that could see through any pretence that hid a demented fan. He saluted Karen as if he were a corporal and she a colonel. In return she let a smile tug lightly at the corners of her mouth. He opened a door that was a hinged slab of glass set in a clear-glass wall, and saluted again.

A humid morning had followed a night of rain, and it was hot inside the piace. Two girls sat at a glass-topped reception desk. They glanced up from their paperwork ready to smile, but didn't. The foyer had a fake-marble floor. The lower four feet of each of the walls was sheathed in shimmering imitation maple. An old man sat at a high desk in a far corner. He wore archaic sleeve garters and an outdated green eyeshade that gave him the look of a card dealer in an old gangster movie. Karen didn't know what his job was, and had never been interested enough to enquire.

The doors of the studio swished open on her approach. She was momentarily sickened by the perfumed smell of makeup that was layered on the heavy air. Having seen what she believed to be Jay Clifford's car parked outside, she was worried. That low-life could have no business here other than to make trouble. As she moved forward the glare of bright lights added more heat. Two overhead fans turned the air round in an attempt at fooling her into thinking that she was cooler. Cameras were being raised and lowered as they were wheeled across the floor. Scattered about were cheap-café plastic chairs with jackets and sweaters draped over them. Actors and technicians stood around waiting. They had the kind of tension and uncertainty noticeable in athletes as they wait to be called on to the track.

Karen was the only celebrity. There were five or six oldies recognisable only because of programme repeats on television. They were outnumbered by the hangers-on, the twilight people who lived on the fringes of show business.

This was the first day of taping *Beach of Fear*. The four-parter for television was a true-life tragedy of a glamorous British holidaymaker who had been murdered in Barbados. Though contemporary, it was hoped that the series would rise far above costume dramas in the ratings. Karen was to take the lead as Laura Cass, while Lei Linden, a nice-looking but limited young actress, was to play her teenage daughter, Helene Cass.

Karen spotted John Brighton, who was standing pounding a clipboard against the back of a chair to emphasise whatever he was saying to a young blonde girl. She was wearing the briefest black bikini that Karen had ever seen. The black of the bikini made only the barest of slashes against milk-white skin. She was shapely and luscious and more desirable than a teenager had a right to be.

As usual, the hairy-legged Brighton was wearing shorts. Ever conscious of his diminutive stature, he ludicrously kept his body stretching upwards. It gave the impression that he was constantly looking for something on a high shelf.

When he saw Karen coming his way across the floor he first shouted instructions across to a camera crew, then called for a ten-minute break. The whole assembly came to life, collected sweaters from backs of chairs, throwing them over shoulders and loosely tying the sleeves. Excitement on their dull faces, they all talked and nobody listened as they headed for a serving hatch in a wall that was distanced from the set.

Eyes averted, the girl in the bikini passed Karen. A phoney-blonde, she had an inverted V of fine dark hair running up to her navel. She had a nice wiggle-fanny walk and her figure was every bit as good as Karen's had been at that age. Perhaps it was better than hers once was. Karen never injured her self-esteem by making that sort of comparison.

Smiling didn't come easily to John Brighton, but he was doing his best as Karen approached. He lit a cigar and had a comfortable halo of smoke above his head when she asked, "What's with the fair-haired girl, John?"

"Paula Monroe," he announced, shaking his head in wonderment. "Just imagine a kid choosing a name like that." He nasally and breathlessly sang one line of a song. "Happy birthday, Mr President!" He grinned at Karen. "Kennedy's ghost is probably hanging around in here somewhere with a king-size hard-on." He laughed with the cigar clenched between his teeth and made a show of cupping his crotch. "She's a looker, though. I like the way her bikini line goes all the way up to her tits. A real turn-on."

"You're dated, John. Shaved cunts are in." Karen thought for a moment, then threw an unseeing glance towards the wall behind the director. She experienced a sudden and inexplicable feeling of disquiet. "What's the kid doing here?"

"There's been a change in casting, Karen. That little blondie is the new Helene Cass."

Karen was shocked. "What do you mean? What's happened to Lei?"

"Indisposed."

"What the fuck does that mean, John?"

"I'm just repeating what I've been told," he said defensively. Taking the cigar out, he studied it, knocked off the ash. "Seems like bringing in the new girl was Alan Marriott's idea. I don't know why he wants to bugger things up by changing them. Young Lei Linden would have soon fitted into the part."

"I wonder why Marriott made the switch," Karen mused. "He's not shagging that kid. He likes them older than him and fat."

"That Oedipus thing figures. I can believe that bastard murdered his father," Brighton grunted. The cigar went back into his mouth. He dragged on it and let out a thin stream of smoke. "You'd better get changed, Karen. See Martha, she's got everything ready for you. We're starting with the scene by the hotel pool when the mother gives way and lets the daughter go to some kind of rave on the sands."

"The new kid will be playing opposite me, John." Karen had a worried frown. No matter how good you were, how well you'd studied a scene, some prat could easily fuck it all up. The blonde girl might be juicy, but she certainly wouldn't be a Katherine Hepburn.

"How well do you react to advice these days, Karen?"

"Depends on the source. From you, John, no problem. Where are you coming from – the wisdom of Solomon or the sexology of Krafft-Ebing?"

"Neither. More like nous Alfred Hitchcock," Brighton replied. "I know how to shoot a scene, make a film, Karen. Paula's read the script and I've tested her on it, as well as telling her exactly what I want. She's a bright kid. Leave the worrying to me. Just go and get into your gear and we can make a start."

"I'm on my way, John," Karen said, giving the director a backward wave as she walked off. But the strange feeling she had been experiencing increased and swept over her. She somehow connected it with having seen Jay Clifford's car outside. It was as if she were dropping into a swirling vortex of time and sound and colours. A prickling sensation travelled across her shoulders and her stomach muscles tightened painfully. As she turned to look over her shoulder, her stare at Brighton was a lifeless one, hiding things. "Is Jay Clifford here in the studio?"

"He was earlier, setting up his gear to do some stills for

Marriott," Brighton replied. He made a wry face. The most significant part of his answer was in his eyes. "But seems like he's gone now, which suits me fine."

Giving a nod of thanks, Karen walked away, more slowly this time. She reflected as she went. Jay Clifford's presence in the studio was ominous. Of late she had been hearing things about Alan Marriott, and Clifford was one of those he used for his dirty work. She thought back over the months, putting the pieces of incidents in slots so familiar that they were worn smooth at the edges. She had only suspected, but now she knew for sure. Alan Marriott had become her husband's deadly rival. It was more than that: he was Matthew's enemy. Karen realised that both Matthew and Richard Neehan were aware of this. That was why they had so desperately wanted to cover up what had happened at the ill-fated party. Alan Marriott would fully exploit even a whiff of scandal concerning Matthew or her. Karen knew that all she could do right then was to put her faith in the cool, self-sufficient Cheryl Valenta.

The blonde kid was in Karen's dressing room talking to Martha, who greeted Karen with a hug. Embarrassed, the girl went to hurry out. Karen stopped her. "Stay, if you don't mind. We'll need to have a chat before we go on set. I'm Karen Cayson."

"I know," the girl muttered reverently, looking as if she was about to drop into a curtsy.

Martha Abel chuckled. She was a retread, a performer from the 1960s who was now a dresser. An attractiveness still lurked despite – or maybe because of – her middle-aged chubbiness. A summer dress of yellow flowered material accentuated her heavy breasts. The dress was short and added to the attractiveness of her trunky but firmly muscled legs. Martha's hair was up under a turban that made her look as if she'd just stepped out of a harem. As always, the sight of her caused an uncontrollable warmth and wetness between Karen's legs.

Being aware of Karen's carnal interest in her caused Martha to take liberties. Karen didn't like that. Sex was the great emancipator, and emancipation always raised the servant above the mistress.

There was a deliberate equality in Martha's eyes now as she gently stretched the bright-orange one-piece swimming costume Karen would be wearing in the first scene. She asked, "Can I fix you a drink, Karen, or is it too early in the day?"

"I could really use one," Karen answered truthfully.

Passing Karen a glass of a good whisky blend and plenty of ginger ale, Martha looked at Paula and asked, "Do I pour the kid one?"

Still wearing just the black bikini, the blonde was perched stiffly on the arm of a chair. Karen looked and saw a little country girl with starry eyes. A girl who missed the smell of new-cut grass and the coolness of an evening breeze sweeping down from green hills. The little sexpot had given up the security of the unknown to walk the plank of show business. She was now among pirates – producers, directors, assistant directors, and fat-lipped parasitical agents.

Moved by compassion, Karen said, "Of course. Give the girl a drink. And get her a robe, Martha."

The blonde shyly introduced herself. "My name's Paula Monroe."

"Hi, Paula."

Karen spoke lamely as she started to get out of her bright, turquoise, button-through dress. In her skimpy bra and panties, aware of Martha blatantly and the girl covertly watching her, she did a burlesque stage walk towards the dressing table. She revelled in their silent appreciation.

Looking at herself framed in the eight lights that encircled the vanity mirror, Karen concentrated on getting her false eyelashes properly fixed. Then she rested one hand upon the other to steady it, like an artist at the easel, to apply black eyeliner. Satisfied with a good job well done, she sat back.

The lovely image stared back at her. Then the eyes dropped to take in the firm, swelling breasts that required no support from the flimsy bra. They came up again to meet hers with a direct, peculiar, almost alien stare. Beautiful, she mused. Yes, she was perfectly feminine, grossly beautiful, the fantasy lover of men and boys the world over. She was a fleshy piece of bait for suckers who were in love by proxy with a creature they didn't know and never would know.

As she stood and walked to a full-length mirror, Paula was talking to her. "I feel like a lamb to the slaughter. Mr Marriott said I'd be fine." She let out a little-girl giggle. "But now I'm struggling not to run away."

"First-night nerves, Paula, so to speak. You'll be fine," Karen said consolingly.

Karen stood. Reaching behind to unclip her bra, she let it fall for Martha to pick up. In a western gunfighter pose with a hand at each hip, she used her thumbs to hook into the elastic of her panties and push them down. Naked, she kicked the flimsy knickers from her feet, enjoying the feel of Paula's hot eyes on her. The first sighting of Karen's mass of pubic hair was always a shock, and Paula Monroe was no exception. Though she knew she was staring, and that caused her face to flush a dark red, the girl couldn't pull her eyes away.

Posing in front of the full-length mirror, Karen was pleased. Her lovely body was as fit as ever. The big, pushy breasts were crowned by two prominent and dark Walnut Whips of nipples; the wildly triangular dark snatch of hair hid the slippery entrance that men dreamed about and yearned for. Seeing herself look so good was a boost after all the problems of late. "Whatever they say," she whispered to the mirror, "I still like me."

The image looked back without showing any response. Then, slowly, it smiled.

As Karen turned, Martha was holding up a black satin robe that she slipped easily into. Paula was wearing one of her dressing gowns, the apricot one. It would have a subtle odour of girly sweat to it the next time Karen went to put it on. She liked that thought.

Tying the sash, Karen looked around for her copy of the shooting script. The organised Martha was holding it out to her.

Taking it, Karen turned the pages, folding them back as she walked over to sit on a stool across the room from the girl. "John tells me you're up to speed on the scene we're going to do, Paula."

"Mr Brighton talked me through it, yes."

Brow creased, Karen read some of the script, then looked up at the girl. "Neither of us has much to say. You're standing off from me, looking sulky because I have forbidden you to go to the rave."

Paula giggled, childishly holding her hand over her mouth.

"What's so funny?" Karen smilingly enquired.

"It's just trying to think of someone like you, someone so beautiful, as my mother," Paula explained, her voice shaken by another little giggle.

"That's not being very complimentary to your mother," Karen said, pretending to rebuke her.

"It's being truthful."

"You naughty girl," Karen chuckled. "You better get me into your head as Mummy, Paula. I'm sitting by the hotel pool, and when I relent you rush over to thank me, hugging me and giving me a kiss on the cheek before you run off to join your young friends."

"Do you think," Paula asked hesitantly, "that we could try it now? It would help me."

"Sure, go ahead."

"Hold it!" Martha held both arms up, palms facing away from her. "I got errands to run. Let me out of here before you start your *Gone with the Wind* stuff."

She went out. Paula stood, glanced at the script, then put it down.

"Oh, Mummy!" she cried out. "Thank you so much. You're a real darling."

Running to Karen, who sat with her legs crossed, she embraced her.

Their cheeks were soft and warm against each other. Paula's

crotch was against Karen's knee. Suddenly there was a pubic thrust and Paula turned her head so that her lips brushed Karen's. It was a fleeting contact but Karen could feel the tiger behind it, the savage need, the urgent desire.

Clasping Paula by the shoulders, moving her a little away, Karen said, "No more, Paula. There's a generation gap separating us."

That was bullshit, Karen scolded herself. Their faces were close together; Paula's sweet breath was mingling with hers. The sexual ice had been melted and was dripping. Cause and effect. A real kiss was now inevitable.

A knuckle rapping on the dressing-room door had Paula jump back from Karen. A male voice called, "John is ready for you, Miss Cayson."

"Thanks," Karen called back.

She ran her fingers down the side of Paula's face and lightly pinched the skin under her chin. "We'll have to put it on hold, Paula."

The telephone woke Jay Clifford. Daylight filtered weakly through the blind, giving no hint of the time of day. The digital figures on his electric alarm clock were no help. They were just a green blur. Blinking his eyes only succeeded in changing the pattern of glowing green. Clifford kept his head still on the pillow, which was the only way to ease a buzzing ache. It had been a heavy night. He hadn't got home until 4.30 that morning, and his eyes felt scraped. What time was it now? He tried the clock once more but the sharp-cornered digits defeated him yet again. An insistent electronic bleeping was still coming from the telephone. Clifford had a strong hunch that it was Ralph Remington, the club owner, ringing to put pressure on him to settle his bill. There wasn't much hope of that happening. An account at a Soho club wasn't exactly like having a slate at *Corrie*'s Rover's Return.

Clifford was wrong. It was Alan Marriott. Not Marriott himself but the tubby Tasmin. Marriott always had her place his calls. He did it to create an impression.

"Mr Clifford?"

"I told you never to ring me at work," Clifford jokingly complained.

"Mr Alan Marriott is calling," she announced reverently.

Tasmin's voice was as frosty as Norway in January. Jay Clifford wasn't one of her favourite people. Marriott came on the phone. There was a long, presidential-style pause for effect. Hail to the fucking chief!

"Hello, Clifford," he rasped.

"How's things, Mr Marriott?"

"Fine, Clifford, fine. You sound about as lively as a fresh-fucked cat. Did you fix everything up at the studio yesterday?"

"You can rely on me, Mr Marriott, everything's in place," Clifford assured him. "With the lens I'm using I've got every inch of Karen's dressing room covered. You'll be able to count the hairs on their pubes."

"That won't be necessary. You make sure that you stay out of sight."

"You forget that I'm a veteran campaigner," Clifford complained. "Any movement in the room will start the camera, and it will cease filming when there's no movement. I'll simply go back early tomorrow morning and check what's been videoed. That's if there's anything worth seeing. The Monroe kid wasn't there."

"She doesn't start until this morning," Marriott said. "You've met this kid, Clifford. Are you sure she'll go for it?"

Clifford was confident. "Guaranteed, Mr Marriott. Her friend, Nikki, does some work for me, and she's had her. Nikki says she's a goer, a bleeding nymphomaniac!" He sounded puzzled as he went on. "Is there such a thing as a nympho-lesbian?"

"How the fuck would I know? You're the arse case."

"Oh, Alan, that's slanderous."

"It's the truth, and I'm Mr Marriott to you, Clifford," Marriott told him nastily. "There's a lot of difference between two adolescent friends experimenting with each other on the bed, and having a sexual animal like Karen Cayson going mad on top of you. You are pretty sure that she'll go for Karen?"

"It's the other way around, Mr Marriott. Karen won't be able to resist a dishy little blonde, and Paula was drooling over Karen at the Wyndham bash. The chemistry's there, the camera's there, so it's in the bag, Mr Marriott. I take it that I can call round for my money this afternoon?"

Marriott made an explosively hissing noise. "You take it wrong, Clifford. You'll get paid when you bring me the video, and even then it will depend on whether it's what I want."

"Of course, but could you see your way clear to—" Clifford began, intending to ask for expenses in advance because he was broke. But Marriott had hung up at the other end of the line.

Matthew Wyndham had brought Cheryl and Karen to lunch at a hotel where the dining room had been preserved as it had been in Corinthian and Victorian times. It did a lively business at lunchtime, its patrons in the main being the as yet unnamed successors of the yuppies. The diners were happily homogenised in the close cut-and-thrust world of money chasers. The low-ceilinged place had atmosphere, plenty of it. But the olde-worlde charm had no effect on Cheryl when she walked in. Nostalgia was an illusion. Days gone by were no better than today. Probably they were worse.

Even so, her fascination with history had her ponder on the fact that what was once Hogarth's home had become a part of the hotel when it had been built a couple of centuries ago. On a now distant wet and windy night, Byron had been barred after urinating in front of guests in the hotel's entrance hall rather than use the uncovered back yard. The walls were dark with old paintings and Cheryl thought, wryly, that the ghosts of artists and pissers past probably haunted the place.

"It's some time since I was here," Matthew Wyndham remarked, looking around him with great interest. "I find the surroundings somehow incredibly soothing. Though recognising that modernism had its place in the order of things, I abhor the way in which this country is sacrificing traditional standards to spin and sophistry."

Silently concurring, Cheryl didn't like Wyndham enough to agree with him aloud. The faces around them were those of the types of people that were all too familiar to her. They spoke urgently and their talk was of big money, big business. Across the table from her, Karen was looking elegant, almost luminous, in a light-blue suit. Cheryl was very conscious of the fine, clean line of Karen's profile, the proud way that she held her head, the full-lipped mouth and the slender deft fingers.

Anxious to the point of distraction over the Wendi Maylor problem, Karen, while her husband ordered lunch, fixed Cheryl with a steady look. Uncertainty was making a little furrow on her forehead. Her cool blue eyes were no longer cool. She was no longer poised and talkative. She had a trick of looking away suddenly. Then she was back with Cheryl, and the little furrow had become a full-fledged frown.

But Cheryl couldn't put Karen out of her misery, knowing that she must wait for a cue from Matthew when it would be time to introduce the subject of Wendi. Although Cheryl sensed that he was every bit as worried as his wife, Wyndham's iron will made it possible for him to contain himself until they were partway through an excellent lunch.

"Money is no option, Cheryl," he said, dabbing at his mouth with a napkin, "so tell me what a whore's silence costs these days."

"You mean Wendi Maylor?" Cheryl, annoyed that Wendi was being referred to in that way, raised one eyebrow questioningly.

"Who else?" an irritated Wyndham replied with a question of his own.

"She won't be bought," Wendi said flatly, relishing Wyndham's agitation, although regretting the distress her evasion was causing Karen.

"So you strong-armed her by bringing up her past, Cheryl?" Wyndham sat with his hands pressed together chest high, prayer-fashion, waiting for an answer.

Shaking her head, Cheryl said, "That wouldn't have worked, either, Matthew."

"Mission impossible," Karen said with a subdued groan.

"So, you failed, Cheryl."

Wyndham didn't say this angrily or accusingly, but totally unemotionally. He exchanged worried glances with his wife, who sat silently twining and entwining her fingers. When they looked back at Cheryl, they were astounded to see that she was smiling.

"Both of you can forget the whole thing," Cheryl told them. "Wendi Maylor won't cause you any trouble."

"You deliberately held out on us, Cheryl." A smiling, immensely relieved Karen playfully levelled a long and lovely finger at her. She alarmed Cheryl for a moment by reaching her hand across the table to her. But she jerked it back quickly before it touched Cheryl's, and it took her a moment to recover her composure. Though Wyndham gave no sign of having noticed his wife's spontaneous gesture, Cheryl felt sure that he had. For a moment all three of them became lost in a vacuum of quieting emotions.

"Can you be sure of this, Cheryl?" he asked, probably because he hadn't expected it to be so easy.

"Wendi gave me her word, Matthew."

"You believe her word to be dependable?"

"I'd stake my life on it," Cheryl answered without needing to consider the question, aware of the quick and interested glance that Karen shot in her direction.

"Then that's good enough for me." A satisfied Wyndham nodded. "It's doubly pleasing, Cheryl, because it was achieved without the likes of Richard Neehan being involved. I expect you've heard the old tale about the two farmers who each claimed ownership of a particular cow. While one of the farmers was busy pulling at the head and the other was busy tugging on the tail, a lawyer milked the cow."

Cheryl burst into genuine laughter at this as Wyndham beckoned the waitress to bring them coffee, then pulled a chequebook from his pocket and placed it on the table, holding it open with a forefinger. Pen poised, he smiled at Cheryl. "You said that you wanted nothing in return for doing us this huge favour, Cheryl. But you could never imagine what this means to Karen and myself. At the risk of offending you, I would like to show our gratitude."

Dismissing the offer with a wave of her hand, Cheryl said, "It is kind of you, Matthew, but there is absolutely no need."

"It would make me feel better about it, Cheryl."

An idea started as a tiny speck in the back of Cheryl's mind. It grew with astonishing speed to excite her. There was a little catch in her voice when she spoke. "In that case, Matthew, I will accept a small gift, if you will agree to leave the payee blank."

"Whatever you say, Cheryl, although I don't profess to understand."

"It's no big mystery," Cheryl laughed briefly. "It's just that there's a charity I would like to donate it to, but I'm not sure of the name."

"Your wish is my command," Wyndham nodded. He mopped his brow. The lines in his face shocked Cheryl, the ones in his forehead being particularly deeper than she remembered. He had aged two decades in less than two weeks. She felt a sudden rush of compassion for him.

Then his pen scratched at the cheque, which he tore from the book and waved in the air to dry the ink before passing it to Cheryl.

Taking it, she intended to show good manners by just glancing at the amount. But her good intentions deserted her at the sight of the colossal figure on the cheque. She was comfortably placed financially herself, but her mind couldn't adjust to how even the opulent Matthew Wyndham could write out a cheque for £25,000 on a whim.

"Honestly, Nikki, Karen is so easy to be with. She treats me like an equal."

Though aware that she was boring her friend, Paula couldn't stop talking fast and excitedly. All the pieces of the puzzle of her young life were in their correct place and she had personally placed each and every one of them there. Even the way she had matured over the past few days was a part of her success story.

She realised that she was being both selfish and unfair. This was the opening-night celebration of the musical in which Nikki had just managed to scrape into the chorus line. By going on about her much more successful achievement, she was spoiling what was her friend's big night.

This was a private celebration, and Nikki, who knew no one and was an insignificant figure among West End stars with household names, had invited Paula.

"I'm sorry to keep going on about myself, Nikki," Paula apologised. She lifted her glass to her lips. It was expensively heavy and cumbersome.

"It's no problem," Nikki said flatly.

The two of them stood in enforced exile among boasting, boisterous men and smiling, seductive, breast-bared women in expensive linens and flowered silks. They were voluptuous sophisticates with challenging eyes and beckoning hands. The room was pervaded with the disturbing muskiness of their combined scents.

It was a grand affair, with exotically flavoured pâté and caviar and varied cocktail dips all adorned with vegetable-flowered and celery-curled decorations. The early talk was of the show and its well-received first night.

"If tomorrow's reviews are as brilliant as tonight's audience, dearies," a well-known male singer, a glass in his hand, was saying to a small, charmed group, "it will be great. I feel this is my night to howl. First I'm going to get as drunk as a hiccuping hyena, then I'm going to get myself laid."

The man had provoked the subject and the talk of sex ricocheted around Paula.

"Don't get your hopes, or anything else, up," a woman advised, tongue-in-cheek. "I was speaking to your wife a little while ago and she mentioned that she had a headache."

The singer's mouth sneered round the rim of his raised glass. "A wife is for watching the television with. I'm going to get me a whore tonight. Prostitutes are the most honest people in the world. The tenderness of a stranger is golden compared with the mealy-mouthed promises of a wife."

"You're an incurable romantic," the same woman remarked cynically.

"Don't give me any of that sentimental crap about love." The singer took a long a swallow of his drink. "Love is being on the bed with a different woman every night, bouncing together belly to belly, pelvis grinding against pelvis. When it's my time to leave this unhappy world, I want to die in the warm arms of a whore while I'm tasting her particular brand of pleasure."

Rolling his eyes upward in pretend ecstasy, he laughed. His little band of listeners did not laugh with him but at him.

"Women and sex bore me to tears," an elderly man with a purple face announced in a loud voice. "An evening at the Rotary and tinkering with my old car does for me."

A handsome young man, better known for television commercials than he was for acting, indicated the female star of the musical with a jerk of his head. "*Cammy* would be my personal ambition."

Paula looked to where Cammy Studland stood with an elite gathering of the show's hierarchy. She was wearing a polished-bronze cotton dress tightly draped around her narrow waist by a long sash that crisscrossed over her full breasts and tied into a halter around her neck. With her photograph appearing regularly in the newspapers and in just about every issue of all the magazines published, Cammy had the best-known face and tits and bum in the United Kingdom. Right now, she was somewhere on the wrong side of being slightly drunk.

Though admitting that Cammy was lovely, Paula regarded her as immature to the point of being childish in comparison with a fully ripe woman like Karen Cayson. Earlier that evening a disgruntled and perhaps jealous Nikki had accused her of being totally obsessed with Karen. While accepting that her friend could well be right, Paula knew that Nikki would be exactly the same in her situation.

A pianist started playing a 1950s tune from the show and Cammy was swaying with the music. The partygoers began coaxing her. "Come on, Cammy, sing for us, dear."

"Nobody can wiggle like Cammy can wiggle," a girl near Paula and Nikki remarked as everyone settled down quietly and looked to Cammy Studland for a performance.

"Let's move closer," Nikki said, taking Paula's arm and propelling her forward.

Cammy sang the old Floyd Robinson hit *Making Love,* her throaty voice distinctively compelling as she swung her liquid body from side to the beat of the music. As she gyrated, the knot of her halter become loosened, unnoticed by her. There was something almost ritualistic about her wild dance. She had absolute control over every sinuous muscle of her lithe body. As she jerked and twisted, her turquoise print dress lowered, treating the whole assembly to a peek of her pink-nippled breasts, jutting mounds of flesh that were bright white against the bikini-top boundaries of her tan.

Moving in the dance had increased the effect of alcohol on Cammy. She looked bewildered and distressed by the howls of delight from the younger men and women. To Paula's surprise, Nikki struggled through the throng to go to the rescue. Reaching for Cammy's halter ties, Nikki, to booing from a number of the menfolk present, hoisted them up and secured them.

Hurrying to join her friend, Paula was aware of her high heels castanetting over the polished tile floor. Cammy's dark-lashed eyes were slits and there was a nervous tic at one side of her mouth. Recognising this as signs of drunkenness, Paula took one of Cammy's arms while Nikki took the other.

"I know which is her room," Nikki said as they led the tipsy star away.

In the lift, as Nikki fingered one of ten mother-of-pearl push-buttons in a black panel, Cammy began to cry softly. She sobbed, "I've made a complete fool of myself, haven't I?"

Abso-fucking-lutely, Paula thought coldly. The people downstairs had deliberately lured the gullible Cammy into providing them with a cheap thrill. The innocence behind her erotic dance had made her inevitable exhibitionism more sexually arousing than any performance by a professional stripper. Stardom was nothing without dignity, and Cammy Studland didn't have the dignity that a star should have.

"Of course not," Nikki said, comforting the weeping Cammy. "You simply joined in the spirit of the party."

Paula needed to support Cammy against the wall while Nikki opened the door of her room. It was an enormous square room with roses as the theme of its décor. They helped Cammy to a downy-mattressed bed. She sat on the edge, head down, still quietly crying. Sitting down beside her, Nikki murmured soothing words as she took and held the star in her arms.

Watching the scene from where she stood by a kidney-shaped dressing table, a bored Paula saw Cammy cuddle gratefully against the solicitous Nikki. She couldn't understand the problem. The girl had a great pair of tits, so why was she upset about showing them off? Only the exhibitionist was successful in showbiz.

She was toying with the idea of telling Nikki to leave the silly bitch to sleep it off, when the two-woman tableau on the bed showed signs of life. Cammy put a hand gently under Nikki's chin, slowly raising her face, and then a single shiver shook Cammy like a convulsion, and she wrapped her arms round Nikki and kissed her hotly. The memory of the wonder of Nikki's mouth stirred Paula every bit as much as did the sight of the two women on the bed getting carried away by the kiss. Laying Cammy back on the bed without breaking the kiss, Nikki partly mounted her, opening her legs and thrusting herself against Cammy's hip with a rhythmic on-and-off pressure. Slowly at first, Cammy moved her hips until she was matching Nikki's rhythm.

As the couple writhed and moaned in the preliminaries to love-making that was more in depth, an excited Paula walked towards the bed in a slow march, a controlled pacing like that of a disciplined soldier on parade. Heads moving this way and that to get the most from each other, Nikki and Cammy had opened their mouths and were hungrily exchanging tongues.

From the corner of her eye, Nikki saw Paula's approach. Still passionately kissing Cammy, she fumbled with one hand to undo the halter that she had tied up when Cammy's primitive dance had come to an end. With the same hand, Nikki pulled the top of Cammy's dress down. Though Cammy was lying on her back, the big breast stood up in perfect shape, the nipple poking proudly upwards.

Understanding why Nikki had made the move, Paula leaned

over to rest both elbows on the bed and cup the bare breast in both hands to tenderly caress it. Bending her head, she circled the pimpled areola with her tongue. Aware of Cammy's body stiffening under Nikki and hearing her long, drawn-out groan of pleasure, Paula opened her mouth and took the full length of the erect nipple in, sucking as avidly as a baby at the teat.

Enjoying the energetic writhing of a thoroughly aroused Cammy on the bed, Paula covered her teeth with her lips and worked tantalisingly on the nipple. But then everything changed. Breaking Cammy's hold on her, Nikki sat up, apologising breathlessly. "Oh, I'm so sorry. I've had too much to drink and need to go to the bathroom."

She was standing by the bed when Cammy reached out to grasp one of her wrists, preventing her from walking away.

Though reluctant to release the nipple from her mouth, Paula sat up on the bed as Nikki got to her feet. Cammy turned her hungry, heavy-lidded eyes on Paula. Reaching up with both hands, she pulled Paula down on top of her.

Holding Paula's face, a panting Cammy kissed her. Head spinning, lost in deep kissing, Paula recognised that she had started on a sexual journey from which there would be no return until her desire had been completely satisfied. The sound of Nikki closing the bathroom door came from hundreds of light years distant. Then nothing existed for Paula other than the thrill of a demanding, fully aroused – and to all appearances fully sober – Cammy Studland.

Eight

"I trust that your application is for a short adjournment, Inspector," the magistrate said without raising his head from studying the papers before him on his desk. For a long time he stared at the file in front of him, as if he had X-ray vision and could read through to the document at the bottom. He drew in a long, sighing breath as he waited for his question to be answered.

"The police enquiries are almost complete, sir." The policeman stood with his head down like a tired horse. He spoke in the monotones of officialdom. "I apologise for the delay, sir, but the court will appreciate that a charge of attempted murder may well be brought against the accused. We will be ready to proceed shortly.

Seeing the astute, hawk-nosed Detective Inspector Collings again had an already on-edge Karen shaking. She was still haunted by the memory of the night the policeman had sat in Matthew's high-backed chair, judging her like a latter-day Pontius Pilate.

Hoping for reassurance, she looked to where Matthew sat in the court. But he was as inscrutable as a china Buddha. She knew that a terrible rage was seething inside her husband. He was determined to put a stop to all this. He'd had all he was prepared to take of the tenth-rate tittle-tattle, the spite, the scandal, the innuendoes, the you-mark-my-words, and the just-you-wait-and-sees, and the absurd stories with mocking headings in the tabloids. Though a force to be reckoned in the worlds of entertainment and big business, he was a man being slowly destroyed by his own legend.

They had spoken little on the drive from home that morning. Both of them had been lost in their own thoughts, both of them trying to pin their hopes on Richard Neehan's prediction. If it were to prove right, then they would arrive in court to learn that the police had withdrawn all charges. That hadn't happened.

Karen had been pleasantly surprised to see the ultra-sophisticated Cheryl Valenta in the court. Dressed smartly in a tailored blue suit, she sat round the highly polished, heavy press table, which was huge and uncluttered. Her long-fingered hand made notes quickly as she leaned her head to the left to listen to the whisper of the male reporter sitting beside her. She shook her head either in denial or refusal. Sophisticated Cheryl was as coolly aloof with her colleague as she was with most other people. Karen noticed that the journalist avoided looking in her direction. She assumed that the sensitive Cheryl didn't want to embarrass her.

Karen felt that being in court had stripped her of everything, including even her birthright. All of the officials, from a white-faced court usher who was draped like Count Dracula up to the egocentric clowns on the bench who were deluded into thinking they had a God-given right to judge their fellows, made her feel like some kind of nonentity. It was similar to, but worse than, the way hospital doctors stood at the end of your bed discussing you as if you weren't there.

Their attitude diminished her self-esteem. She wanted to shout out, to remind them that she was Karen Cayson, a universal star, while they were nought but pen-pushing pricks. Petty little officials who would never amount to anything outside of their smelly little courtroom.

The whole thing was ridiculous, a farce rather than a tragicomedy. Both Karen, the accused, and Matthew, her victim, wanted the whole thing to be dropped, but the law was intent on pursuing the matter to the bitter end. Karen felt certain that there was somebody, some enemy of Matthew's, who was pulling the strings of the judiciary.

Fixing Collings with a steady gaze, the obviously irritated magistrate questioned him. "How serious the circumstances are has not escaped my attention, Inspector. You say that you will be able to proceed shortly. 'Shortly' is a relevant term. What are we talking about here – weeks, months, years? A hearing at this court is only a stepping stone to the crown court, so delay here has a chain effect that can cover a considerable amount of time. It is claimed that all are equal before the law, but that guarantee wouldn't seem to extend to public figures like the principals in this case. We are all now familiar with the phrase 'trial by journalism', but if this is allowed to drag on I fear that we will witness conviction by journalism, and I will not permit that to happen."

"I share your concern, sir. Yet this is a straightforward case, sir, and I would expect the prosecution to be in a position to commence in two weeks at the outside."

Karen's heart sank. Another two weeks of waiting, wondering and worrying. She thought of Helen and Nellie Drury sitting outside the courtroom, both constantly stirring the prosecution pot. Both eager to give damning evidence against her while they were still in the employ of her husband, well aware that their long service with the Wyndham family afforded them immunity. The snobby servants saw her as a slapper who had used the elastic in her knickers to catapult herself to the top. Fame meant fuck all in the kind of situation that she was in. Though she was witty and terribly literate, and had changed herself from a two-bit stripper into a star who was adored worldwide. But being a celebrity didn't bring respect and respectability to someone born on the wrong side of the tracks. Even Matthew couldn't break with family tradition to support her fully.

"My wife is truthfully innocent," Matthew had told the police. "She has never lifted a finger against me; she has never been anything but a caring and dutiful wife. On that night I was the author of my own distress. I foolishly believed that I could celebrate my birthday as an old man the way I did my twenty-first. I had far too much to drink, and I fell."

Detective Inspector Collings had listened to him, but he had listened more attentively to the accusing Drurys, who had pushed forward their campaign to oust Karen from the Wyndham household, while the Crown Prosecution Service had in turn listened to Detective Inspector Collings.

Once again, Karen's conspiracy theory had her suspect that some third party was manipulating the Drurys against Matthew. Alan Marriott would seem to be the most likely suspect, but when he visited the studios he always treated her with respect and in a friendly manner – although that wasn't anything to go by when money was involved.

Matthew was in a position to test her hypothesis, but she couldn't risk upsetting him by putting the idea to him. Had she been able to, and had Matthew agreed with her, the servants would soon back down if Matthew threatened them with dismissal. But he regarded Henry and Nellie Drury as indispensable, and would not go against them.

"Mr Neehan?" The magistrate made Richard's name a question by the way he said it.

Standing up from the polished table where he sat alone, Richard Neehan preened himself. Karen noticed that Matthew was staring at him thoughtfully, as if measuring how far Neehan would be prepared to stick his neck out. Not very far, she was sure, and guessed that Matthew was just as certain. Neehan had a command of words and was snappy with the quickies of repartee, but that didn't alter the fact that he was a lawyer.

Picking up some papers from the table, Neehan studied them confidently as if they held all the answers he needed. Knowing the solicitor's style, Karen wasn't surprised to see him surreptitiously put the papers back down because they meant absolutely nothing.

It had been simply a calculated act to impress the court. By choosing to be a lawyer, Neehan had deprived showbiz of a talented actor.

"Detective Inspector Collings has told the court that this is a straightforward case, your worship," Neehan began.

"Legally straightforward but, nevertheless, an emotionally convoluted issue," the magistrate interrupted, with no particular sharpness.

"Quite so, your worship," Neehan agreed. "But, with respect, Inspector Collings was referring to it as being straightforward in law. If that is so, why is the prosecution taking so long to present it to the court? Aside from where expert medical evidence is concerned, there are only two witnesses for the prosecution. It is a psychological fact that memories are not infallible and passing time is not conducive to accurate recall. It is my contention, your worship, that it would serve the best interests of everyone, not in the least the taxpayer, if all charges against my client were dropped immediately."

The magistrate was silent. A frown laddered his forehead and the knuckles of a bony fist rubbed at his prominent chin. Hope swelled up in Karen. Sensing Matthew's eyes on her, she turned her head his way. They looked hard at one another. It was no more than a moment, but, in their eyes, their expression, or whatever breath of a motion one makes if only to exist, live, breathe, they had communicated well with one another. For that fleeting second it was as it had once been between them, when he'd been a born pit bull terrier able to smell her on heat from a half-mile distance. They had been really close then.

When? Back when Basil Brush had been a shy cub?

She realised that she was so tense that she had stopped breathing. When the magistrate cleared his throat prior to speaking, the sound seemed so loud that it made her jump. All was at stake here. To the public she was right now the biggest thing there ever was, and then all of a sudden they wouldn't be seeing her any more. For her that would be a living death, which had to be much, much worse than the real thing.

"I see where you're coming from, Mr Neehan, and have noted your application," the magistrate said. "But the court has a duty to ensure that the law takes its due course." He turned to the police officer. "Inspector Collings, the prosecution has exactly two weeks from today to bring a case against the accused. Failure to do that will have this court order that the charges against the accused are dismissed."

Catching Karen's eye, Neehan gave her a conspiratorial, fraction-of-a-second wink. He followed up with an everything-will-be-all-right look. Maybe he thought so, but it didn't look that way from where she was sitting.

Karen closed her eyes and leaned against the nearest surface. It was getting worse. Everything was getting worse. She needed a drink really bad. That was against Matthew's rules: alcohol was something you could either take or leave alone, if you had all your buttons. She was beginning to think that a lot of liquor had flowed under bridge since the time she'd had all her buttons.

Standing as still as a statue in her kitchen, holding the cheque in both hands, Wendi looked incredulously at it, seemingly unable to speak. Cheryl was content to wait, enjoying the chance to study the nice-to-look-at blonde. She felt herself juicing up between the legs by being so close to her. Wendi had on a dress of an indescribable shade of olive, cleverly set off by a dull-finished appliquéd decoration around the neck. It wasn't just that she was pretty all over, but that there was something alive about everything she did. She seemed to be in touch with every part of her lithe young body. Cheryl liked that. A woman who knew herself so well also knew how to please another woman. Wendi was one of a rare type who made the best-ever lovers.

The fact that she'd had a long-term relationship with Karen

Cayson was proof enough of that. Karen was known to be choosy – very choosy. Not that anyone seeing Karen in court that morning would have thought so. Nerves clearly strung tight, her eyes had betrayed the redness of recent tears when Cheryl had spoken to her after the hearing. Devastated by the fact that the case against her had not been dropped, Karen had raised a hand to stifle a sob that had risen from some cold, empty depth within her. Cheryl had felt really sorry for her.

Karen had affected Cheryl so badly that she had suddenly felt deeply for the problems of those in the stories that streamed constantly past her desk, the tragedies, the failures, the mistakes.

Turning to prop herself against a worktop, Wendi gestured for Cheryl to be seated in one of the steel-framed chairs at the table. Wendi struck a tough kind of pose with her thumbs in the thin leather belt at her waist. There was a depth to her that was beyond the senses. There was something compelling about Wendi that made Cheryl realise how long it had been since a woman had ceased to be a separate entity and become part of herself. Wendi gave Cheryl the impression that she was studying her mind, and it made her feel oddly insecure. That was a novel experience. The sun slanted through the window behind Wendi, forming a crosshatch pattern on the tile floor. She gave a little self-conscious laugh before speaking.

"It is an old cliché, Cheryl, but I really don't know what to say."

"You don't even have to say thanks," Cheryl advised with a smile. "It's Matthew Wyndham's money, not mine. It's proof that it is possible to teach an old dog new tricks."

"But it was you who got it for me."

"For a good cause, Wendi."

"I can't tell you what this will mean for the children in Manchester," Wendi said dreamily. "We'll be able to do so much that's needed doing for so long."

"I'm pleased."

"Let me get you something – a sandwich perhaps?"

"No," Cheryl answered. "It's a kind offer, but I have a deadline for a story, so I must get back."

"Well, then, please come to dinner this evening, Cheryl."

"I was hoping that you would ask," Cheryl said half-jokingly.

"Great," Wendi exclaimed, opening a cupboard and taking out a bottle of wine. "Now, let's at least have a drink together before you leave. I brought this back from France a couple of months ago. I don't know what it's like, so I'd better try it first." Taking two glasses down from a shelf, she poured wine into one. "Here goes."

Holding the drink in her mouth, each cheek ballooning alternately as she washed the wine from side to side, she then swallowed. She spoke dubiously. "It's not great."

"Then maybe I'll sit this one out," Cheryl said ruefully.

"I think that I could get you to like it."

Cheryl chuckled. "I doubt it."

"I haff vays of making you..." Wendi began, Gestapo-fashion, as she refilled her glass and drank from it.

There was a mixture of trepidation and daring in the expression on her face as she looked down at the seated Cheryl. Her eyes were glazed, sexy slits of appraisal. They embraced Cheryl's breasts and the tight fit of the black dress over her hips.

Wendi placed the empty glass on the worktop, moving very near to Cheryl as she did so. She glanced at Cheryl again, covertly, her eyes reflecting uncertainty. Cheryl caught the scent of Wendi's hair. The nearness of their bodies caused them both to feel the jarring impact of new and sudden emotions.

Then Cheryl was erotically awash in the body aroma that the warmth in the kitchen had brought out. It was a natural perfume that was Wendi's very essence. Her eyes, just inches away, had clouded so that Cheryl couldn't fathom what was going on behind them. Held in her spell, a powerful entrapment that no witch could cast, Cheryl waited for what seemed an eternity as Wendi's face came closer and closer. Then Wendi's mouth gently connected with hers.

It wasn't a kiss, but merely a fairly meaningless contact. Initially mystified and disappointed, Cheryl then found her senses reeling as Wendi transferred the wine, warmed and sweetened, into her mouth.

The exchange was slow and sexually arousing. Cheryl held the wine, savouring the intimate taste of Wendi. At last, she swallowed it. Wendi showed that she had great style by moving her mouth just fractionally away so that Cheryl could have the exquisite experience of licking the remainder of the wine from Wendi's slightly parted lips.

When it was over, leaving Cheryl filled with longing, Wendi straightened up to do a lithe, feline stretching. She said huskily, "I'd find it easy to love you, Cheryl, but not as a sister, if you get my meaning."

Cheryl tingled, feeling myriad emotions, all with their own elements of arousal, not the least of which was anticipation of the evening to come.

The past few days had been an incorporeal time. Karen couldn't recall them in much detail. She was sleeping little, if at all. The realisation that she might be locked away, bound to obey whatever she was told to do, had been quite a mental shock. A wildness went on in her mind until it was like being caught in an echo chamber, strident voices reverberating and screaming, growing louder and louder. Panic and fear ballooned in her. When her mind quietened, she would lie awake worrying over her husband and her career.

The taping of *Beach of Fear* had continued with Karen acting mainly from habit. She had got away with a mediocre performance mainly because of the unexpected talent of Paula Monroe. The kid had shone. She was good, really good, impressing even John Brighton, something that was remarkable in itself. For all her country ways and teenage looks there was nothing simple about Paula. The girl evoked the protective instinct in Karen, and they had become close without making any physical contact beyond what had occurred on the day they had met.

It was the prolonging of the case against her, and in particular the reaction of the newspapers, that was blighting Karen's life. Press speculation was rife, and sensational stories had been exploding like a string of cluster bombs. Lies are never more easily accepted as truths as when they are put into print. Disclaimers from Richard Neehan were ignored. Matthew's two-day stay at Bristol, where his doctor had arranged for him to see a medical specialist, had hit the headlines as an announcement of their separation. A paragraph of one story in a particularly vicious tabloid read:

> The elderly Matthew Wyndham has discovered that puppy love is no fun when one of the lovers is an old dog. He has packed his bags and left his young and violent wife, an alcoholic who is far from anonymous.

An irate Matthew had wanted to sue, but Neehan had wisely advised him not to. Such a move, the lawyer had explained, would principally serve to add fuel to the raging fire of adverse publicity. Neehan had pointed out that, if the police withdrew the charges against Karen, then the frantic media interest in her and Matthew would die a natural death. Matthew, Neehan stressed, should use his considerable influence and wealth to halt the case.

Matthew saw this as the sensible, and possibly only, solution to the problem. In his impulsive way he had arrived unexpectedly at the studio that afternoon to collect Karen and have her go with him to the home of an old acquaintance of his, Assistant Police Commissioner Emmett Foyle.

Foyle, past middle age and divorced, lived at the top of Belmont Buildings, which were located in a quaintly preserved area of London. It was a classic four-storey building of Portland stone and decorative ironwork, a memorial to an era of horse-drawn buses and barrel organs. Belmont Buildings was an expensive house, in which Foyle's apartment was the most expensive. The ground floors of the fine Victorian buildings in the area around it had been ripped out to accommodate anachronistic shops and fast-food outlets. But Belmont Buildings still stood intact, a breakwater against the turbulent seas of change.

The surroundings disturbed Karen. It was like being in the kind of mysterious half-world visited in dreams. Though it was Thursday afternoon, the movements all round her were deadened by a kind of Sunday-evening hush. It was as if the place were still populated by the unquiet dead of yesteryear, and the presence of the living were resented. For a long moment there was fear in her throat, dry fear. She couldn't see how good could result from a visit to such a place as this.

Her earlier depression had deepened when Emmett Foyle opened an ornate door to invite them into his four-room, corner apartment, a bachelor pad with all the snazzy furnishings. He extended a thin, mottled hand to each of them.

Matthew apologised. "I'm sorry about disturbing you, Emmett."

"Not at all. It's always a pleasure to welcome an old friend." Foyle smiled. A formidable, stocky, severe-looking man with Richard Nixon jowls and opaque blue eyes hidden behind heavy glasses, he had reached that point in life where ageing proceeds at a gallop. He looked at Karen. "And it has been a long-held dream of mine to meet your beautiful wife. I would venture to claim that I am your most ardent fan, my dear."

"I regret destroying the image you have made of me," Karen said in self-deprecation.

She had sunk into the sofa beside Matthew, her legs high. She had crossed her knees, and the hem of the red dress she wore had retreated to her thighs. This had obviously presented Emmett Foyle with a problem. Karen smoothed her dress further down her legs in a semblance of modesty.

"Quite the opposite, Miss Cayson. Uniquely, the fantasy comes a very poor second to the reality."

"You are very kind." Karen smiled politely while hating the smug, droopy-faced bastard. But she guessed the egotistical Emmett Foyle would have taken a rebuff badly, and they wanted him on side.

For a moment she watched a pigeon stretch its wings and take off from the windowsill, riding the currents high above the rooftops. She saw the bird hover outside the window, then suddenly dip away to the street and out of sight.

Turning his attention back to Matthew, Foyle said thoughtfully, "You are a busy man with little time to spare, Matthew. Therefore it has to be something important that brought you here."

"No doubt you can surmise what it is." Matthew spoke in his customary incisive manner.

"I have an inkling, old chap. Is it connected to your, er, accident at your birthday party?" Obviously not caring for the subject, he kneaded the arms of his chair with his hands.

"It is. And 'accident' is a precise description, Emmett."

"That's what I thought." Foyle nodded sagely. "The damned press has blown it up out of all proportion."

"The press would be stymied, Emmett, if the police did the sensible thing and let the whole matter drop."

Moving uncomfortably in his chair, Foyle was noncommittal. "I would like to help you and your wife, of course, Matthew, but this is a veritable minefield for someone in my position to enter into. Even a most innocent enquiry made on behalf of someone in your position can provoke allegations of corruption."

"Ours is a simple problem, Emmett, in the form of a Detective Inspector Collings," Matthew said bluntly.

"Frank Collings," Foyle said in a slow, memory-searching way. "Yes, I remember him. Frank was a DC when I was with H Division. He was born out of his time, Matthew. Frank Collings's style of policing belongs back in the first half of the twentieth century. He won't cut corners and he's like a dog with a bone once he gets onto something."

"Tell me about it." Matthew rolled his eyes heavenward.

"He's not an easy man to handle," Foyle said quietly, almost speaking to himself, "but there are certain strings that I can pull. However, I must caution that I can offer you no guarantee of success."

Irritated, Matthew momentarily forgot that he was a guest in Foyle's home. "Surely you're not asking us to accept that you have no power over someone with the rank of inspector?"

"You know that is not so, Matthew," Foyle mildly reproved his friend. "The problem is that your case is media-sensitive. To paraphrase an old adage, I will have to ensure that injustice isn't seen to be done."

Matthew Wyndham glared, his eyes full of profanities. "Injustice? There can be no injustice, Emmett, as my wife has not committed any crime."

"Quite so, Matthew."

The way that Foyle spoke those three words told her that he did not for one moment believe her husband. Assistant Commissioner Emmett Foyle knew that she had come close to killing Matthew by whacking him over the head with a bottle. She consoled herself with the thought that Foyle was at the upper level of society where whom you knew was much more important than whether or not you were guilty.

For the first time since that terrible drunken night, Karen Cayson was really hopeful.

Outside the hotel, shivering in the chill night air because her exit has been so rushed that her coat was flying open, Paula signalled to a passing cab. Behind her the revels of the cast and production staff of the musical could be heard still in full swing. What was she doing out here? If a team of brutal and highly skilled inquisitors questioned her she would be unable to give an answer. To run away from the most exquisite physical sensations of her life, a totally erotic, mind-busting adventure, now seemed such a stupid thing to do. But at the time she had known that it was the right thing, the proper thing. Imagining Nikki and Cammy still making passionate love in the hotel room, Paula prayed that the conviction that had caused her to leave them would soon return. If it didn't she would begin to doubt her sanity.

With Nikki still in the bathroom, her tongue had been sliding wetly into Cammy's welcoming mouth, while she had caressed the star's firm and responsive left breast with her right hand. Finger and thumb first manipulating the nipple, Paula had then got an extra reaction from Cammy, who (as Paula had suspected) no longer appeared to be intoxicated whatsoever, by covering the breast with her hand so that the hard yet conversely beautifully soft to the touch nipple, dug lightly into her palm. An intuitive little movement of Paula's hand had sent shivers of delight through them both. Cammy was vibrant and naturally sexy.

A tinge of guilt still affected Paula when she recalled her momentary annoyance when Nikki had returned to the bed. It wasn't right to be affected in that way by a friend, and Nikki was a good friend. Yet for Paula it had briefly been a case of two's company but three's a crowd. Not that the feeling had lasted.

Within minutes all three of them had been carried away by the kind of crazy and totally out-of-control sex that pays no heed to the number of people involved, and recognises no inhibitions.

Nikki and Cammy had ganged up to ravage her. They had been up over her on the bed and, initially, their faces so close to hers had been intimidating. Some possibly primitive kind of fear had held Paula rigid, unresponsive. But then, first Nikki's and then

Cammy's sweet breath had been mingling with hers. Within a split second the sexual ice had thawed. Paula had felt it melting wetly and warmly between her legs. Blood had been pumping hard through her, throbbing at her temple. Excitement had been making her light-headed.

Out here in the night the taste of Cammy's kiss was still on her lips, and she could find Nikki's perfume about her now. The thrill of their hot mouths on hers, their wet eager tongues licking at her skin, and the erotic memory of their intruding, invading fingers probing inside her body was still with her. It made a girl from the placid and conservative county of Hampshire wonder where the sweet Nikki and Cammy, who were little older than she, had learned such things as they had done to her.

Cammy's crotch had been against Paula's hip as they had undressed her. Her lithe, silk-skinned body had driven them sex-mad. Ripping her dress in their eagerness to bare her breasts, Nikki had kissed and sucked the left one while Cammy had licked at the light film of sweat that had formed in the flesh valley between them. Paula had felt excitement curling through her genitals like a hot snake.

With a deep groan of desire, Cammy had buried her nose deep into Paula's armpit to savour the aroma of feminine perspiration before opening her mouth to get the taste of it. As she had sucked on Paula's skin, Cammy had wriggled out of her dress and panties to work her bare cunt hotly and wetly against Paula's thigh. While this had been going on, Paula and Nikki had kissed long and passionately. Naked, tight-together kisses.

A flash of coldness, a brief moment of feeling terribly alone and sexually frustrated, had then blighted Paula when Nikki stopped kissing her. But Paula had then caught a trace of the fragrance of her own sweat as Cammy's mouth had claimed hers. Thrilled by the musical star's kiss, Paula had known that there was a lot of movement going on around her, but had been too preoccupied with the probing of Cammy's tongue in her mouth and the sweet taste of her saliva, to bother about what was happening.

Ending the kiss, Cammy had then slid her mouth down over Paula's chin, down her neck, kissing each breast as she went. Closing her eyes, Paula had ecstatically felt Cammy's lips travel lightly over her stomach, moving on until it reached her pubic hair. Cammy's mouth pressed against the bushing of hair while her nose breathed in its very special perfume. Animated both by instinct and sexual desire, Paula had opened her legs to present Cammy with first prize in the game of sex. Holding Cammy's head in a light grip between the thighs, Paula felt Cammy's mouth and tongue part her swollen lips. Her slit was squelchy with arousal when Cammy's mouth opened ready and eager to devour it. The sex session with Nikki in their rented room had faded into childish insignificance in comparison with what had been going on then. A tongue slid into her, and Paula had felt her first orgasm run electrifyingly through her body, trailing a series of convulsions in its wake.

Relaxing then as skin touched skin, Paula responded to the slithery, indescribable feel of three bodies moving gently and rhythmically against each other. Her mouth had opened in surrender as Nikki's lips came against it. Nikki's delicious mouth had tasted of something extra, something too exotic, too erotic, and too wonderful to be described. Realisation had dawned on her. While she and Cammy had been kissing a few moments ago, Nikki had gone down on Cammy. In their kiss, Nikki and she had been sharing the exquisite taste of Cammy's love cream.

Making odd, strangulated half-screams as Cammy had sucked and nibbled at her clit with lip-covered teeth, Paula reached up with both hands to hold Nikki's head so as to get every last morsel of pleasure from the kiss. Heart racing, eyes closed, she had striven to imagine that it was Karen she was kissing.

That had been a drastic mistake. Though sex with Cammy and Nikki had her on the outer verge of excitement and was threatening to push her across the border into unknown but even more intense sensations, bringing Karen Cayson to mind had swiftly cooled Paula's passion. She had been unable deny to herself that she wanted sex with Karen, but there was more to it than that. Much more.

Though jolted by the impact of the discovery, Paula had suddenly known that she was in love with the beautiful Karen. Cammy was straddling her face now, lowering herself slowly. The scent of Cammy's vulva was pungent. As she pursed her mouth, a wave of shock ran through Paula, in her tautened abdomen and where Nikki was licking between her legs. Gripped in the erotic sensation of kissing another woman's secret parts, she felt her conscience suddenly battered by guilt over Karen. Paula broke away. "No, Cammy. Don't, please."

Mortified by the thought that she was right then being unfaithful to the woman she loved, Paula had gone instantly cold. To the protestations of Nikki and Cammy, she had freed herself from them and clambered off the bed. They had tried to coax and cajole her to return to their arms. Perhaps she was tempted for a fleeting moment by the sight of their naked bodies and the mingled aroma of their sex.

She needed to get away from them. She had to let the passion die right down so that she was able to think clearly. After getting dressed, she had hurried from the room, leaving the startled and bewildered Nikki and Cammy sitting up on the bed, gaping at her. Now, as the taxi pulled in to the kerb and she got in, it occurred to Paula that she had acted foolishly. Fun was fun, and the three of them had been having a great time in the hotel room before she had become so ludicrously romantic.

Giving the cab driver directions, Paula sat back comfortably. She told herself that she had not acted ridiculously at all by abdicating from the *ménage à trois*. She had done so on a matter of principle, and that was something to be proud of.

Getting into the rear of the limousine, Jay Clifford sat unmoving and unspeaking beside a menacing Alan Marriott. The silence was extraordinary. The night birds swooping and diving around the high buildings made no cries. In the dark sky of a new night, a low bright star painted a silver line through a thin mist. Clifford grimly accepted that it wouldn't be a star of hope where he was concerned. Watching a moth stupidly and repeatedly smash its dusty head against the windscreen added to the tension that was building in him. The driver sat as rigid as a corpse, looking straight ahead, both hands on the steering wheel, awaiting an order from Marriott. An order that didn't happen.

They were in a poorly lit side street that was too isolated for Clifford's liking. There were a few pedestrians around, but they passed the limousine in the hurried pace of city dwellers. Only tourists walked slowly in London, and in this area of the city you were more likely to see the ghost of one of the Krays than you were a tourist. Clifford knew that he could be murdered here and no one would stop to help him, or even care. Not that Alan Marriott was capable of murder. But he couldn't be sure of that. Alan Marriott was an impresario, not a Mafia godfather, but Clifford didn't know him well enough to know what he was capable of. What he did know was that Marriott was one of those lucky prats who could break all the rules and get away with it.

"You wanted to see me, Mr Marriott." He tried to make it a confident statement, a comment from one businessman to another, but the tremor in his voice betrayed him.

"You're full of crap, Clifford," Marriott rasped. "You promised to deliver the goods three days ago, but I had to hunt you down tonight."

This criticism wasn't fair. Clifford had diligently set up the camera and the sensor, and had driven three miles to the studio every evening to collect a tape that was useless. All he'd managed to get so far was a shaggable but running-to-fat dresser having a sly sniff of a pair of Karen Cayson's dirty panties, and Paula Monroe furtively fingering herself while reading a raunchy magazine. He hesitantly tried to explain the situation to Marriott.

"I've done everything I can, Mr Marriott. It's just a matter of waiting."

"Waiting? I don't have time to wait, Clifford. You led me to believe that the first time the new kid bent over to put on her shoes, Karen Cayson would mount her like a dog."

"And she will," Clifford affirmed with a nod that was useless in the dark inside the car. "The problem, well, the biggest problem, is Martha Abel."

"Martha Abel?" Marriott questioned in a way that said he couldn't understand what Clifford meant.

"Yes, she was in that 1960s thing about the—"

Marriott angrily interrupted. "I know what she was in, prick-face. What I *don't* get is how she could be causing problems on this."

"She's Karen Cayson's dresser, Mr Marriott."

"And she's screwing her," Marriott guessed.

"Not as far as I know," Clifford reply. "But she has got the hots for the kid, Paula Monroe, and she hangs around in the dressing room all the time to make sure that Cayson doesn't get into the kid's slit first."

Marriott fell silent again. He took out a gold-plated cigarette case that glinted in a stray beam from a street light, and opened it. His fingers crossed the tightly packed row of cigarettes. About to pull one from the case, he hesitated. The silence gained depth, worrying Clifford. Then the flame of a lighter flared, dramatically illuminating Marriott's hard face. He blew a horizontal column of smoke through the long car, and coughed an explosive cough.

When Marriott spoke his voice was even more hoarse than usual. "You have two days, Clifford, no more. Bring me pictures of the Cayson woman shagging that blonde kid, or else."

Clifford didn't ask what "or else" meant.

Nine

As she didn't feature in any of the scenes being shot, Karen had taken the morning off. Except for the absence of her idol in the studio, it had been a perfect morning for Paula. Getting up early when the grey sky was still greasy with leftover night, she had arrived punctually. In dramatic takes with close-ups predominating, she had excelled in scene after scene, delighting John Brighton by relieving him of any need for retakes. He had congratulated her long and often, expressing his expert opinion that she would be a world-renowned star within a year.

Paula, though elated, was finding it difficult to believe that her lifetime's dream had come true so swiftly. Here she was in a top studio, changing from one set of expensively glamorous clothing to another, as the script required. The highlight of life at home was when an item ordered from a catalogue arrived. Yet she was afraid to trust what was happening to her. Maybe it wouldn't end when the ball did, exactly at midnight, but it surely wouldn't last. Glass Slipper time was sure to come. She had met enough wannabes to convince her success in showbiz would always elude her as it had eluded countless others.

Though prepared to accept that hers was a natural talent, she knew that she owed much of her success that morning to Martha Abel. In a short while, Paula and Martha had become good friends. Paula liked Martha, who was one of those rare women who seem immortal in their feminine beauty, and Martha enjoyed the attention and youthful companionship that she got from her.

With Karen not present that morning, the veteran actress had voluntarily exceeded her duties as a dresser to become Paula's mentor. Enduring the close-to-intolerable heat of the studio, Martha had stayed close to her throughout to impart invaluable tricks of the trade that had put a gloss on Paula's performance.

In the dressing room now for the lunchtime break, Paula voiced her heartfelt thanks. "I owe you so much, Marty. I didn't know any of those things you taught me. I feel rotten for taking the credit."

"Forget it, Paula," Martha advised with a laugh. "I had my moment of glory long ago, now it's your turn. You owe me nothing." Then, as an afterthought, she added, "You can buy me a pint some night."

"I'd buy you champagne if I could," Paula assured her.

"A pint of bitter will do," Martha chuckled. "No one bought me champagne when I was using those gimmicks to improve my act."

"Someone should have," Paula said gallantly as she watched a totally unselfconscious Martha unbutton her short red dress. Letting it fall to the floor, she reached down to the puddle of fabric around her ankles. Lifting her feet from the skimpy dress, she picked it up and folded it neatly before laying it on a chair. Martha did everything meticulously.

Standing unmoving, Paula felt very unexpectedly shy and awkward. Other than her mother, which was very different, she had never seen a mature woman naked. The sight of Martha's stocky but well-shaped body unnerved her. No, maybe that wasn't accurate. To say that it made her feel somehow inexplicably disoriented would be nearer the truth. Finding herself unable to look away, she had to swallow hard.

Though she had to be hovering around the age of fifty, Martha was truly lovely to look at. She wasn't wearing a bra, and her soft skin was nicely tanned except for a strand of white across breasts that were every bit as firm as those of a teenager. She had a body that was lushly ripe with hidden sensuality in the mounds of her brown-tipped bosom. The tiny nylon panties she had on had surrendered to the dense bushing of dark hair that escaped from each side of the crotch and from above the thin material.

Exhaling in a rush, Paula found it impossible to get her breath back in as Martha pulled down her panties, releasing a wonderfully luxuriant growth of glossy pubic hair, so thick that it totally obscured her slit.

"Come on, don't be shy," she admonished Paula with a smile. "You must be absolutely boiling in that dress. Don't worry about me. I've shared a dressing-room with everything from a Billy Holiday to a billy goat."

Paula laughed. "I don't believe you, Marty. Not a goat."

"Well, he shagged like a goat." Martha quietly searched her memory for a moment. "Come to think of it, he stank like a fucking goat, too."

"You're really funny, Marty," Paula said after recovering from a fit of laughter. "You must have had a few propositions in your day."

More at ease now, Paula took off her blouse, then her skirt, and stood in the matching red bra and panties that Nikki said made her look really good. But now, compared with Martha, she knew that she must appear to be nothing but a gawky kid.

"Being propositioned is one of the hazards in this game, Paula," Martha said, adding, pointedly, Paula was certain, "but I turned all the guys down."

"All of them?" Paula raised both eyebrows.

"No, I tell a lie," Martha confessed. "There was one guy, a famous crooner."

"Who was he?"

"I couldn't betray him by telling you that, Paula."

"But you had an affair with him?"

"Not bloody likely," Martha was indignant. "He's a really sad case, Paula, a great sexual performer on stage, but a nonstarter off. Like I say, he was, and still is, very sad. All he wanted to do was dry-fuck."

"What's that?"

"Rub himself against a woman till he came."

"And you let him, Marty?"

"You ask too many questions, nosy parker." Martha tapped her own nose with a finger.

But as she finished speaking, Martha changed noticeably. Her eyes went catlike and were moving over Paula, sizing her up. A surge of fear welled up in Paula. She had an urge to run, not because she was actually afraid of Martha, but from fear that she would make an absolute fool of herself with an experienced woman.

But something kept her rooted to the spot, and the moment passed. She saw Martha go through another transformation to return to her usual self. But her pupils remained dilated, and a faint flush of colour stained her cheeks.

Reaching behind herself with both hands, Paula fumblingly unclipped her bra. An unintentional movement on her part caused her breasts to swing free the way a stripper puts on an exaggerated display. Her nipples were hard and pointed.

"Jeeeeewiz!" Martha's long-breathed exclamation was complimentary. Her obvious indecision was strange to see in so self-assured a woman. Taking a hesitant step, she stopped near to Paula, who stared unblinkingly at Martha's disconcertingly close breasts. The older woman's nipples were standing proud of the large, dark areolae.

Moving forward again, Martha let her naked breasts lightly contact Paula's bosom.

"Snap," Martha said in jest, but her eyes had narrowed and a sultry expression changed her face.

She gave a planned, quick wiggle of her shoulders that made her erect nipples brush against the smaller but equally thrusting crowns of Paula's breasts. The erotica of this simple movement plunged Paula into a state of frantic sexual arousal. The intense feeling was a new experience for her – exhilarating and frightening at the same time.

In that fleeting moment of nipple contact with Martha, Paula seemed to have matured ten years. Aware of Martha's eyes following her movements, she hooked both thumbs in the top of her red panties and eased them down. Though she couldn't match the older woman's luxurious growth of pubic hair, Paula was confident that she hadn't been at the back of the queue when fuzz triangles had been handed out. She was conscious that the top of her V was springing out as the panties were lowered, and saw the spontaneous and impressive appearance of pubic hair register appreciatively in Martha's eyes. The older woman took in a deep breath and held it. A furrow appeared between her eyes and she took the edge of her heavy lower lip between white, even teeth.

There was a mixture of dread and regret on Martha's face then. Paula guessed that her friend was troubled by the thought that she had gone too far. Martha confirmed this by taking a step back and saying, "Forgive me, please, Paula. I don't know what came over me. It was wrong of me to take advantage."

"It was only a bit of fun," Paula lied to console Martha.

But instead Paula felt that the sexual exchange had matured her dramatically. Smiling briefly and confidently at Martha, she knelt in front of her as if in worship. Clasping Martha's warm buttocks in both hands, Paula eased her closer. Her slightly parted lips made a lingering contact with the soft, hot skin of Martha's stomach.

Remembering what the more experienced Nikki had taught her about the special place where you could inhale the soul scent of a woman, Paula moved her head a little until her open mouth was just above where Martha's thick growth of pubic hair ended. Moistening the skin of Martha's stomach with her tongue to coax out the flavour, Paula breathed in a heady incense.

She felt Martha clasp her head with both hands, her fingers entwining in her hair somehow anchoring Paula's mind and stopping her from drifting away into what she thought would be a sex heaven. Seemingly coming from inside her head rather than separate from her, Martha's voice sounded worried.

"Stop, Paula. We shouldn't. Where is this going to end?"

Who cared where it would end? All that mattered was that it didn't end soon. A startling lust suddenly burned through Paula like a fork of lightning. She moved her mouth down through Martha's profuse hair. Reacting, Martha opened her legs and Paula's head went between them. A little muffled cry of delight came from Martha as Paula's tongue lightly, ever so lightly, touched her outer lips. Then the older woman's whole body shuddered as Paula tenderly and slowly and lovingly gave the wet folds of her gaping cunt a long lick from its back end right up to the clit. Martha released a strangled cry of pleasure.

Gasping, Martha thrust rhythmically with her hips as Paula, crazy for her flowing juices, avidly licked and sucked at her. Martha was saying something, mumbling and muttering inaudibly, as her hip thrusting changed into a frantic thrashing, and Paula held her face tight against Martha's cunt. Crying out, still inaudible, Martha began to make odd, strangulated half-screams as Paula suckled at her.

Both of them were building fast to a mammoth climax. But then the door of the dressing room opened.

The four of them sat in the lounge of the servants' quarters on the upper level of the house. Through the high window a few fluffy white clouds could be seen in the sky. Down below, the buildings of New Malden were pink and white and ugly and unfledged, like young birds in a crowded nest. The room was as shiny and bright as a temple of faith, with icons that were ornaments and heirlooms and pictures lovingly displayed. There were a dozen roses in a vase. Now, the flowers were limp. A scattering of black-edged petals lay on the table. Karen wondered why other people's places always smelled oddly. What worried her most was that your sense of smell soon adjusted to it, and you sat breathing in unpleasant air without being aware of it.

It wasn't a happy get-together. Henry and Nellie would have welcomed Matthew, the "young master", into their home, but Karen's being with him made them hostile. She fuelled their horrible habits and prejudices.

Nellie sat stern-faced and upright, knitting furiously, click, click, click. The facetious Henry was on the verge of schizophrenia, caught between the desire to please his master and frantic worry over the reason for Matthew's visit.

Assistant Commissioner Emmett Foyle's telephoned message to Matthew had been curtly to the point. "You must do your bit, Matthew, by calling off those servants of yours. They're like a couple of baying hounds, and your wife is their prey."

"I know that," Matthew had admitted, but Karen was aware that he wasn't happy being asked to do something nasty. Matthew preferred to pay someone else to do his dirty work. "But what will happen then, Emmett?"

"You can leave everything to me, Matthew. But you have to silence that pair of geriatric witch hunters, once and for all."

"How?" Matthew had plaintively enquired.

Foyle had snorted angrily down the telephone line. "Sack the old cunts if you have to."

"But they started in service with the Wyndham family when my parents were first married, Emmett."

"The choice is yours, Matthew. It's your servants or your wife," Foyle had advised sharply before hanging up.

So Karen had sacrificed her eagerly anticipated morning away from filming to come here with Matthew in the hope of finding some solution to their problem. She didn't hold out a lot of hope unless Matthew kicked his sycophantic servants into touch. That wasn't likely, but Karen's anger at her husband was checked by her concern for him in his illness. Of late, his face was grey and his voice had an old tiredness.

"This is something of a delicate situation, Henry," Matthew began. There was awkwardness between employer and employee that made them talk to each other like second-rate actors in a poorly scripted film. "Far be it for me to transgress on the honesty and integrity of Nellie and yourself, but—"

"That was something Mr Jonathan Wyndham always complimented us on," Henry interrupted in proud reminiscence.

Karen's heart sank. Henry Drury had used his main weapon, mention of Matthew's late father, to open up the defence. It would all go downhill from now on. The ghosts of Wyndhams past were on the march to the beat of Nellie Drury's knitting needles.

They should have put this to arbitration, have someone like Richard Neehan show the Drurys the folly of biting the hand that fed them. But she didn't like the solicitor. He was unfeeling. To men like him all females were objects just waiting to be used. Turn women upside down and there is no difference to any of them – that was one of his favourite expressions.

Perhaps Cheryl Valenta would have been the best choice to handle it. The journalist had been most sympathetic in court. As the hearing ended she had risen up from her chair and pulled down the jacket of her suit. Karen had noticed her breasts particularly. When she'd thought of Cheryl's body before, it had been to consider it as lean and hard-muscled, like a pugilist fully trained for a boxing match. In an instant in court she had become a woman. Intuitively aware of this and the effect it had on Karen, Cheryl had touched her arm with a gentle pressure. It had surprised Karen to find that the thrill she had felt with Cheryl's touch had been new to her. She was physically drawn to the writer, but of late had been weary of dynamic, sophisticated people. Karen longed to find a woman it would be restful to be with. Just a nice, quiet girl with no distracting ambition or talent of her own. Fame made it easy to get laid, but the side effects were a right bastard.

"I'll come straight to the point, Henry," a suddenly resolute Matthew was saying when Karen tuned back in to the sounds of the present. "Mrs Wyndham does not deserve to suffer the way she is suffering right now, and she certainly shouldn't be facing criminal charges."

Henry gave a vehement shake of his head, eyes a blank dark blue as he slanted a look at Karen. He spoke in the tone of a man who was supremely confident that he knew right from wrong. "Our first duty is to you, Master Matthew, and you were badly hurt. We seek only justice for you."

"You have it wrong, Henry. My being injured was rough justice. I was caught cheating on my loyal wife, breaking my marriage vows, a transgression for which I got my just deserts."

The clicking of needles slowed as this had the Drurys thinking. Karen was excited by the step Matthew had taken, and putting something over on the old fuckers was even more exciting. She needed an uplifting victory, however small. In recent days she had passed through too many emotional phases: apprehension, indignation, revulsion – everything but love.

Henry Drury changed position in his chair, making a lot of noise. This would seem to indicate that he had reached a decision. Nellie Drury suddenly ceased her knitting, as if unconsciously conditioned to react to the scrape of a chair leg. It had become warm. The sun struck the skylight obliquely to cast a bright and uncomfortable reflection in the room, resurrecting the smell that had sickened Karen on arrival.

"You will appreciate, Master Matthew," Henry said sombrely, "that what you are asking is an important matter of conscience to us. At this stage I am prepared only to say I will discuss this with Mrs Drury and inform you of our decision. "

It was obvious that this was all they were going to get at that time. Karen, who was due back at the studio in less than an hour, stood ready to leave. Getting slowly to his feet, Matthew issued the nearest thing to a threat he would ever make to the Drurys. "This matter requires your urgent attention, Henry, and I hope to have an answer from you first thing tomorrow morning. It will be best for all concerned if your answer is favourable to Mrs Wyndham."

When they were back in the main part of the house, Henry said that he would drive her to the studio, but Karen insisted that he should spend the afternoon resting. Getting her Mercedes-Benz 380SL convertible, her prize possession from the garage, Karen drove as fast as the London traffic would allow.

On her right a huge building was under construction. As yet a steel and concrete embryo, it had the usual gathering of people, those who were doing things and those who like to watch them doing things. A typical London scene.

The buildings along the Embankment seemed friendly, somehow almost human in the steamy halo of a summer afternoon, and no longer aloof as they did in the harsh glare of winter. Stopping at traffic lights, Karen watched a woman carefully tending a window box outside of a white-painted house, training the tendrils of a pot-grown vine. It was pleasant to imagine that with care and patience the little garden would one day grow. She was pleased not to have lost interest in the simpler things of life.

A driver on the opposite side of the road was covertly eyeing her, either wondering if she was who he thought she was, or mentally shagging her. His face reddened and he turned away, made gauche and embarrassed by the steady gaze Karen had turned on him. Sitting beside him was a sultry dark-haired girl whose brown-skinned shoulders were bare. Lighting a cigarette, the girl blew a long column of smoke out between her red-painted lips and looked at Karen.

The lights changed and the brief encounter was over. There was said to be no meeting without consequence. What could the lustful stare of a man and the jealous glare of his woman possibly lead to? That theory was probably just another load of balls, the same as the crap that reckoned it was better to journey than to arrive. Karen couldn't wait to get out of the nose-to-tail traffic and into the studio. Once she was there, doing what she was good at, her self-esteem would be restored. She needed that, as her mind had curled into a tight grey ball on the night of Matthew's birthday bash. Would it ever unwind? Karen doubted that it would.

She was driving along residential streets now in which other families lived, and other homes housed their own secrets and sorrows, their own hates and boredoms, frustrations and troubles.

Nobody could know what went on in any of the houses she passed. Or why.

She turned the car into a deserted side street, then gunned the motor to swing with a squealing of tyres into the studio car park. Manoeuvring into her personal car space, she parked, took her handbag from the car, and reached to the back shelf for the Stetson she would be wearing in a Spanish nightclub scene that afternoon. After putting the wide-brimmed hat on her head at an angle, she locked the door of the car, shouldered the handbag, and walked away.

Outside the studio's main door, several young women were waiting like predators for the chance of meeting someone famous. Karen's arrival caused a stir among them. They were ardent fans who probably knew the dates of her menstrual periods better than she did. One of them, tall and slender, obviously urged on by the others, detached herself from them and walked confidently towards Karen.

Dodging round the girl, leaving her gobsmacked, Karen hurried on in through the door. She felt nothing at having snubbed the pathetically keen fan. People had to stop being people for celebrities, the way money stops being money for a bank clerk.

As she entered the studio, John Brighton noticed the Stetson and greeted her with the lines of the song *Una Paloma Blanca*: "No one can take my freedom away..."

"Get fucked," Karen moodily muttered.

"OK. When you have fifteen minutes free," Brighton willingly agreed.

"One and a half minutes, if my memory serves me correctly," Karen sarcastically remarked as she passed on by.

She went along the dark corridor that was flanked by dressing rooms, determined to throw herself into her work that afternoon. That way she might be able to blank out worry over whether the Drurys would let her off the hook. Sex was another means of escape. After the shooting was over and providing she could get rid of Martha, who constantly hovered like a shite-hawk, she would give the blonde what she had been asking for, begging for, since coming to the studio. Paula was a nice kid who had a nuclear-reactor effect on Karen's libido, while, conversely, having an almost mesmerising calming effect on the rest of her.

Opening the dressing room door, Karen stood transfixed by shock. Martha was standing, backside against the dressing table, head back, eyes closed, mouth open, with Paula Monroe crouched in front of her, head between her legs. Several more Marthas with more Paulas going down on them met her gaze in the mirrors of dressing tables; the fornicating couple were multiplied all around the room.

Karen screamed an unearthly scream that had John Brighton running down the corridor. Slamming the dressing room door in his face, a wrathful Karen advanced on the new girl star and the ageing dresser, who, having disengaged, cowered before her.

The evening sun was filtering through London's heavy air, pressuring a golden light onto the city. Sitting on the balcony of her apartment at the top of the tall, elegant building with Cheryl, Wendi was both pleased and a little amused by her companion, who was looking in wide-eyed awed at the London skyline stretching away into the blur of a far distance. Immediately below the balcony was a communal garden, the pleasant greenery of which set South Kensington above the rest of London,

"What a magnificent view, Wendi," Cheryl complimented her hostess.

"It offers two different worlds," Wendi said. She pointed out at the rooftops. "That sounds like an estate agent's spiel, doesn't it? Seriously, though, out there is twenty-first-century London, while down there" – she indicated the communal garden – "the nineteen twenties and thirties are preserved. It really is a time warp. In the summertime it's a scene of old England at its best. The ladies from the houses around the square invite their friends to sit with them among tubs of varicoloured flowers on the flat roofs of their dining rooms. Like gorgeous birds of prey in their colourful summer frocks, they genteelly sip tea and look down at the green lawns below where their well-schooled children play."

"I often think we are unfortunate not to have known that era," Cheryl wistfully remarked.

"And I'm up high enough to ensure privacy. On a hot summer's night I often come out here starkers to take an air bath. In a less adventurous way, I'm copying that great star Ava Gardner. When filming in Africa years ago she had all the local people horny by persistently walking around completely naked."

Cheryl smiled to herself.

Recognising this apparently innocuous expression as a sexual gambit, Wendi paused to find a way of putting into words a decision she had earlier made. They had enjoyed an intelligent conversation over dinner, during which they had stumbled on a rapport that had come as a complete surprise to them both. The same harmonious atmosphere was still with them as they sipped their drinks in the peace of an approaching twilight. But Cheryl was hinting that she was anticipating something more. Though

Wendi also felt a compelling physical urge for her new friend, she felt that to venture into intimacy now would ruin all that had gone before that evening.

Unsure of herself, she looked out of the window to where a mute melody of sunlight played off the windows and stonework of an office block. "I realise that I came onto you strong when you were here this morning. That's something that I intend to speak to you about, Cheryl. I suppose it would be best to begin by saying that I don't recall ever having enjoyed the company of anyone as I have being with you this evening."

"That's a compliment I can return," Cheryl said seriously. "I've had an absolutely wonderful time."

"I'm pleased to hear that. It helps with the point I'm trying to make."

"A point that you're having great difficulty with," Cheryl chided her good-naturedly.

"I am," Wendi confessed. "My problem is that I feel that there's something special between us. I know that I'm making a complete fool of myself."

"I can assure you that you're not, Wendi. I feel the same way."

"In that case, I hope that you, like me, will want our relationship to develop slowly and surely," Wendi, gaining confidence, said. "I've had all I can take of relationships that are heaven in bed and sheer hell out of it. To put it crudely, a mouthful of tit one moment, a mouthful of abuse the next."

Cheryl nodded. "Having experienced the kind of thing you're talking about, I'm unable to disagree with anything you've said, Wendi. But where do we go from here? Paths leading into the unknown can be dangerous. I'm physically attracted to you, and I'm pretty certain that you feel the same way about me. But it seems that you are suggesting a platonic relationship."

"I suppose that I'm looking for someone to change my life, to rearrange all the millions of cells that are me," Wendi confirmed.

"If we start off on a social basis, as we have this evening, then we can let everything find its own level. Sex will become a natural part of things, not some unstable cornerstone that we attempt to build on."

Going silent for some time, a silence so deep that it was almost audible, Cheryl had Wendi worried. She knew that she was seeking a relationship in reverse order, so to speak. The usual problem was that you inevitably became friends with whomever you were having sex with. You shared their hopes and ambitions, their sorrows and their joys. Love might grow strong but passion would weaken as you listened to their problems. Wendi's novel idea was that love could survive if it came first, with sex following at a sedate pace.

"It's an intriguing proposition, Wendi, and it could work."

"I'd like to think so, Cheryl."

"So would I, but it will require honesty from the very beginning, and I have to own up to something. When I called on you the first time I..."

A sense within Wendi, a familiar voice, told her to interrupt. "You came on behalf of Matthew Wyndham and Karen to silence me. Having gone into my past, you were ready to threaten to expose me."

"Good heavens, Wendi. What are you, a psychic? A Mystic Meg?"

"Wacky Wendy, more like," Wendi laughed. "No, I'm just intuitive. Research is a major part of your job, and you would be easily able to find out that I went off the rails when I was younger."

"What you say is true," a shame-faced Cheryl admitted. "You made the threat unnecessary, but I don't believe that I could have carried it through, anyway."

"Having got to know you, I don't think that you would have been able to," Wendi assured her with a smile. She added soberly. "I make no excuses for my past, except perhaps for dropping out of university, which was entirely my fault. All of the rest, travelling the

West Country fairgrounds, stripping with a show, and starving in a bedsit while I tried to sell double-glazing, was down to me. I was good at striptease, but a bloody awful salesgirl. Eventually, more from good luck than good planning, I made it into show business."

"Where you met Karen Cayson?"

Detecting a hint of jealousy in Cheryl's voice thrilled Wendi. She would be more than jealous if she knew the truth. That time in Karen's flat with Frankie had become more torrid as each minute had passed. While Frankie and Wendi were tongue kissing, Karen had slid her mouth up the inside of one of Frankie's thighs. Obeying some instinctive command, Frankie opened her legs and Karen's mouth, her tongue parting dark pubic hair to clear the way, was sucking and licking at the blood-engorged, distended lips of Frankie's cunt. Enjoying the kissing as the other woman had teetered on the edge of sexual insanity, Wendi slid a warm hand up between her own thighs, parting the drooping lips of her own cunt to slide a finger in, slipping and sliding up her, moving to create suction and friction.

Fingers slippery with her own juice, eyes closed, Wendi had heard Frankie give a little squeal. Then Frankie had taken Wendi's lower lip between her teeth. An oddly whimpering bleat had escaped from Frankie as she reached orgasm. It had been a dramatic, traumatic come, and Wendi had quickened the movement of her finger to bring herself off at the same time.

"That was when I met Karen Cayson," Wendi replied to Cheryl, after winning the struggle to push the erotic memories of that night to one side in her mind.

"The start of a wonderful romance," Cheryl commented cryptically.

"The start of something," Wendi confirmed with a nod.

She accepted a cigarette from Cheryl. When Wendi's gold

lighter flared modestly, the little glow revealed and accentuated Cheryl's features in close-up. Wendi found her breathing quickening. The yellow flame lit Cheryl's face dramatically. She was stunning, radiating a sensuality that was heightened by her dark-brown watchful eyes.

"Karen is a nice person and fun to be with," Wendi continued. "But she couldn't offer what I'm looking for."

"The impossible dream."

"Do you believe it to be impossible, Cheryl?"

Cheryl shrugged. "Maybe, maybe not. You and I have got along so well together tonight that I think if any two people can dream the same dream, then we are the two."

"I'm more than willing to try."

"So am I," Cheryl volunteered quickly. "I imagine that Karen's very demanding. As a lover, I mean."

"Karen's demanding in many ways," Wendi replied. She could have added *especially* as a lover.

That night when Wendi had been lying on the bed with a half-conscious Frankie in her arms, Karen's head, her red hair in total disarray, had come up from between Frankie's shapely thighs. Reaching up to put a hand behind Wendi's head, she had pulled her towards her. Eyes heavy-lidded with sex, lips parted ready to kiss, Karen had brought her face close to Wendi's.

Deterred for a split second as she had caught the strong aroma of Frankie's sex from Karen's face and mouth, the scent of it had suddenly changed to become aphrodisiacal for Wendi. With a driving urge for both the taste of Karen's mouth and to savour what the actress had licked from Frankie's cunt, Wendi had kissed her passionately.

The kiss had gone on and on. Stirred deeply by it, Wendi had become aware of the insistent pulse of her throbbing cunt. Her fingers and toes were tingling in time with the sexual rhythm between her legs as Karen had laid her back on the bed beside a still lifeless Frankie. She had made no protest as she felt Karen, still holding the kiss, push her dress up, feel for her panties and pull them down.

Hating the slump of passion she had experienced when Karen had stopped kissing her to stand up, Wendi had watched her own black panties thrown to one side on the bed. Then she had allowed Karen to spread her legs. The actress had stared avidly at her cunt. Wendi had become a little frightened of her own passion, which had been building to the point of being overpowering.

Turning Wendi onto her side, Karen had run her face across the cheeks of her bum, giving little kisses all along the way. Then she was nosing into the cleft between Wendi's buttocks, her anus and the insides of her upper thighs before kissing the underhang, where a veil of sweat had formed in the heat of the room.

To Wendi's chagrin, Karen stopped suddenly and stood up, exclaiming, "Now it's your turn, Wendi."

"I came when Frankie did," Wendi had breathlessly told her.

"That was a feeble puff compared with the thrill I'm about to give you." Karen had wagged a finger at her.

Puzzled, Wendi had watched Karen walk off to the drink cabinet. Not knowing what to expect, Wendi had heard the scraping sound of ice being taken from its container. Frankie had been stirring beside Wendi on the bed as Karen walked back. The actress had had two small and chunky lumps of ice, glistening like clear crystals, in her right hand. Smiling a sensual smile at Wendi, Karen had popped the ice cubes into her mouth and lowered herself between Wendi's thighs. She had felt Karen's mouth gently kiss her puffy-lipped, sopping-wet cunt. It had been a pleasant sensation, but nothing spectacular for a woman as experienced as Wendi. It had thrilled her to realise that Frankie had propped herself up on one elbow to observe what Karen was doing to Wendi.

Then everything had changed for Wendi in an instant. Karen's mouth had opened her up. The tongue Karen slid into her had been icy cold. Never had Wendi known anything so mind-blowingly exciting inside of her. She had been licked, sucked, titillated, all in an icily cold way, an ecstasy that was in contradiction almost unbearable. She had felt Karen slide both hands under her buttocks. She had been lifted a little and her cunt pulled tightly against Paula's mouth.

The exquisite torment increased as Karen's tongue went even further into her. Karen started up a rhythmic in-and-out sliding movement. Each time her top teeth had brought excruciating pleasure to Wendi's clitoris, so had the icy tongue gone deeper into her. Allowing herself to be guided by the expert Karen, Wendi had begun to move her lower body in time, thrusting and jerking in the sweeping rhythms of love. Hearing a scream of pleasure, Wendi had been shocked to realise that it had come from her as her body arched violently, writhing from side to side. Then she had let out another wild shriek as she reached dynamic orgasm.

With difficulty, Wendi brought herself out of an erotic past into the convivial present as she heard Cheryl say, "But it's all over between you now?"

"It has been for quite a long time," Wendi answered. "Perhaps it's because I'm getting older, but all of my relationships seem so frivolous in retrospect."

"You sound as if you're ready for the female-on-female equivalent of the pipe-and-slippers syndrome," Cheryl observed with a light laugh.

"I hope I'm a long way from being in my dotage," Wendi giggled. "But I do seem to need stability. Do I frighten you, Cheryl, with this unexpected deluge of words, emotion and love?"

Reaching out a hand, laying it gently on Wendi's, their fingers entwining, Cheryl said, "No way. Honestly, you are the most marvellous woman I have ever met. Mind you, I think that maybe you're some kind of a witch. But I want what you want, and nothing worth having comes easily."

Pouring each of them another glass of wine, Wendi raised her glass. "Here's to an uncertain future."

"To a happy future."

They clinked glasses.

Ten

"I thought that you would be terribly angry with me," Paula said in a fearful, quiet voice. Until Karen had walked in on her and Martha in the dressing room, Paula's new life had been a happy, rolling-along thing, energised each day by thrilling new experiences.

Wishing that everything could revert to what it had been, clean and fresh and eternal, she was having a break for refreshments with Karen while John Brighton organised the next shoot. One of the hardest tasks Paula had had was to become friendly and stay friendly with the crude John Brighton. She abhorred the way he vulgarised the acting profession by advising Karen and her before each scene to, "Accentuate the orifices in your body for the camera. When it comes down to it that's really the only parts of you that those fuckers out there are interested in."

There were noisy arguments going on ow between Brighton and the floor manager, Brighton and several cameramen, Brighton and the props man. Foul language turned the air blue. Standing across the studio, as aloof as ever, was Don Ricci, the male lead in *Beach of Fear.* Though not tall, he was dark and handsome and smiled continuously but coldly. There was never any warmth in his eyes. He seemed only half human, an example of what self-regard can do to a man. Paula, like Karen and most of the rest of the cast, detested him.

Pushing the ice around in her Coke with her straw industriously for several seconds, Karen then said, "You weren't responsible, Paula. I put full blame on Martha."

Paula had tried to blame Martha for changing both her and her unquestioning adoration of Karen. But that was unfair. She had been as eager for sex with Martha as Martha had been to make love to her. But, dreading that being caught i*n flagrante* would mean her being sacked from the studio, perhaps even before *Beach of Fear* was in the can, Paula wasn't about to sacrifice herself. Even so, she felt real bad about Martha, who was said to be on sick leave. Paula suspected that "on sick leave" was a euphemism for "dismissed".

"I feel that I'm to blame, Karen," she answered coyly and her little-girl coyness moved Karen to put out a hand to touch her shoulder.

"You mustn't. Just leave me to deal with it," Karen said firmly. There was an odd note to her tone and her eyes were watching Paula carefully. "I should tell you that there are going to be some big changes here in the very near future."

"You don't mean...?"

Convinced that she was about to hear bad news, Paula was unable to complete her sentence. She waited for Karen's reply, barely breathing, barely *able* to breathe.

"You're expecting to get the big E, aren't you?"

"Well, I... I'm... I thought..." Paula stuttered and stammered.

"I know what you thought." Karen smiled fondly at Paula, slipping a reassuring arm around her waist, moving her hand up to slyly cup a full breast. "Take my word for it, Paula, your future lies here. In a very short time you will be this studio's hottest property, its biggest star."

"Second biggest," a blushing but deliriously happy Paula modestly corrected her. "I could never equal you, Karen."

With a shake of her head, Karen insisted. "The *biggest* star, Paula. As I said just now, there are going to be some big changes here. I will be concentrating on the management side of things after we've done this film."

"You can't be serious, Karen," Paula protested. "Your fans would never allow it."

"Perhaps I'll find time to appear in the occasional film," Karen's vanity had her concede. "But right now we'd better get back to work. Here comes the poor man's Alfred Hitchcock – more hitch than cock, believe me."

Seeing Brighton heading their way, Paula used a hand to conceal her laughter. "You are terrible, Karen."

"John is a sure and certain cure for penis envy," Karen chuckled.

Still on a high from bossing his inferiors around, wearing his studio rank like a cape of royalty, John Brighton swept up to them. A garlicky smell hung over him from the previous night. He looked Karen over, taking in the silken Pucci minisheath that she wore. Though he managed to show a smile, annoyance crossed his red-purple face like a quick shadow.

Brighton consulted the clipboard he held in the crook of one arm. "This is the scene where Paula rushes excitedly into the house to tell you about this great guy that she's met, Karen. That means that right now you should be casual, in jeans and a sweater."

"But you're shooting that in between the two disco scenes that have me wearing this dress," Karen argued. Her face was expressionless, but the tendons in her neck were taut against her skin as she went on. "If you shoot the two disco things first I'll need to change clothes only once instead of twice."

Thumping his forehead with the heel of his hand, Brighton groaned before angrily rebuking Karen. "I'm running this show, Karen, and I choose the shooting schedule." He went on sarcastically. "You can give the orders when you are in charge."

"That may well be sooner than you think, John." Karen shrugged, but that simple gesture implied much.

Throwing his head back in uproarious laughter, Brighton spluttered, "If that should ever happen, then I won't be here."

"Many a true word spoken in jest, John," Karen warned as she flounced off to the dressing room.

Seeing a suddenly serious John Brighton watching Karen go, Paula was shaken to realise that he appeared to be a worried man. A very worried man. She was shocked into staring silence. The strong-minded Karen was planning something big. The star was obviously going down a route that was well plotted, and appeared confident that the challenge had been met and the prizes already attained.

Paula discovered that she inexplicably felt every bit as uneasy as John Brighton looked.

Late that afternoon, the obsequious Henry Drury, freshly efficient in a brilliant white coat that was as stiff as a straitjacket, black tie and knife-creased trousers, admitted Richard Neehan to the Wyndham residence. Neehan, for all his confidence both in everyday life and in the courtrooms of the land, felt apprehensive as always when about to meet Matthew Wyndham, especially when they met on the mogul's home ground. Apprehension was perhaps the wrong word. It was a strange telepathic thing, as if Matthew consciously or unconsciously used some kind of mental energy to prise Neehan's mind loose from its moorings so that he couldn't get his thoughts properly organised. Matthew's relationship with Karen confused Neehan further. Though Wyndham worshipped his wife and Neehan didn't doubt that Karen loved him, they both had opposing, secret agendas. This caused constant battles in the unseen world of the mind that had a powerful effect on Neehan. It was like being in a house that was haunted not by the dead but by the living.

Matthew rose to greet him with the same direct action he would have shown in a pub or club. Despite his effort to appear his old hard-driven self, there was a lethargy about him that he couldn't hide. Neehan glimpsed a Matthew Wyndham who was no longer so sure of himself as he appeared to be. At times a slight hesitation betrayed that something was wrong at the centre of the man. He was saddened by the speed at which the signs of Matthew's terminal illness were showing through.

"Take a seat, Richard," Wyndham offered genially. "I'll delay playing the perfect host and pouring you a drink until after you've given me the good news."

Sitting on a downy-cushioned sofa with his briefcase across his knees, Neehan looked grave as he announced, "I'm afraid there is no good news, Matthew."

"Henry Drury hasn't been in touch?"

"I'm afraid not," Neehan replied. "I fear that the Drurys feel that their position here is secure regardless."

"I impressed upon them that Karen must come first." A dismayed and disappointed Matthew put his head in his hands.

Looking at him, Neehan didn't know whether to feel pity or contempt. The old guy was using love as a pretence to justify sex with a lovely young woman. It probably wasn't worth the charade. It was Neehan's guess that Karen Cayson was as selfish in bed as she was out of it. One shot at marriage had put Neehan off for life. He had since tongue-in-cheek wished many couples good luck and within a year the ones not having an affair were desperate to do so, and the ones having an affair were desperately unhappy.

At the very beginning he had joined Doc Williams by tactfully advising Matthew that marrying Karen could well be a mistake. But the madly-in-love Matthew had declared that he could handle it.

"Ignoring the rules is the key to my success. Everything comes with a set of rules, Richard," Matthew had explained at that time, "and to make anything work, even a relationship, like a marriage between Karen and myself, we are supposed to be addicted to the rules. Take the so-called Christians. They are not worshipping Jesus Christ, but jumping idiotically up and down to a set of rules he never even mentioned when he was on earth."

There were some rules that Matthew would do well to obey, Neehan thought as he brought his mind back to the current business. "I regret to say that the Drurys seem to believe it safe to ignore your warning, Matthew." Opening his briefcase, he took out a legal document and passed it to Wyndham.

"What's this?" Matthew, taking the paper, held it at arm's length.

"It's what I suggest you allow me to serve on the Drurys. Read it through, Matthew, and I'm sure that you'll concur it is the way ahead."

Matthew passed it back to Neehan. "I can't read a frigging thing without my glasses. You tell me what it says, Richard, but spare me the legal jargon."

"Fundamentally," Neehan began in his best courtroom voice, "it terminates the Drurys' employment and their tenancy of the servants' quarters here in exactly four weeks."

"What!" Matthew Wyndham shouted in anger and disbelief. "This would give them a cast-iron case to drag me through every industrial tribunal in the land. I'm dying, for God's sake. I'm preparing to meet angels, not a bunch of pricks in silly wigs and gowns. I don't want the hassle."

"Neither do you want your wife in prison," Neehan calmly reminded him. "If you had read this through as I asked, Matthew, you would know that I have protected you. This notice tells the Drurys that you urgently require the quarters they occupy to house the nursing staff you are engaging to take care of you in your illness. I've been in touch with Doc Williams, and he is preparing a letter to that effect."

With a long, whistling sigh of admiration, an incredulous Wyndham exclaimed, "You're such a devious fucker, Richard, that you scare me."

"I'm on your side, Matthew." Neehan sat back in his chair and folded his arms.

"Only because I pay you," Wyndham cynically observed. "Financial consideration and friendship are not necessarily joined to the same body, Richard."

"I would like to think there is something other than money between us, Matthew."

"My time is too short to indulge in sentimentality, Richard," Wyndham said. "Even so, because I'm a soft old prick, I feel sorry for the Drurys."

"That's not necessary, Matthew. I'll take this down to them now, and within an hour they will come running to me ready to withdraw their statements against your wife. Think what that will mean to you and Karen, Matthew."

Neehan looked at his client, puzzled as to why his prediction didn't have Wyndham as elated as he'd anticipated. He was citing illness for the surprising lack of response, when the sick man, speaking despondently, came at him from an unexpected angle.

"Why isn't it possible to pinpoint when the loving stopped and the hating began, Richard? I'd like to be able to set a date for it, to mark it on the calendar like some kind of anniversary."

Neehan was unable to reply because he didn't know to what Wyndham was referring. Then it dawned on him that the old man was talking about Karen, and Neehan didn't *want* to reply. Karen Cayson would allow nothing, not even a very sick husband, to stand in the way of her eternal pursuit of fame and fortune.

It was late in the evening when they went in through pretentious mock-gilded double doors of the Oceanic club. Cheryl found that entering the place was like landing on an alien planet. She regretted having accepted Karen's mysterious but insistent invitation. "It's both business and pleasure, Cheryl," Karen had half-explained on the telephone. "I need your brains for the business, and where pleasure is concerned I owe you for the Wendi Maylor thing." But Karen had offered nothing further since collecting Cheryl from home and driving her here.

The building was a modern slab of polished concrete and blue-toned glass. The club was crowded, the air was stuffy with perfume and body heat and the noise was close to intolerable. Couples writhed on a cramped dance floor. Together, but separated by modern dance, they performed movements that were oddly convulsive, very sexual but at the same time impersonal. A few girls weren't dancing but stood as onlookers, minor attendant-goddesses.

Leaning close to Karen to compete with the thump-thump of music, Cheryl said, "I've always preferred the behaviour of the plebs to that of the patricians, Karen. But right now I'm not so sure."

Laughing, Karen shouted back, "Whose side will you be on when the revolution comes, Cheryl?"

"My own."

Together they cautiously weaved through the dancers to reach a far corner of the room, where a small office was partitioned from the rest of the club by glass. Cheryl saw a Pierce Brosnan lookalike sitting behind a desk inside. He stood as they walked in.

Resplendent in a velvet tuxedo, a lace shirt and a drooping bowtie, the club owner wore a defensive expression as the two of them walked softly across the carpeted, brightly lit room. Then he put square, brilliant-white teeth on show in a welcoming smile.

"I'm glad that we found you here, Malcolm," Karen said as she shook his hand. "This is Cheryl Valenta, my friend. Cheryl, meet Malcolm Reay."

Cheryl was acutely aware of Reay's dark-blue eyes turning black as he looked at her when Karen introduced them. Yet, despite this odd feature, Reay had an unexpected and easy friendliness as he took Cheryl's hand. "Not Cheryl Valenta the columnist?"

It was plain Reay was expecting a rewarding response. A platitude is a great icebreaker, and has the best effect when spoken by an attractive woman. But Cheryl only confirmed her identity with a curt nod. She knew Reay's type. They had the values of a caveman, and the instincts of a piranha. Before moving from a neutral position, she needed to know what Karen and she were doing here.

"Then, as a devoted admirer, let me welcome you to the Oceanic," Reay gushed. He turned to Karen. "I'm usually here at this time of an evening. The fact is that I make a point of visiting each of our clubs every evening. That way I can keep an eye on things. Drugs have become a matter of great concern in this business."

Indicating the dancers with a nod, Cheryl pulled a face. "They'd have to be on something to enjoy that racket."

"It's an acquired taste, Cheryl," Reay said, unable to conceal that he was slightly offended. "Sadly, perhaps, the days of Dean Martin and Perry Como are long gone. Days that would mean nothing to those youngsters out there."

"Times change," Karen said pseudo-philosophically, "and I'm going to make sure that the studios keep up with the times, Cheryl. Malcolm is exactly the kind of high flyer I will need to drag the Wyndham organisation belatedly into the twenty-first century, and he is interested."

Cheryl heard a cautious Reay say a soft-voiced, "Tentatively interested," as the full import of what Karen had said hit her. It brought a chill down her back. As far as the soulless Karen was concerned, Matthew was already dead and buried.

"How interested?" Karen sharply quizzed the club owner.

"Not enough to stop me wondering why I'm being offered a stake in a thriving company, Karen," Reay hedged. "I'm a naturally suspicious person."

"You are a go-ahead entrepreneur, Malcolm, who is well known and highly respected in America," Karen said. "Last year, Matthew put out some feelers in the States, and got promising responses from a high number of television companies. Cheryl did a piece on it at the time. At the studios we have the technical knowledge, the facilities and the actors to turn out exactly what they are looking for. I've presently got my eye on a girl who will be the biggest UK star since Diana Dors. I've told Cheryl nothing about the negotiations between us, but I'm sure that, as an independent party, she'll support what I am saying."

"Cheryl?" Reay invited with a raised eyebrow.

So, this was why Karen invited her along! Though she didn't care for being used in this way, Cheryl was capable of shrugging off her annoyance. What upset her was that she had been drawn into Karen's cold-hearted plot against her ailing husband. She resolved to keep her involvement to a minimum.

"I do recall that there was tremendous interest in Matthew's proposals," she told Reay. "But I also remember that what the people in the States wanted would mean expanding the studios considerably."

"Exactly," Karen put in. "Which is why I need your input, Malc."

Still not convinced, Reay asked, "Why didn't Matthew expand?"

"Matthew, despite his amazing business acumen, has never managed to lever himself free from the nineteen sixties," Karen explained. "Now, of course, it's too late even if he could be persuaded."

Cheryl's sympathy was with Matthew. At his time of life, the capacity to be moulded into new forms had been lost. This was a serious handicap in a fast-changing world. The eternal conflict between age and youth was quietly raging between him and his wife.

"Let's say for the sake of argument that I am interested, Karen. What do you see as our next move?"

Karen became thoughtful. "Well, I don't want Matthew to get wind of this, so I can't have Richard Neehan draw up a document. What do you suggest, Malcolm?"

"There's nothing personal in what I am going to say, Karen, but you will appreciate that I need something more than blind trust. If I have my solicitor prepare a document that meets with your approval, will you sign it?"

"Of course, most willingly."

"I'll need to know what share I'm being offered."

Nibbling at her lower lip, Karen said, "Would ten per cent be acceptable?"

"Most generous," a surprised Reay answered. "I'll get everything organised and give you a buzz when your signature is required."

Karen and Reay shook hands, but Cheryl gave the club owner no more than a curt nod in parting. Then she and Karen cut themselves a new route through the dancers and out into the comparative coolness of late evening. Not for the first time, Cheryl noticed how a London dusk descended straight from the sky, whereas in rural areas it rolled in from the horizon. She did not know why that bothered her, but was aware that a need to fathom the unfathomable had long been a curse for her.

The balmy languidness of the soft summer twilight gave them a false feeling of freshness. In contrast to the discordant blare of music they had just escaped from, the sounds of a gospel choir practising in a church across the road had a sedating effect.

"That's a load off my mind," Karen breathed thankfully as they got into her car. "I owe you a double thank-you now, Cheryl. Let's go to my place and we'll order a takeaway, then crack open a bottle in celebration."

Smiling contentedly, Karen started the engine and drove off, heading for her flat in Holborn. There was a mean glassiness to her eyes, and there was a pouty bitterness about her kissable mouth. Cheryl had noticed that Karen's business discussion with Malcolm Reay had awoken something primitive within her. That wildness hadn't completely subsided. It remained with her now, semidormant and menacing in a peculiar way.

Sitting silent in the front passenger seat, commiserating with the unsuspecting and terminally ill Matthew Wyndham, Cheryl Valenta had not the slightest desire to celebrate.

The fashionable King Henry wouldn't have been Matthew Wyndham's choice. Unlike the nearby Molly Maguire, with its

Irish music and lively characters, or the George, which had stayed back in his beloved 1960s when the rest of the world moved on, the King Henry had no personality, not even with its curved windows that seemed to be part illusion, part glass. Good pubs had clocks that didn't work and poor ventilation, so that you could spend a great evening totally ignorant of the time and the weather.

But Emmett Foyle had said to meet him here, and the assistant commissioner was calling the shots right then. The illuminated mirror clock behind the bar advertised the local brewery and told Wyndham that it was 8.35. Feeling absolutely shagged, he rested both elbows on the bar and wondered what he was doing in this poxy place, when he could have insisted on meeting Foyle at Molly's, where the atmosphere was gracious. Or, better still, at home in bed. That was where Karen thought he was, and where he should be. Never in his life had he felt so totally fucked up as he did right then.

The barman came up to him now. He had one of those haven't-I-seen-you-on-television? looks on his young and effeminate face. But he had the good sense not to enquire, and restricted himself to the professional necessities with, "What will it be, sir?"

Wyndham broke into a sweat as attempted a reply. Then he stopped sweating because his body had rapidly dried out and his tongue did a thick, rasping working across his lips. A lot of thoughts rushed through his mind, but most of all he thought of how ill he felt and the shame he would feel if he collapsed in public. A burgeoning regret at coming here was swiftly defeated by his determination to help his wife. For all her tough public image and her Mae West-style wisecracks, Karen was a tender-hearted girl pushed to breaking point by the criminal charges against her.

"Sir?" the barman questioned.

Still unable to summon the energy for a reply, Wyndham was saved by the voice of Emmett Foyle, which came from behind him. "I'll get these. Two Scotch on the rocks, please, barman. Bring them to that table in the corner." Foyle's smile vanished when he spotted how sick Wyndham looked.

Wyndham had to blink twice in quick succession before he could see Foyle clearly. Helped psychologically rather than physically by Foyle's hand under his elbow, Wyndham sank with relief into a chair. Feeling a little easier, he was able to take heed of his surroundings. There was more than a touch of class in the dark-wood walls, blue carpeting and blue velvet draperies. Despite the casual dress of some of those around him, it wasn't a cheap crowd. There was no strobe lighting or chromium. The long bar was an antique mahogany masterpiece. A quartet played soft, sweet music from a niche that could double as a stage if necessary. Body fragrances were mixed into a potpourri of heady smells that had no individual identity.

"Drink up, Matthew, you look terrible," Foyle said.

"It'll pass, Emmett." Wyndham spoke with a confidence that he didn't feel.

"If I'd known how ill you are I would have come to your home, Matthew," a regretful Foyle said. "I do hope that coming here hasn't put too much of a strain on you. Nothing is important enough for you to take a risk like this."

"I came here for Karen, who is the most important thing in my life, Emmett."

"I appreciate that.," Foyle smiled kindly. "And you will welcome what I'm about to tell you, Matthew. Whatever method of persuasion you used on your servants, it worked brilliantly. Karen will receive a letter from the Metropolitan Police in the morning. All charges have been dropped. The case is now closed."

"Thank the Lord," Wyndham sighed, his eyes closed. This put a blessing on everything. "Dear Karen will be so relieved."

"Shall we drink to her?" Foyle suggested as he raised his glass.

But Wyndham, who had become suddenly and strangely detached, didn't raise his glass. With both hands on the table, fists knotted, he was summoning the strength to get to his feet. He lowered his voice to a confidential whisper. "I need to get to the gents', Emmett, urgently."

Standing up quickly, Foyle reached out to assist the sick man, but before he could reach him, Wyndham keeled over sideways and crashed flat out on the floor.

"Why do you ask?"

Sitting with her legs curled under her on a settee, squinting against smoke from her cigarette, Karen studied Cheryl, making her feel uncomfortable for having enquired about Paula Monroe. They'd had an excellent meal delivered, and had sipped expensive wine. The conversation should be flowing easily now as they sat enjoying coffee, but it wasn't.

"It's just that I met her when she first arrived in London. She seemed a nice kid, but very vulnerable."

It occurred to Cheryl that she was making excuses to herself. Maybe what she had said wasn't true. Her interest in the blonde Paula may once have been as carnal as it had been caring, but Cheryl had changed since meeting Wendi Maylor. No longer promiscuous, the young Basingstoke girl – having been taken under Karen's wing, so to speak – now worried her. Being rocketed fast to the top in show business often proved to be far more problematic than never making it. Cheryl doubted that Paula was equipped to cope successfully with the trauma that was a part of either success or failure. She was definitely a candidate for exploitation, for the young girl had the vacuous look of an eternal student with no interest in anything other than the next game of tennis. It would be a crime if Karen killed the child in Paula, the fairy-tale believer.

Karen's lips struggled with a tentative smile. Then the smile took hold and moved up to include her eyes. "I think that you're fibbing, Cheryl. Come on, now, own up. You fancy the sweet little Paula?"

"Not particularly," Cheryl shrugged. "That's an honest answer, Karen. Now it's your turn to be frank."

"Paula's different, excitingly different." Karen's pale brow creased. Then she smiled. White teeth flashed and dimples dimpled. "I launched her career, Cheryl, and if she wishes to show her gratitude I won't stop her."

"The lesbian version of the casting couch," Cheryl remarked, sounding more critical than she had intended.

"You make it sound seedy," Karen complained. "The casting couch was an altar on which the would-be actress sacrificed herself. Paula is under no obligation. She's going places whether she comes across with the goods or not. It would be better for her if she did, as an actress is at her best if she has sex immediately before a performance. It gets the adrenaline coursing through the system."

"That sounds like a crafty excuse for a shag." A disbelieving Cheryl smiled.

"No, it's true," Karen contradicted her. "I know several singers who fuck in the dressing room just prior to going on stage. They swear that it mellows the voice." She casually tacked on a question that was far from casual. "Do you feel like singing right now, Cheryl?"

Karen stood and stretched, catlike. The olive-green dress that she wore was as tight as a second skin. Cheryl was certain that she was red-haired upstairs and downstairs. Tall and full-figured, with long legs that went on for ever, Karen was beautiful, gorgeous, exquisite, divine, the whole shebang. Her question had been blatant, but it surprised Cheryl that Karen didn't push for an answer. Her slinky walk as she went behind a Formica-topped bar stirred Cheryl.

Looking around the spacious expensively furnished apartment, Cheryl thought that Wendi had once sat where she was sitting now, also waiting for Karen to pour drinks. It made her jealous to think of Karen and Wendi having sex here in this room. A quick analysis suggested to Cheryl that she was in love. Madly and deeply in love for the first time in her life. She still wanted the luscious Karen, but now that urge had become something to resist rather than be indulged. The pact that she and Wendi had made demanded fidelity.

Was hope of a monogamous relationship a delusion? They both desperately wanted it to work, but Cheryl feared that was wishful thinking. Reality had a way of invading the most strongly defended mythical kingdoms. Now she regarded Karen as the first big test. A test that she was determined to pass.

Karen Cayson came out from behind the bar with two glasses, each a tall gin and tonic. She gave one to Cheryl, whose fingers slipped a little as she took it, causing a tiny amount of drink to splash over the rim. An embarrassed Cheryl got out of her chair to place the glass on a table. Sitting on her heels she dabbed at the small damp spot on the blue and gold carpet with her handkerchief.

"It's nothing, Cheryl, leave it," Karen said as she came over to squat beside her.

Cheryl realised that the summer skirt that she had on still covered her upper thighs, but the fullness of it allowed it to drop away below. Though struggling to find something to concentrate on, Karen could not keep her eyes away from the darkness between Cheryl's legs.

"Don't worry about it, Cheryl. It's only that one tiny spot," Karen said, looking around.

Thoughtlessly, Cheryl spread her thighs apart as she, too, looked for more alcohol stains. She realised her mistake as Karen's hand slid up between her legs to reach where the crotch of Cheryl's bikini briefs tightly contained the bulge of her quim.

Attempting to get away, Cheryl only succeeded in falling over backwards, which to Karen doubtlessly looked both lusty and intentional. Closing her legs was another mistake, as in doing so she trapped Karen's hand between them. Expertly getting a crooked middle finger inside of Cheryl's panties, Karen gave a practised tug that freed the crotchpiece away. Karen's middle finger straightened to part Cheryl's pubic hair and locate and open lips that were already swollen and pouting.

Slowly but relentlessly in small, shunting movements, the finger moved further into her. Cheryl's body disobeyed her. Love juices overlubricated Karen's finger, and her thighs were slackening and tensing to the rhythm set up by Karen's hand. Her head picked up the beat that had the pace of a ticking clock, as it turned sideways, back and forth, to avoid Karen's kisses, though her hips were jerking forward to the same pulsing rhythm.

Then she felt an awful coldness as Karen's finger slipped out completely. Then, joined by another finger, it was back, entering deep, filling her with a sensation of total eroticism. As the finger took on an irresistible, fucking movement, Karen's wrist sliding hotly against her clit, Cheryl's legs flew apart. Trying to recover herself, she caught her left foot in the leg of a chair. In a few moments she was out of control and squirming towards Karen, as Karen's mouth claimed hers.

With Karen on top of her, Cheryl clasped her tightly, running her hands over the firm swell of her buttocks as they kissed. It was a gasping, open-mouth, breath-and-saliva-exchanging kiss. One coherent thought ran through Cheryl's mind, telling her that if there was such a place as paradise, then she had entered it. Karen's two thrusting fingers speeded, threatening Cheryl with a fast-approaching orgasm.

Sensing that Cheryl was close to climaxing, and wanting to delay it, Karen ended the kiss, and Cheryl cried out in protest as Karen fully withdrew her fingers. Standing, a sultry Karen looked down at Cheryl through half-lidded eyes. Karen reached down to the hem of her green dress and pulled it off over her head, mussing her red hair in the process. Quickly, abstractedly, she removed her bra and panties. She stood posing for a moment, legs apart, pelvis thrust forward.

Looking up from where she lay on the thick-pile carpet, Cheryl thrilled at the sight of Karen's well-defined face; the firm set of her lean jaw; her long neck; her full breasts that proudly stood out from her body without the slightest sign of sag; the firm, the slightly bowed-out belly; her smooth thighs; the dark-red, bushy triangle of her womanhood.

But Karen had broken the spell when she had broken the kiss, bringing Cheryl's mind back from the verge of sexual abandon. Having retrieved at least some control, Cheryl was determined to resist the powerful temptation that was Karen. She raised herself up on one elbow, but Karen was too quick for her.

Tenderly using one hand to gently push Cheryl back down, the naked Karen came to kneel with a leg on each side of her chest, like a wrestler pinning an opponent to the floor. But Karen applied neither force nor her weight. Her pubes were only inches from Cheryl's face.

In a deliberate, seductively slow movement, Karen reached her hand down to her crotch. Intently watching Cheryl's face, pleased by the reaction she saw there, Karen stroked and pulled gently at her own pubic hair. Delving into it, she parted her labia and eased her fingers into her cunt. Thrusting and twisting, she widened the gap with movement that sounded wet and syrupy. Fingers glistening with her own love juice, she spoke huskily: "I know that you're longing to eat me out, Cheryl."

Unable to stop herself, Cheryl raised her head a little, while an obliging Karen thrust herself closer to her. Entranced by the mini-forest of hair that went on up into the crevice of Karen's bottom, fringing round her smaller opening, Cheryl pushed her face into it. A heady carnival of aromas assailed her nostrils. She opened her mouth and her tongue stretched up between Karen's held-apart lips. Breathing became difficult, but Cheryl didn't care. Suffocation meant nothing: she was ready to drown here.

Putting her right hand between own her legs, Cheryl fucked herself with her finger, manipulating her clitoris as she greedily licked Karen's saturated, throbbing cunt. She could tell from

Karen's movements and groans of ecstasy that she was about to come. Masturbating faster and faster, Cheryl climaxed as wildly as she ever had in her life, as Karen, in the grip of multiple orgasms, thrust hard against her mouth.

After a long moment of blissful relaxation, Karen rose up on one knee to get off Cheryl. As Karen's cunt slowly separated from her mouth, Cheryl was aware of a cobweb of silvery strands of juice stretching between them. Fascinated, she watched as the strands of Aphrodite's nectar thinned and then broke, ending the lovers' connection between them.

Sitting up, Cheryl saw an insatiable Karen standing, pushing her hair back with both hands as she spoke. "That was just for starters, Cheryl. We'll have another drink, then get down to some real loving."

Getting to her feet, unsuccessfully trying to straighten out the creases in her rumpled skirt, Cheryl objected. The massive orgasm she'd experienced had lowered her sex energy so that she had full control of herself. Confused by a mixture of guilt and loving thoughts about Wendi, she found solace in the thought that no one, Wendi included, could have resisted what Karen had so provocatively put on offer.

But it had been a one-off and it was over. Cheryl was determined never to fall by the sexual wayside again. She was surprised to hear how resolute she sounded when she said, "No, Karen. You are lovely, and I still want you. But, for personal reasons, reasons that I can't explain, I have to go now."

"You mean...?" a stunned Karen gasped. Her ego had been bent. Not fractured. Just slightly bent. "Obviously, I'm disappointed, but I won't stop you from leaving. I wouldn't dream of forcing you. Sex is only fun if everyone involved really wants it."

"I'm sorry, Karen," Cheryl said, but was stopped from going further by the telephone buzzing.

Going to answer it, Karen nodded several times, said, "I see," and "Thank you for letting me know," before replacing the receiver and turning smiling to Cheryl. "Great news, Cheryl. That was Emmett Foyle, a policeman friend of Matthew's. All charges against me have been dropped. Oh, God! I just can't believe that it's over!"

"I'm so pleased for you, Karen," Cheryl said as Karen went to the bar.

"Thank you. I feel really great. At least have another drink before you go," Karen said, placing two glasses on the bar and starting to pour from a bottle. As an afterthought, she added. "I've got to go out, too, damn it. Emmett said that Matthew has collapsed and been rushed to hospital."

Cheryl's skeleton turned to ice, the coldness radiating out into her flesh. Selfishly delighted at hearing that the charges against her had been dropped, Karen had all but forgotten that her husband had been rushed to hospital and could possibly be dying, or even dead.

The regret that she had felt about having sex with Karen increased a hundredfold. Fetching her coat, she said dully, "Forget that drink, Karen," and walked out without saying farewell.

Eleven

The lengthening shadows of evening had darkened the corridors of the studios. Except for Paula and Karen, the huge building was unoccupied. There was a silence so profound that it seemed to have an echo to it. Everyone else had long ago left the studios, and Paula would have gone at the same time if an unusually subdued Karen had not called her back. Close to tears, Karen had tried to say something, but her voice had splintered into the shards of mounting hysteria, and Paula had tried to comfort her idol. But by taking Karen into her arms she had triggered a sexual nuclear bomb, an explosion from which only now were they slowly recovering. The fallout would surely last an eternity. Already there was a renewed fire in Paula's limbs, and her sex ached for Karen, who was looking at her now with unquestioning love in her eyes. If Karen thought that what they had done had changed anything, then she did not show it.

"This is our secret, Paula," Karen cautioned, tidying the flounced chintz cover on the divan they had used. "No one must even suspect for one moment that we are lovers."

"Are we lovers?" an insecure Paula enquired, dependent now on finding refuge in Karen's arms and kisses and the deep warmth of Karen's love.

"Of course we are, you little silly. You're a great lover. You should be loving all the time. There is so much wonderful love in you. I want to keep on loving you all through your rise to stardom and beyond."

Her hands seeking and finding Karen's face to tenderly caress the silken hair that had fallen loosely across it, the pronounced cheekbones, the soft yet firm mouth – a consuming mouth that had sought and fought and discovered and divined every last inch of her – Paula said humbly, "Without you I wouldn't I wouldn't be going anywhere, Karen."

"Hush, my darling," Karen whispered.

Paula hushed, snuggling in Karen's arms, happy to be there and nowhere else.

As the videotape ejected automatically, Alan Marriott stooped over to grasp it. His dark night had finally got bright, and he smiled at a seated Jay Clifford. Clifford felt no warmth from the wide smile. It had come from a smugly contented spot somewhere deep inside the gangster-like Marriott.

"A masterpiece," Marriott acknowledged, lighting a gnarled, black, evil-smelling cigar. "I'd have defied Liberace to watch those two red-hot girls and not get a boner. It took you a while, but you earned your money, Clifford."

"We agreed cash," Clifford said, a little panicky, raising his voice as Marriott reached for a chequebook.

With a grunt of annoyance, his face looking slightly sweaty, Marriott tossed the chequebook to one side. Taking a wad of banknotes from the back pocket of his trousers, he peeled some off, counting them one at a time onto a table. Clifford greedily snatched each note up as it landed.

"That's one real steamy tape, Mr Marriott," he said contemplatively. He didn't want to push too hard in asking for more, to overdo the Oliver Twist bit. But the essence of good pornography lay in the fact that the participants did not know they were being filmed. That was beyond question in this case, but the fact that both Paula Monroe and Karen Cayson had big tits could affect its appeal. Fashions and fancies were ephemeral. The voyeurs these days liked a big arse and small knockers. "You got it cheap. Too cheap, I reckon now."

"I got it for the price we agreed." Marriott's face seemed to flatten out into a mask as he inhaled the foul-smelling cigar deeply.

"Maybe so, but we didn't know how good it was going to be then," Clifford argued. He looked at the money he held in his hand. There was a childish pout of dissatisfaction on his fleshy face. "You'll be able to put a plethora of copies on the market and you'll make a fortune."

Clifford had heard Jeremy Paxman use the word "plethora" on television last night, and had looked up its meaning. Little tricks like using special words put you a cut above the rest. But Alan Marriott was not impressed by his pseudo-erudition.

Grabbing him by the lapels of his jacket, Marriott yanked Clifford up out of his chair, holding him so that his dangling feet were inches from the ground. Face close, Marriott hissed a warning. The cigar smell had linked up with something even viler on his breath to become nauseating. "It isn't going on the market, sonny. In fact, this tape doesn't exist, so keep that in mind when you walk out of the door. You ever hear of a guy named Vincent Argo?"

"No." A choking Clifford half coughed his one-word reply. That was a lie. He had heard of Argo, a tough and ruthless Greek-Cypriot heavy. The man was bad news. Really bad news.

"He works for me, and you'll meet him if you even mention the video to anyone. Vince'll rig a bomb under that clapped-out obscenity that you drive around in. It will blow up through the driver's seat and they'll be picking stardust out of your arse for a month. Do you understand me?"

Jay Clifford understood, and he said so.

"How is Matthew?"

Facing Richard Neehan across his office desk, Cheryl hesitated.

There had been a certain amount of guarded talk at cross-purposes since she had entered the office and taken a seat. Now she wasn't so much afraid to give the lawyer a straight answer as she was scared of hearing herself say the truth. The Wyndham story had begun as a bedroom farce and had graduated as a tragedy. Lying unconscious in a hospital bed, Matthew Wyndham had looked like something the River Police had fished out of the Thames after three days. Any recovery he might make, which she doubted, would be very short-term. Pity for him and admiration for his faithfulness to Karen had edged their way into her own churned emotions as she had stood there looking down on him.

"He's not good," she answered. "He didn't know that I was there, and even if he had come round he was in too bad a way for me to have mentioned the purpose of my visit."

"Which was?"

Cheryl again delayed her reply. Though her conscience prevented her from leaving Matthew in ignorance, to enlighten him would be to betray Karen. To tell Matthew to his face would have caused Cheryl problems, but informing Neehan would have her feel an absolute traitor. Added to Cheryl's problems was the possibility that Karen was simply an opportunist with style rather than a wicked woman.

Delaying answering, Cheryl idly watched flying insects fuss and fidget against the glass outside of the window. The air was light and soft, and yet she knew it would be hot again today. Oppressively hot. Neehan had taken off his jacket and draped it over the back of his chair.

At last she said, "This is very difficult for me, Mr Neehan."

"Call me Richard."

"OK," Cheryl said with a false smile and a nod, knowing that she could never address the reptilian lawyer by his first name. She started her story slowly. "I'm telling tales like a vindictive schoolgirl, but only because I like things to be fair. Karen is already planning for when Matthew is no longer with us. It won't take her long to destroy everything that Matthew built up in a lifetime. She intends expansion of the studios, and is bringing Malcolm Reay in."

"Malcolm Reay!" Neehan repeated the club owner's name musingly. "Perhaps Reay is not everyone's idea of the ideal bedfellow, Cheryl, but capitalism is an immoral system. You can't promise to close down the brothels while inviting the brothel keepers to dinner."

Neehan's easy acceptance of Malcolm Reay discouraged Cheryl. "I'm speaking out of turn here. I was present when Karen made this arrangement, and as I am her friend she has a right to expect confidentiality. I came here to see you for Matthew's sake."

"That's understood," Neehan assured her. "Trust me to be discreet, Cheryl. You have my word that nothing you tell me will ever be traced back to you."

This made Cheryl feel better. "Thank you. Karen has agreed to give Reay a ten per cent share in the business in return for his help in expanding the studios."

"That won't work, Cheryl," Neehan calmly informed her. "Matthew would need to countersign any agreement to that effect."

"Thank goodness," Cheryl exclaimed, but her thankfulness was short-lived. A very real possibility occurred to her. "But it will be different when Matthew dies?"

Neehan shook his head. "I will be able to put a block on Reay then, Cheryl. Even if both Karen and Reay fought me, I could tie them up legally for so many years that Reay would lose interest in the project."

"But what if they made some arrangement now, before Matthew's death?" Cheryl asked, still uneasy.

"As I explained, it would require Matthew's signature," Neehan insisted.

"Reay is having his solicitor draw up something for Karen to sign right now."

Face paling, the lawyer stared open-mouthed at Cheryl. He swallowed hard, swallowed again, then asked, "Are you sure of this?"

"Absolutely certain," Cheryl confirmed. "Does it change anything?"

"Everything. It could change everything. Reay is cunning enough to lure Karen into signing away more than ten per cent in an agreement that will come into effect after Matthew's death."

"What can be done about that?" Cheryl asked.

"Probably nothing," Neehan admitted unhappily. "If I may say so, you are taking a very personal interest in this, Cheryl."

"I suppose there are really two reasons for that," Cheryl said frankly. "I don't particularly like Matthew Wyndham, and, though I regard Karen as foolish rather than heartless, I don't like to see anyone taken advantage of. Also, Karen is promoting a young girl who hasn't been in London very long. The girl is being used unscrupulously just to boost the studios' reputation."

Sliding open a drawer in his desk, Neehan took out a newspaper and laid it on his desk, opening it as he asked Cheryl, "Have you seen today's paper?"

"No, not yet."

He slewed the newspaper on the polished desktop, and Cheryl saw a photograph of a happily smiling Paula Monroe shopping in Oxford Street. The headline dubbed her the new showbiz "sensation", while the story below was an imaginative tale of a Paula that Cheryl didn't recognise. She noticed that Paula's "little girl" look showed through the studio-imposed veneer of sophistication. It was funny: the things that recalled someone most clearly to you were the unimportant things, the things you had forgotten about the person. These were the real memories, unchanged by thought. Nevertheless, the spin had begun. If Paula did ever have a grip on reality, then it was about to be snatched away from her

"Is that the girl?" an astute Neehan asked. When Cheryl confirmed with a nod that it was, he went on. "Is she a relative or close friend of yours, Cheryl."

"Neither." Cheryl shook her head. "I met her soon after she'd arrived in London. She's a country girl and terribly naïve. I feel responsible because I introduced her to Alan Marriott, and he got her a part in this latest Karen Cayson film."

"You acted out of kindness, Cheryl, so no one can hold that against you."

"I'm sure that the girl will when they shatter her dream."

"I sympathise, Cheryl," Neehan said. "But you will appreciate that my duty is at present to Matthew Wyndham. That may well change in the near future, when I'll be responsible to Karen."

Expecting support, Cheryl had met nothing but the blandness of a lawyer interested only in furthering his practice and his finances. Neehan's shirt was wet under his arms as he studied her briefly. His eyebrows drew down. "Having said that, there is, of course, nothing to prevent you from diplomatically approaching Matthew as a friend."

Cancelling out that possibility, Cheryl decided to call on Paula. Matthew and Karen Wyndham were hardened veterans who probably deserved each other, but blonde Paula was worthy of being rescued from her own ignorance.

Thanking Richard Neehan for his time, Cheryl rose from her chair, ready to leave.

For some of the time, he had not been actually unconscious. It had been dark and gloomy when Matthew Wyndham had first woke, to find himself in some kind of a time slip. Convinced that he had been shanghaied by a press gang and would be serving at least two years before the mast in the China Seas, he had sat up. Roughly pushed back down, he'd had an oxygen mask rammed over his face. Everything was rocking and swaying, and his last ludicrous thought before blacking out once more was that they must be doing at least ten knots in rough waters.

Next time he came round he was in the present, half aware of being pushed about and rolled and lifted out of an ambulance. He had an impression of strong sunlight and then dimness and occasional voices. But he didn't entirely know what was going on. There was a hazy time when it seemed Cheryl Valenta had been standing by his bed, and he couldn't fathom why she would visit him. The Valenta woman was a respected columnist, not a hack thrashing around for a STUDIO BOSS MATTHEW WYNDHAM RUSHED TO HOSPITAL story.

Karen hadn't been around, he was sure of that. He excused her as being incapable of coping with sickness or anything she considered ugly. It wasn't possible to really know anyone, due to the countless facets that came under a heading of personality, but Karen was an even more complex character than anyone he had ever come into contact with. Of late she had gone to great lengths to keep her body covered from his gaze. That struck him as really odd in someone who had always earned a living by exposing herself to some extent. Yet everyone was entitled to their little quirks, and he considered himself to be a lucky old bastard to have such a beautiful young wife. Wyndham knew that she would be there to care for him when he returned home. If he ever did return home.

It was imperative that he do so, if only for a short time. There were arrangements to be made with Richard Neehan. For a start, his will had to be altered. He would still leave everything to Karen, including the studios. But empires that take long years to build can disintegrate in months under the wrong leadership. As much as he loved her, Karen was too impulsive, too erratic, to run a business. With Neehan's help he would appoint someone trustworthy to oversee the running of the studios.

Right now he felt really groggy. A nurse, who had carbolic as a perfume and a starched uniform that made a squishing noise with her every move, hovered round him like a shitehawk. When she stuck a needle in his arm he knew no more until there was a doctor at the end of his bed, smiling at him secretively, as if they shared a naughty secret after having been out on the town together last night.

Going misty at first, the doctor then disappeared in a blackness that engulfed Wyndham, filling his mind. When he regained consciousness it was to see an anxious Henry and Nellie Drury at his bedside.

Henry bowed his head of Brylcreemed grey hair closer to Wyndham with a solicitous enquiry: "How are you feeling, Mr Wyndham?"

"Just able to sit up and take nourishment," he jokingly replied. "It's nice of you both to come."

"We couldn't stay away," Nellie said, going on to covertly convey their regret at having withdrawn their statements against Karen. "It was the blow to the head brought this on, Master Matthew. You were perfectly well until that time."

"I don't think we can say that, Nellie," Wyndham warned.

"Perhaps not. The important thing is to have you back home so that we can nurse you back to good health," Henry Drury said.

"You're a good, loyal man, Henry," Wyndham complimented him. "Now, how is Mrs Wyndham coping?"

"Your guess is as good as ours is, Master Matthew. We haven't seen her since you were brought in here."

"She was staying the night at her apartment in Holborn, Nellie," Matthew said, to excuse his wife. "She won't have heard about my having been taken ill."

"We telephoned her apartment countless times, and left messages on the answerphone," Henry bluntly pointed out.

"I'm sure there's some explanation," Wyndham said, aware that there *was* an explanation, and that it was one that he didn't like.

He suddenly felt very old and very tired, but he cursed the fact that he wasn't too tired to care.

*

Gina Bey El Araby was out when Cheryl arrived at her house that evening. Paula already had Nikki Graham as a visitor. Nikki's presence was a threat to Cheryl's plan to have a heart-to-heart talk with Paula, warning her as delicately as possible that a difficult time lay ahead for her. There was a distinctly hostile atmosphere between the two young friends that Cheryl found to be embarrassing. Paula was strangely remote and Cheryl sensed that the girl wasn't pleased to see her, and actually resented her having called.

Maybe, Cheryl reasoned, I am oversensitive because I've had a bad night followed by an appalling day. Having gone to Wendi's place anticipating sex, she had returned to her own apartment pleased with the new-style relationship Wendi had proposed, but agonisingly frustrated. Love was bouncing on the bed, tits against tits. It was belly to belly, cunt to cunt, not a load of sentimental gibberish.

Despite having been bone tired she had considered telephoning Wendi to ask if she could return to her apartment for the loving she was so desperately in need of. But they had made incontestable rules together and Cheryl had long ago learned never to mess with definite rules.

Her restlessness had increased, so she had put on a Carpenters CD in the hope that their special sound would soothe the nerves. But she had found herself pacing from room to room, the Carpenters becoming a background sound that she had hardly noticed. "Yesterday Once More" wasn't a lot of use to someone with a fucked-up today. Pouring herself a drink, she had then needed to open a window because she had been sickened by the onerous smell that whisky always has. She had placed a hand between her legs; her finger had dutifully located her clit, ready to assuage the raging demand. But she had desisted. Even an act of self-relief seemed to be a gross disloyalty to Wendi.

Now she was discovering that her enforced and temporary

chastity had disturbing side effects. Although she had come here on a mission of mercy, sexual desire had become uppermost at the sight of the luscious Paula. Accepting that this rampant hunger was ludicrous in a mature woman who had been around, who had turned down far more opportunities than she had taken up, Cheryl was baffled by it.

"What brings you here?" Paula asked, gesturing for Cheryl to be seated. "I hope it's something that will cheer me up."

"I called to see how you're getting on," Cheryl explained, miffed by Paula's attitude. "I don't understand."

"It's just that Karen's coming for me later this evening. We've been invited to a pretty important award ceremony of some kind. But then Nikki turns up, all weepy because she's been dropped from the chorus. I must admit that going suddenly from a successful musical to the job centre isn't a career move to boast about."

How could someone change so drastically in such a short time? Cheryl wondered. Life had suddenly exploded into a carnival of music, colour and gaiety for Paula, who was obviously gloating over her friend's misfortune. Witnessing this, Cheryl considered leaving right away. It occurred to her that Paula merited what was soon to happen to her at the studios. The way she was now, it would be a good thing to bring her down to earth with a bump. But Paula was young, and instant success had turned her into a spoiled brat. She had yet to learn that fame was fleeting, and would be particularly so in her case.

Yet she had been particularly cruel to her friend, and Cheryl was not surprised to see Nikki stand and reach for her coat, saying, "I'd better be going, Paula." She turned to Cheryl, her face very sad. "It was nice meeting you, Cheryl."

"It was a pleasure to meet you, Nikki. Try not to worry. Something will turn up soon."

Nikki gave her a wan smile that said she appreciated Cheryl's kindness in lying to her. They were both aware that it was likely to be a very long time before show business gave Nikki another break. If ever.

"I'll be seeing you, Paula," the girl called listlessly as she walked towards the door.

"Yeah, see you," an uninterested Paula replied, making no attempt to see her friend out. She then started to fuss over Cheryl. "I'll make us both a drink, and then we can chat. I expect that you want to do a story. I'm being chased all ways by reporters, but you take priority."

"Oh, God!" Cheryl groaned inwardly and silently. This once sweet kid was now absolutely full of herself

Able to see Paula in the kitchenette, efficiently measuring out milk and coffee, she called to her, "I expect Karen's very worried about her husband."

Paula remained silent. Women were at their most unguarded when doing household chores, and Cheryl studied Paula's profile through the partly open door. The girl's overconfident manner had been sheer bravado. She looked scared now, and her childish aura had returned. Cheryl realised that it was going to take a lot of courage for her to prick Paula's bubble by telling her that she was not an emerging star at the studios, but merely a means to an end as far as Karen was concerned.

"She was to start with, but I understand that he's on the mend now," Paula replied in a way that said the subject was closed.

To ease the situation, Cheryl called conversationally, "Being dropped must have come as an awful shock to Nikki."

"I think she could have been expecting it. I like Nikki, like her a lot, but I don't think she has what it takes in showland."

Having brought two mugs of coffee on a tray, she placed them on an occasional table and sat opposite to Cheryl.

"Two sugars. It was a guess. I hope that I got it right," Paula said with a natural smile that showed her beautiful teeth.

"Spot on." Cheryl smiled her thanks.

She covertly watched the gorgeous blonde girl raise her cup to her mouth. Even the way she tasted her coffee was a sheer sex act. Paula had gained much carnal knowledge in a short time. Cheryl's eyes travelled slowly down her smooth white neck and her full round breasts, which, unsupported inside the flowered summer dress, managed to stand out without the slightest sign of sag. Projecting nipples of magnificent circumference proudly made convex impressions on the thin material. Cheryl imagined stroking the blonde hair, closing her eyes and pressing her face into the creamy softness of Paula's breasts. She could almost feel a brown crest harden against her cheek, and she mentally turned her head to take it in her mouth. Faint tendrils of sensation first uncoiled then built into a warmth that spread through her thighs and belly.

Embarrassment made her face flush hotly when she realised that Paula was watching her amusedly.

"You syndicate the stories you write, don't you, Cheryl?"

Glad of the diversion offered by Paula's question, Cheryl was pained to see the girl's disappointment at her truthful answer. "I haven't come here for a story, Paula. I wanted to warn you that there's likely to be some big changes at the studios."

"Warn me? I don't understand." Paula frowned.

"The changes are sure to affect you, Paula."

"No." Paula gave a vehement shake of her head. "Karen told me that there would be changes, but that they will be to my advantage."

"I hope that's true, Paula."

"I *know* that it's true," Paula retorted, gripping her mug tightly with both hands, knuckles showing white. She was angered by Cheryl's implied criticism of Karen. "Karen said so, and I trust her completely."

"Believe me, Paula, I pray that you're right. I worry about you."

"Why should you worry about me?"

Cheryl shrugged. "Because you're a nice girl and I like you."

"That's obvious from the way you've been looking at me,"

Paula said, confirming for Cheryl that Karen Cayson was both her mentor and her lover. "If you've finished your coffee, perhaps you'll leave so that I can get myself ready for Karen."

Hurt by Paula's coolness towards her, Cheryl stood up from her chair and followed the girl, who was heading for the door. In the hallway the girl paused, leaning her back against a doorjamb, breasts thrust out provocatively as she looked archly at Cheryl.

Recognising that Paula was motivated principally by an urge to boost her already overinflated ego, and not so much by sex, Cheryl planned a rebuff. Keeping to the far side of the doorway, she went to pass the girl. But Paula showed a sudden repentance. Reaching out, she gave Cheryl's hand a light squeeze.

"I'm sorry, Cheryl. I've been perfectly dreadful and mean and nasty. As friends we should part with a kiss."

This was the Paula Monroe that Cheryl remembered. The quick rapport, the tender eyes, the warm smile, the soft voice. It put her in a dilemma. Her commitment to Wendi loomed large in her mind again. Wendi's adoration made her feel secure, smugly complete and deserving. She was suspicious of Paula. Though the offer of a kiss seemed genuine, Cheryl suspected that the girl was testing the strength of what sexual power she held over her. It could be that Paula was coming at a different angle to enhance her self-image.

But she was breathing in the heavenly fragrance of the girl, and there was no way that she could resist. The earlier animosity was forgotten as Cheryl moved close to kiss Paula warmly on the lips. Paula raised her hand and put it behind Cheryl's head to hold the kiss warmer and closer and longer.

Mouth to mouth, lips touching, Paula whispered, "Do you forgive me for being such a little bitch, Cheryl?"

Cheryl said, "Of course I do." But the words had no real meaning. Though she found talking through a kiss to be frantically arousing, nagging away at the back of her mind was the worry that Paula was playing some kind of a game. But the compelling sexuality of the girl was getting to her.

They kissed again, their tongues meeting, lapping together in full unison. Paula tasted divine, and Cheryl obligingly parted her legs a little as the girl slid a hand stealthily up under her skirt. She felt two of Paula's enterprising fingers slip beneath the silky material of her panties to find a readily lubricated pussy that Cheryl knew was begging to be explored. One finger started to gently stroke her velvet lips, then moved to tease the clit for no more than a few seconds before seeking entry.

Cheryl's gasping response broke the kiss. Clutching Paula tighter as she probed her, she nibbled her way over the skin of Paula's cheek to one of her ears, stabbing her tongue inside. But Paula's mouth sought hers again, and Cheryl realised why when she thrilled to feel the girl's second finger being inserted in her. Then Paula was devotedly frigging her, both fingers sliding in and out of her with the force and rhythm of a piston. The fingers stroked Cheryl's inner walls, searching for and then finding her G-spot. A sensation of ecstasy raced through Cheryl, a feeling so exquisite that it was difficult to bear. She gave a grunt that expelled hot breath into Paula's mouth, which the girl sucked down deep into her lungs.

Thoroughly sexed up, Cheryl cupped Paula's heavy left breast. Paula moved herself a little away, an unexpected reaction that baffled Cheryl. Then the two fingers were withdrawn, leaving her feeling rejected. Raising her hand, Paula sucked at her fingers, looking impishly at Cheryl.

Aroused far beyond the point of no return, Cheryl reached for the girl, needing to embrace her, to kiss her, to love her properly. But Paula had changed from a temptress into a tormentor. Wagging a finger exaggeratedly at her, Paula grinned, "Naughty, naughty! That's your lot."

"But Paula!" Cheryl pleaded.

"I have to get ready, Cheryl," Paula complained. "Karen will be arriving soon. Please leave."

As the fog of sexual desire thinned a little in her head, Cheryl realised that she had been toyed with by a girl suffering from megalomania brought on by gaining too much fame too soon. Though she felt that the blonde was silently mocking her now, she blamed Karen Cayson's influence, not Paula. The young are pliable and formed by those around them, and Paula had not reached the age when the capacity to be moulded into new shapes is lost.

The moment Wendi Maylor saw the once familiar buildings and shops, she recognised them. But it pleased her to know that, if someone in London had asked her for the name above any of the shops, it would have taken her a long time to remember one. The street was squalid, and as she stopped her car by the kerb it felt good to know that it was no longer her street. That she had lived here at all had been accidental, and she hadn't remained a moment longer than it was necessary to grow up and achieve a modicum of independence. The scene viewed through the car's windscreen was a dreary one. A group of shabbily dressed little girls were skipping to the chant of "Salt, mustard, vinegar, pepper... salt, mustard, vinegar..." while some boys energetically kicked a rubber ball around in the street where she had once played.

Summoning up at least some of the resolve that she knew she would require, she was about to get out of the car when her mobile phone trilled. Closing the car's door, she answered it.

"Hello."

"Wendi, can we meet, now, either at your place or mine?"

"Cheryl!" Wendi was perturbed to hear how agitated the normally cool and self-possessed Cheryl Valenta sounded. "Whatever is the matter?"

"It's just that something's happened that's left me badly

needing to love and be loved, Wendi."

"What does that do to the agreement we made?" Wendi worriedly enquired. Cheryl's obviously high sexual drive had caused her to fear something like this. It was plain that somebody had started making love to Cheryl but had left her high and far from dry. Was it Karen Cayson? That probability made Wendi jealous.

"I'm not looking for an orgy, for God's sake, Wendi. If necessary I'll sit under a tree with you and read fucking poetry. All I need is just to have the comfort of your arms around me."

"We both know what that would lead to."

"Please, Wendi, you'll have me begging in a moment. Can I come to yours right now?"

"I'm in Bristol, Cheryl."

There was a lengthy silence at Cheryl's end, and when she spoke her voice was flat, dispirited. "What – what are you doing in Bristol?"

"My sister telephoned to say that my father is very ill."

"Oh dear, I am sorry."

"Don't be. He was a drunken, ignorant pig when I left home, and I'm sure illness hasn't changed him. The only reason I've driven down here is out of some stupid sense of duty. Hypocritical, isn't it?"

"You haven't seen him yet?"

"No. I'd just pulled up outside the block of flats when you rang."

"But you'll be back home later tonight?"

"No, it's too long a drive, Cheryl. I'll be back tomorrow and I'll call you then."

"I hope everything works out for you down there. Goodbye, Wendi."

Cheryl had sounded so terribly disappointed, so low, that Wendi, desperate to help her in any way that she could, called her name loudly: "*Cheryl.*" But Cheryl had already ended the connection.

Getting out of the car, Wendi walked past women gossiping on doorsteps. They looked at her critically as some well-dressed toff from Planet Janet. Some snobby, stuck-up, bitch. She wasn't of their world, a world that had them trapped but from which she had escaped.

What had been her home was squeezed between two other decaying tenements. Time had washed over the cramped buildings, leaving the scars of fading paint and crumbling brickwork. As she went in through double doors, the smells of ages ago were still there to be smelled. There was a pet rabbit in a small hutch, incongruously out of context in the surroundings. It didn't look much like a rabbit, but it stank like one. Tilting her head back, she looked up four stone-staired flights, stairs she had run up and down a million times as a child. She saw Thelma, her sister, smiling down at her.

Thelma was a depressing sight. Aged far beyond her thirty-two years, she had grown heavier than Wendi believed. The dress she wore was torn and grease-stained, and she was far too young for the immense tiredness around her eyes. Despite the smile, she had an air of absurd unhappiness, like someone who has never known laughter.

"Wow, is that your car out there, Wend? Look at you, all dressed up," she said as, embarrassed, she tried to hold the tear in the dress together with one hand, and hopelessly attempted to rub off some of the grease with the other. My God! Wendi thought. Though I'm two years younger than she is, I'd look as she does now if I hadn't got away from here. It had all been worth it – the drugs, the struggle to get ahead, even the necessity to sell her body in order to survive. Anything was better than this.

"It's great seeing you, Thelma," Wendi said tonelessly.

"You'll have to excuse the mess. It's been real hard since Dad took sick."

"How is he?"

"Not too bad now. Mum's given me a break by sitting with him now. She's not too clever herself, Mum isn't. Dr Coombes says if Dad goes on a light diet and gives up the fags and drink he'll be all right."

Placing her bag on the floor, Wendi immediately recognised every single inch of the poorly furnished, untidy flat. Not a thing had changed. She detested this building, where the sun never entered. She had a feeling that there had been a time, long ago, when her feeling for her father had changed from worship to shame. Maybe that was a false memory and she had never worshipped him. Her years of hating him made it academic, anyway. "And is the old man prepared to follow doctor's orders?" she enquired. "Has he stopped drinking?"

"You know Dad," Thelma sheepishly answered. "He reckons he'd rather be dead."

Then why didn't the old bastard die? To do so would be his only kind act ever. Turning to her sister, who had once been attractive compared with the present version, Wendi felt a huge sadness. Thelma's tired face was swollen so badly that her once expressive brown eyes were just slits. She was ugly, transformed.

"You look ill, too, Thelma. Tell me about yourself."

Looking away self-consciously, Thelma said, "You don't want to hear about me."

"I do. Just because I've been away for so long doesn't mean that I don't care about my sister."

Eyes filling up, Thelma spoke in a half-whisper. "I'm as daft as ever, Wend. Had to go and get myself pregnant, didn't I?"

"Oh, no," a shocked Wendi groaned. "Who was the father?"

"Bert Clements. I expect you remember him. He used to live up on the next floor."

"Yes, I remember him," Wendi said, able to see the scruffy, permanently unemployed Clements in her mind. He had to be a good fifteen years older than Thelma, and he was married. She said unnecessarily, "He's a married man, Thelma."

"He was. Rita left him when she learned he'd got me into trouble, and he left soon afterwards."

"So you were all on your own?"

"Yes, but I had a miscarriage early on. Worked out for the best, I suppose."

"Do you manage?" Wendi asked. "Can you pay the bills?"

"I—" Thelma began, but she was interrupted.

Twelve

Karen didn't have to tell the barman at the Ocean Club what her preference was. Was that a sign of fame, a reason to rejoice, or an ominous signal that she was leading a bloody boring life? "Who gives a shit?" she muttered as she raised her glass to her lips. She shouldn't be in such a grumpy mood. The evening had gone really well. The award ceremony had been recorded for television, and she had cunningly involved Paula when she had been interviewed. That had to be something of a record, an unknown kid getting a plug on the telly. Paula had it made. Karen intended to make her world-famous before *Beach of Fear* hit the screens.

The place was crowded. In the company of couples and elite cliques, she was alone at the bar. But that didn't matter. A night of hard drinking would take care of any feeling of social isolation. She had dropped Paula off on her way back, and then had parked her car and taken a taxi. Once she'd had a talk about business with Malcolm Reay, she was going to get as drunk as a hiccuping hyena. The alcohol would see her through a night during which she needed to forget that she was going to the hospital to see Matthew in the morning. It would have been easier, with no recriminations, to have visited him earlier, but she had been unable to force herself to do so.

She was pushing her empty glass across the bar for a refill when Malcolm Reay walked up and signalled to the barman that it was on the house. Reay placed a hand on her shoulder. "You're downing 'em fast tonight, Karen."

Reay had an oddly contemptuous look that had permanently settled into the lean lines of his handsome face. It was like an interesting scar or his own trademark.

"Medicinal purposes, Malc: I need a good night's sleep." She gave him her thrifty smile, learned in the no-animation school of sophistication. "How do you slow down after running this place at night?"

"I've got a great psychiatrist who has an answer for everything. I get to bed about two in the morning, after taking two Seconal tablets that knock me out with shameful swiftness."

"Geez, I envy you, Malc," Karen said. She turned her head to left and right, studying the dancers.

"Don't," he advised her solemnly. Brow sweating a little, he picked an ice cube out of his drink and popped it in his mouth. "The same two Seconals mean that I'm drowsy for about three hours after waking up. I blunder around like a prick in a stocking."

"Surely your shrink's got an answer for that?"

"He's working on it," Reay drawled. "He's more interested in why I shy away from relationships with the opposite sex, but love prostitutes. My hope is that analysis will discover that a friend of my mother's seduced me when I was thirteen. It would be like watching a video of it in my head. That would be a real turn-on."

"Hasn't this psychiatrist ever told you that you're incurably mad, Malcolm?" a smiling Karen enquired.

"As long as I keep paying good money he won't," Reay answered. "Now, let's get down to business. Ralph Laker has the papers all ready for us to sign. Which would be easiest for you tomorrow morning, go to his place in Knightsbridge or shall I get him to come here?"

"I don't know where his office is, so it would be best if he came here," Karen answered. Then she exclaimed, "Oh, shit!"

"Hair appointment?" Reay sarcastically enquired.

"I've arranged to visit Matthew in hospital tomorrow morning."

Though disappointed, Reay shrugged. "Don't worry. We'll put it off until another day."

"No." Karen was adamant. "I want to get this fixed up between us. I'll be here tomorrow morning. Will ten o'clock do?"

"Ten o'clock's fine. But what about Matthew?"

Karen banged a drained glass down on the bar. She had begun to feel strange for no reason at all and was imagining that the deep facets of the glass had sliced into her fingers. "Fuck Matthew."

"No, thanks," Reay grinned, then, looking at her with undisguised feverish desire, he added suggestively, "But his wife – now that would be a different matter."

Karen fixed him with a steady look, uncertainty making a little furrow on her forehead. Her cool blue eyes were no longer cool. She was no longer poised and talkative. The barman had filled her glass again, and there was a tremor in her hand as she reached for it. Her legs twitched involuntarily from time to time as a sickening fear in her transformed itself into rage. She drank deeply, coughed on the straight alcohol, and drank again.

How dare he make such a preposterous suggestion? Her glare at Reay was contemptuous now, her voice rasping as she warned him, "Don't you ever say anything like that to me again. You got that, creep?"

"I've got it," a shaken Reay said as she slid down from her stool and walked, slightly unsteadily, through the crowd towards the door. Bewildered, he called after her, "What about tomorrow morning, Karen?"

She replied without turning her head, shouting above the music, "I'll be here. Make sure that it's strictly business."

"Who you talking to, Thelma?" their mother's voice called.

"It's Wendi, Mum, she's home."

"Wendi?" The voice went quiet. Then asked, "Then what's she

doing out there? Ain't me and your dad worth saying hello to?"

The superior feeling that had sustained her since leaving her car deserted Wendi. Her nerve went with it and she felt a flooding sensation of dread. She didn't want to see her parents. There was nothing any of them could say, nothing for any of them to listen to.

"Don't be surprised, Wend," Thelma advised as she placed a hand on Wendi's back to ease her towards the bedroom door. "They've both altered, gone down. They won't be how you remember them."

Which would be worse, seeing them as she remembered them, or as they now were? Not seeing them at all would suit Wendi fine.

The curtains were drawn on the one window. The room's odours were of medicine and urine and the mustiness of the decaying old couple, one a human scarecrow lying under the covers, the other bent and shrivelled sitting on the bed. Wendi was aware that Thelma was standing in the doorway behind her, wearing a faint and nervous smile when there was nothing at all to smile about.

"How are you, Mum, Dad?"

"Come here, and give your old mum a kiss."

Trying to push herself towards the bed, Wendi couldn't move. They were her parents, but there was no way she could move close to them. Feeling ashamed of her own callousness, and sickened by the sight of the old couple, she wanted to run out of the room, but even that was impossible.

The two giants who had once dominated her life had shrunk to become half-human beings.

"Don't just stand there," her father complained in a reedy voice that she wouldn't have recognised as his. "Come here, girl."

Slowly, very slowly, Wendi advanced with her body stiff, shoulders erect. Though not wanting to, she took in the sagging bed with its brass rails. The quilt was dirty and ripped, and the pillows were without cases. Newspapers and magazines were strewn on the bed and floor. On the windowsill was a framed, fading photograph of her father standing beside a steam railway engine. The sight of it made Wendi guilty because she'd even forgotten that he had once worked on the railway.

"How about that kiss?" her mother demanded. "You too bleeding high and mighty to kiss your own mother now?"

"Don't, Mum," Thelma tearfully begged. "Let's all be happy, 'cos Wendi's come to see us."

"Not afore time," her father squeakily complained.

Bending quickly forward, Wendi pecked her mother on her wrinkled cheek. Planning to step away immediately, she was prevented by the old woman, who wrapped both arms around her waist and hugged her tightly. Her mother smelled like rotting meat and Wendi fought to keep her breathing shallow. She was aware of the old woman's dirty fingernails digging into her fashionable, expensive clothes. Wendi had the cringe-making notion that the nails had laid tracks across her skin like an ugly tattoo.

Forcing herself to look at her mother's worn and pleated face, Wendi was tortured by the sight of the loose skin loitering in creases, heavy folds of it burdening the too-small eyes. Frighteningly aware that she had been drained of strength, Wendi fought to free herself. She made it, breaking free of the clasping arms, but an abysmal lack of balance made her stagger. She would have fallen had not Thelma caught her.

"Look at your father," the old lady commanded. "Your poor sick father weighing eight stone, can't eat, can't drink. I bet you never gave him a thought while you've been swanking up there in London."

Oh yes, Wendi had. She often thought of both of them and their constant, shouted rows. She had thought of her father staggering, stupidly drunk. There was the day her mother had used a carving knife to slash to pieces the new suit he had got from the catalogue, in case he found another woman while out in the pub. Did age and illness excuse them all that? Wendi thought not. She would betray herself and her own principles to ever forgive them the hell they had caused her as a child.

Her mother's eyes started to leak tears. She made a sound like a laugh but it turned into the first of a succession of sobs. Wendi's father turned his skull-like head to look at her, his eyes as bright as coals. "Now, see what you've done, Miss High-and-Mighty. What did you come back here for, just to gloat?"

Thelma saved her by saying, "Wendi's very tired, Mum, Dad. She's had a long drive. Let her get a good night's rest, and we'll all have a good chat in the morning."

Wendi felt ill. Something had made her come *home* today. Driving down the motorway she had accepted that it really was neither love nor a sense of duty. But she had been resigned to staying there a few nights, perhaps to gain some undefined perspective. Now she realised that was out of the question.

Ushering her from the room, Thelma whispered, "You'll find it easier with them tomorrow. You'll have to sleep with me tonight, Wend. It will be like old times. We can have a good old natter. I want to hear all about your life in London. You go on into my room now and make yourself comfortable. I'll settle Mum and Dad down and then I'll be with you as soon as possible."

Thelma's bed hadn't been made and the sheets were a grubby grey. Knowing that she couldn't stay in that room, couldn't sleep with her slovenly sister, Wendi tried her mobile phone, crying softly at the sadness of it all. Relieved to find she had a signal, she dialled Cheryl's number. She had to get back to her proper life as soon as possible, and Cheryl was going to share that life with her. It had been foolish to try to arrange an emotional and sexual relationship as if it were a United Nations charter. She got Cheryl's answerphone.

"Cheryl, it's me. I'm coming back to London tonight, and I'll ring you in the morning. I was stupid to impose all of those rules and regulations on us. From now on, we'll play it as it comes. I love you."

Opening her handbag, she counted out three hundred pounds

in twenty-pound notes. Then she quickly scribbled a note:

My dearest Thelma,

I am so sorry, but I just can't face it. Please try to understand. This money is for you. Ring me on this number if you can ever get away and come to London.

Please forgive me.

Your loving sister Wendi.

Placing the note on the banknotes on a rickety chest of drawers, she put an empty perfume bottle on top of them. Then she picked up her bag and crept from the room.

Passing her parents' room on tiptoe, she could hear voices but not what they were saying. From the rise and fall of the tones, she surmised that Thelma was defending her against fierce opposition from their parents. Moving quietly, she went out, taking care to make no noise when closing the door of the flat behind her. She went down the stone stairs, very aware that it was for the last time.

Out on the street she walked swiftly to her car. Driving away, she rolled the windows of the car down, as if the odours of the flat still clung to her. She felt awful about having deserted Thelma, but found some consolation in the thought that she would have caused her sister more trouble by remaining at the flat. Needing to get away, she drove fast.

It was always a mistake to try to go back.

Going in through the park gates, Cheryl passed a few old-timers sitting on benches. With limited futures they were animatedly discussing the past. You should never hurry in a park, Sheena, her erstwhile West Indian girlfriend, had always maintained. Sheena claimed too much would be missed by doing so. Cheryl stepped off the tarmac path onto the grass, enjoying its softness and resiliency after the hard pavements of London. She walked close to the pond that was ornately framed by its summer border of water lilies and fragrant bluebells.

Alan Marriott had telephoned to ask her to meet him here at lunchtime. He hadn't explained why he wanted to see her. But Marriott had put her onto some great stories in the past, so it was worth the gamble. Anyway, she was always intending to come to the park more often, but never got around to it.

Sunlight dappled the soft turf like gold coins, and she felt good. Arriving home last night, she had retrieved Wendi's heart-warming message from the answerphone. It had gone some way towards calming the sexual frustration Paula Monroe's teasing had inflicted on her. It was good to know that within a few hours she would be with Wendi, who had thrown her restricting rule book out of the window.

Cheryl smiled at the mallard duck that waddled up awkwardly to stand by her. Satisfied that she was carrying no sandwiches to share with it, the duck waddled off in feathered disgust. Watching it go, she caught sight of a dark suit through the corner of her eye.

An unsmiling Alan Marriott approached her at a steady pace. He was one of those men who dressed the same summer and winter, with only the presence or absence of an overcoat denoting the different seasons. As if stepping straight out of an old Hollywood gangster movie, he politely raised his George Raft-style hat to her. "Cheryl."

"Hello, Alan. Meeting out here is very mysterious," Cheryl joked. "Shouldn't I say something like 'The cats favour the high walls tonight,' and you reply, 'The tabby cats climb the highest'? Then we exchange briefcases."

Giving what passed for a smile with him, Marriott mused, "I suppose we are spies in a kind of way."

"You'll need to explain that to me."

"I will do so," he told her with an emphatic nod. "Shall we talk as we walk? It's such a nice day."

Cheryl fell in beside him as he left the path to walk on soft grass that felt hospitable under their feet. The sweet scent of earth rose from the ground. A lurking squirrel observed them suspiciously from its home in a hollow tree.

"I'll come straight to the point, Cheryl," Marriott said in his gravel voice. "What I'm about to say can't be excused by the old business-is-business cliché. I know that Matthew Wyndham is ill, very ill, but I'm determined to take over his studios."

"As you said yourself, Alan, there's no way of excusing that."

"I know what you're thinking, Cheryl, and I confess to being a hard businessman." Marriott stopped walking for a moment and looked Cheryl straight in the eye. "If things are left as they are, then Wyndham's business will die shortly after he does. Though I, of course, admit that to own the studios will benefit me, I also want to save what is a major part of the British entertainment industry."

"Even though he's sick, perhaps even more so because he is sick, Matthew won't welcome an approach from you, Alan. Maybe it would be easier for you to speak to Karen when, you know..."

"No," Marriott said as they started walking again, a leisurely stroll. "Karen Cayson's talent as an actress is dubious, but her business acumen is zilch. I see her as a disaster waiting to happen."

"I've a feeling that you are about to get to where I come in, Alan."

"You catch on quickly," Marriott praised her. "Your intelligence is a flaring beacon in a dark world peopled by dickheads, Cheryl."

That was indeed a compliment, coming as it did from a man frequently heard to proclaim that all women were totally stupid. Tosser.

"I've learned to be on the alert when Alan Marriott waxes lyrical. My guess is that you are trying to flatter me into making representation on your behalf to Matthew Wyndham."

"You do know him better than I do."

With a brittle little laugh, Cheryl said, "I know him well enough to have 'I wouldn't touch him with a ten-foot bargepole' spring to mind when your name is mentioned, Alan."

They had climbed a small hill and stood together, looking down. Although they were encircled by the city, there was a solitude here, a meaning to the landscape that was almost oppressively mysterious. They were standing beside two twisted trees, almost ludicrous in their stance, like petrified dancers. It was a silver birch and a pine curved unnaturally round each other. Their branches were locked together, and they seemed to be like dancers waiting for music to move to the rhythm. Or perhaps they were about to make love. The birch and the pine had grown there, had remained there for years, frozen in an embrace, sorrowfully unfulfilled.

"There is a way to bypass Wyndham's hatred of me, Cheryl." The fact that Marriott spoke tentatively unnerved Cheryl. He patted his jacket. "I have a videotape of Karen in my pocket that will change his mind. I'll be offering a fair price for the studios, and I'm certain he'll accept when the alternative is to let Karen take over."

Cheryl was shocked to the core. Having always known that Marriott was a ruthless operator, she would never have considered that he could be this cruel. An educated guess said that the content of the videotape was sex. She spoke her mind. "You don't know me as well as you think, Alan, if you believe that I will be party to the blackmail of a dying man."

"I can't argue that's how it appears to be on the surface," Marriott agreed unhappily. "But however odious my method may seem to be at this moment, Cheryl, please believe that it is for the good."

"For your good, maybe."

"For the common good." Marriott rolled his expressive eyes upward.

"It will take a lot to convince me of that." She reminded herself that she was a veteran, too experienced to stand naïvely listening to treacherous male persuasive talk. Cheryl prepared to make a stand.

"I'm sure that I can convince you," Marriott insisted. "For the moment I ask only that you take the tape with you. When you have had the opportunity to view it, we can meet again."

Cheryl disagreed. "I don't feel that I can take the tape, Alan. Neither do I want to meet you again about this."

"I'm hopeless with quotes, Cheryl, but some sage once said that the most dangerous mind of all is a closed mind."

"Now you're trying psychological blackmail on me," Cheryl complained with a tight smile. "Without any commitment whatsoever, I will take a look at your tape. But I want your assurance that Matthew Wyndham won't be hurt. The poor man looked absolutely terrible when I visited him in hospital."

Holding up his right hand like a man taking an oath, Marriott said, "You have my word, Cheryl. If you don't join me in this, then I can go no further. If you should decide to help me, then you will be my go-between with Wyndham. Only you will be talking to him, so you will have full control."

Far from certain that she was doing the right thing, Cheryl held out her hand for the tape.

The sun warmed Paula as she lay on the airbed beside the small swimming pool. Its bright dazzle was so uplifting that she could not feel guilty about Nikki any longer. Cammy Studland had telephoned the studio that morning with the unexpected invitation. With Karen out of the studios all day, and a rapt John Brighton involved in overseeing a change of scenery for shooting the following day, she had been able to slip away to the small but luxurious property the theatre company had rented for its star singer.

It had been awkward at first, with Cammy explaining that she had been charmed by meeting Paula at the party, and wanted to renew their acquaintance. Neither of them had mentioned the torrid sex with Nikki in the hotel bedroom. Recalling how drunk Cammy had been at the time, Paula wondered just how much, if anything, the singer remembered of that night.

"It's a wonder the studio hasn't said something about electrolysis," Cammy remarked, stretching out an arm from her lounger to run a forefinger through the fine, silky hair that ran from the top of Paula's bikini up to her navel.

"Are you implying that I have bad breath?" Paula asked in an offended tone.

Withdrawing her hand, Cammy appeared to be astonished at her new friend's ignorance, and then she realised that Paula was joking, and they laughed together.

"If you do have any faults, which I doubt, Paula," Cammy smiled, "halitosis certainly isn't one of them." This time she reached to slowly and caressingly run three fingers through the inverted V of pubic hair. "If anyone ever suggests removing this, then ring the cunny police and have them arrested."

Paula giggled at that, but her laughter stopped as Cammy leaned down from her chair to press lightly parted lips on the hair. Thrilled, Paula wanted the stolen kiss to go on, to develop into something more adventurous, but before she had the chance to run her fingers through Cammy's hair, the singer lay back in her lounger and made small talk.

"Do you see your friend Nikki very often, Paula?"

Up to that moment, Paula had felt rotten that Nikki was not there with them, but now she felt a little irritated that Cammy had brought her into the conversation. This was their time together, just the two of them.

"I haven't seen her for a while," she replied. "She was very down about being dropped."

"I can imagine, Paula, but it's all part of the process. It's all a matter of willpower, really. You have to be really dedicated. No one ever got anywhere by skimming through life unfeeling. I wouldn't like to count the number of mammoth disappointments I've had. Have you ever been to the Midnight Blue, a little club in the West End?"

Paula gave a shake of her head as an answer. She had yet to visit the West End, but she wasn't about to admit her ignorance.

"I used to sing there night after night," Cammy went on. "I did it for no pay, just to gain experience, and it paid off. Nikki has something, I'm pretty sure of that, but whether she's prepared to work hard in order to improve herself is something else. I know she's your friend, and this is not a criticism, but have you noticed Nikki's eyes? They are a lovely blue, but they have a cold look, a blueness that's neither soft nor unyielding, a cold blueness that says she takes all and gives nothing in return. Nikki makes a better friend than she would an enemy."

"I guess that I must consider myself lucky getting ahead so quickly," Paula said happily, letting the soothing sun's marvellous feel of contentment reach her.

"That's not luck, it's natural talent," Cammy corrected her. "You'll go to the top, with or without Karen Cayson helping you. It will just be quicker with Karen behind you."

Mention of Karen's name brought her to Paula's mind. It was an odds-on bet that the beautiful actress wouldn't be happy about her being with Cammy. But there was simply nothing for Karen to be concerned about. She was a mature woman, wonderfully experienced and with all the special and natural aromas and scents that accrue in a woman of her age. In contrast, Cammy had the sweetness of youth and the eagerness. Equally attractive in a sexual sense, Karen and Cammy differed so greatly that each of them was desirable for different reasons. After all, the sex urge was an advanced version of the appetite, and it would be boring to have stew for dinner every day.

Though pleased with Cammy's compliment, Paula couldn't take all the credit for her success. "I've been fortunate since coming to London. A friend introduced me to an agent, the agent placed me in the film with Karen, and Karen has been invaluable to me. Honestly, Cammy, I would be nowhere without her."

"Does she frighten you, Paula?"

"No, not in the least." Paula laughed at the odd question. "Why on earth should she do that?"

"I've never actually met Karen Cayson, but she strikes me as a woman with a forceful personality."

"Karen's very direct, very much to the point," Paula conceded. "But her bark is much worse than her bite."

"Bite." Cammy repeated the last word of Paula's sentence with a giggle. "That reminds me. I heard a whisper that she's a dyke, but most people say that's rubbish. Come on, Paula, put me out of my misery by telling me the truth. Is she?"

Replying light-heartedly, Paula said, "I think you only asked me here to give me the third degree."

"Nonsense," Cammy protested. "I asked you because you are you, and I enjoy being with you."

"Not exactly scintillating company, am I?" Modesty caused Paula to put herself down.

"I don't want to embarrass you," Cammy began, "but I will say that you are the most marvellous girl I have ever met."

"You're joking with me, Cammy."

"I'm not, Paula, I'm serious," Cammy insisted. "I don't remember too much of what went on at the hotel that night, which is probably a good thing, but I do have a vivid memory that you don't kiss with your lips."

Puzzled, Paula asked, "What do you mean?" She suddenly had a shaking feeling of inadequacy, fearful of what Cammy's answer might be.

Leaning to one side on the lounger so as to bring her mouth close to Paula's ear, Cammy murmured as if they were among a crowd and she were imparting a secret. "You kiss with your whole body. And it is wonderful, really wonderful. No one has ever kissed me like that before."

She nibbled at Paula's ear, her cheek. Paula shielded her eyes, ostensibly from the sun, but really to conceal the look of startled pleasure in having Cammy come onto her. Feeling excited, she couldn't tell whether it was the warmth of the sun or Cammy's closeness that was the cause of the blissful sinking, the melting of her very bones.

"I want to kiss you and make love to you," Cammy whispered.

"I may not want to," Paula teased.

"I know that you want to. I can see it in your eyes. I want to remember it this time."

Sliding down from the lounger, Cammy pulled Paula to her. She kissed her with lips open, tongue seeking Paula's. Feeling herself go all soft and warm, Paula dissolved against the other girl. She felt every pore unlock and open up to Cammy as the kiss gained power.

When it was over and Cammy drew away from her, Paula was devastated by the feeling of despair in losing the warmth of Cammy's body. She said, "This is why you were asking about Karen, isn't it?"

"Yes," Cammy admitted. "Has she had you?"

Paula's confirming nod inflamed Cammy's passion. Pulling Paula to her, she took her chin in her hands and brought her mouth close to hers. Fusing into the soft yet firm curves of Cammy's lovely body, Paula felt her own body blending fluidly with Cammy so that they were touching completely from head to toe.

They kissed, and this time Cammy was fiery, demanding. Her mouth covered Paula's lips, and the breath went out of her. She lost herself completely in the warmth that radiated from Cammy. It fanned the flames of Paula's desire, quickly igniting the deep untapped roots of her so that they burned with an overwhelming passion.

"God, I think I love you," Cammy said, her lips against Paula's cheek. "For today, anyway. Maybe tomorrow. Maybe even every day to come."

"Don't talk of love," Paula said huskily. "There is no yesterday, no tomorrow, there is just the *now,* Cammy, and I want sex."

"Then kiss me."

Paula kissed her. The kiss was long and sweet and consuming. Paula took a deep breath, relishing the afterglow of Cammy's sweet tongue in her mouth and the nectar that had drained from Cammy's mouth into hers.

Caught up on a feeling of urgency, she stroked Cammy's hair. It was soft and fine and the noonday sun sparkled in on the golden flowing waves. Paula was in awe of a new emotion assailing her. Never, never before had she felt her body triumph completely over her mind, telling her what to do, when to do it, and how.

For an instant she was terrified at totally losing control. Fear made her try to free herself, but Cammy's arms tightened around her, and the warmth of Cammy's body flowed into her. The terror subsided swiftly. Desire raced through her, sparking every nerve, turning her bones into liquid things. Down, further down, deep down to the dark placid pool at the very centre of Paula, desire churned into a sea of stormy yearning.

"You pushed me away," Cammy complained with a smile. "You little minx, you little tease. You know that I'm going to have you. I'm going to drive you crazy."

Her hand reached down and lifted one of Paula's breasts from her bikini top. Cammy kissed the nipple, a hard projection in the firmed white flesh overflowing from her cupped palm.

They kissed again and Paula slipped back into a delicious void, unthinking, uncaring. Their hands eagerly sought the taut, hot, straining places of each other's needs. The sun's heat beat down on them, but the friction of their bodies was producing an even more exotic glow. There was an ecstatic interchange of smell, taste, glow, touch, breath and sweat. In those magic moments there was a plundering of pleasure that no sun could outshine.

The roar of a car engine and a squealing of tyres jerked them apart. "Oh, shit!" Cammy groaned, hurriedly adjusting her swimsuit and tidying her hair with combing fingers. "It's Arnie from the theatre. The prat's here to explain a change in the choreography of tonight's show."

As the doorbell rang at the front of the house, she kissed Paula quickly, saying, "This is just a postponement, darling. Next time we'll make sure that we are not disturbed."

It was four o'clock that afternoon when Karen Cayson switched off the engine of her car in her allotted place in the studio car park. She sat for a moment in the uncomfortable heat inside the vehicle, head back, eyes closed. It was necessary to get her head back together before entering the noisy hurly-burly of the studio. Karen was worried. She knew that she was right to be worried, but it was made worse by the fact that her worry was indefinable. It had to do with the negotiations, such as they were, at Malcolm Reay's place. Reay and Ralph Laker, his solicitor, had been friendly and plausible. Too plausible, Karen suspected now.

They'd had no problem in persuading her that she was doing the right thing. It was simple, plain and straightforward, Laker had explained to her. On her inheriting the studios after Matthew's death, Reay would own ten per cent of the business. Everything either of the men said seemed to carry suspicion with it, but she had tried to tell herself that it didn't.

"What power does that give him?" Sharp concerned had tightened Karen's voice. "I need Malcolm's drive and expertise, but not at the expense of my overall control being under threat."

Spreading both hands wide, palms up, Laker had made a what-can-I-do? gesture to the filing cabinet in Reay's office.

"Miss Cayson, Karen." The solicitor had opened his eyes wide as a sign of total honesty. "Malcolm's ten per cent is a tiny drop in the sea of your business. He can offer his opinion, he can advise if you request him to, but you will remain the boss-lady throughout."

"That's the deal," Reay had said, reaching out to shake hands.

But she hadn't been able to take his hand. To do so would have been to feel the touch of every man she had ever been with. So she pretended not to have seen the proffered hand and, probably against her better judgment, she thought now, she had added her signature to the document. The small print had been there, masses of it. But even if she had not signed, but had brought the document home and studied it all night, she probably wouldn't have been able to grasp any of what it said.

Reassuring herself that, after Matthew had gone, she would be able to have Richard Neehan handle any problems with Reay, she got out of the car. It was still early enough for the summer's day to have retained its beauty. It consisted entirely of sky, a great expanse of cloudless blue, a brilliant sky that was an empty, meaningless smile. The sun was too bright, and the heat came up from the tarmacadam so that she could feel it through the soles of her feet.

She had made a tentative plan to visit Matthew in hospital that evening. She owed it to him, and her conscience was punishing her day and night for abandoning him. It had been the insecurity of someone whose early life had been poverty-stricken that had made her neglect her ailing husband. But, now she had been able to guarantee her future by ensuring that Malcolm Reay would be there to help her in an uncertain future, she could set time aside to comfort Matthew.

Entering the studio, she saw Paula talking to a cameraman at the far side of the large room. Then, catching her immediate attention, was a slender honey-haired figure who stood with John Brighton's friendly arm around her narrow shoulders. Karen's first thought was that she could be Brighton's daughter, a girl she had never met, coming straight from school to see her daddy at work.

But when she got nearer, and the girl looked at her through long-lashed eyes, Karen realised that this was no child. The girl met her eyes steadily, although a lack of confidence made her a little tongue-tied as she asked, "Could you spare me a minute or two, please, Miss Cayson?"

Noticing the girl's awkwardness, Brighton gallantly sprang to her assistance. Lighting a cigar, he slanted a look at Karen through the smoke. "This is Nikki Graham, Karen. She's just left Cammy Studland's musical, and is looking for work. I told her to see you."

Not particularly interested, Karen enquired dully, "Whose idea was it to leave the musical, yours or theirs?"

"Theirs," Nikki, eyes downcast, blushing a little, admitted.

"Then you don't exactly come highly recommended," Karen coldly remarked.

"Don't let that worry you, Nikki," John Brighton advised the girl loudly. "You don't need to act, but just show off enough of yourself to give the Johns a hard-on. A standing prick ain't no art critic."

Paula came towards them then. Noticing her sun-reddened skin, Karen knew that Paula hadn't spent the day in the studio. Where had she been, and with whom? Suppressing her anger, Karen postponed subjecting Paula to a barrage of questions.

"Nikki is a friend of mine, Karen," Paula fluttered.

"That is a recommendation of sorts," Karen said briskly to Nikki, who was waiting anxiously for Karen's decision.

"I would be most grateful for the chance to show you what I can do," Nikki murmured.

The girl had a uniqueness that intrigued Karen. Though tired and faintly ill through worry about the business, she found that she couldn't dismiss the golden-haired, doll-like little creature out of hand. But the implications of her deal with Reay suddenly became starkly clear. One of the technicians had a radio playing and the music wound round her like ribbons of grey mist, blurring everything. There was a high note singing in her ears, and her feet felt stuck to the floor so she couldn't move them. She was conscious of Paula signalling behind her back to Nikki, trying to get the girl to say something they had probably earlier agreed on.

"I've a thousand and one things to contend with right now, Nikki," Karen explained. "And I have to visit my husband in hospital this evening. Ask Paula or John for my telephone number and give me a ring later on."

"Later this evening?" Nikki checked, struggling to hide her elation.

"Later this evening," Karen confirmed.

As she walked away from the group she was aware of Paula looking at her in a kind of disappointed-disapproving-unforgiving manner. Let the kid stew in her own juice. That was a pretty good metaphor, very apt. It would do Paula good to be jealous, pay her back for sloping off for sex in the sun with someone that afternoon.

"Give Matthew my best regards," Brighton called after her.

Giving him a backward wave, Karen walked on, weighted down by dread of visiting the hospital and having to face Matthew. It seemed a million miles to her dressing room, and it felt as if her legs were shackled.

Thirteen

All in all it had been a good day for Cheryl Valenta. It began with the news that a cabinet minister had suddenly and unexpectedly resigned for personal reasons. He was a controversial, arrogant figure on whom Cheryl had been compiling a dossier. She even had his obituary on file, among others, in readiness. Usually there was a sordid story behind the bland official resignation announcement – the did-he-fall-or-was-he-pushed? syndrome. Cheryl soon learned that was how it was in this case. At nine thirty that morning, Deborah Hurley, Cheryl's super researcher, had telephoned.

"Cheryl, this government minister," Deborah had begun in the laid-back manner that she used to hide her enthusiasm for a blockbuster piece of news. "I've found the whore he's probably resigned to spend more time with."

Cheryl had jotted down the girl's name and Hampstead address and telephone number. There are rules in the civilised jungle that even apply to prostitutes, and Cheryl had politely telephoned first to make an appointment. Half an hour later she pulled up outside an impressively large redbrick house. It had a veranda with four white columns, and a large chimney at either end. Business had to be good, really good, Cheryl decided as she rang the doorbell.

The girl who answered the door was a stunner. Her black hair was short, her breasts self-supporting, and her wide mouth a provocative pout. She had long violet eyes, a straight nose and cheekbones that were high and patrician. Eighteen, that was

Cheryl's guess, but the girl's eyes were older and bolder than that. Her face, as a whole, had a sensual quality.

"Hi, I rang you a little while ago. I'm Cheryl Valenta."

"Wow!" The girl's bright-blue eyes widened in surprise. "I was expecting some old librarian type with a face like a fresh-fucked cat. Pardon my French. Hi, I'm Janey Starr. Come on in."

Janey's walk was a practised little parade that gave a tantalising fillip to her hips. Her full breasts swayed slightly under a yellow high-necked sweater, and her long exquisitely proportioned legs were brazenly bare under the short blue-denim skirt.

She led Cheryl into a lovely room that was decorated in shades of mauve with discreet accents of old rose and muted green. Totally feminine, the room suited Janey Star perfectly, and it told Cheryl that there was no man in the house. Gesturing for Cheryl to be seated on a velvet-covered settee, Janey perched on the upholstered arm of a chair.

She was talkative and absolutely frank. Cheryl found her easy to get along with and instantly likable. Janey readily explained that she was a student studying for degrees in design and media presentation. Without the hint of a blush, she admitted that she financed her academic ambition by working as a call girl at the top of that profession. When Janey claimed that she was pulling down £1,000 a night, Cheryl didn't doubt her. She was a young woman, indolent and sensual, with a truly lovely face, great looks and of startling scholarship and brilliant capabilities.

As she bubbled with excitement at the thought of being interviewed, Janey's violet eyes were bright with thoughts of the vagaries of her profession. Getting her to talk about the cabinet minister was no problem. She assured Cheryl that she would tell her nothing but the truth.

"You can quote me with confidence," she said with a crooked grin. "It's a topsy-turvy world, Cheryl. If you are looking for honesty you come to a hooker. If you want to get fucked you go to a solicitor."

"Nicely put," Cheryl smilingly remarked. Taking her pad and pen from her handbag, she said, "Fire away."

Janey gave the full story. The government minister, a regular client of hers, was a crack addict. A young man who helped out at his constituency headquarters had complained to his parents of the minister's conduct. The police had been informed, and the minister had immediately jumped ship.

When Cheryl had all the information she needed and stood ready to leave, Janey came close enough for Cheryl to catch the fragrance of expensive perfume. She recognised it as a scent that she could afford to buy but would be reluctant to spend so much money on.

"This probably sounds like a Mae West one-liner, Cheryl," Janey said, less up front than she had been until then, "but if you want to come and see me some time, just give me a buzz to let me know you're on your way."

Taken aback by this unexpected invitation, Cheryl asked, "Why would you think I would want to do that, Janey?"

"I suppose it's the old adage that says it takes one to know one. You see, Cheryl, I'm a lesbian too. With me, men are for business while women are for pleasure. If I could get away with it I'd wear asbestos gloves when touching the weirdoes I service."

"Thanks for the invite," Cheryl said, adding regretfully, "I'd like to fix up a date here and now, Janey, but I've just begun a very special relationship."

"Then all I need do is bide my time," Janey grinned cheekily. "Nobody as yet has made monogamy attractive enough to last, and I don't think that you'll change that."

"I'd like to believe that I can," Cheryl said wistfully.

"So would I," a serious Janey agreed. Then she was thoughtful for a moment before wonderingly asking, "Am I right in thinking that you wrote up the Karen Cayson assault thing?"

"For my sins," Cheryl smilingly admitted.

"Her old man should have reversed the charges and whacked her over the head with something."

Cheryl was surprised. "You know Karen?"

"Well enough to say how she operates when she becomes vicious, and I think Karen Cayson is the most vicious person I have ever met. Is she a friend of yours?"

"Loosely speaking," Cheryl replied, wanting to know more. But Janey swiftly changed the subject.

"I really do admire your writing, Cheryl. Perhaps you could spend an hour or so to help me put the finishing touches to my autobiography. I've got most of it done, actually. I thought long and hard to eventually come up with a great title: *I'm Going to Fuck For Ever*."

"That could be just a tad over the top," Cheryl warned.

"OK, I accept that none of us go on for ever." Janey had shrugged, hurt by the mild criticism. "But I do have an alternative. What do you think of *Prostitutes Don't Give a Fuck*?"

"That's better. I like the witty double meaning," a defeated Cheryl said before she bade Janey a fond farewell.

In fairness to the other side, Cheryl then contacted the minister's office, to be told that he didn't wish to comment. Two hours later she had written up the story and was satisfied with it. Her agent's approval of the piece had been mirrored through the lens of his glasses. He made a few telephone calls, and the story was sold at a good price.

Cheryl felt good about earning enough in a few hours to comfortably keep her for a month, and she had decided to call it a day. She was a high earner now, and if every day was like this, she would in a comparatively short time rank among the wealthiest women in the United Kingdom. But, in the way of most writers, Cheryl had times when she completely dried up. During those periods she could not compose a saleable story.

Success in her work invariably acted as an aphrodisiac for

Cheryl. Added to that was the fact that being with Janey Starr had left her juicy between the legs.

In her car outside the agent's office she took counsel with herself, and rejected a dozen resolves. The memory of a delicious and petite blonde, however, decided the matter, so she had telephoned Wendi. While waiting for the receiver to be picked up at the other end, she had mentally titillated herself by imagining having sex for the first time with the Wendi. But the minute Wendi picked up the receiver and listlessly gave her number, Cheryl knew that something was wrong.

"I'm so sorry, Cheryl, but could we leave it today? I want to be right for you, and I'm completely worn out and terribly depressed after my visit home. I'll tell you about it when we meet. I feel that I'm letting you down."

"Don't worry, Wendi. You have a good rest."

"Will this make any difference to us, Cheryl?" Wendy anxiously enquired. "I can't tell you just how much having a one-to-one relationship means to me. I suppose that it's something that I've always wanted but was never lucky enough to find until I met you. Knowing there's someone who loves me, and is always there for me, is very important to me, Cheryl."

"I want that every bit as much as you do, Wendi," Cheryl said truthfully. "I'll ring in the morning to find out how you are."

After switching off her mobile, she drove through London's chaotic traffic, taking her sexual frustration out on the other drivers who were idiotic enough to be caught up in it. She responded to the blast of a horn from a purple-faced cab driver by miming, "Up yours, fuck face!" The cabby replied with a clearly mouthed "Get fucked!" If only, but not by an ugly bastard like you, Cheryl thought as the traffic lights changed and she and the taxi driver parted, probably for ever. Two ridiculously angry ships that passed in the night.

Now she was home alone, with a long and boring evening stretching ahead of her. Pouring herself a glass of white wine, she put the tape Marriott had given her into the video recorder. Settling back comfortably in an armchair, she pressed the remote control.

Startled by the sudden brightness of the video picture, she saw Karen Cayson in a studio dressing room. To Cheryl it was if she had stepped into a brand-new, wholly irrational world.

Karen was looking at herself framed in the dressing table mirror, concentrating on peeling off false eyelashes. Assuming that Karen had just finished filming, Cheryl was made uncomfortable by the absurd thought that this was live and she was peeping timidly at Karen. It wasn't just ordinary timidity, but some little-girl reflection of guilt from her childhood.

This was secret filming, a despicable practice that she really didn't want to involve herself with. But the voyeur part of her personality took control, the force of its excitement astounding her. Cheryl looked at the lovely image of Karen reflected in the mirror. Then her eyes dropped to take in the firm, swelling breasts that required no support from the flimsy black brassiere. Beautiful, she mused. Karen Cayson was breathtakingly beautiful.

Then Cheryl found herself foolishly cringing back in her chair as Karen turned suddenly from the mirror and appeared to meet her eyes with a direct, disturbingly peculiar stare. She was being stupid. An unsuspecting Karen was simply facing a hidden camera.

Paula Monroe then came into shot, jolting Cheryl. Maybe Paula no longer had the dewy, dewy eyes she'd had the night Cheryl had met her, but there was still an untouched quality to the girl that moved Cheryl, both emotionally and sexually. Paula was wearing a simple flowered frock, but the cheapness of it couldn't conceal what was underneath. Though vaguely ashamed of herself, Cheryl could not take her gaze from the girl's luscious, bursting breasts. She wanted to get her hands on them, pull down the dress, undo the brassiere and take a full peak in her mouth.

Enthralled by the scene, Cheryl gave a startled little jerk as Karen commented, "You're all ready to go?"

"Yes, but I'll wait for you if you wish, Karen."

"If you want to." Karen shrugged. Standing up from the stool, she walked to a full-length mirror to view herself. Observing her made Cheryl remember the warning words of the mystical Sheena when they had lived together. "Staring into a full-length looking glass is a short cut to schizophrenia. Remember that, Cheryl." Knowing that it was sensible to listen to every word Sheena said, Cheryl had remembered. God, she still missed Sheena terribly, and not only for her offbeat words of wisdom.

Yet now everything but Karen went from Cheryl's mind as she watched her reach behind to unclip her bra, and let it fall. Striking a western gunfighter pose with a hand at each hip, she used her thumbs to hook into the elastic of her panties and pushed them down. Naked, she kicked the flimsy knickers from her feet. Her first sighting of Karen's mass of pubic hair was a stirring experience for Cheryl. She was shocked to find that her own hand had taken on an independence and slid up between her thighs.

Posing in the mirror, Karen was obviously pleased with what she saw. Her lovely body was in superb condition. The big, pushy breasts were crowned by two prominent nipples; the triangular dark snatch of wild hair hid the slippery entrance that Cheryl had always found herself excitedly imagining when she had been in Karen's company.

Turning away from the mirror, Karen reached for a black satin robe that she slipped easily into. As she was tying the sash, Paula spoke in a shaky voice. "I'll wait for you if that's all right, Karen."

"Of course it is, Paula," Karen smiled. "I won't be long. I put the robe on because of the way you were ogling me just now."

"I wasn't looking... I was..." Paula stammered.

Laughing, Karen gave Paula's shoulder a playful push. "I was only joking, you silly. You can look all you want. It would shock you to know what I'd like to do right now."

"What do you mean?"

"I'd like to undress you."

"But I'm all ready to go," Paula giggled girlishly.

Ignoring this, Karen sat on her heels in front of the girl. Lifting one of Paula's legs at a time, she took off her shoes and threw them to one side. Lifting Paula's right leg slightly, Karen cupped the calf and rubbed her cheek against it. Then she ran her lips over it in a series of light, feathery kisses. Sliding both hands up under Paula's dress, she ran them up and down the outsides of her soft, responsive thighs with lightly fondling fingertips. She reached the girl's panties and she pulled them down. As she stepped out of the flimsy underwear, Paula automatically spread her legs.

Karen's hands moved to stroke the length of the insides of Paula's thighs, long strokes that at first stopped short of their soft target. But her hands stroked upward and still more upward to inevitably come to the tantalising, droopy-lipped, moist and shadowy place between Paula's open legs. Twitching heavily, Paula gave a loud groan of pleasure. Quickly withdrawing her touch, Karen lifted her head.

"I've wanted to do this, dearest," she whispered, "since the day when you came into these studios for the very first time."

Paula threw her head back. Her eyes were closed and her mouth was open as she panted in ecstasy. Finger-fucking herself, Cheryl imagined kissing the girl's sweet, open mouth while Karen got to work on her down below. She found that she was sitting stiffly in fear that any movement, a single sound, would shatter what had to be a hallucination and the scene of rampant sex on the television screen would disappear.

Karen suddenly stood up and undid the sash of her robe. A shrug of her shoulders freed the shiny black garment, and it slithered to the floor. Cheryl noticed the tremor of excitement on Paula's face as she looked at the shapely nude body.

Standing stark naked in front of Paula, Karen said, "You're trembling, Paula. Are you frightened of me?"

"No," Paula gasped, "it's just that I've never been with a real woman like you."

"That's no reason to be afraid," Karen said huskily. "I want to make love to you, and love is something to be shared. It can even be the light touch, the soft kiss. Now, kiss me and tell me that you're not afraid."

Cheryl opened her legs and used her left hand to hold her labia as the fingers of her right hand softly teased and caressed her clit. She watched Karen put both hands on Paula's shoulders. Then she kissed her, first on the forehead and then on the lips. Paula pulled away. Reaching with both hands to grasp the skirt of her dress, she pulled it up over her head and off in one swift movement. She then dropped the dress on the floor and used a sideways movement of one foot to kick it away.

Then she moved back to Karen, who deftly unclipped the girl's bra before taking her in her arms. Her hands went down to hold and fondle Paula's round, soft buttocks. This time Paula returned the older woman's kiss. At first it was a gentle, sisterly kiss. But then their passion flared instantly. The kiss lost every vestige of innocence as the mouths of Karen and Paula smeared wetly together. The concealed microphone picked up their coarse breathing. The sound seemed to fill Cheryl's room, somehow increasing her arousal to an almost unbearable pitch. Everything but Paula and Karen lost importance for her. She desired the delectable young Paula, but she was also crazily hungry for the beautiful, magnificent Karen.

Stroking Paula's hair as they kissed, Karen drew her down on a divan. Cheryl could hear and feel the pounding of her own heart as Paula instinctively rolled onto her back and Karen sat astride her, panting heavily.

Tossing her glorious mane of red hair back from her face, Karen then bent to kiss the girl again. Her hands moved to caress Paula's breasts, causing the nipples to jut upward proudly as she teased them between a thumb and forefinger. Then she was kissing Paula's neck before moving a licking tongue down Paula's moist skin, circling an erect nipple tantalisingly before travelling on down through the fine hairs on her stomach.

Seeing Karen slide lower and push Paula's knees apart and dip her head between her thighs, Cheryl stopped rubbing her fingers up and down inside the sopping lips of her cunt. Instead she held them rigid and actually mounted them. Jerking her hips frantically and spasmodically, she literally fucked herself as she heard Paula's cry of pleasure when Karen's mouth met her nether lips in a tender kiss.

With one of Karen's hands on each of her hips, Paula began to gyrate her lower body. Able to hear the sucking, grunting noises that Karen was making, Cheryl knew that the older woman was setting the tempo for Paula's rhythmic movements with the pressure of her licking, sucking, nibbling, and the thrusting of her tongue.

Knowing exactly what was needed to work Paula to a fever pitch, Karen was relentless with her oral manipulation of Paula's cunt. Close to coming as she worked herself on her fingers, a watching Cheryl felt herself to be an intruder as the intimacy between the two women on the screen reached an erotic intensity. She reached with her spare hand for the remote control, and her finger sought the OFF button.

But then Paula convulsed as she hit orgasm. Never had Cheryl witnessed such a sexually charged sight as the shuddering girl's head thrashed from side to side, an expression of wild abandon on her lovely face.

Karen didn't stop as Cheryl had expected her to. She was merciless. On and on she went, lapping away at Paula's exposed cunt, slurping up her juices, teasing Paula's clit and probing both of her holes with an insatiable tongue. As she trashed about on the divan, Paula's moaning grew louder and louder. Then she was coming again, over and over, each orgasm closer to, and obviously stronger than, the previous one. Asking for nothing, but giving her all, Karen seemed to feed on Paula's pleasure.

It was all too much for Cheryl. The sights and the sounds on the screen made her climax in an eruption of excitement. It was an explosion so powerful that, as the delicious sensations coursing through her body peaked, she nearly blacked out.

Cheryl found herself sprawled in the chair, her head supported by the backrest. Sitting herself upright, she brought her attention back to the screen. A drained and exhausted Paula lay on the divan with Karen lying at her side, propped up on one elbow, smiling down at her

Moving a hand slowly, Karen lightly cupped Paula's left breast. Bending her neck, she kissed the girl's cheek. Then she kissed Paula on her full, ripe lips. Karen didn't press the kiss deeply. It was an exploratory kiss, a test to see how Paula would respond. The observing Cheryl saw that Paula shivered a little at the touch of Karen's lips, but the girl's only reaction was to nestle closer.

Karen kissed her again, more deeply this time, while she moved her hand a little to take Paula's nipple between her insinuating fingers. She kissed Paula a third time on the lips, a real, passionate kiss this time.

"That was nice, wasn't it?" Karen murmured dreamily. "You loved it, didn't you?"

Turning her head to bury her face in Karen's naked chest, Paula answered in a barely audible voice. "Yes, it was lovely."

"It's you that's lovely," Karen said, taking Paula's chin tenderly between a thumb and forefinger to turn her face out from where it was hidden against her chest. "So very lovely. I want to kiss you again."

This time Karen put everything into the kiss. Her tongue reached to gently prise open Paula's lips. Keeping her mouth closed for a few moments, Paula then gave a muffled cry and opened her mouth. Her tongue was there to eagerly meet Karen's.

Holding the kiss, enjoying it, with Paula's response becoming more pronounced by the second, Karen suddenly parted herself from the girl. Getting up from the bed, she turned and walked away. The watching Cheryl was puzzled.

"Karen!" Paula cried out pleadingly.

Not answering, Karen went to a small refrigerator and took out a bottle of white wine. After pouring two glasses, she replaced the bottle. Then she took something else from the fridge and closed the door before returning to the divan and holding out one glass of wine to Paula.

"Drink up," she said. "Sex makes you thirsty."

There was something familiar about a small pot that Karen had surreptitiously placed beside the divan before joining Paula on it. While the two of them drank the wine, Cheryl leaned closer to the television and was able to identify the pot as a carton of yoghurt. Peering closer, she was intrigued when reading the side of the carton to discover it was strawberry flavour.

Placing the now empty glasses on the floor beside the divan, Karen picked up the yoghurt and passed it to a mystified Paula.

"I'm not hungry, Karen," Paula said, revealing that she was still an innocent to quite a degree.

"You will be," Cheryl heard Karen confidently predict. "Just open the carton and pour it out."

Lying on her back, a smiling Karen said, "Spread it over me." She pointed to each of her breasts, her tummy and pubes, saying as she did so, "Here, here, and down there."

Cheryl held her breath and watched a bewildered Paula kneel between Karen's legs and tip the yoghurt over her. Following whispered instructions from Karen, Paula spread the yoghurt over her breasts and down over her flat stomach. As she reached the mound of dark red hair surrounding the engorged lips of Karen's cunt, an obviously fully aroused Paula took time and care. Her hand moved in a slow caressing movement as she smeared the yoghurt through the hair, then gently opened Karen's labia. Pulse racing, Cheryl heard Karen draw in a long breath that she let out as a moaning sigh as Paula tenderly spread the yoghurt on the pink flesh inside of Karen's pouting cunt.

Paula, needing no instructions from Karen, then moved up to start licking the yoghurt from Karen's breasts. The girl held them together and licked deep into the valley between them. The watching Cheryl could almost imagine the raunchy flavour of strawberry yoghurt garnished with the salt taste of Karen's sweat.

Karen released a second moaning sigh as Paula closed her mouth on her fully erect nipple and sucked gently. Then Karen was writhing a little and moaning softly and continuously as Paula licked down over her stomach and started to suck yoghurt from her. In case she brought on another massive orgasm and blacked out, thereby missing something, Cheryl didn't dare to even think of the special taste the girl must be enjoying down there.

Good as it must have been, Paula was now too eager to linger in the pubic forest. She moved lower and Karen gave a small scream of pleasure as Paula sampled her first taste by dipping her tongue inside her.

Sitting forward in her chair, one hand between her legs, working frantically on her own cunt again, Cheryl saw Paula close her eyes and savour the taste of Karen's cream. Head going down once more, Paula again entered Karen with her tongue, deeper this time, and Cheryl recognised the first stirrings towards orgasm in Karen.

Cheryl, accepting that Paula was young and relatively inexperienced, reasoned that everyone must have an innate set of sex instructions, as the blonde girl got to work with the technique of an expert. Paula slipped first one finger, then a second, inside Karen's vagina. At the same time she licked at her stiffened clit. This made Karen gasp with delight and raise her hips towards Paula.

"More! More!" Karen cried out pleadingly.

Not ceasing even for one moment to tease Karen's swollen bud with her mouth, Paula answered Karen's plea by slipping a third and then a fourth finger into her. Feverishly fingering her own clit, Cheryl could see that Paula had put her free hand down between her own legs and was fingering herself as the tempo of Karen's thrusting hips increased as she was caught up in the throes of a mighty orgasm.

The two women on the screen climaxed simultaneously, and Cheryl came off just a split second behind them. This time it was an aftershock, not an earthquake, and she remained fully conscious. She saw that Paula had collapsed on the divan, half lying on top of Karen. A sultry Karen, eyes heavy-lidded, combed her fingers through Paula's hair and spoke huskily.

"Now I'm going to do something really special to you, darling."

"Oh, no!" Cheryl groaned aloud. "Don't go on. I can't stand any more."

But that wasn't true. She avidly moved forward in her chair again as Karen's open mouth, as hungry as ever, claimed Paula's mouth. But then there was a loud click and the screen suddenly went blank. The tape had come to an end.

Slumping back in her chair, Cheryl first thought of what the tape's existence would do to the terminally ill Matthew Wyndham. She promised herself that she would not allow Marriott to pressure her into threatening Wyndham with it. But, if she wouldn't, Marriott would find someone who would. She decided that she would visit Wyndham in hospital tomorrow and somehow try to persuade him that it would be a sensible move to sell out to Alan Marriott. She was unlikely to succeed, but she had to try.

Then she was starkly aware of her own needs, which had been brought to a pitch by the video. The tremendous power of sex, its terrific energy, had built up in her. She was in the grip of compulsion to sip a dry martini and kiss a wet mouth. Wendi was her first thought, but it was now twenty minutes to midnight.

Wendi had troubles after visiting her sick father, and it would be cruel to disturb her now.

Aware that she would never sleep that night because of her high state of arousal, Cheryl looked up Janey Starr's telephone number and dialled it. Janey, not surprisingly for someone in her profession, answered cautiously and suspiciously by just giving her number.

"Janey, it's me, Cheryl Valenta."

"Hello, Cheryl. Don't tell me, I forgot to tell you some important part of the story."

"No, nothing like that," Cheryl said. "I want to give you whatever help I can with your autobiography, and I thought about coming over."

"Now?" Janey exclaimed. "It's coming up to the witching hour. You're a fibber, Cheryl. I don't think it's my etchings that you're after. What's happened? The love of your life got the decorators in?"

Embarrassed, Cheryl answered truthfully. "No, she went to see her sick father and came back really depressed."

"I was right about monogamy, Cheryl. You've managed to stay loyal for, what, ten hours?" Janey said with a good-natured laugh.

"I don't want a lecture from you, Janey," Cheryl chided as a joke.

"I know exactly what you want from me," Janey chuckled. Then her breathing became erratic and her voice had lowered an octave when she went on. "I can come to yours if you like, or you to mine. Whichever, I don't mind, Cheryl."

"I'll come to you."

"Please hurry," Janey pleaded breathily.

Karen Cayson regretted having at last visited the hospital. It had been the kind of experience that made you want to crawl back into the void. Matthew had lain in bed shrivelled and with pained eyes staring at four walls that were the horizon of his future. There had been no complaining that she hadn't been to see him, no recriminations of any kind on his part. Genuinely pleased to see her, he had been anxious to avoid the present by reviving old memories, to talk about a past of which a good section already lay dead.

"What wouldn't you give, Karen, to be living it up in Los Angeles again?"

"They were good times," Karen had said, reminiscing as he expected her to.

"We were really somebody then, you and me," he had laughed spasmodically, before wincing in pain and falling quiet until the spasm had passed. Then he continued, his voice stronger than before. "The new Rita Hayworth, they called you. That made me proud, but it didn't do you full justice, Karen. You are unique, not a copy of some other person. We should have stayed on there longer. You'd have... been the queen of Hollywood... by now. The Nicole Kidmans and... the Sandra Bullocks... couldn't hold... a candle to you..." The pain had returned. Matthew's face had twitched horribly. Then he had lain quiet.

He had looked very tired, very old, but still present was the aura of pride that was so much a part of Matthew Wyndham. There had been no expression on his white and lined face, only the sadness of his suffering in the reflected light of his eyes.

"I'll fetch doctor to give him a sedative," a nurse had told her.

Having to turn her head away as the doctor had injected her husband's painfully thin arm, Karen had quietly asked the nurse, "What is it?"

"Morphine," had been the nurse's whispered reply.

At that moment it had come home to Karen how far down the road to the end Matthew had gone. She had expected aspirin, codeine at the worst.

"He'll sleep for a while," the doctor had told her, and she had stood up from her chair.

She had wanted to get away. Antiseptics had made the air unbreathable. Every sound was muted. The voice of everyone around her had been too low, and the footsteps of the nurses were so soft that they had been ghostly.

Standing by the bed, she had looked down at the white sunken face. She had known that Matthew deserved a kiss of farewell. But when she had bent over him she hadn't initially been able to bring herself to do it. Even touching his thin, cold hand had been too much for her. Yet she had kissed him tenderly, and then had straightened, turned and started for the doorway.

There had been a greyness at the hospital that had followed her home. The summer evening she had driven through should have been alive with colours, but she saw it only in a depressing monochrome.

The morbid air clung to her now. It seemed to fill the house. She had to get out for a few hours. She needed to be where there were bright lights, alcohol, and an interchange with people. But she didn't want to go alone, couldn't stand to be alone. The animals had it right when they'd insisted on going into the Ark two by two so that they'd have companionship while waiting for the Flood to subside. On impulse she had phone Cheryl Valenta, but on getting her answerphone she had hung up without saying a word.

"What is it?" she answered irritably to a knock on her door.

The handle turned and the door opened just far enough for Henry Drury to put his grey-white head into the room. "There is someone here to see you, Madam."

"Who is it?"

"A young lady, madam."

"Does the young lady have a name?" Karen snapped.

"I would regard that as a distinct possibility, madam," Henry sarcastically conceded. "One moment, please."

Withdrawing his head, he poked it back in a few seconds later. "The young lady does indeed have a name, madam. She is Miss Nikki Graham."

For a few moments the name meant nothing to Karen. Then it

clicked. The doll-like little creature who had arrived at the studio seeking fame and fortune. A kid with the looks of a young Audrey Hepburn, but lacking her elegance. A wet little bitch to whom Karen would enjoy giving the bum's rush. She had told the stupid little fucker to telephone.

"Show her in, Henry," she said flatly.

Minutes later the girl sheepishly entered the room. It would be an understatement to say that she was underdressed. Wearing a shabby anorak, she was absolutely unglamorous. In that state she wouldn't have got a job as a factory cleaner.

She apologised self-consciously to Karen. "I'm sorry if I'm intruding, Miss Cayson."

"I was expecting you to telephone," Karen said curtly. "How did you find out where I live?"

"It wasn't difficult."

"I suppose not, but getting here must have been a problem. Do you have a car?"

"No," a blushing Nikki answered. "I came so far on the Underground, then caught buses."

"Goodness, you really must want to join the studios," Karen remarked.

"More than anything in the world, Miss Cayson."

An idea came suddenly to Karen. A solution to her dread of being alone that night. The kid's appearance was unprepossessing right then, but the fact that she had looked good that afternoon meant that she "scrubbed up well", as the saying goes.

"I plan to go clubbing tonight, Nikki," she said.

"I'm so sorry," the girl muttered humbly, misconstruing Karen's meaning. "I'll go. Will you have an answer for me if I came to the studios in the morning?"

"You've got it wrong." Karen, feeling strangely better now that she had female company, smiled at her. "I take it you've got a decent evening dress where you're staying."

Nikki nodded. "Yes."

"What if I got myself ready, then drove you to your place? Would you be interested in giving yourself a quick makeover and joining me?"

"You mean..." Nikki stammered. "You mean... go clubbing with you?"

"That's exactly what I mean," Karen assured her. "If you want to pack yourself a bag you can come back here and stay overnight."

"I can't..."

"You can't what?"

"I can't believe it."

"Fuck me, Nikki," Karen swore impatiently. "It's a good job that Cinderella had more faith than you, otherwise a lot of us would be out of work every Christmas." She waved a hand towards a drinks cabinet. "Pour yourself a drink and I'll be with you in two shakes of a donkey's dick."

From the corner of her eye when she left the room, Karen saw Nikki advancing slowly towards the cabinet with the stiff-legged pacing of a sleepwalker.

Fourteen

"I'm sorry to rush off like this," Cheryl apologised to Janey Starr in the hallway of Janey's house.

Baroness Thatcher squinted at them from a framed photograph hanging on one wall, while Fidel Castro stared sternly from the opposite wall. Cheryl didn't question this political paradox. Janey was too complex a person to give a logical answer. A dozen roses in a vase were a testimony to Janey's femininity. The flowers were limp. A scattering of black-edged petals lay on the hall table.

"Love 'em and leave 'em," Janey commented in a low voice used deliberately to cement the joking bond between them.

"There was certainly plenty of love, Janey."

"How are you spelling that – l-u-s-t?"

Cheryl couldn't argue. Janey certainly was something else. Cheryl's maxim was that if you can imagine what it would be like to have sex with a particular person, then that person wasn't worth having sex with. Trying to imagine a fuck with Janey would have had Walter Mitty beat. Janey had absolute control over every sinuous muscle of her body. It was a body that, despite her calling, had a virginal look, with uptilted small breasts, a narrow waistline and snaky hips. Not in the least pretentious, but an unashamed extrovert, Janey was one of those lucky people who broke all the rules and got away with it.

She had welcomed Cheryl with a voice that was the soft purr of a kitten. Her violet eyes had been glinting, sexy slits of appraisal.

They had passed caressingly over Cheryl's breasts and on down to the tight fit of the black dress over her hips. Cheryl had again felt the electric, chemical reaction of earlier that day, but now it was far more potent. She had known similar sparks with other women.

With Janey it had been different. Very different. "I take no prisoners," was the warning she had whispered in Cheryl's ear after they had shared their first kiss. Electricity had zigzagged between them. They had spent more than an hour in Janey's bed. Each had savoured the particular brand of pleasure the other had to offer. She had discovered Janey to be a thrilling sexual combination, capable of both mating like a savage and, in contrast, rolling Cheryl's saliva and vagina excretions around her palate like a sophisticated connoisseur of wine. Janey's "party piece", as she called it, was to ease Cheryl's legs wide apart and lie on top of her, putting her hand down between them to open the lips of them both, then wriggling her hips until their sexes were hotly glued together.

In a session of hot sex they had demanded and received everything from each other, everything but commitment, which was something neither of them wanted. It was free love at its best, with their only regret being that it had to end.

Able to think clearly once her supercharged sexual energy had been drained, Cheryl planned to get home and have a few hours' sleep before beginning what would be a busy day. Top priority was a visit to Matthew Wyndham in hospital. For his sake more than Karen's, she had to take whatever measures necessary to ensure that he would never see the video of his wife engaged in abandoned sex with a young woman.

"Will you tell the love of your life about having been with me?" Janey enquired as she held Cheryl's light coat for her.

"It wouldn't be much of a relationship if I didn't."

Having been thinking of Wendi since her last explosive orgasm with the tasty Janey, Cheryl had decided to throw herself on her mercy. She would explain everything and leave it to Wendi to decide whether forgiveness was possible. The circumstances must make it so. After all, they weren't a couple of schoolgirl virgins making vows to each other. Both of them had been round the track a few times. Looking at it from a philosophical rather than a romantic angle, a slice off a cut loaf was never missed.

"It probably won't be any kind of a relationship if you do," Janey logically pointed out. She turned Cheryl to face her, and moved in close, saying, "As this is likely to be our last-ever kiss, let's make sure that it's a long one." Her voice sighed away. Cheryl noticed that her eyes were bright and smoky at the same time, hiding the thoughts behind them.

They kissed, mouths twisting this way and that, lips mashing against lips, tongues doing the Sabre Dance. Each of them wanted to get as much as possible from the kiss for pleasure then, and to store the memory of it for the future. Wilhelm Reich said that the sex drive is nothing but the motor memory of previously remembered pleasure. Sex was as much etheric as it was physical, and Cheryl enlarged on Reich's theory by the rather Freudian belief that, although you thought that you were going to bed with just one woman, all those who had ever fucked her, and all those who had fucked you, were there joining in.

When the kiss ended, Janey kept their opened lips in light contact, breathing her sweet, warm breath stirringly into Cheryl's mouth. Eventually and reluctantly, Cheryl pushed her gently away. "It would be so easy to go back into the bedroom, Janey."

"This easy," Janey agreed, taking her hand and attempting to lead her away.

Cheryl recognised this as a crucial moment. A word here, a gesture, or even a careless smile at the wrong time would prevent her from leaving. The huge difference between Janey's way of life and her own meant that she had to go quickly. If they stayed together, neither of them could guess what lay ahead. They could never openly be a couple, but lurk and love in the shadows, prepared for their love for each other to come second to the opinions of everyone else.

"No, no," Cheryl protested, terrified of her own lack of willpower.

They stood apart, silent, looking at each other, marvelling at what they had just done together. They had opened themselves up completely to each other, an act so intense that it had been a rite. Their souls had mystically touched during their embrace. Now they had reached a point when both of them accepted that only lies were permissible.

Shaking her head sadly and reflectively, Janey said softly, "You will keep in touch, won't you, Cheryl?"

"Of course," Cheryl tearfully replied.

Turning, she opened the door and went out through it without looking back. The door closed behind her.

Proud to be seen with Karen, who as a celebrity was being covertly eyed by the people around them, Nikki Graham was having a great night. The fast-moving twenty-first century had narrowed the generation gap to just a few years, so the difference in their ages didn't affect them. Karen's long dress made of white silk chiffon traversed time. It looked modern while at the same time seeming to belong to the 1960s, but, with one shoulder bare and the other draped in the style of Ancient Greece, it couldn't be dated. She looked absolutely stunning in it. The strobe lighting somehow picked her out and projected her. The switching of light and shadow across her face accentuated her high cheekbones and brought out the strong planes of her jawline.

Even so, Nikki didn't feel in the least upstaged by the famous star. Her own yellow dress was as close to her as body paint. She was a living doll that, judging by the looks she was getting, plenty of grown-ups, both men and women, would be happy to play with.

This was the fourth club they had visited this evening, and it was packed. A young guy afflicted by one of those "Oh God, I'm going bald!" ultra-short haircuts, was playing "I Left My Heart in San Francisco" on the piano with a talent that belied his very ordinary looks. Karen was nodding her head in time to the tune. She had loosened up a little more with each drink, something that Nikki welcomed because it brought them closer. It seemed impossible to her that she had gone to Karen's home earlier that evening in an act of desperation. At best she had hoped for nothing more than a grudging appointment for a routine test before the cameras. At worst she had expected hostility, to be turned away. Now, just a couple of hours later, she was out on the town with the magnificent Karen Cayson, and being treated as an equal. This would be one in the eye for Paula Monroe, who was a nice friend but had got a little too big for her boots since playing opposite to Karen.

The piano had fallen silent and the disco was back on. The music started up again, pounding, and dancers were out on the floor, convulsing as if they were plugged into the mains electricity.

Overcoming Nikki's objections, Karen pulled her out onto the floor. They danced facing each other, experimentally at first as they sought a rapport, like first-time lovers in the sex act. Then the alcohol she had consumed fumed into Karen's brain, blanking out her inhibitions. She began dancing with sinuous movements. Twisting and turning with her head thrown back, eyes partly closed and mouth partly open, she moved animatedly. The clinging silken dress proved to Nikki, and to several appreciative onlookers, that Karen had no underwear underneath. It was a display hovering somewhere between immodesty and indecency.

The sight stirred Nikki, and her arousal was increased collectively by drink, the heat in the club, the gyrating bodies around her and the crashing, intrusive beat of the music. Karen was laughing and clapping to the beat. Then she suddenly froze, her raised hands stopping in mid-beat as her eyes met Nikki's.

Something special flashed between them. It was something that neither of them could comprehend. Then it was gone. But it left Nikki with an icy prickling creeping all over her scalp. Dancing again, Karen swayed close, and Nikki, eager for the sweating scent of her, breathed in deep. Like a dog sniffing a bitch on heat, she scolded herself.

When the dance ended, she had to put a steadying hand under Karen's arm as they headed for the bar. "Boy, do I need a drink!" exclaimed Karen, who'd already had too many.

"Do you think we should call it a night, Karen?" Nikki suggested tentatively, worried that Karen would soon become unmanageable, while at the same time frightened of sounding bossy.

A girl sitting sideways on a stool at the bar was attempting to catch Nikki's eye. She had a lean face with a long, thin nose. Her sensuous red mouth was a provocative pout, and it must have cost her a fortune to have her hair mussed up in the modern untidy style. The skirt of her polished bronze dress was ultra-short, and when she slowly and deliberately parted her legs, Nikki saw that she was wearing crotchless panties. Her profusion of dark nether hair bridged the gap created by the missing nylon. A gaudy but cheap ring was prominent on a finger of her left hand.

The girl invitingly licked her lips, and Nikki was tempted. But she reminded herself that the fleshly delights the girl was offering were ephemeral, whereas being with Karen was a career move. The girl raised an arm to check the time on a wristwatch that was as cheap as the ring. Nikki recognised the move as a signal for her to hurry up.

Head bowed, Nikki studied the drink she was holding is if it were the most interesting thing in the world, and switched off the sexual sensor that had picked up the girl. She heard Karen answering her question.

"Just this one, and then off we'll go to beddy-byes," Karen giggled.

A spotlight was playing over a girl singer. She wore a shiny red dress that exposed a lot of bosom. The girl was making better music with her hips than she was her voice. The sensuality of the swaying black girl had grabbed the attention of just about everyone in the club. A strange hush had descended, and Nikki had the perhaps not so ridiculous notion that everyone there was having mind sex with the girl as well as with everybody else in the room.

Lazily raising her glass, Karen let her eyes flick over its rim at Nikki. Indicating the singer with a nod of her head, Karen moved close to Nikki, a grin twitching at the corners of her mouth. She said in a low tone, "I'd like to have that beauty across that piano. She'd be playing *Land of Hope and Glory* with her arse while I fucked her."

Hearing this language of the gutter from a star she was accustomed to seeing cool and elegant on cinema and television screens knocked Nikki mentally sideways for a few moments. But she recovered, and realised what Karen had just said confirmed both that she was drunk, and that the rumour that Nikki had heard was the truth. The lovely, desirable, edible Karen Cayson was a lesbian.

Leaning closer so that her forehead was touching Nikki's, Karen said in a confiding whisper, "I'll let you into the secret of my success, Nikki, the power that brought me an army of fans. What got me to the top is sexual magnetism. I'm one red-hot babe, and you'd better believe it. I had my first orgasm when I was three years old. It was self-induced, of course, but I'm buggered if I know how I did it. I didn't even know what it was that had happened, until I worked it out years later. Crazy, isn't it? I sometimes dry up in front of the camera, forgetting lines learned ten minutes before, yet I can remember coming in my cocoa thirty-five years ago. Now, here's another little secret. If I try to move away from this bar I'm going to fall flat on my fucking face."

As the shock of this vulgar, one-way conversation eased, so did the realisation seep into Nikki's head that she had a drunken

Karen becoming more and more dependent on her. Only a silk chiffon dress separated her from Karen's superb body. She would be staying the night with her. The two of them alone in the house. Although becoming increasingly worked up by the prospects that lay ahead, Nikki was aware that it would come to nothing. There was no way she could bring herself to take advantage of someone who was drunk. Especially Karen.

"You'd better get them to call us a cab, Nikki."

At last some sound sense had come from Karen. If Nikki didn't get her out of here right away, then she wouldn't be able to. Even now, the task of getting her to the door was a daunting one.

Propping both of Karen's elbows on the bar to ensure that she would remain upright while she was gone, Nikki turned to leave her, but a man stood in her way. With his black hair having a hint of a wave, and his brown, deep-set eyes, he had what it took to pull women. But an uninterested Nikki just wanted him to move.

"Excuse me," she said, doing a sidestep.

But he moved to stop her passing. He stood with his right hand spread against his grey-suited chest, like an American when the US national anthem is being sung. With a smile he said, "Don't be alarmed, miss: I'm a friend of Karen's.

"Hello, Malc." Karen turned to greet him after hearing her name called. "Nikki, this is Malcolm Reay, my soon-to-be partner. Malc, meet Nikki Graham, the next Diana Dors."

"Another one," Reay said cynically under his breath. There was the hint of something romantic in his smile, but it was dangerous and threatening, too, as he said, "Time to go, Karen."

Moving Karen's still nearly full glass across the bar away from her, he turned to Nikki, using her name as easily as if they were old friends. "Can you help me to get her to my office and out the back way, Nikki? There's quite few newshounds in here tonight, and if we're not careful there will be a picture of a drunken Karen

Cayson, her eyes shut and her legs open, on the front page of every tabloid in the morning."

That was something that Nikki was dreading, and she readily volunteered.

"You get that side of her, and I'll get this side," Reay instructed. "Stay close enough to support her without appearing to do so."

Nikki did as she was told, and they were able to steer Karen through the crowd to the office without anyone noticing her condition. They plonked her down in a chair while Reay telephoned for a taxi. While the dial-out sound pulsed and he awaited an answer, he said to Nikki, "Once I've got the taxi fixed up, I suggest that you taken Karen outside. She's not really a drinker, but I've seen her like this before. The strange thing is that she can snap out of it suddenly, drunk one minute and sober the next. The fresh air could well work a miracle."

"I hope so," Nikki said fervently. Then she found the courage to ask a question. "Do you own this club, Mr Reay?"

"Yes, and the name's Malcolm."

Smiling, pleased at being accepted into what she regarded as an elite circle, she enquired, "Do you mind me asking what Karen meant when she said that you would soon be her partner?"

"I don't in the least mind you asking, but I think it best that you put that question to Karen when she's back in working order," Reay replied. "Now, you'd better make your way out, Nikki. The taxi will be here any minute. If you have any problems, don't hesitate to come back in to get me."

Thanking him, Nikki got Karen up out of the chair and out through the door. A couple of minutes of being outside in the comparative cool of the moonless night proved that Reay had been right. Supported by Nikki one minute, Karen was standing upright the next. She held herself with invisible discipline, but in the concentrating way of a circus performer in mid-act. When the cab arrived, she walked to it unaided, and as they moved off in it she spoke to Nikki without the slightest trace of any slurring of her speech.

"I've made a prick of myself tonight, haven't I, Nikki?"

"No," Nikki lied because she guessed that it was expected of her. "You wanted a good time, and you had it. One drink too many, perhaps, but that's not a sin."

"It is if anyone noticed. I could make tomorrow's headline."

"No one did notice, apart from Mr Reay."

"Malcolm doesn't count, Nikki," Karen assured her. "Thank you for taking care of me. You're a nice girl, and I don't know what I'd have done if I hadn't had you for company tonight."

"I've really enjoyed myself," Nikki told her truthfully. "It's been great being with you, Karen."

"I don't usually behave like that, you know."

"I wouldn't imagine for a moment that you did."

Karen smiled at her in the dim illumination of the cab's interior. "Thanks for saying that. It's just that I've a lot on my mind at the moment, and there's Mr Wyndham's illness on top of it all."

"I don't know how you handle everything so competently and professionally," Nikki complimented her, not wanting to mention Matthew Wyndham, who she'd heard was on his last legs. Having read just about everything there was to read about Karen Cayson, she wondered how long Karen, despite her talent, would survive without the dynamic support of her husband.

As the taxi swung round Marble Arch and headed down Park lane, Karen was thrown closer to Nikki on the back seat. They looked at each other and neither of them could look away. Nikki's thoughts were turning to other things, and she guessed that Karen's were, too. She gazed into Karen's beautiful eyes and could see that the pupils were dilated: a symptom of sexual excitement, she had long ago been told. They sat in silence, staring at each other. Nikki recognised what it was leading up to, and was sure that Karen also knew.

They leaned slowly towards each other. Nikki willingly moved into their first embrace. She felt Karen's right hand go round the back of her waist, while her right hand cupped the back of Nikki's head to pull it towards hers. Their first kiss was brief and tentative. Their lips touched and then parted again. The two of them smiled at each other, each seeking the permission of the other to continue.

As if moved by an invisible force, they came together again. This time there was passion in their kisses. Karen's hand was flat on Nikki's stomach, rubbing gently over her dress. Nikki caressed the smooth, warm skin of Karen's bare shoulder, then moved her hand down towards her left breast. When Karen made no attempt to stop her, she closed her fingers round the breast, finding it to be a thrilling handful as she lightly squeezed it through the silky material of her dress and felt the projecting hardness of the nipple in her palm.

Karen's response was to move her hand down to Nikki's crotch and grope her through her dress. They were both caught up in desire for each other when the taxi entered the drive of Karen's house and they had to part.

Entering the hall, a fully aroused Nikki turned to Karen, expecting them to take up where they had left off in the taxi. But Karen was cool to the point of being cold. She said matter-of-factly, "I've had Nelly Drury prepare your room. It's on the first floor, second door on your left at the top of the stairs."

Totally bewildered by the sudden and drastic change in Karen's mood, Nikki stood close enough to make herself available for a kiss, and said, "Goodnight, Karen."

"Goodnight, Nikki," Karen responded only verbally. Something had happened under her skin and was reflected in her eyes and the set of her mouth to take all the attractiveness out of her face.

Disappointed by the transformation, Nikki turned away and headed for a flight of wide, majestic stairs.

*

Finding that her legs were a little shaky and her knees felt week, Cheryl knew that it was delayed reaction. If it was possible to overdose on sex, then she had done so with Janey. Having tried to relive it all over again on the drive home, she now the alternated between regret at having left Janey, and relief that she had done so. The reward for staying would have been a full night of sizzling sex, which would have to be paid for with all the emotional disasters that befall couples who have nothing but carnal desire linking them.

She locked her garage door and walked towards her apartment. Always alert at this hour of the morning, Cheryl noticed the car parked across the street. She was apprehensive at first, but her fear subsided a little as she recognised the car as Alan Marriott's grey Mercedes. The silhouette in the driving seat drew on a cigar, and the red glow dramatically illuminated the hard face of Marriott. In black and white it could have been a scene from an old Hollywood gangster movie.

Walking across the road to the car, Cheryl reached the driver's side as the electric window purred down and a cloud of cigar smoke enveloped her. Playing softly on the car's CD player was Aled Jones's "Panis Angelicus".

"Cheryl," Marriott said cheerfully. "I was wondering if you've had a chance to look at the tape."

"At two o'clock in the morning, Alan?" a disbelieving Cheryl questioned.

"I don't sleep good, Cheryl."

"Having seen the tape, that doesn't surprise me. You play dirty, Alan."

"Not as dirty as Karen Cayson," he said, and Cheryl suspected that he was smirking in the dimness of the car's interior. "That tape will have Matthew Wyndham ready to sell out to me."

Marriott had understated the tape's potential, and Cheryl

corrected him. "That tape will kill Matthew and ruin Karen."

"That's bullshit, Cheryl." She sensed rather than saw Marriott's dismissive shrug. "Wyndham is dying anyway, and without his guidance Karen will ruin the studios first and herself second."

Having to accept that what Marriott said was true, but hating it, Cheryl tried finding solace in listening to the song, which was one she liked. But she failed, able to think only of a sad, dying man and his neurotic wife. Neurotic? Was that fair? Cheryl had to admit that it was a pretty accurate description of Karen.

"When are you thinking of going to see Wyndham, Cheryl?"

"This morning. I want to get a few hours' sleep, then I'll go to the hospital."

Marriott reached to the seat beside him for a brown C4 envelope and passed it out through the window to Cheryl. "I've had some stills made of the raunchiest shots for you to take to show Wyndham."

He looked at Cheryl angrily as she passed the envelope back into the car. She explained. "I can see that it would probably be best for everyone concerned if Matthew sold the studios to you, Alan, but I won't use either the tape or the photographs. I'm not into hurting people."

"That isn't strictly true, Cheryl," he advised in a calm but steely voice. "If you refuse to do it, then it will hurt Wyndham a whole lot more, and ruin Karen a whole lot quicker, if I pass copies of the tapes to the newspapers."

"Could you bring yourself to do that, Alan?" Cheryl asked, expressing her very real doubts. In a way, Alan Marriott and she were two of a kind. Not twin souls. That would be going too far. But they shared a dedication to their work, and both of them were capable of a degree of ruthlessness if it was necessary to get the job done. What misery Alan had caused entertainers with his hiring and firing, she had probably equalled by denting celebrity egos with her often caustic writing. Even so, she found it hard to believe that he was capable of the viciousness required to carry out his threat.

Again there was a shrug from Marriott. "Where business is concerned I don't have many scruples, and none at all when it comes to saving the Wyndham studios from oblivion. Either you change your mind, Cheryl, or I unleash the dogs of dirty tricks."

For some time, Cheryl had attributed Marriott's hatred of Matthew Wyndham to envy. Though a man of considerable vision as well as being astute in business, Marriott lacked that special something, perhaps an innate gift, that set Wyndham above the rest. The problem was that, although he probably refused to consciously acknowledge it, deep down Marriott knew that he was inferior to Matthew Wyndham.

The outcome of what Marriott intended doing was too horrific for Cheryl to contemplate. She raked through her mind for a possible alternative. Though Matthew Wyndham was a stubborn old cuss, she just might be able to persuade him that the way to ensure that his studios continued as a memorial to him, and to secure Karen's future, would be to sell up. Trying to have him sell to his archenemy Alan Marriott would be the hardest task of all.

"Give me time to try it my way," she pleaded.

"How much time, Cheryl?"

"A week?"

"Out of the question!" Marriott came close to shouting. "A week may be a long time in politics, and it's certainly too fucking long in this game. Wyndham's likely to be dead in a week!"

"Then how long will you give me, Alan?"

"Today, Cheryl, you've got today, that's all. I'll ring you at ten tonight, and if you haven't clinched it with Wyndham by then, I'll do what I have to do."

Cheryl wanted to object, to ask for at least three days, but the electric window was rising, cutting her off from Marriott, separating them into different worlds from where they couldn't hear each other.

Then the car roared away, leaving her standing in the middle of the deserted street. She felt somehow exposed, even though the subtle starlight was discreet. Her eyes caught a flicker of redness as Marriott braked before turning left at a junction. Then he was gone, but his threat remained to harass Cheryl as she walked to her apartment.

Carrying a mug of steaming Ovaltine, Karen walked steadily up the stairs. She felt better now, almost completely relaxed. A terrible black mood had settled on her immediately on coming in the door with Nikki. The hollowness of the empty house had been a stark reminder for her that life was about to change, and change drastically. She had experienced a debilitating terror at the thought of being without Matthew. It had stripped her of every vestige of self-confidence, turning her big plans into pie in the sky, and making it clear that Malcolm Reay wasn't to be trusted. For the first time in her life she had gained an insight into what it was like to be suicidal. There was no way that she could muster enough resolve to face the immediate future.

To her delighted surprise, the heavy fog of despair had lifted reasonably quickly. She found herself remembering Nikki's kisses in the cab, and had tried to recapture the heat, the taste and the sensation. That didn't work. What made sex addictive was that it largely eluded the memory. Even the most imaginatively created masturbatory exercise was a very poor runner-up to the real thing.

With the excuse to herself that she owed Nikki an apology and the hospitality due to a guest, she had made her a hot drink. Naked under a silver silken robe, she paused at the girl's bedroom door. Aware that it would be polite to knock, Karen realised that to do so would run contrary to her motive for coming to the room. Twisting the handle in a swift movement, she pushed the door open fast and stepped inside.

Wearing a wispy, crimson shortie nightie, Nikki was bent over the bed reaching into her bag for matching crimson panties. Her white buttocks were invitingly on display. A surprised expression on her face, she turned her head to face Karen.

"Don't straighten up," Karen said.

With a shaking hand, she placed the mug down on a dressing table. Bewilderment on her face, Nikki, her body rigid, remained bent over the bed. It dawned on Karen that her sexual need had turned what she had intended to be a request into a sharply barked order.

"I'm sorry," she cried, running across the room to drop to her knees behind Nikki.

Placing a hand on each of the cheeks of the girl's bum, she opened it up and leaned back to study the dusky-stained valley at arm's length. The sight was too much for Karen. Moving her head forward, she cushioned her forehead against Nikki's soft-skinned buttocks. Resting momentarily, Karen then avidly breathed in the girl's natural scent. It was a stimulating, pungent smell that caused Karen's head to swim.

Though unable to get enough of the smell, Karen had had a greater need to taste. The first contact with the Nikki's plump youthful lips sent shuddering waves of shock through Karen's body. Mild convulsions continued as she kissed and licked the glistening pink slit that was running wet. Nikki's juices filled her mouth and filled her mind with rampant desire. She heard Nikki moaning softly in accompaniment to the waves of pleasure she was giving her. Then in a quaking voice she heard the girl ask what had to be a rhetorical question.

"What are you doing to me?"

Letting her tongue slide out of Nikki, Karen ran it tantalisingly slowly up the dark valley. Her arousal was brought to a new peak by the heat of the anus against the tip of her thrill-seeking tongue. The coarse hairs in that area titillated Karen's sense so much that she allowed her tongue to do a lap of honour. Then she ran on up, finding a different kind of erotica in the taste of sweat before she reached the end of her journey at Nikki's coccyx.

Catching hold of Nikki's hips, Karen deftly turned and manoeuvred the girl until she was lying flat on her back on the bed. Moving athletically, Karen knelt on the bed straddling the girl's head. Lowering herself a little, Karen let her cunt kiss Nikki full on the mouth. It was a kiss that Nikki wanted to prolong, but Karen teasingly moved slowly on down with her cunt kissing Nikki all the way from her chin to her breasts, leaving a shining damp trail of love juice in its wake.

Above Nikki's left breast, Karen let her body gradually lower, aiming accurately so that Nikki's standing up nipple parted Karen's labia and entered her. Moving her hips gently back and forth, causing Nikki's nipple to run and up and down her slit, breathtakingly contacting the clitoris each time, Karen was in awe of the magic that made it possible to take so much pleasure from someone else's body while giving equal pleasure in return.

Moving so that her cunt could give the same pleasure to Nikki's other nipple, Karen slid down over the girl's stomach. She deliberately slowed so that her wet, sensitive lips caught pick up the mega-sensation of contact with the first wisps of pubic hair.

Sliding further down, Karen let their cunts come together. Hearing Nikki's grunt of pleasure at their uniting, Karen gave just three rhythmic thrusts, causing Nikki to kind of yodel in delight, before purposefully breaking the contact and moving further down the bed.

As she came closer to Nikki's gaping cunt she caught the girl's heady aroma again. Karen could smell herself, too. Normally her own scent was something to be avoided, but now, trembling helplessly in total abandonment, she put her hand down in between her legs, running her fingers through her moist pubic hair and opening her lips to get her hand as wet as possible.

Bringing up her hand, she got a tremendous thrill from sniffing it. Then she moved it on up unseeingly, searching for Nikki's face. She found her target and was rewarded by the feel of Nikki licking her hand and sucking on her fingers.

With her head between Nikki's legs, Karen teased Nikki's clit with her tongue and let her nose slide in between the hot, glistening lips. Nikki was writhing on the bed now, and her lips jerked and swelled at each rasp of Karen's tongue.

Retrieving her hand from Nikki's mouth, Karen moved both her hands so that she could dig her fingertips into the hollows on each side of Nikki's quim and spread her open as wide as possible, allowing her to kiss deeper and increasing the girl's pleasure at the same time.

Panting ecstatically, Nikki started to cry out, "More! More! More!"

Making her wait so as to heighten the girl's passion and her own, the experienced Karen then stopped licking and sat up. Reaching out, she opened one drawer of a chest drawers that stood close to the bed. Taking a strap-on dildo from the drawer, Karen, watched by a sultry-faced Nikki, put it on. There was a short projecting piece on top of and at the base of the dildo. Puzzlement made Nikki frown as she looked at this little "extra".

Then Nicki obligingly welcomed Karen between her legs, bending her knees in readiness. Arms spread, resting on her hands, which were on each side of Nikki, Karen aimed the massive cock at Nikki's swollen, throbbing, dripping labia. Nikki had her middle finger stroking her own clit and was groaning softly. She reached down with her other hand to firmly grasp the dildo and guided it so that it gradually parted the heavy lips of her vulva.

Pleased by the girl's active participation, Karen fed the dildo slowly into her. Nikki's wet folds moved accommodatingly aside and the dildo went all the way in. Karen thrust with her hips to make sure that it was in right up to the hilt, and Nikki yelled out, driven half crazy by the small projection coming against her clit, and moving against it thrillingly as Karen wriggled her hips.

Karen came down so that their breasts kissed. Then she was kissing Nikki's sweet mouth. Sucking on Karen's tongue, giving it little painless bites, Nikki moaned into Karen's throat as Karen speeded up the movement of her hips. "Fuck me! Fuck me!" she moaned and panted as Karen licked the saliva from her mouth as she did as the girl asked.

With no prompting from Karen, Nikki slid her hand down between them. Pushing it through their respectively sodden pubic hair, she bent her thumb as it went into Karen's slit. The knuckle of her thumb came into contact with Karen's clit, causing her to groan loudly as, each time she thrust into Nikki, Nikki's thumb caused a pleasurable friction against her clit.

As Nikki's movements quickened and her breath was coming in frantic gasps, Karen slid a hand under her buttocks and first lubricated a finger in Nikki's juice, then squirmed it into the tight hole of her anus. That was the last straw to break the back of a massive orgasm for Nikki.

"Now! Now! Now!" Nikki screamed.

Karen skewered her with the dildo, and worked her anus with a finger, so that Nikki seemed to light up like in a fluorescent glow as she rolled from side to side under Karen, her head thrown back, open mouth rimmed with a coating of saliva as she orgasmed noisily.

As Nikki fell back exhausted, Karen got off her and undid the dildo while sitting on the bed facing Nikki. Then, as Nikki dizzily raised her head, Karen rocked back a little and used both hands to stretch her vulva open and present it to Nikki's view.

"Please, do something," she begged Nikki.

Scrambling up into a sitting position, Nikki stretched out a hand to the abandoned dildo, but Karen, in an agony of ecstasy, called to her, "No. No! Please! There's no time."

Lying back as Nikki came over to her, Karen groaned as the

younger woman mounted one of her thighs, pressing a soaking-wet cunt against it. They kissed wildly, madly, as Nikki worked two fingers into Karen. But it wasn't enough. Mumbling through a kiss, Karen told her what to do.

At first not understanding, and then hesitating so that Karen had to break their kissing to scream at her to get on with it, Nikki slowly eased in a hand and then fist-fucked her. Her excitement exacerbated by Nikki's astonishment at her first sighting of a grown woman in the throes of what amounted to a sexual fit, with Nikki's fist up inside her, Karen felt that she was about to explode.

It wasn't a lie to say that that was what she did. Shouting and yelling, scaring her younger partner, she came with all the power and noise of a steam engine. Then they both collapsed in each other's arms and lay still and Nikky carefully slid out her hand.

Neither of them spoke or moved for more than five minutes. Then Karen said softly, "I'm sorry."

"What for?" Nikki asked, a mystified smile on her doll-like face.

"The Ovaltine that I brought you has gone cold," Karen spluttered.

They both collapsed with laughter, clinging to each other, and when the laughter subsided they lay quietly together, holding each other, mouths just touching, breathing each other's breath.

Karen and Nikki were at peace.

Fifteen

The hospital was enclosed within a head-high thick green hedge. Reached by way of a gravel drive, it was a large seven-storey building that was modern and plain-looking and made ugly by iron fire escapes positioned on all sides. An attempt to add brightness by planting rhododendrons along the walls had failed due to the poor soil. To Cheryl it seemed a million miles from the car park to the entrance.

The day had started badly for her. Straight after breakfast, moved by her conscience, she had telephoned Wendi to confess to her Janey adventure, as well as the other "slips" with the other women. A devastated Wendi had given her no chance to relate any extenuating circumstances. Though one circumstance included the steamy video of Karen and Paula, Wendi would not excuse her lapses and, shattered by being betrayed by Cheryl before their relationship had really begun, had sobbed piteously before ending Cheryl's call.

After dialling Wendi's number again, Cheryl waited for fully two minutes, but Wendi obviously guessed it was her calling, and she didn't pick up the receiver.

Now offering up a silent prayer that Matthew was still alive, Cheryl entered the hospital. Sucking air hard into her lungs, she willed them to fill up. She held the air down there, and her throat closed so that it couldn't get out. Then she started along a maze of corridors that were long and glaringly white, with potted cacti sticking up dangerously everywhere. There was a reek of disinfectant and a stench of stale people along the way.

The waiting room was large and mellow with an enormous anachronistic fireplace, importantly framed prints on the walls, and several brilliant leather chairs and a sofa. There were several people there, sitting in the stiff self-consciousness of strangers confined together. Their only common denominator was worry over a sick loved one, and they gave furtive, sideways glances that slid off each other. Cheryl took a seat as two white-coated doctors came out from a side room, their conversation clinically cold-blooded.

"He complained that he couldn't sleep, so I started him on tranquillisers. He proved allergic to some of them, and got no help from the others."

"I see," said the second doctor. "I see."

"So I switched him to Nembutal."

"I see. I see."

They passed out of the room into the corridor, and Cheryl suddenly found herself to be in the middle of a conversation with an elderly woman without ever having begun it. They spoke the way strangers do until familiarity eases the awkwardness between them.

"You never know what you're going to find when you get to these places, do you?" the woman remarked worriedly. "Mind you, our Jennie's well on the mend now. Is it your mum you're here for, dear?"

"No, a friend. Just a friend," Cheryl answered.

Addicted to self-searching, Cheryl questioned whether what she had said was the truth. Matthew Wyndham couldn't be described as her friend. Why was she here? It would take months of psychiatric analysis to come up with the real reason, which was probably Karen Cayson. No one in the world could really be sure of anything. Did she simply fancy the glamorous star or did she subconsciously envy her as well? Or was her being here at the hospital a symptom of a deep psychological problem? Living through someone else was the easy option – a kind of semi-suicide.

She gave an involuntary little jump then as a young man sitting in a corner suddenly shouted out, "Peter! Where's Peter?"

"He's not all there, poor thing," an elderly woman said, leaning close to Cheryl to state the obvious.

Everyone there looked acutely and oddly embarrassed as people do in the presence of someone unstable. The waiting room door imploded and a tall, big-built, long-jawed woman with grey hair pulled away from her face in a bun, and wearing an outdated Florence Nightingale nurse's cap, swept in. Her manner was military, and her severe blue dress rustled as she advanced on the young man, who was about to shout again.

"That's quite enough out of you, Garry. I'll go and help you look for Peter in a little while." The sister's small, close-set hard dark eyes swept over the other waiting visitors. "You can all go in now, but please go quietly."

There was a screeching and scratching of chair legs against the floor followed by an orderly exodus. Cheryl went with the flow, branching off into Matthew Wyndham's room. Cheryl stepped nervously into the small room, her high heels click-clacking on the tiled floor, an intrusion in the deathlike quiet. She moved slowly towards the narrow bed to look down at the sunken-cheeked figure that had been Matthew Wyndham before illness had removed him.

"Cheryl, so good of you to come to see me again."

"How are you, Matthew?" she enquired.

He looked brighter than last time she was here, and he had the strength to raise his head a little from the pillow. She walked to stand by the window and he talked to her back as she looked at the get-well cards lined up on the sill. A huge card with embossed roses was signed, "From your ever-loving Karen". There was a card from John Brighton and another from the "Boys and girls at the studio". Testifying to Wyndham's importance was an impressive, albeit coldly official, card from 10 Downing Street.

"I didn't think that I'd ever hear myself saying this, Cheryl, but

I'm feeling quite a bit stronger."

"I'm delighted to hear it, Matthew." She rested her forehead against the cold glass of the window for a moment. There were things to be said, and she had to say them right. Turning, she grasped a light iron chair with a plastic seat and brought it over to sit close to the bed. "You're going to need plenty of rest when you leave here, Matthew."

Up close, his face was old and wasted, with deep lines of pain engraved permanently across his brow. But he mustered a smile, and his hand came out to her in the jerky movement of a robot. "You are a professional wordsmith, Cheryl, so I know that you're trying to tell me something. So, cut the crap and cut to... What's the modern lingo?"

She caught hold of the thin, cold and bony hand. "Cut to the chase."

"That's it." Wyndham smiled again. "But first indulge a nostalgic old man who's been lying here thinking of the good things that have happened in his life. I can trace all of those good things back to Karen. Before Karen I was all sharp edges, Cheryl. I was made up of jagged pieces that scratched against myself as well as everyone else. That horrible scratching ended the moment she came into my life.

"Most prominent of my memories are of our times together in bed. I'm not going to shock you with sexual details, my dear. Oh, no. I'm talking of those tender moments that come after the lights-out of erotica. That's when we would lie there, perfect bedmates exchanging secret stories of our lives. That after-sex time is the grown-ups' version of *Jackanory* on kids' television, Cheryl. It is truly wonderful. Most of the time in here I'm so sick that my mind doesn't work properly, but yesterday's memories live on in my heart."

Weeping inwardly for the sad old man, Cheryl told herself that she had a duty to perform and she had to do it. But how can you say to someone, Look, you're going to die soon, so there are things that you must immediately attend to – business things?

Instead of saying that, she said, "That was beautiful, Matthew. You have just described for me what love really is."

"It's the only thing in the world worth having, Cheryl."

"Then you now want to do what is best for Karen and yourself," Cheryl said half as a question, half as a statement.

"Especially for Karen." He nodded his shrunken head. "She's the important one. You have something to say, Cheryl?"

"I would like to offer some advice, if that's not presumptuous of me."

"Of course not. As a long-time admirer of yours, I'd welcome hearing it."

"I was going to suggest that you retire."

The strange bright glow of sickness in Wyndham's eyes dimmed. "That's out of the question, Cheryl. I love Karen dearly. There isn't a pedestal high enough for me to put her on, but with her kind of beauty a business sense would be superfluous. She couldn't run things."

"Then sell the studios, Matthew."

His initial shock at this suggestion gradually turned into at least a modicum of interest. Wyndham expressed his reservations. "The studios are my life's work, my empire, Cheryl."

"And they always will be," she stressed. "You've made your mark in show business, Matthew. Whoever may own them in the future, those studios will always be thought of and talked of as yours."

He accepted this. "You make sound sense, Cheryl, but it's a little more complicated than that. The way modern business is, only some giant, impersonal company could afford to buy me out. That would mean that my studios would lose the personal touch, the individualism that is so vital to them."

"I think that I may have the answer for you," she said with temerity.

"You have?"

Dragging in a deep breath, she blurted out, "Alan Marriott is willing to give you a fair price, and he'd be personally in charge."

"No," Wyndham hissed. "You are a good friend with the best of intentions, Cheryl, so I will not vent my spleen on you. But never would I enter into any business dealings with that man."

Though bitterly disappointed, Cheryl knew that it was wise to drop the subject. She spent another hour with Matthew, and they talked of many things. But the earlier accord had gone. There was a tangible undercurrent of awkwardness between them, and she wasn't sorry when it came time for her to leave.

The telephone was ringing when she got home. When she rushed to pick it up, she found that it was Karen inviting her out to lunch.

"I'm sorry, Karen, but I can't spare the time. I'm absolutely loaded down with work and besieged by deadlines."

Karen sounded subdued and unhappy, and Cheryl heard her refusal provoke a long sigh.

"I understand, of course, Cheryl. Don't worry, we'll make it some other time."

"Are you all right, Karen? You certainly don't sound it." Karen was, obviously, very worried about Matthew.

"Nothing that a stiff drink won't cure," Karen said with a patently forced flippancy. "Don't worry about it, Cheryl."

"Worry is one of my vices. Listen, Karen. I'm having a working lunch here. It won't be anything much, just a salad. But you're welcome to come and share it."

"Are you sure?"

"Absolutely."

"You are a gem, Cheryl. I'll be there at around twelve. Is that OK?"

"That's fine," Cheryl replied.

"Karen won't be in today," John Brighton announced to the actors and crew, "so we have some rescheduling to do."

Standing among six cameras that were loaded and ready, Paula Monroe wanted to ask Brighton why Karen wouldn't be in. She wanted to ask what Nikki Graham was doing here in the studios. Nikki could be here only because Karen had arranged it, and Paula needed to know how this came about, and what the arrangement with Nikki actually was.

Consulting a clipboard, Brighton then put it under his arm and addressed them all once more. "First of all, though, I don't suppose any of you know her, so allow me to introduce Nikki Graham."

There was a chorus of shouted, "Hi, Nikki," and the doll-like little creature blushed prettily and waved a hand in general acceptance of the greetings. She stood several feet away from Paula, often covertly glancing in her direction, but clearly afraid to approach her even though they were supposed to be friends.

Resenting Nikki's being there, as her presence somehow diminished the self-esteem she had enjoyed since joining the studios as a budding star, Paula felt anger rise in her as Brighton continued.

"Karen wants Nikki to have a camera test, so that's how we'll kick the day off. Here's the script for the scene we had intended to shoot next, Nikki. You'll take Karen's part for the test shoot, playing opposite to Paula. All you need to do, kid, is to forget the cameras and act natural. Give your best and they'll fix your teeth, invent an image for you, use ice on your nipples so that that stand to attention at all times, and even fit you up with a new arsehole if that will make them money. Within a week your own mother won't know you. Two weeks and your mother won't want to fucking know you. So get ready to say goodbye to Nikki Graham for ever. I understand that you and Paula are old friends, so take fifteen minutes to go through the script together in the canteen."

Paula walked off the set with Nikki, unspeaking. In the canteen they got a coffee each and, as they sat at a small table, Nikki asked, "Have I done something to upset you, Paula?"

"You're encroaching on my territory," Paula replied, ashamed at how childishly sulky she sounded, "and I don't like it."

"But I don't understand. We're friends, so it will be really great to work together."

"I don't think so. How did Karen come to take you into the studios, Nikki?" Paula asked, not realising until that very moment how much her relationship with Karen really meant to her.

"I just asked, and she said yes," Nikki said, but the faint pink colouring of her face hinted at the worst for Nikki.

"You telephoned, and she agreed just like that?" a disbelieving Paula enquired.

"I didn't telephone: I called at the house."

What had happened between Karen and Nikki? That was a stupid question. Paula felt terrible. The illumination in the canteen seemed to dim, and she was buffeted between a terrible anger towards Nikki and an urge to cry. She regained control only because John Brighton put his head in round canteen door to call, "Right, girls. Let's be having you."

"Have you ever felt yourself being slowly tortured, Cheryl, with your inside being ripped loose from your frame and torn into little pieces slowly, agonising slowly? You try to absorb all the hurt, but the inside of you is too raw."

"What brought this on, Karen?"

Across the table from Cheryl, as Karen picked at her meal, her eyes looked older and more tired. She was tense, holding herself tight as she looked at Cheryl. She was a long time answering. "A couple of nights ago, in the darkness, I sat alone with a feeling of aloneness such as I had never experienced before. It was then that I knew that I had brought all this on myself. I have been terribly selfish, Cheryl, using people, even my dear Matthew, heartlessly. Now I'm afraid. Terribly afraid."

"I have a problem with imagining Karen Cayson afraid," Cheryl remarked, trying to lighten the conversation.

"She is." Karen gave an emphatic nod. "Before I met Matthew I was nothing. An actress of sorts, I suppose, but no different from a lot of others. I'd probably be a lap dancer or perhaps even a hooker now if it weren't for him. I owe everything to Matthew, Cheryl. What am I going to do when he's gone?"

"You are a strong person, Karen, and I'm sure that you'll survive," Cheryl said, reaching across the table to give Karen's right hand a gentle squeeze. "Richard Neehan is there to help you with the legal side of things."

Close to tears, Karen said, "There's something you don't know, Cheryl. I've done a very silly thing. I've become involved with Malcolm Reay."

"Involved?" Cheryl questioned, feigning surprise.

"Not in that way. Of course not," Karen replied. And all at once the whole story of Malcolm Reay and his stake in the studios was pouring out of her, hard and tough and real, and she was crying.

"Hey, come on, Karen," Cheryl said. "It can't be that bad."

"It is," she choked. "It was silly of me. I just wanted to make sure that the studios would go on, and didn't have enough confidence in myself."

"But surely this agreement will depend on Matthew's will."

Karen's shoulders dropped, a kind of shrug in reverse. "No, Malcolm's lawyer made certain that he owns part of the business immediately upon Matthew's death."

"Are you sure that he gets only ten per cent?" Cheryl queried worriedly.

"I can't be sure of that. I just signed the document without question. I've made a mess of everything and it can only get worse. You're the only one I can turn to, Cheryl."

"The only advice I can give," Cheryl said sympathetically, "is that you put this to Richard Neehan straightaway."

"Do you think he'll be able to do something?"

"Neehan's a sly old fox, Karen. He's clever enough to block anything that Reay's solicitor can think up."

"I'm sure that you're right. I'll go to see him first thing tomorrow morning," Karen said. She went quiet. She looked down at the lettuce wilting on her plate, then she slanted a look at Cheryl. "I've been so thoughtless and selfish, Cheryl. I've promised two young girls the earth in show business, and I'm frightened that I'll let them down."

I've seen you with one who won't expect to be let down, Cheryl thought wryly, and no doubt you've had what you wanted out of the other one. But Karen was in such a state that she now felt only pity for her. She said, "Get this legal business settled first, Karen, and then I'll do whatever I can to help you in an other way."

They got through what remained of lunch reasonably happily by exchanging only small talk. Karen took her mind away from her troubles by concentrating on her favourite subject – the studios.

"I have big plans for next year, Cheryl. We are big here in the UK and in Europe, but I want us to be renowned globally. It's early days yet, but I have put feelers out and hope to have Michael Caine over here to make a film. But that means expansion, and that has to be done fast. It's an exciting prospect, isn't it?"

"It certainly is, and I'm sure that you'll make it," Cheryl said, discovering to her horror that lying came easy with a little practice.

When Karen was ready to leave she promised that she would be in Richard Neehan's office first thing in the next morning.

At the front door she moved so that Cheryl couldn't open it. Her customary poise had deserted her and she spoke in a garbled rush. "There is something that I've always longed to do, Cheryl, and it would mean a lot to me right this minute if you would let me kiss you."

Acute awareness of Karen's high sex drive made Cheryl cautious, but she had long secretly wanted to kiss the beautiful Karen. But that urge was nothing when compared with her determination to restore her relationship with Wendi. So she offered what she hoped would prove to be a compromise. "Just one kiss, Karen, and nothing else."

Cheryl relaxed as Karen's soft but firm body came against hers, gently moving her back against the wall. Karen's body was supple and warm, and she smelled all womanly, every bit as exciting as she looked. She watched entranced as Karen brought her face close, drawing a red tongue over ripe lips so that they glistened wetly, pleading to be kissed. Karen's eyes swirled into a smoky grey that rose up from the depths of an inner fire.

It was a long, slow, deep kiss that sent a sparking fuse down Cheryl's body until she curved inward against Karen with a fierce undulation that left no gaps between their bodies.

With a strength of will that amazed her, Cheryl ended the kiss. Karen leaned back slightly. Her eyes had narrowed. Her lips, moist, slackly apart, invited more kissing.

But Cheryl was adamant. Seeming to be embarrassed by her own obvious sexual excitement, Karen hugged her briefly, said "Thank you, Cheryl," and hurried out of the door.

The insistent bleeping of the telephone awakened Cheryl. It took her a little while to work out what was happening, and then she quickly sat up to snatch up the phone from the bedside table before the answerphone cut in. The clock told her that it was twenty minutes past one. It was Richard Neehan calling: "My apologies for waking you at this time in the morning, Cheryl, but I thought you would want to know. Matthew Wyndham died a half-hour ago."

Karen was speechless, numb. The news was inevitable and it shouldn't be a shock, but Matthew had seemed so much stronger when she had visited him yesterday. She said, "I know we expected it, Richard, but this sort of thing still hits you hard."

"It certainly does. I suppose it is some comfort to know that he went peacefully in his sleep."

"But it's left the big problem of Malcolm Reay and the studios. Karen planned to come and see you this morning, but now it's too late."

Neehan chuckled, the apologised. "I'm sorry, that was out of order at a time like this. But Karen's projected trip to my office would have been wasted. You underestimate your powers of persuasion, Cheryl. Matthew telephoned me shortly after you left him yesterday morning. He had decided to sell the studios, and by four o'clock in the afternoon the sale was completed."

"My goodness, that was quick. Who's the new owner?"

"Alan Marriott."

"Good God!"

"The description of your being good at persuading is inadequate, Cheryl. You are a miracle worker. Everyone comes out of this a winner."

"Except for Karen. How do you think she'll take this, Richard?"

"I won't be telling her until after the funeral, Cheryl, so please keep this to yourself. Once I explain it all she is sure to see it's for the best. Matthew has left her everything, so she will be a wealthy woman. I personally believe that if she'd inherited the studios she would have been penniless in a very short time."

"That was my feeling, Richard."

"I know. Now I'll let you get back to sleep. Remember, Cheryl, mum's the word where the sale of the studios is concerned."

"Trust me, Richard. I won't breathe a word. Goodnight."

Goodnight, Cheryl."

The morning rehearsals had gone as well as could be expected in the circumstances. Everything in the studios had been in limbo over the three days since Matthew Wyndham's death. Tomorrow was the day of the funeral, so no one expected to hear anything until that had passed. The uncertainty had increased the bad feeling between Paula and Nikki. Out of necessity, John Brighton had moved ahead to shoot scenes in which Karen didn't appear. It boosted Paula's ego that she was in all of the scenes, while Nikki, who wouldn't know the result of her screen test until Karen returned, was hanging around the studios like, in the vernacular of John Brighton, "a spare prick at a cow's wedding".

With the future of the players and the crew in doubt, it was a relief for everyone when Karen arrived that morning. Pale and haggard-looking, she was accompanied by a tall, dark and handsome man who Paula assumed was an actor being introduced to the studio. This lifted her spirits, as Karen would not be bringing in a new actor if everything were going to go on as before.

"Would you all gather round, please?" Karen called.

Within minutes, anxiety for their futures had everyone standing together in an arc facing Karen and the newcomer. She addressed them in a strong voice.

"First I must thank you all for your kind messages of sympathy. I know how Mr Wyndham was popular with all of you, and that he would appreciate your condolences in the same way as I do. Now, you all must be wondering how the death of Mr Wyndham is going to affect you. So let me put your minds at rest. As far as every single one of you is concerned, your positions here in the studio are rock-solid safe."

There was a concerted sigh at these good tidings. Having moved closer to Paula, Nikki whispered, "This is great news, isn't it, Paula."

"Yes," Paula agreed, and in her relief she realised how churlish she had been. She said quietly, "I am sorry to have treated you so badly, Nikki. Can we be friends again?"

"That would make me very happy."

They caught hold of each other's hand as Karen started speaking again.

"There will, however, be some changes. Allow me to introduce

Mr Malcolm Reay, who will be taking an active part in the day-to-day running of the studios."

"In other words," a belligerent John Brighton called out, "he'll be doing my job."

"That is not so," Karen contradicted him. "I have already said that all of your jobs are safe, and that includes yours, John. Now—"

Karen stopped speaking at the sound of a car stopping outside. A car door slammed and a man carrying a briefcase walked into the studios. He walked up to where Karen and Reay stood, and Paula recognised him as Alan Marriott, the man who had started her on the road to success.

"Good morning," Marriott said. "Might I have a word in your office, Miss Cayson?"

"I'm talking to my people, Mr Marriott. Anything you wish to say can be said right here."

"As you wish." Marriott shrugged, opened his briefcase and took some papers out. "As Mr Neehan, your solicitor, will have told you, I now own these studios."

"Richard Neehan has told me no such thing," Karen said angrily. "I must ask you to leave, Mr Marriott. Right now!"

Passing her the papers he had taken from his case, Marriott said, "I apologise for barging in like this, Miss Cayson. I honestly believed that you knew. As this document attests, I purchased these studios from your late husband four days ago."

As she looked at the document, Karen's knees sagged. Paula realised that she was on the verge of collapse. Peering over her shoulder at the papers, Malcolm Reay then turned on his heel to stride angrily away and out of the building.

"Will someone please help Miss Cayson?" Marriott called, as Karen swayed and had to clutch at him for support.

Paula and Nikki came up to support a trembling Karen and take her to a sofa that was part of the set. After sitting her down, they sat each side of her as Alan Marriott spoke to the assembly. Paula listened but didn't really hear. A wildness was going on in her mind until it was like being caught in an echo chamber, strident voices reverberating and screaming. She was aware of Nikki continually and anxiously glanced sideways at her.

"While I have you all here together," Marriott said, looking apprehensive and pausing a long while before speaking again, "I will take the opportunity to explain. I am afraid that it is not good news for any of you. I bear a heavy responsibility. My plans for these studios include refurbishment and expansion. This will take some time, and I am sorry to say that each and every one of you is redundant from this moment."

A scurry of shock that ran through the group of listeners. Marriott added, "Progress is always painful."

"Not for people like you, it isn't," Brighton remarked, getting a few cheers from those around him.

"I will honour all employment compensation arrangements, so none of you will lose out."

"We've lost our jobs," John Brighton pointed out angrily.

"That is true, and something I deeply regret," Marriott said. "I assure you that when, in six months at the earliest, a year at the latest, when I advertise vacancies, the applications of those among you who wish to apply will be given top priority."

"What about *Beach of Fear*? We're in the middle of filming."

Marriott gave Brighton a straight answer. "That film is scrapped. It will never be completed, at least not in these studios."

The impact of this hit Paula, and brought all else Marriott had said with it. Made faint by disappointment, she was glad of the consoling hand of Nikki, who reached past Karen to squeeze her shoulder.

"Am I welcome?"

That was all that Wendi Maylor could think of saying as Cheryl opened the door of her apartment. It sounded pretty trite after what had happened between them. But there was no space for any other words between the two of them. They would have to be neutral words, and neutrality solved nothing. She waited expectantly, wondering how long it would take to repair the damage to their relationship. Whatever happiness Cheryl and she could find together, it was guaranteed to be one hundred per cent better than what she had witnessed in Bristol. Whenever she thought of home, she shuddered in distaste, and worried about how much longer her sister could survive in that environment.

"I didn't think that you would call," Cheryl said emotionlessly, so blandly that it disheartened Wendi.

Keeping this to herself, she shrugged. "I guess that I got lonely. I've missed you, Cheryl."

Cheryl's lips struggled with an incipient smile. Then the smile took hold and moved up to include her eyes. "I'm just so astonished by your turning up like this, Wendi."

"I wanted to tell you the good news," Wendi said, relieved by having a solid excuse for being there. I'm playing the lead in a musical at Richmond, starting next month."

"That's great, Wendi. It makes me doubly pleased to see you."

"Does that mean that I'm forgiven?"

"I'm confused about who should be forgiving whom," Cheryl admitted. "I've missed you, too. You'd better come in and we'll talk."

Following Cheryl into the flower-scented cool air of the lounge, Wendi felt herself melting inside – the wonderful, liquid desirous melting that comes with high-powered sexual desire. It felt as if she were on a soft cloud, floating dreamily somewhere far above the world.

"I hope you've not come to give me a lecture on morals," Cheryl said.

"Far from it," Wendi said with a shaking of her head. "I've come to say that I was wrong to take such a pompous attitude. I'm in no position to lecture anyone. You're looking at the woman once voted as Bristol University's Miss 69."

"You lying little minx," Cheryl smilingly scolded her, adding with surprising innocence for a worldly-wise woman like herself. "You are not old enough to have been Miss 69 at any university."

Laughing uncontrollably, Wendi was at last able to say, "You sweet old thing, Cheryl. My title had nothing to do with 1969, but was won for my skills as the best taker and giver of sex in the 69 position."

The fun and laughter had broken down all remaining barriers between them. Hitting her forehead with the heel of her hand as she sat down in an armchair, Cheryl exclaimed, "I'm a dumbo. But I don't believe you even now. You're going to have to prove it to me."

"A demonstration will do that," Wendi purred.

Leaning over Cheryl to hold the hair off her neck with one hand, Wendi nuzzled behind her ear with her lips. Then she moved slowly around Cheryl's neck, tasting the warm skin with little sucking kisses. Cheryl closed her eyes as if listening to her favourite tune as Wendi's kissing veered to move along Cheryl's jawline, heading for her full-lipped mouth.

Standing at the window of the bedsit Nikki had taken in Crystal Palace, Paula was thrilled by the view. The panoramic skyline of high buildings provided her with an angle on London that would have been impossible to perceive in her imagination. The sun had gone and long shafts of sullen light poured through the still silhouettes of buildings in a rolling urban landscape. There was a sultry feel to the air, a breathless heat that increased her growing depression caused by being out of work.

"You have a wonderful view here, Nikki," she commented as she took a mug of coffee from her friend.

"But for how much longer?" Nikki asked, pulling a face. "Landlords have a nasty habit of wanting rent paid."

"Something is sure to turn up."

"I wish I had your confidence."

"I live in hope," Paula said. "Although in my lowest moments I suspect that I'm deluding myself."

Holding her coffee mug with both hands, Nikki took a sip before answering. "I'm sure that you are. The competition in this business is overwhelming, Paula. The only thing we can hope for is that the studios open up again in six months. And that's a vain hope."

Turning from the window, Paula anxiously faced her friend. "What are we going to do, Nikki?"

"I thought that when we've finished our coffee we could take a walk in the park near Crystal Palace Station. It's nice there in late evening."

"I meant what are we going to do about work?" Paula tried to smile at Nikki's having misconstrued her meaning. But smiling was becoming increasingly difficult.

Nikki made a decision. "Finish your coffee, Paula, then we'll take a walk."

"Let's agree not to come back here until we've agreed on what to do," Paula suggested.

"That's one hell of a burden to lumber ourselves with," Nikki said doubtfully. "But let's give it a whirl."

They discussed their situation quietly as they followed a footpath that made a series of steps leading up a grassy rise. A row of untended evergreens provided them with a welcome screen that limited the horizon, helping them concentrate.

"You'll think I'm mad if I tell you what I've been thinking," Paula said wistfully as she and Nikki passed in and out of the shadows of some pines, from where they could see the last ray of sunlight snatched over the horizon.

"Try me, Paula, and I'll tell you," Nikki said, her voice sounding strange as it reverberated in the twilight.

"More and more, it seems to me," Paula continued, "that it's much more fun living the dream than it is experiencing the reality."

"Of showbiz, you mean?"

"Yes."

"So what conclusion did you come to?"

Hesitating, sensing that Nikki was dreading the answer she might give, Paula said, "I've been thinking of going back home and staying there."

"There's nothing to stop you."

"I can't go because of you," Paula explained. "You said that you've no home to go to."

"My mum chucked me out when I was fourteen, for objecting to one of her countless sleazy boyfriends. But that doesn't mean that you have to stay in London if you don't want to."

"Would you consider moving to Basingstoke with me, Nikki?"

"Where would I find a room there, Paula, and what would I do for money?"

"That's no problem. You can stay with my family and me," Paula offered. "I'll be going back to the supermarket to work, and I'm sure that I can get you a job there."

"I've never had a proper home."

"You have now," Paula said, hugging her tight. "And since Susie, my sister, got married, I've a double bed to myself."

"It's getting better by the minute," Nikki giggled happily. "Let's hurry back to my room and celebrate."

Hugging her friend once more, Paula said, "Great idea, but first I want to find a phone box and ring Cheryl Valenta to tell her that I'm leaving London. She's been very good to me."

When Cheryl and Wendi called at the Wyndham house to find out how Karen was, they found her sunning herself by the pool. In the briefest of bikinis, of a shiny black material, she stood up from the airbed she was lying on and led them into the house, talking as she went.

"First thing I did was sack the fucking servants. That settled their hash, the geriatric bastards. Then I made some phone calls to my contacts in America, and got myself fixed up with a part in a Hollywood film. I'm way down the billing, but it's a start."

Waiting while she poured drinks and passed them a glass each, Cheryl said, "We're very pleased for you, Karen. You seem to be coping very well. Will you be selling the house?"

"No, that's part of the Hollywood deal. A property is put at my disposal over there, and in return the film company's executives have the use of this place when visiting London."

As they stood drinking and chatting, Cheryl was keenly aware of Wendi's impatience. That lunchtime, in what had been an unbelievably passionate hour of sex, Wendi had established beyond doubt that she was indeed a 69 expert. That session had left them wanting more, and they were now on their way to spend the night in Wendi's apartment.

"A nice arrangement," Cheryl said, complimenting Karen on her astute business dealings. "You can start your new life with a clear conscience about those two girls who thought they were going places with the studios. Paula phoned me a short while ago to say that they were giving up show business and moving out of London."

"Wise kids. I often wish that I'd never got mixed up in this game."

"I'm sure that you don't mean that, Karen," Cheryl smiled. "When are you leaving?"

"First thing in the morning."

"Phew! It's a good thing we called in, or we wouldn't have been able to say goodbye."

"It's hardly *Brief Encounter*, I know, but I'd welcome a goodbye kiss from you both," Karen told them, her eyelids growing heavy as lust pushed its way through her. Cheryl raised an eyebrow, remembering that Karen had used that line on her once before. "Do you want to go first, Wendi? You're a great kisser and I know that for a fact."

Karen tilted her head back a little to make her parted-lip mouth available as Wendi took her in her arms. Aroused by the sight of them kissing hotly, and seeing Wendi's hand slide down into Karen's bikini briefs to finger her, Cheryl joined in the action. Pressing herself against Karen's side, she kissed her neck, shoulders, and back.

Karen was moving herself in time with Wendi's probing finger, as Cheryl gently got her hand inside the back of Karen's briefs. She slid a finger down the hot and ever so slightly damp crack between Karen's buttocks. When her finger reached its goal, Cheryl crooked the end of it and entered Karen's anus.

The film star stopped kissing Wendi to pant and gasp a question: "Why don't we say goodbye properly on the bed upstairs?"

"Have you got that rule book of yours with you, Wendi?" Cheryl asked.

"I burnt it two days ago," Wendi cheerily replied.

Arms around each other, the three of them walked side by side up the majestic stairs of the Wyndham house. As they went, Cheryl marvelled at how the story had ended exactly where it had begun.

New erotic fiction from Red Hot Diva

Cherry
Charlotte Cooper

It's sexy. It's sassy. It's so, so slutty.

Desperate to pop her lesbian cherry, Ramona soon finds that shagging women in real life bears little resemblance to the dirty books she's been reading under the covers. Every dyke has to ditch the theory and put herself out there if she wants to get some action and *Cherry* goes all the way... Ramona pursues and is pursued by the coolest, hottest, richest, wildest – and sometimes the saddest – girls around.

RRP £8.99 UK/ $13.95 US
ISBN 1-873741-73-1

Scarlet Thirst
Crin Claxton

Lesbian vampires on the prowl!

Sexy Rani is initiated into the vampire lifestyle by the butch dyke Rob and embarks on a hedonistic trip through a sex-fuelled underworld, seducing and being seduced by more and more women who live the Life...

For once, the lesbian vampire story is not just a metaphor: this novel is as upfront about sex as it is about biting into beautiful young necks. They're butch, they're femme, they're out for blood.

RRP £8.99 UK/ $13.95 US
ISBN 1-873741-74-X

The Fox Tales
Astrid Fox

Bizarre. Perverse. Moving.

The dazzlingly filthy erotica of *The Fox Tales* spans the gamut from sacrilege to Scandinavian myth, from prison dykes to Victoriana, from smug straight boys to mermaids to the devil herself.

These are eighteen of the best of Astrid Fox's sleazy stories, including favourites from previous anthologies and brand new fantasies. Pandering to every taste, her work combines unapologetic West Coast lust with the darker tones of Angela Carter-style magic realism.

RRP £8.99 UK/ $13.95 US
ISBN 1-873741-79-0

The Escort
Kay Vale

Kinky power games, romance and sex, sex, sex

Our heroine is a "tart with an art" – she satisfies scores of women as a high-class lesbian prostitute and pumps the profits into her real passion – designing opulent jewellery.

Enter Naomi, a spoiled princess who buys a night with Harriet and works her way into her affections. But Harriet has a jealous girlfriend – a sexy police sergeant who's not afraid to use the cuffs...

RRP £8.99 UK/ $13.95 US
ISBN 1-873741-84-7

Peculiar Passions

or, The Treasure of Mermaid Island

Ruby Vise

Fun, saucy sex and rip-roaring adventure

Aboard a pirate ship in 1670, runaway Elizabeth meets Jack, who has been disguised as a boy from birth. They both wear lockets that together form the map of a treasure island. They join forces and find themselves...

... battling the pirates for treasure; solving an ancient lusty mystery; performing amazing feats of derring-do; discovering the delights of some serious Sapphic pleasure.

RRP £8.99 UK/ $13.95 US

ISBN 1-873741-83-9